Praise for the novels of Maisey Yates

"Yates brings her signature heat and vivid western details to another appealing story in the excellent Gold Valley series.... Fans of Kate Pearce should enjoy this."
—*Booklist* on *Rodeo Christmas at Evergreen Ranch*

"Yates's outstanding eighth Gold Valley contemporary... will delight newcomers and fans alike.... This charming and very sensual contemporary is a must for fans of passion."
—*Publishers Weekly* on *Cowboy Christmas Redemption* (starred review)

"Fast-paced and intensely emotional.... This is one of the most heartfelt installments in this series, and Yates's fans will love it."
—*Publishers Weekly* on *Cowboy to the Core* (starred review)

"Multidimensional and genuine characters are the highlight of this alluring novel, and sensual love scenes complete it. Yates's fans...will savor this delectable story."
—*Publishers Weekly* on *Unbroken Cowboy* (starred review)

"Yates' new Gold Valley series begins with a sassy, romantic and sexy story about two characters whose chemistry is off the charts."
—*RT Book Reviews* on *Smooth-Talking Cowboy* (Top Pick)

Also by Maisey Yates

Secrets from a Happy Marriage
Confessions from the Quilting Circle
The Lost and Found Girl

Four Corners Ranch

Unbridled Cowboy
Merry Christmas Cowboy
Cowboy Wild
The Rough Rider

Gold Valley

Smooth-Talking Cowboy
Untamed Cowboy
Good Time Cowboy
A Tall, Dark Cowboy Christmas
Unbroken Cowboy
Cowboy to the Core
Lone Wolf Cowboy
Cowboy Christmas Redemption
The Bad Boy of Redemption Ranch
The Hero of Hope Springs
The Last Christmas Cowboy
The Heartbreaker of Echo Pass
Rodeo Christmas at Evergreen Ranch
The True Cowboy of Sunset Ridge

For more books by Maisey Yates,
visit maiseyyates.com.

MAISEY YATES

The Holiday Heartbreaker

CANARY STREET PRESS

CANARY
STREET
PRESS™

Recycling programs
for this product may
not exist in your area.

ISBN-13: 978-1-335-60079-0

The Holiday Heartbreaker
Copyright © 2023 by Maisey Yates

Wild Night Cowboy
Copyright © 2023 by Maisey Yates

For questions and comments about the quality of this book, please contact us at CustomerService@Harlequin.com.

Canary Street Press
22 Adelaide St. West, 41st Floor
Toronto, Ontario M5H 4E3, Canada
CanaryStPress.com

Printed in U.S.A.

CONTENTS

This book is dedicated to the mothers and mother figures,
the ones who make magic at the holidays
but, most importantly, give unconditional love.

THE HOLIDAY HEARTBREAKER

CHAPTER ONE

"IS THAT A FOX?"

"I think it's a bear," Elizabeth said, knowing that she sounded as distracted as she was, her eyes flickering from the sign her son was commenting on, then back to the highway.

It wasn't a real bear, obviously, just a rusted-out metal representation of one, one of the many that they had seen on the long drive out to Pyrite Falls.

It was cold, and she knew that the temperature outside might be above freezing, but that didn't mean there weren't slick patches in the shade on the road.

It wasn't her first time out here, but it was her first time bringing Benny. He wasn't happy about the move, and she knew that it was because he didn't like change. He was upset that he was leaving his grandma, and she understood that. But she wasn't upset to put some distance between herself and her former mother-in-law.

There had been a lot of promises about how their relationship wouldn't deteriorate after Elizabeth's marriage ended.

After all, Elizabeth hadn't *chosen* to end it.

Elizabeth hadn't *wanted* Carter to start a new life with a different woman, to have children with her. Act like Benny was a leftover from a life that he had never really wanted to begin with.

It wasn't that her mother-in-law was awful to her. Or like they'd had a fight. It was just…easier. Easier for her mother-in-law to just visit her son's new wife and children, and to let her relationship with Elizabeth grow distant.

To trade in afternoons spent over tea at Elizabeth's kitchen table for dinner with Carter and Ashley.

She had Benny over to her house still, of course. Usually when Carter and the other kids were there.

She was trying to foster a relationship between Carter and Benny, that was what she'd said, and Elizabeth knew it was true. When his mother didn't get involved, Carter missed more weekends with Benny than he managed to make.

The twins have soccer. Benny would get bored.

Ashley has a dressage clinic. Benny won't want to sit through that.

But when his mom brought Benny over, he was always delighted. There was usually a cookout and games in their huge backyard and time spent at the stables, riding the horses.

Stables that had been hers.

But were Ashley's now, for her sweet little children to learn to ride horses in while Benny's bedroom-window view was a parking lot.

Carter was always so *nice* on those weekends. As if it wasn't his mother who had arranged visits. As if it wasn't Elizabeth who supported them. And then, of course, he had been furious when she had announced that she was moving three hours away. As if he saw Benny all time. As if he was father of the year and she was cruelly ripping his son away from him.

And so close to the holidays!

Because of course. *Of course.*

Benny was sad. Even though she'd told him it would be so much different than living in the little apartment they were in now. No, they wouldn't have a community pool, but there would be space to run, and there was a creek, she was told.

Of course the idea of letting him swim in a creek made her nervous and anxious.

But her son *deserved* more. And the truth of it was *she* was going to have to work to give him more. Because God knew Carter wasn't going to do it. At least, he wasn't going to give him what he should get.

And maybe... Maybe *she* deserved more. Deserved to find the life that she would've had if she had never fallen in love when she was fourteen years old. If she hadn't followed it to the conclusion of marriage and having a child before she was strictly ready.

Carter had always been in a hurry. She'd never been certain what he was running toward, but she'd gotten caught up in it. Until he'd gone on to someone else.

Left her behind. Struggling to pay her bills, struggling to remember who she'd been before. If she'd ever even known who she was on her own.

She'd been Carter's girlfriend, Carter's wife, Carter's ex-wife.

Who was she when he didn't define her?

Maybe she deserved to find out.

She kept her eyes on the two-lane road ahead of her, trying not to get distracted by the scenery. The town itself was nothing to behold. A little strip of buildings made of timber that blended in to the trees. But the sight of them signified that they were close to Four Corners Ranch, which was where they would be living.

Specifically McCloud's Landing.

Four Corners itself was a ranching collective that functioned like one large ranch, but it was actually four, run by the four founding families.

The McClouds had been equestrian focused since the founding of the ranch in the late 1800s, and now they were expanding to offer equine therapy.

She'd met all of the McCloud brothers, who were handsome, intense, and a whole thing.

Gus, the oldest, and the one she'd had the most dealings with, was now happily married to a woman she'd met briefly on her last visit. Tag and Hunter were married too, and she harbored hopes of finding a friend among at least one of the wives. Lachlan and Brody McCloud were both single.

Lachlan didn't bother her in the least.

Brody, on the other hand…

There was something about him. Something that made her feel prickly and uncomfortable. Worse, during her every interaction with him, she had the sense he knew it.

She didn't like it.

"We're here," she said, happy to distract both Benny and herself. The sign that proudly proclaimed the dirt road they were turning on to be the main-entry point for Four Corners Ranch had horses on it, and Benny didn't seem overly impressed by that.

It was her greatest sorrow that her son did not seem even half as enthused about horses as she was.

But then, he hadn't been able to have a lot of exposure to them.

Carter had left when Benny was two, and it had changed their lives dramatically. They had gone from living in a lovely house on the outskirts of town, with ten acres and several horses, to only being able to afford an apartment.

While Carter had kept the house.

And her horses. They would always be her horses, because in her mind nothing living was property in the sense of who bought them or was awarded them by a judge. And she didn't think of them as hers in that way.

As something she owned.

They were hers, in her heart. Because she loved them and always would.

But he'd taken those like they were assets.

He had eventually moved his girlfriend in, and she'd been pregnant already. They'd married, and started a family. Right over the top of Elizabeth's life.

Right over the top of *their* life.

Like she and Carter had never been there at all.

Ashley'd had twin boys, which always felt like an insult to Elizabeth. Like she'd been doubly efficient when giving him children too.

Two to Elizabeth's one, in a single pregnancy.

And now there was a girl, and another baby on the way.

The worst part about Carter was when he'd told her, he hadn't been cruel. He'd looked at her with that familiar, handsome face and said he'd made a mistake. But that the mistake had opened his eyes to problems he'd been ignoring in their lives, in him.

His fault, his mistakes.

It's not your fault, Elizabeth. It's me.

Like that was supposed to make her feel better? They'd been *married*. Everything was supposed to be about *them*. But this was all him, which meant there was nothing she could do to change it or fix it.

He'd been the one to lead her, she'd always felt that. But suddenly in this story he told her about them that wasn't true at all. In this story he'd made no real choices, he'd made it sound like they'd drifted together, then drifted apart.

He'd been on a path he didn't feel like he'd chosen. He hadn't understood what love was until he met *Ashley*. He had married Elizabeth because it had seemed logical. They'd been in love since high school, you married your high school sweetheart.

He'd never really known how happy he could be, not until he met Ashley.

Well, she called absolute *bull crap* on that. They'd been happy. They *had been*.

And it wasn't fair for him to say all of that when… In the end, she…related to his words. That was what hurt so much.

He wasn't wrong.

He had *acted* wrongly. But when it came to assessing the state of their marriage, he wasn't wrong.

She had married him because he'd been there. He'd been the only guy she'd ever dated, ever been with, ever kissed. He'd asked her to marry him, and she hadn't been able to imagine a life without him – not because their love was so intense – because she could hardly remember not being with him.

She hadn't loved him passionately, but she'd loved their life.

She'd spent the last six years trying to figure out what her world looked like now, and it had taken her all this time to get brave enough to really change things.

They had built a life and now the life was gone. It didn't seem right or fair. It wasn't because she was still in love with him.

It was because he'd left her without the skills to figure out what the hell she was supposed to do.

But she was over that. Done living in wreckage.

And he could be as mad as he wanted to be, but it wouldn't change a damned thing.

He'd claimed a new life for himself. Wasn't she allowed to do the same?

"I hate it," Benny said.

"You haven't even seen it. The house is really cute. I saw it a few months ago when we were first planning the move." Of course, it hadn't been livable yet, but the bones had been nice.

It had taken time to get everything in order, it had taken time to get the custody arrangement adjusted so that the move could be approved.

It was frustrating, because she knew that Carter didn't actually care. How could he? He was an absentee dad when he lived nearby. He was just pretending that he cared, and that he had never been so outraged, because he intended—of course—to spend endless quality time with his son at the drop of a hat.

All of that had somehow gotten in her mother-in-law's head, and eventually she'd made comments in front of Benny, who had taken his grandmother's opinion on everything to heart. She found it all enraging.

Because of that she was stuck with a sulky eight-year-old boy who felt like she was the enemy because every other adult around him treated her as such.

"I miss my friends."

That *did* make her feel guilty.

"I know," she said. "But there's a better life for us here. You get to go to school in a one-room schoolhouse."

"That seems weird."

"It's an adventure. It's like *Little House on the Prairie*."

"I hated those books," he said, sullen.

That made her heart kick hard. She had read him those books when he was little. He hadn't seemed to hate them.

Not then.

But maybe she had lost him even more than she'd realized. Maybe occasional visits to Carter and the Xbox, PlayStation and everything else at that house had won.

She was the real parent. The one who made him go to bed on time, brush his teeth and do his homework. The one who had to discipline him. Carter got to step in on weekends and give him fun, only fun.

She had a small apartment and books.

Carter had everything.

Who could blame Benny for being more into his dad than he was her? When he went to see Carter it was like being on vacation.

She was just his real, boring life.

"They're good books," she said. "And this is an adventure."

"As long as there's Wi-Fi."

"There's Wi-Fi," she said, rolling her eyes. "I think even the one-room schoolhouse has Wi-Fi."

"I'm bored."

She tightened her grip on the steering wheel. "We're almost there."

She gritted her teeth as they continued on down the

dirt road, and she wished that she were even half as patient as she pretended she was on the outside. She was an expert at keeping her emotions to herself. She was fantastic at keeping a placid expression while she listened to all manner of nonsense being spoken directly to her face.

She did it professionally, as a therapist, but that wasn't personal.

She didn't know when she had gotten quite so good at applying it to her personal life. When the skill had first eventuated, it was difficult to say. But she had honed the skill during her divorce, and even more in recent years.

She was now absolutely fantastic at it.

It took several minutes to get from the main road back onto the narrower one that took them to McCloud's Landing. There was a small sign made of planks of wood with the name McCloud hand carved into it.

"That looks like pirates," Benny said, looking suddenly intrigued.

"Well, maybe they are pirates," she said.

She could see Brody McCloud as a pirate. He was... Well, he was a rogue.

She didn't know that much about rogues, but she could recognize one when she saw him. Or maybe he just gave off such a vibe that it was easy enough even for women like her—with no real experience of dating and men—to see it.

"Well, that would be cool."

"Super cool," she echoed, with absolutely no conviction behind the words.

The road began to climb a mountainside, and she knew that the back portion of the property was flat, perfect for horses, but the area where all the houses were nestled was protected by this mountain and by a river, right below.

She knew that if nothing else, Benny would be temporarily impressed by the scenery. For one moment, he quieted, and she took that as a win. Because there could be no complaints over this place. The tall pine trees reaching up toward the fathomless blue sky and the rushing white water below. She had been driven to the cabin once by Gus when she had come out to visit, and was shown around, and she had made great mental note of exactly where it was so that she could find it again without having to ask for help.

She recognized a particular mossy rock, a bend in the road, and a change in the river. It was still where the cabins were. A watering hole that would be nice for swimming.

Though, she might have to make sure that he had a life jacket on at all times when he was anywhere near the water.

He would hate her for that. Maybe *hate* was a strong word. Maybe she was just channeling how she felt the teenage years would likely go.

She didn't have high hopes that she would be any sort of hero.

No. Of course it would be his distant father. Because he didn't have to do the hard days. He didn't have to do school routine on homework. He got to blow everything off on the weekends when he actually did take Benny and do whatever he wanted.

She put that out of her mind. Things were different now. Now, if Carter held to it, Benny would spend a month in the summer there, rather than visiting on the weekends. He would also spend some school breaks with Carter, and while it would be hard to be away from him for long stretches of time she did feel like it would force Carter to actually plan and be present with him.

"Look how much space there is," she said.

Of course, she would have to figure out a way to feel comfortable letting him explore that space, and she had a feeling that would be easier said than done.

She hadn't had a consistent model for what it meant to be a family, to be a mother, and having Benny was her chance for that. She'd wanted something better for him. The nuclear family she'd never had and…

Well, she hadn't been able to give him that.

Consequently, she probably hovered over him more than she should.

She breathed a sigh of relief when the little house came into view. It was rustic, but neat, and Gus had told her that there would be some updates made before she and Benny moved in, which were now presumably there.

But her relief was cut short when she saw a blue truck parked in the driveway.

She had been here for months, and she knew exactly whose truck it was.

It wasn't Gus who had come to greet her, or any of the other myriad McClouds who it might have been. Of course not.

It was Brody.

THE PRETTY LITTLE ice queen was right on time, but Brody wouldn't expect anything different. Not from her. She had been officious and sniffy from the moment he'd first met her.

He had the strong urge to ask her why she was so damned uptight.

He also had the strong urge to undo the neat, low ponytail that she kept her blond hair in.

He could see, even as she pulled up to where he was standing, that her hair was styled in that same fashion now. He wondered at that. At the commitment to being quite so sedate.

Her car came to a stop, and she looked through the windshield, right at him.

He *felt* it.

That was the problem. The urge to undo that ponytail was a very grown-up version of wanting to pull her pigtails.

Of course, the attraction that he felt for Elizabeth Colfax was clearly not reciprocated, and if it was, it wasn't reciprocated *happily.*

She had been prickly and dismissive of him from the get-go.

Him, specifically. She seemed much friendlier to each and every one of his brothers. But yeah, *friendly* was not a word you would use to describe the way that she treated him.

She turned the engine off and got out of the car.

Her blond hair was sleek and shiny, her face colored by only the slightest bit of makeup, a hint of blush, a pale pink lip gloss. She was wearing a navy blue top and white pants. She was dressed a good twenty years older than she actually was.

A single string of pearls completed the look.

They made him think dirty, dirty thoughts.

"Nice to see you," he said.

She smiled, but it didn't reach her eyes. "Yes. Nice to see you too."

The back door of the car opened, and a little boy tumbled out. Blond, just like her.

For a moment, he felt disoriented. He hadn't realized she had a kid. Did that mean she had a husband? Because that sure put a damper on some of his fantasies.

Well, depending on how happily married she was.

But no. He wasn't a homewrecker. Wasn't his style.

There was no point to go in for any drama when a man could just as easily go in for a no-strings-attached, simple affair that didn't hurt anyone.

"Who is this?" he asked, smiling, because he was good at that. He was a charming son of a bitch. It was his best quality.

"This is Benny," she said, her answering smile tight. He stressed her out.

"Hi, Benny," he said.

The kid looked up at him, and he noticed that his eyes were the same blue as Elizabeth's. "Hi. Are you a pirate?"

Standing there in his T-shirt, jeans and cowboy hat, it had never occurred to Brody that he might be confused for a pirate.

"No," he said. "At least, not on Saturdays."

"Why not on Saturdays?" Elizabeth asked, her nose wrinkling slightly.

Why was that adorable?

"Because today is Saturday and I'm obviously dressed as a cowboy."

"Oh," she said. "I guess that…that makes sense."

The woman could hardly take a joke. He shouldn't find her hot.

"You're a cowboy?" Benny asked, clearly interested.

"Yes. This is a ranch, or did you not realize?"

"My mom just said something about horses." He shrugged. "Horses are boring."

"Horses are boring," he repeated.

Brody had never been so offended in his life. And by a half-grown piglet. "Horses are the furthest thing from boring, kid. Horses are the Wild West."

"Not the way my mom does it. She just rides in a circle."

"I do not just ride in a circle," she said.

He'd seen her ride. In those heaven-sent English-style riding breeches. The way this woman rode wasn't boring, not at all.

"The reason what your mom does looks boring is that she makes it look easy. You don't see all the work that goes into it because that's what it's like when someone is an expert."

"She's an expert?" The kid looked skeptical.

"The best there is, or we wouldn't have hired her to work here. You know why?" The kid shook his head. "There are going to be some people who have injuries. And not just injuries to their bodies, things that have frightened them or hurt them inside. In places you can't see. Horses help heal those things."

Benny frowned. "How?"

"Because horses understand you. Without you needing to talk. Without you needing to do anything at all. And sometimes all a person needs is to be understood." He realized that Elizabeth was staring at him. He returned her gaze. "Don't you think?"

"Yes," she said, as if it surprised her. "I do."

He straightened. "Gus asked me to show you around the place."

That wasn't strictly true. He'd volunteered to do it. Because he liked the look of her. Though, Gus had given him a stern warning with that scarred-up face of his. And Brody'd done what he did best, and ignored it.

Anyway, Gus was a lot tamer now that he had his little woman. Who would've ever thought?

Gus and *Alaina*. Together. Like that.

Certainly not something Brody would ever have picked out.

But the man was the proudest husband and father-to-be anywhere, and Brody couldn't begrudge his brother that happiness. Especially not when he'd spent so many years being the most *miserable* son of a gun Brody had ever known.

"Come on in, I'll show you around. Didn't realize you were coming with a kid in tow."

He waited to see if she would say there was a husband coming too.

"Gus knew," she said.

Well, he hadn't, and he didn't know why it felt notable. Or why it mattered.

You know. It's because you think she's hot, and now she's off-limits.

"Well, he didn't mention it. That's all." He'd suspect that Gus had left it out to throw him off on purpose, but his older brother wasn't like that.

Gus could be a dick, but he was straight up.

"Unless you were involved in the preparation of the cottage, I can't imagine that it would be your concern."

"Well," he said. "This way."

She walked on ahead of him, and Benny had already trotted up to the porch.

"You got any bags?" he asked.

"A couple."

"Got a moving truck coming or anything?"

She shook her head. "We basically did everything we could to downsize before coming. But we lived in a pretty small apartment, so there wasn't a whole lot."

It was strange, the idea of this woman living in a small apartment. She *felt* like money to him. There was that rich simplicity to the way that she dressed, a style that didn't take trends into account at all. Then, there was the sort of haughty manner with which she conducted herself, the way she acted like she was too good for the likes of him.

And the way he kind of liked it.

Because it made him want to take her down a peg or ten, and he knew exactly how to do it.

He hadn't really thought that he would get off on the fantasy of the uptight girl. But she made him want to undo every button on one of her twin sets. See if he could get her to mess up that sleek hair.

Well, fantasizing about undressing a woman while her kid was standing right there was a low, even for him.

He went to the car and grabbed the duffel bags, and a small suitcase that he found, and hefted them up before following her to the porch. "My brother's wife, Nelly, did a little bit of landscaping for you. She thought you'd like it."

He indicated the fresh flowerpots on the porch.

"I do," she said. "It's nice."

"You don't live here, do you?" Benny asked, his eyes suddenly going round.

"I live on the ranch."

"You're not my mom's new husband or anything, are you?"

He couldn't help it, a guffaw of laughter escaped his lips. Elizabeth's mouth dropped open. She was not laughing.

"No, Benny. What would've given you that idea?"

"Tim at school said that his mom has new husbands in the house all the time. I thought maybe you were going to do that."

She looked genuinely confused. "I've never done that. Why would I start now?"

"We've never moved before either." Kid logic.

"Not since you can remember," she said, her voice tight. "I moved here for a job not a... There is no husband."

"I'm just a pirate cowboy, kiddo. Sorry." Then Brody cleared his throat and pushed the door open, revealing the clean and newly renovated cabin.

"Oh," she said. "This is... Well, it's... It's just so much... I don't know what I expected, but this exceeds it."

"We have a little bit of an advantage now because we married into the Sullivan clan and the Garrett family, which brought a bit more support for the venture. So... We were able to significantly upgrade some of the living quarters."

"It's beautiful," she said.

And for just one moment, he thought he saw her eyes go glassy with tears. But she blinked, and was back to smooth, porcelain perfection.

"I imagine you don't need me to show you around every room."

"I might need you to show me how some of these appliances work."

Benny had raced away down the hall, and he let out a holler.

"What?" Elizabeth asked, hurrying down the hall, and Brody followed her.

"Look at my room!"

The room was a little-boy's paradise, and he had to wonder which one of his brothers had been responsible for that. Brody hadn't even realized.

He'd been busy, he supposed. Doing whatever outdoor-labor task Gus asked him, and additionally, heading to the bars and getting drunk whenever possible.

There were bunk beds with lanterns hanging on them, and the bottom bed was done up to look like an outdoor tent. The entire room was like camping. There were glow stars on the ceiling, and a light on the floor that glowed like a fire.

"I told you that you'd like it," she said.

The little boy's face went flat. "Well, I don't think I'll like it for forever."

He suddenly felt sympathy for Elizabeth. Because he recognized when a kid was trying to make their parent miserable. "Hey," he said. "Don't talk to your mom that way. She's doing her best. And from what I can see, her best is pretty damned good."

"That's a cuss word," the kid said.

"Yes," Brody said, realizing he did not know how to talk to kids. "It is. But it's true. And if you really think it's boring here, then you just wait. Tomorrow, I'll show you and your mom everything."

"Everything?" Benny asked.

"Hell yeah. I mean… Heck yeah. Tomorrow I'm going to show you why horses are exciting, and why you're going to love it here."

"A real cowboy," Benny said, looking at his mom. "A real cowboy is going to show us around."

When he looked back at Brody, Brody didn't need to have any experience with kids to realize that he had gotten himself into a bit of a hero-worship situation. And when he looked back at the kid's mother, and saw the cool fire banked in her blue gaze, he realized that when it came to her…

Well, it was anything but.

"As long as it's okay," he added.

"Of course," she answered, her expression frosty. And hell, even he realized that he'd walked her into a situation where she couldn't refuse.

"Great. I'll let you all get settled. And I'll see you tomorrow."

CHAPTER TWO

ELIZABETH WAS CERTAIN that as soon as Brody left she would be able to catch her breath. But she found that her elevated heart rate lingered long after he walked out of the cabin.

Benny disappeared into his room, and honestly, she couldn't blame him. It was an incredible room. So far beyond anything that she had imagined. Gus had promised that they would fix the place up last time she was here, and he had not disappointed.

She wanted to thank him. Of course, she hadn't seen Gus. Or any of the other McClouds. Just Brody. A one-man welcome wagon. It made her feel… Off-put. Not in a terrible way, it was just that…

You think he's hot.

No. She was twenty-nine years old, she was divorced. She was a *mother*. She did not think men were hot.

Okay, she thought men were hot. There was a reason she watched superhero movies and it wasn't for the plot. It was the one perk of having a child who was obsessed with that kind of thing. She thought *those* men were hot. But those men were actors. They lived far, far away, they didn't really have superpowers, and they had nothing to do with her real life. She could fantasize about them all she wanted.

No. She didn't think that men that she actually had

to deal with were hot. There was no point to it. She was raising a child, and things were complicated enough without introducing...

She leaned over the kitchen counter and groaned when she thought about what Benny had said about Brody being her new husband.

And really, she needed to ask him what else his little friend at school had told him about his mother. Because she had follow-up questions.

She didn't do that kind of thing. For six years she had done nothing but concentrate on raising Benny and working as hard as she could to keep their life stable. She did get child support from Carter, but she still had to work full-time. She had experience at several ranches in the area and had given private lessons. At one of the ranches she'd gotten to observe the STRIDE program, and she'd become fascinated with it. So she'd decided to work toward getting certification as a STRIDE instructor. Which was an acronym for Successful Training Rehabilitation Integrating Disability Education. Kind of a mouthful. But it was something that she believed in really deeply. She had gotten her start working with veterans, and the whole program had been incredibly successful.

And when she had seen the ad go up on a job website for the position at McCloud's Landing nearly a year ago, she had replied to it, beginning her communications with Gus. The thing was, the move here was well considered. She was tired of feeling stuck. She was tired of feeling like she was living a life she hadn't chosen.

So she had chosen this.

She looked around the kitchen, which was small, but brightly lit and absolutely beautiful. The cabinets were white, with a marble backsplash behind a gas stove with beautiful gold knobs. She wandered over to the white fridge, all smooth and fancy with handles that matched the stovetop, and opened it up. There was food.

A loaf of bread wrapped in cloth, pre-prepared stew.

And it would taste really good on a night this cold.

She gave thanks to whoever had provided that, and set about heating it up. When she got dinner on the table, she hoped that when Benny appeared his mood would be improved.

Well, it wasn't his overall mood, because he was perfectly happy when talking to Brody. He was impressed with Brody. Brody was a pirate cowboy.

In spite of herself, she laughed as she ladled stew into the two bowls for herself and her son.

She had not expected Brody to be that good with kids.

But he seemed to talk to Benny easily. Even if he had used a little bit of salty language. It had only increased Benny's awe of him. She could tell, because Benny wasn't in awe of her at all.

"Dinner," she called.

When Benny didn't appear, she walked down the hall to his room, where he was tucked away in the tent bed. "Dinner," she repeated.

He poked his head out between the flaps. "I'm not hungry."

"I don't care. You have to come and at least sit at the bowl and look at it. And take two bites."

"That's not fair," he said, worming his way out of the bed and falling to the floor in a dramatic fashion.

She ignored it. He finally stood up and padded down the hallway, then flung his chair out with far too much force and plopped down onto it. "This looks gross," he said.

"Joke's on you, kid. I didn't make it, so it doesn't hurt my feelings. But I don't know who did make it. And you better be careful saying something like that, because it might hurt their feelings."

"Do you think Brody made it?"

"I don't," she said. "But, we can't be sure. You wouldn't want to hurt a pirate cowboy's feelings."

"You probably can't," Benny said, putting his elbow on the table and resting his cheek on his hand as he dug his spoon into the stew.

Well. That was probably true. Brody McCloud was likely one of those men whose hearts were like Teflon. She would never have thought that her ex-husband's heart was like that, but then it had turned out it was. At least where she was concerned.

It was so deeply unfair, because Carter never acted mean or impatient. Because Carter didn't have Benny for long enough to ever feel stretched thin. Because he wasn't the one who did homework. Or bath time or bedtime or parent-teacher conferences. Because he wasn't buying school supplies and counting every dime. Because he didn't have to do discipline and consistency.

Carter just got to be Teflon with everything sliding right off, and it all stuck to her.

Yeah. Brody was probably one of those Teflon men.

For all she knew, he had several kids of his own, and not a single wife. Maybe he was used to these casual interactions with kids because he was often patting them on the head and sending them to be dealt with by their mothers when it came to anything serious or real.

Yeah. That sounded about right.

This imaginary Brody made her angry, and she welcomed it.

It didn't matter how hot he was. It didn't change the likely truth.

Anyway, she was not the kind of woman who could afford the cost of hot men. She didn't know how to do that whole thing. She had forfeited her youth to Carter. And now what was left of it was being given to Benny. What it amounted to was: too many men in her life already.

"It's not gross, is it?" she asked, lifting the spoon to her lips and taking a sip.

It was actually amazing.

"No," he grumbled.

"Have some bread and butter," she said, pushing the bread down toward him, along with a pat of butter and a small wooden knife that was more like a spatula.

After he had about six pieces of bread and butter, she quietly called dinner a triumph. She wasn't going to say anything to him about it, because she didn't want any attitude.

She did not know how she was going to survive this boy's teenage years. The very thought of it made her chest ache, and she felt guilty for what she had just been thinking. That she was sacrificing anything for Benny.

She loved him.

The worst thing wasn't him thinking Carter was more fun than she was. The worst was the pain that would inevitably come when he realized exactly what kind of man Carter was.

He didn't see it now, and sometimes that frustrated her. But she should be grateful. Because eventually, he'd see it all too clearly.

He yawned.

"You sleepy?" she asked, smiling.

"No," he said.

"You know, cowboys keep pretty early hours, so I have a feeling that when Brody comes by to give us the grand tour it's going to be a lot earlier than you want to wake up. And then next week you have to start school, so it's going to be a lot of early mornings then too."

"I hate getting up early."

"I know. But no matter how many times I called the school system, they don't see the point in changing the schedule just to suit you. Bummer, right?"

"You never called anybody."

"You don't know that."

"Yes I do," he said. "You hate calling people on the phone."

Of course the kid paid unerring attention to her and her behaviors when it suited him.

"Maybe I sent an email," she said.

Even though he was still grumpy, this felt better. More like a return to their usual relationship. As far as she was concerned, it was them against the world. She just knew that he didn't see it that way. And again, she should be grateful for that. He loved his dad. He loved his stepmother, and his half siblings. And she might only see the flaws in the way that relationship worked, but Benny saw good things in it, and for as long as that lasted, she should be glad.

"Bedtime," she said.

She ushered him off to his room, and then a few minutes later, once he had his pajamas on, she got down on her knees next to the tent bed. "You want a story?"

"No."

He grabbed a flashlight from inside the tent bed and shone it at the canvas ceiling.

"That's fine," she said, trying to be cool.

"Good night," he said.

"Good night, buddy. I love you." She stood up slowly and walked to the door, turning the light off and pausing in the doorway for about a minute longer than she needed to. Then she turned and closed the door behind her, looking down the unfamiliar hallway, out into the living room.

And she had a visceral memory of the day she had moved into the apartment in Portland. When she had moved away from the property that she and Carter had called home.

That was her last move. And it hadn't been her choice. It hadn't been because she was moving toward something better. It was because what she was leaving behind had crumbled. Had fallen apart beyond repair, and had been left rubble that defied recognition.

She had chosen this place. This ranch. The future.

She just had to be firm and follow what she knew. And what she knew was that Benny might not understand now. But it would be a better life.

She would be happier. She would have more resources. More to give him.

She was exhausted. And she realized she hadn't gone into her bedroom at all.

With a strange heaviness in her heart, she turned and walked all the way to the end of the hall, pushing open the door and revealing an oasis. The room was white, with a large bed in the center of it. There was a geometric rug on the floor, and potted plants all around. It was simple, but it was beautiful. She opened the door to the bathroom, and her heart lifted. There were more plants, and a large soaking tub. There was a window, right next to the tub, and she paused there for a whole thirty seconds, trying to figure out what the view might be. And for some reason, imagined Brody being in proximity to that view.

Her heart gave a stutter, and she grabbed the edge of one of the white linen curtains and swung it shut. And decided she was going to take a bath. There was also a shower with a glass door in the corner of the bathroom, but she couldn't remember the last time she had taken a bath. The bathtub in her apartment was so small she had to make that terrible bargain. Boobs or knees under the water? It always ended chilly. But here, she would not have to make that bargain.

It felt like a metaphor. A very strange metaphor, but a metaphor nonetheless.

She started to run the water, and it just wouldn't warm up. Persistently, she waited. And she waited. And she had been given a phone number to text if there were any issues, but she felt bad, because it was going on eight o'clock, and it was dark and cold outside, but she figured the text could go ignored if it was an issue. Because she wasn't going to be silent if she needed something. She was trying to start something new. She was trying to do a new thing, be a new thing, and maybe that included saying something if she couldn't get the hot water to work.

Because she really did at least need a shower.

After the whole of today, she wanted to get refreshed before she got into bed.

She sent off a text, and wasn't sure who the recipient might be.

Brody.

Stop thinking about Brody.

Maybe it would be Lachlan. Easy Lachlan McCloud, who was just as handsome as his brother, but for some reason, didn't get under her skin. Lachlan, for her, was more like one of those movie superheroes. Great muscles, beautiful to look at. A little bit thrilling. But not…

Whatever it was Brody was.

Or maybe it would be Gus, who was happily married and totally safe. Hunter, who was the same, or Tag.

But as soon as she heard the swift, hard knock on the door, she knew exactly who it was. Didn't know how, only knew that her stomach did a strange tightening, shivering sensation. *Maybe you're projecting.*

She was not projecting. It was Brody. And she knew it.

She swallowed hard, and then walked to the front door, opening it. And yes. There he was.

"Are you my official contact point?"

His lips curved upward. "Yep."

He still had that cowboy hat on. Dark whiskers covered his jaw, and those eyes—more gold and green than brown—hit her with the impact of a physical blow. He was so tall. He made her feel petite. Carter was only a couple of inches taller than her, and while he was handsome, he didn't make her feel…little.

What a weird thought.

"The water just isn't warming up," she said. "Which I sent in the text. So you know that."

"Yeah," he said. "Care to show me the offending tub?"

And walk him through her bedroom. To her bathroom.

Lord.

"Back that way," she said, gesturing.

He stepped inside, and again, she was struck by the way he filled up the space. "The bedroom… Bathroom. That one."

She was so flustered words were deserting her.

He lifted a brow. "Back there?" And by the way his lips curved, she could tell that he was teasing her.

"Yes," she said.

"Okay."

He walked past her and went through the bedroom, and she stood at the end of the hall, peering after him. She did her best not to look at the way his jeans show-cased his muscular thighs, and an equally muscled rear. But the fact that she had noted all of that was muscular meant she had looked. What was the matter with her?

She could hear the water running.

She paced back and forth at the end of the hall for a few minutes until he came out to her. "I have a theory," he said. "Come on."

He moved past her, jerking his head. And then he opened the front door.

"Outside?"

"There's a pump house out here that goes to a couple of different cabins. I suspect your issue is out there."

"Hang on," she said, looking at her suitcases and things, which were sort of haphazardly just there by the door. "I need a coat."

"Yeah."

And he watched her. She felt exposed by that. By that green-and-gold gaze and the way that he seemed to track her every movement. It made her feel clumsy, and like every single thing she did was amplified. From her breath to the movements of her fingers.

She grabbed her coat and slipped it on. And for some reason, the silken liner of the navy blue jacket felt sensual as it slid over her long-sleeved shirt, which was a lot thinner than she had been conscious of until that moment.

It was him watching her.

"Let's go," she said, sliding her hands beneath her hair at the nape of her neck and flicking them, getting her hair out from underneath the collar of the coat.

"All right," he said.

He reached into his pocket and took out a keychain, which had a small flashlight on it. He clicked the button. "This way."

She followed him, her hands in her pockets, yet again making a valiant effort not to look him over. But at least the dim lighting made it harder to see him. Their feet crunched over the pine-needle-covered ground. Every so often, there was a pinecone or an acorn that made a big round lump beneath her tennis shoes. They went around to the side of the cabin, and she could see another cabin just a few feet away.

"What does the bathtub window face?"

She hadn't meant to say that out loud, but she had.

He stopped. "I... I would assume it faces the mountain. Off to the side of it. No one can see up this way."

"Okay," she said.

He cleared his throat and kept on walking, and it was impossible to know what he was thinking in that moment.

She was glad.

There was a small outbuilding that stood between the two cabins, and he pushed the door open. "Come here."

With great hesitation, she followed him inside. It was

a shed. And she was quite concerned that there might be spiders. It was surprisingly warm inside, though, clearly insulated.

"This is the hot water heater to the cabin. So it has to travel a little ways to heat the water up inside. But I don't think that's your issue. I'm just going to check the pilot light. And after that I'll check for blown fuses and that kind of thing."

"I don't know about any of this stuff. I've had a landlord for the last six years and before that…"

"Yeah?" he prompted, moving around to the side of the appliance, fiddling with something that she couldn't see.

"I had…" And she didn't know why she was embarrassed to admit that she'd been married. She wasn't usually. She had a child from that marriage. It was a huge part of her life, that relationship and the fallout from it. "My husband. My husband used to fix everything."

"Right," he said, and he sounded like he had some questions, but he didn't ask them. "Yeah, the pilot light is out," he said. "Come here. I don't mind if you text me every time there's a problem. And I'm going to suggest that we get a new hot water heater for the buildings out here, but until then, if there's an issue, and you want to fix it yourself, let me show you. We just need to get it relit." She came around to where he was, and he pointed to a place that he highlighted with his flashlight. She leaned in, and she realized that their faces were very close together. "There should be a flame here."

She nodded, and found that she could barely breathe. He was right there. He was… He was right there.

She swallowed hard. "Okay. So we need to have a flame."

"Yes," he said, grinning. "We need a flame."

He smelled like pine and skin. A masculine scent that she hadn't been in proximity to for a long time. And even then, it hadn't been quite like this. Because it hadn't been him.

"A flame," she repeated.

It was on the tip of her tongue to say that there was a flame now, and why the hell would they try to ignite anything hotter and more dangerous than what was already there? But it was in her head. It was totally in her head, and she needed to get it together.

"So this is how you reignite it," he said. "First you need to check the gas line. That's down here." He crouched, and for some reason, that made her feel completely thrown off her axis. He was down in front of her, and it made her so uneasy, especially when he looked up, and the light caught those eyes, and they clashed with hers. "Looks like the gas is flowing. So I think we just need to click the ignition point up here."

He straightened, and it made her feel dizzy.

"And just like that," he said, pushing a button at the same time he turned the knob. "Flame."

"Right," she said.

Flame.

Her chest burned. Her stomach burned. Everything burned.

"Thank you," she said, her voice sounding thin and breathless.

"You're welcome."

She backed away, and her boot caught on something on the floor, maybe a loose board, she didn't know, but she found herself pitching backward, and then he reached out and grabbed hold of her arm, that large, strong hand steadying her, pulling her back up, keeping her from tumbling down to the ground.

"Hey there," he said, that deep voice sending sparks over the surface of her skin. "Careful."

Careful.

This didn't feel careful. It felt dangerous.

She needed to be *careful*.

It would be so easy to take a step toward him...

So she took a step back.

And out into the fresh, cold night air.

Where she didn't find any kind of clarity. She still felt... Warm.

"A husband, huh?" he asked, and the question felt weighted in a way that seemed to add to that warmth. Stoke it.

"Ex-husband," she said.

"Right. Right."

She didn't know if she should've told him that or not. But what would be the benefit of keeping it to herself? Anyway, like he cared. Just because she was having a hot flash and some inappropriate feelings didn't mean that he was.

"There's a staff meeting tomorrow. Seven o'clock. In the main barn. You know where that is?"

"I... I think so. I think I remember seeing it when I came last time."

"I can come by and pick you up, if you want."

"I don't want to leave Benny."

"You can bring him. And we can go do the tour that I promised you after. He might be bored. But he can hang out in the barn. I'll make sure there's some hot chocolate for him."

"Thank you." She took a step away from him. "I'm going to go… Have my bath now."

And for some reason, she imagined herself in the tub, but envisioned rough hands moving over her bare, wet skin. And that was her cue to leave.

Quickly.

"See you tomorrow."

"Yeah. Thank you. Thank you for…for all this. Thank you." *Say thank-you one more time, Elizabeth.*

"You're welcome."

He lifted his hand and touched the brim of his hat, nodded once firmly. Then he turned and walked away, and it was only then that she started breathing again.

CHAPTER THREE

HE WASN'T HALLUCINATING THAT. She'd felt it. She had been a little bundle of nerves the whole time they had been in that pump house together.

Ex-husband.

Doesn't matter. She's got a kid. It's all complicated.

Brody didn't do complicated.

He walked back to his own cabin, where he found his brother Lachlan still waiting for him, along with Lachlan's best friend Charity. They had been in the middle of a poker game, the singles of McCloud's Landing. All right, maybe Charity technically didn't live at McCloud's Landing. But she lived close enough.

"You get that sorted out?" Lachlan asked.

"Yep. Pilot light. I just had to relight it. So now she's…"

In the bath. Naked. Wet and slick and far too interesting for his peace of mind.

"Yes?" Lachlan asked, not about to ignore the fact that Brody had just trailed off.

"She's taking a bath, I guess," he said.

"She's pretty hot," Lachlan commented.

"If tonight is going to devolve into this sort of talk, I'm going to go home and call Byron," Charity said.

Byron was Charity's fiancé, though Brody had never met the guy, since he lived across the country, per Lach-

lan. Someone Charity had met at veterinary school.
That she'd gotten engaged to someone else only made
Brody that much more mystified by the connection be-
tween his brother and the sweet little veterinarian.

It wasn't sexual.

Lachlan liked an obvious sort of woman, the kind
that was there for a good time, just like him. Lachlan
was an obvious sort of guy. Not really any different
than Brody, actually.

Charity was… She was cute. But, she was really just
cute. She had long blond hair that curled at the ends,
and wore prim little dresses and ankle socks. If she'd
ever applied makeup, he'd never seen it. And yet she
was the one person in the world that Lachlan seemed
to have a strong bond with outside the family.

He was like her guard dog. Always standing with her.

"It isn't going to turn into that," Brody said. "Because I have nothing to say about her, pretty or not.
She's got a kid."

Lachlan grimaced. "Oh."

"If a woman has a child, that disqualifies her from
the two of you objectifying her?" Charity asked.

"Well, now I'm confused, Doc," Lachlan said. "Because you distinctly said that you did not want us getting into this kind of talk, and now you seem kind of
upset that we're not going to."

"I just think it's weird and sexist that suddenly the
two of you can't think she's pretty because she has a
child."

"No, it moves her outside of the arena of women that
we would ever hook up with," Lachlan said. "There
are rules."

"Scoundrel rules," Brody said.

"Lord give me strength," Charity said, looking up at the ceiling.

"No family members of friends—especially not sisters," Lachlan said.

"Hunter blew that," Brody said.

"Hunter is an asshole," Lachlan said. "I would *never*. No friends, no wives of friends, no single moms unless you don't know the kid exists. As in, the kid is nowhere around, because she's just out to have a good time. So basically, if you don't know she's a single mom, it's fine. Because it has nothing to do with you, and neither does the kid."

"Please tell me you don't have this written down somewhere," she said.

"No," Lachlan said. "In fact, I've never actually said it out loud until right now. But it's true."

"It's true," Brody confirmed.

Charity rolled her eyes and reached out toward the center of the table, taking a handful of chips out of the bowl. "You guys are a couple of sketchy characters."

"And yet here you are, on a lovely Friday night, sitting with us."

"Well, it would either be that or sitting at home."

And he knew that Charity had been doing an awful lot of that lately. Her dad was sick, and his health was declining.

"It's good to get away when you can," Lachlan said, all of the teasing gone from his eyes.

His brother really did care about his friend.

"Yeah. It is getting late, though. I should go. Thank you for giving me a chance to kick your butt soundly. I will take my five dollars, and next time I'm in Copper Ridge, maybe I'll buy myself a fancy coffee drink."

Lachlan got up and walked Charity to the door, opening it for her, then standing there watching as she walked to her car. Then he closed the door and turned back to Brody. "Bummer about the kid."

"It's fine."

"You like her, though."

He shrugged. "I think she's hot. But that's it."

If only that were true. *Hot*, in his experience, had a broad definition and was cheaply had. He liked women. He liked how they looked. He liked how they felt, how they smelled, and how he felt when he was with them. In them.

This was more than that. More than hot.

But it couldn't even be that.

"Yeah, I think it's a little more than that."

Damn his brother for that.

"I don't do more than that, bro. As you well know."

"I didn't mean like that. I just meant… I saw the two of you when you met. Kind of obvious chemistry."

"I thank you not to remark on my chemistry. It's creepy."

He laughed. "Sorry. I don't have a social gauge. Which I think *you* know."

"Yeah. Yeah."

He stood and looked at his brother. Lachlan had scars on his face. A line that ran through his eyebrow, and one that disrupted his lip. From his father's fists. He and Lachlan looked the most alike of his brothers, but Brody didn't have a single scar.

Brody had been his dad's favorite.

He gritted his teeth. "She's divorced. The whole thing is like baggage, in a way that…"

"Yeah. I get it. I don't blame you. I don't do that

whole thing either." And Brody chose not to remark on the fact that Lachlan's relationship with Charity looked a whole lot to him like a relationship without the sex.

But then, that kind of made sense. It allowed him to have someone in his life. Somebody soft and sweet, a female influence. That wasn't... Marriage. Love. All that.

Keep your sex and your other stuff separate. Made sense to him.

Actually, sometimes he wondered if Lachlan was a genius.

"Staff meeting tomorrow," Brody said. "Early."

"I know. You don't have to keep tabs on me," Lachlan said.

"Force of habit."

"Yeah. I know. As if you don't need tabs kept on you."

Lachlan was... Well, correct.

Charity was probably the best stabilizing force in his life. And Brody didn't even have that. That was the thing. Hunter and Tag had been part of their posse until they had gotten married. But even they had never been quite as given over to the debauched arts as Lachlan and Brody were.

Drinking, sex... They ranched hard, they played harder. It was the thing they were into. But that sometimes meant they were spotty when it came to keeping commitments and schedules and things like that.

Their life had been hell growing up. Well, Lachlan, Tag, Hunter and especially Gus's lives had been hell. A particular kind of hell, where they had earned their father's fists and ire just for breathing wrong.

And Brody?

He had been the favorite child of the devil.

He was thirty-four years old and he still hadn't figured out what the hell to do with that.

He didn't think he ever would. He would probably just drink about it. It didn't solve anything. But it numbed it. And that was often the best solution, in his opinion.

SIX A.M. CAME around early, and Benny was cranky when she dragged him out of bed and set him down at the table in front of a bowl of oatmeal that he dramatically declared he didn't want.

"You need to eat something," she said.

"Why?" he asked, sounding exceptionally whiny.

"Because, if you don't eat, you're not going to have any energy for the day. And you're going to be in a bad mood." Though, she was struggling now to identify how that would be any different than he was behaving currently. Clearly, he woke up ready to be in a fight with her.

"I want to talk to Dad," he said.

"You can call Dad later. But he probably isn't up yet."

Carter was good about picking up FaceTime calls from Benny, so there was that. But he probably wouldn't welcome one at six.

It was funny that she cared. About boundaries. She was Benny's full-time parent and there was no one going "Whoa there, Tiger, maybe Mom wants to sleep in today."

She couldn't figure out who she was actually protecting here.

Benny, from his dad's annoyance. Carter, from being woken? Surely not.

Herself, because the lack of boundaries was actually a privilege and meant she was more important?

Maybe.

Finally, she cajoled Benny into eating, got him dressed, and got him coherent enough to begin the trek down to the barn.

She had bundled him up in multiple layers, and she was glad that she had, since it was freezing outside. The brown leaves on the ground were outlined in frost, the pine needles like tiny icicles. She looked around, and for a moment, she was completely stunned by the beauty. The mountains were huge, all around them. The trees looked blue in the distance, the furred branches dusted with ice.

"Beautiful," she whispered, the word escaping on a cloud.

Benny grumbled. And she knew that he didn't agree. Well. Fine. He didn't have to agree. She had not asked for an eight-year-old's opinion. Especially not a surly one.

The light was on in the barn, the doors open, a glow emanating from inside. It was clean and warm, and she really couldn't focus on it, because as soon as she walked in, her gaze went straight to Brody.

There were a lot of people there.

But Brody was the one that captivated her. From moment one.

"Elizabeth," said Gus, grinning. "Good to see you."

He was standing with his arm around his wife, who was very pregnant, a gold band gleaming on his finger.

"Yes," she said. "Good to see you. Alaina, remember?"

"Good to see you."

She was reintroduced to the other brothers, and their

respective partners, then to Lachlan, who was alone. "And I helped you with your hot water last night," Brody said.

"I recall," she said. "This is Benny." She reached out and grabbed Benny's hand, drawing him forward slightly.

"Hi," he said, kicking at the ground.

"Hi," all the adults said in return, and it was funny to see a group of people who clearly did not have a whole lot of experience with kids. Alaina was pregnant, but she looked possibly the *most* terrified of Elizabeth's child of everyone in the group.

"How old are you, Benny?" Gus asked.

"I'm eight and a half," Benny said.

"Well. What grade is that, then?" Gus pressed.

"Third. I like my old teacher. I don't think I'm going to like the school here."

"Of course not," Brody said. "School sucks."

Benny's eyes went round. "I didn't think adults were allowed to say stuff like that."

"That's the thing about being an adult," Brody said. "You can say whatever you want."

He looked over at her, and he didn't wink. But she *felt* as if he had. Philosophically. And she didn't know why she found that so confronting.

"Well, now that everybody's acquainted," Gus said, "let's go over the incoming guests. There are going to be three of them, which is good, because it's a nice, slow start. We have Daniel Wheeler and his mother Sarah. The therapy is for Daniel, but Sarah will be here overseeing. Daniel is autistic, and he was recently adopted by Sarah and her husband. The adjustment period, and dealing with some of the trauma that he experienced in foster care has been really difficult. Then, we have Loralee Summers. She was in an abusive marriage and she's been suffering from PTSD. She's hoping that time out here, time with the horses, and doing some physical work will help. And we also have Peyton Smith and her dad, Austen. Peyton has muscular dystrophy, and her dad is hoping that this will be a positive experience for her. A chance for her to get out of her wheelchair and get some different exercise from the normal. So it's a whole spread of different therapies."

"Great," Elizabeth said. "I assume you've all started the online training program."

Everybody nodded. "Do you have anything you're feeling the most or least comfortable handling?" This was easy, slipping into the role of coordinator. She had been observing a successful program and participating in it for a few years now, and this felt natural. It was much smaller than the operation that she'd been part of in Portland, but now she was in charge, so it was different.

"I feel pretty confident in making sure that Peyton is safe on her horse," Elsie, Hunter's fiancée, said. "I did a lot of reading on the specifics of how to help with that. And since I'll have her dad there, I think it will be pretty easy to gauge her comfort level."

"That sounds great, Elsie. You can go ahead and start the week with Peyton, but I want a few different therapists to work with her."

"I'd like to try to help with Daniel," Gus said. "I don't have a whole lot of experience with kids. I don't know a ton about autism. But I do know what it's like to feel abandoned. And I know what it's like to have the adults in your life to have not taken care of you. I know what it's like to have to rebuild trust."

"Good. So you and I can consult a little bit more about that before Monday, if it would be helpful."

Daniel's story was the one that cut closest to Elizabeth's heart. She was good at separating her own issues from therapy—she wouldn't be good at her job if she didn't. But that didn't mean it didn't get to her sometimes.

"I'm happy to start the week off with Loralee," she said. She might not have been abused by her husband, but she knew a little bit about what it meant to start a new life. She had also worked with abuse victims before, so it wasn't an entirely new experience for her.

"Great," Gus said. "And in the meantime, I guess we all keep brushing up on the online courses."

"Yes. Finish those, and once you log a certain number of actual hours working with patients, you can get your certifications. But as long as you get that online piece done, it will make the rest of it go a lot smoother. Plus you won't feel totally like you're going in blind."

"Excellent. Coffee?"

Benny was looking bored and irritated in the corner of the barn. Shuffling pieces of hay around with his shoe.

"Hot chocolate?" Brody asked, directing that toward Benny.

Who looked a little bit brighter at the offer. "Sure."

"And I'll take that coffee," Elizabeth said. "Thank you." She directed that at Brody.

She could be polite to him. She didn't have to be standoffish just because he made her insides feel strange. That wasn't his fault.

And she reminded herself yet again that it could

all be in her head. Could all be one-sided. And if she started acting weird just because she had some feelings and he picked up on them... Well, that was so horrifying she couldn't bear to think of it.

She was handed a Styrofoam cup with steaming hot coffee in it, and the little pot of creamer. And Brody handed a frothy hot chocolate to Benny.

"You ready to get this tour on the road?"

"I guess," Benny said.

"Remember," he said. "I'm a pirate cowboy, so it's not going to be too bad."

Behind Brody, there came a guffaw of laughter. "A pirate cowboy? You're barely a cowboy, Brody."

"Hey," Brody said back to his brother Lachlan. "Don't damage my street cred."

"Yeah. You're well-known out here on the mean streets in Pyrite Falls. The cows tremble, but you have to be careful not to get in the middle of a gang war between the sheep and the goats." That jab came from his brother Tag.

"I have," Brody said. "It was ugly. Come on," he said, directing that at her and Benny. "Let's go."

He led them out of the barn and to his truck. "I'm going to show you around all the different stables, and then, the arenas. But after that, we can go look at some of my favorite spots."

"Do you have a PlayStation?" Benny asked.

"I don't even know what that is," Brody answered.

Elizabeth laughed. And when Brody got into the driver seat of the truck, she realized she had a very awkward decision to make. Either make her child sit next to a stranger, which she knew was the most horrifying thing a child could ever have happen to them, or, she was going to have to sit in the middle.

Well. She *had* to be a good mother. And protect her child from uncomfortable situations. Which meant she couldn't protect herself from this one.

She got into the truck and slid to the middle of the bench seat, and Benny got in beside her, closing the door. There was the slimmest space of seat between their thighs, and Brody looked down, then up at her, those gold-green eyes clashing with hers.

Her chest went tight, her heart starting to beat faster. She swallowed hard.

"So, this has been in your family for…"

"Since the 1860s. Pretty cool. Us and the Garretts, the Sullivans, and the Kings. You'll meet them all when we have our next town hall meeting. Assuming you want to go to it."

"What's the town hall meeting?"

"We have them once a month. All the families get together, all the employees of the ranch. We review the business of the ranch, and how everything's going, and then afterward, we have a big bonfire. Lots of food. The equine therapy center is kind of a gamble. Different to the kind of thing we've ever done here before. But it means a lot to Gus."

She thought of Gus, of his horribly scarred face that definitely spoke of trauma. She didn't know what had happened to him, but she knew it was something, and she had to wonder if that was what had inspired him to do this here.

"If you're wondering why Gus decided to start this place, you're probably right."

"Is he the one with the ugly face?" Benny asked.

Her son didn't say it with malice, it was a genuine question, but it still filled her with horror. The kind that made you hot and dizzy all at once, and she could only be thankful that Benny hadn't said that in earshot of Gus. "Benny. You *can't* say that about him."

"Sure he can," Brody said. "We say it about him all the time." But to Benny he said, in a more serious tone, "Gus got burned. Really badly. When he was a boy. Older than you, but still. Just a kid."

"Oh," said Benny, and she could tell her son felt bad, even though Brody had waved off him saying *ugly*.

"He was in a lot of pain for a long time," Brody said, his voice grave. "He got hurt helping our youngest brother. Saving him."

"That's brave," said Benny.

"Gus is the bravest guy I know," Brody said. "So we might tease him sometimes, but when I look at him, what I really see is the biggest, strongest, most courageous guy around. I think he's always wanted to help people. Because nobody really helped him. He's the oldest of all of us brothers."

"I'm the oldest," Benny said, as if he was suddenly pondering that very deeply.

Those kinds of things always made her feel conflicted. Because for her, he was the only. But of course he considered his half siblings *siblings*. And he should. The issues were hers, not his.

"Oh yeah?" Brody asked, and he looked at her with mild curiosity.

"My dad has other kids," Benny said, explaining not because he had picked up on Brody's curiosity but simply because it was what kids did. "And a really big house. His wife is really nice."

She bit the inside of her lip. And didn't say anything.

"Well. That's good," Brody said, looking at her, as if he was trying to gauge her response to that.

"Yeah," she said. "Ashley is lovely."

"She likes horses, though," Benny said. "Like my mom. It's not any more interesting when she does it."

Elizabeth supposed she could give thanks for the fact that he thought his stepmother's equestrian pursuits were equally dull. Honestly, it would be even worse if he thought it was interesting when Ashley rode a horse, when it was boring that Elizabeth did it.

Except.

Ashley wasn't as accomplished as Elizabeth was. Not even close.

So there.

She was petty, perhaps. But she kept it inside so it didn't infect Benny, and that was all that mattered.

"Seems we have a lot of work to do to convince you that horses are actually amazing."

"And why do you like horses, Brody?" Elizabeth said. She hadn't really meant to ask that, because she wasn't sure she wanted to know the answer. She wasn't sure she wanted to begin to turn this paragon of masculinity into a fully fleshed out human being.

"Because I never liked people all that much, Elizabeth. And horses consistently proved to be better companions. It was the best thing about growing up on this ranch." There was some other truth underlining the words, and she couldn't quite get at it.

They came to their first stop, a beautiful, white stable in pristine condition. And inside were some of the most stunning horses she'd ever seen. Older and docile, horses that would be past their prime to a lot of the people who came to look at them, but she thought they were glorious. It was a roan mare that really caught and held her affection.

"Over there you've got Blueberries and Flowers. This here's Strawberries. Strawberries is a good girl," he said. "Hunter and Elsie got her from a ranch up in Washington a few months ago. Actually, that was the trip where they hooked up. That's a whole story."

"What does *hooked up* mean?" Benny asked.

Horror hit Elizabeth in the chest, and she looked at Brody, who looked equally horrified. And she decided she was going to let him answer that question. See just how he did it. Because he was going to have to learn how to talk around Benny.

No, he doesn't. Benny isn't his child. He does not spend any time with Benny if he doesn't want to.

This wasn't going to be a regular thing. There were tons of people on this ranch. She wouldn't always need him to play tour guide. Realistically, they were never going to have to see each other. Or at least, they shouldn't have to see each other all that much.

"They started *dating* each other," Brody said. "They were, um… She… Well, she's Hunter's best friend's sister, so it was a little weird at first, but it's…well, it isn't…weird now."

Elizabeth laughed, because she knew there had to be a lot of drama going on in that situation.

"Yeah," he said, looking at her with an expression that was far too close to wicked. "It's exactly what you think."

"Well, the horse is glorious. And even if it did cause a little bit of family drama, I think the trip was worth it."

"Seeing as they're engaged now, I think it was worth it either way."

She wondered if he meant that. He didn't seem like a romantic, and Elizabeth had a hard time not being cynical about romance. Even when people seemed as happy as Gus and Alaina, and Elsie and Hunter. Or Tag and Nelly. They all seemed ridiculously happy with each other, and with their love. But Elizabeth knew that those things didn't last. And the promises that somebody made in the first blush of those feelings didn't necessarily stand the test of time. Not when somebody prettier, somebody *better*, came by.

And she really did try not to be bitter about that. It wasn't bitterness, it was just a healthy measure of cynicism. How could you not be cynical when a man you had been with since you were fourteen years old turned into an entirely different person one day? As if there had been some finger snap that had created a before and after that made no sense at all.

It was different than being heartbroken. She wasn't. It was just that she had learned that you might think you know somebody, but you don't really. And maybe they didn't even know themselves.

Because if she believed what Carter told her, he was just as surprised as she was. And while she had a hard time trusting that, she had a feeling there were shades of truth to it.

"Definitely," she said, rather than giving voice to any of the strange thoughts rolling around inside of her.

And supernaturally handsome Brody just smiled.

"How many horses are in here?" Benny asked.

"Fifteen," Brody said. "And most of them used to be in rodeos. Barrel racers, bucking broncos."

"Were you in the rodeo?"

"No. I'm not a rhinestone cowboy, Benny, I'm a real cowboy."

Benny wrinkled his nose. "I don't know what that means."

Brody laughed. "Right. Well, do you want to go for a ride?"

"I don't know how to ride."

And that made her chest get tight. He had been on horses before, she had taken him out to the ranch that she worked at, but there were limited opportunities for her to do it. Because it would mean picking him up from school and taking him back over there when she was done for the day, and there was dinner and homework and a hundred other things to do.

"It's time we remedy that, then. Come on. Why don't you get Strawberries out?" he said to Elizabeth.

"Do you have a really gentle one for him?"

"It's a therapy ranch. Temperament is what we've been focusing on the last few months. Making sure everything is as safe as possible."

It was just impossible to reconcile the idea of Brody, and anything he did, being safe.

But she realized that the precarious feeling that she had inside of her had nothing to do with Benny or riding. It was the fact that he put her so on edge when he was around. The fact that she felt so precariously close to the edge of some cliff she couldn't see the bottom of.

Because he's handsome? You should have started dating a long time ago, you might not be so weird and desperate feeling.

And so, instead, she had moved herself to a place

where dating was probably going to be impossible, because she worked with every eligible man in the vicinity.

She decided that rather than asking him for every bit of information she might need, she would hunt around and see how much she could figure out on her own. By the time she got her horse tacked up and ready to go, he had Benny's horse ready, had a helmet on her son's head, and was ready on his own mount, who was clearly not a rescue animal of any kind.

He was beautiful. Sleek and athletic looking, black and glossy. And the sight of Brody on the back of that horse...

She was perspiring. Actually *sweating* from looking at this man. And her heart was beating two times faster than it should have been. She could feel a burning restlessness between her thighs, and she really could not believe that this was happening to her right now.

Carter hadn't been interested in horses, not ever. She couldn't recall ever seeing him on the back of one. She hadn't realized that a hot man on a gorgeous mount was a very particular kind of catnip for her.

She was around men who rode dressage and English-style all the time. But she was not often around cowboys.

She knew how to ride Western, but still, she had chosen English tack, and had decided to go with what she was most comfortable with.

She noticed that Brody had given Benny a Western saddle and reins.

"I hold mine with one hand," he said. "You don't need to worry about that just now."

"The horse is really big," Benny said, looking up from his position on the ground.

"You'll be just fine," he said.

She walked over to her son and instructed him on how to put his foot in the stirrup, a quick refresher, even though he had done it before.

And then she helped him get up on the back of the animal.

"Hold the reins like this," she said. "There you go, just like that, and if you start feeling insecure, you can just grab hold of the horn on the saddle. He's the kind that's not going anywhere."

"Yep," Brody said. "You'll be just fine."

She wondered if they should have stayed on the ground, and taken him with a lead rope, but she knew that a horse like this would just follow the other two, and would keep a steady pace.

"There's an arena this way. Let's go there. The ground is soft."

Her stomach clenched. She was realistic about the fact that if you rode, you were going to fall off sometimes, but it was disconcerting to think about her child tumbling from a horse.

Brody took the lead, and she couldn't help but watch the figure he cut on the back of that beauty.

She maneuvered herself so that she was behind Benny, and when he looked at her, there was a wide smile on his face that wasn't like anything she'd seen for months now.

And she was tempted to say something. To say "See, it's actually fun." To tell him it wasn't so bad. But she was worried that any kind of insertion from her would only cause problems. So she tamped down her own joy, held it close to her chest, and just kept it private.

They rode in circles in the arena, and Benny had

the time of his life. Maybe it was because this wasn't like the gentrified stables they rode at sometimes in the Portland area. It was rugged out here. Wild. And even in the arena, there was a sense of adventure. And she really hoped that he felt it.

They stayed out there until the sun was in the center of the sky and Benny was complaining about being hungry.

"It's probably time for us to head back to the cabin. I'm sure he's exhausted."

"We didn't really make it very far on the tour," Brody said.

"It doesn't matter. This was exactly what needed to happen. Thank you."

"Can we go riding tomorrow, Brody?" Benny asked.

He had never once asked Elizabeth if they could go riding.

"Sure, Ben," Brody said.

Benny seemed to beam from the attention. "Sweet."

"If you're up to it, why don't the two of you come to dinner tonight? My brother's place. Gus's wife always cooks up something great."

"Oh," she said, "I don't…"

"Can we? I want to ask Gus about what it's like to get burned in a fire."

"Please don't do that," she said.

"No," Brody said. "Ask him. I'm sure he'd like to tell you the story."

He looked over Benny's head and made eye contact with Elizabeth. "He'll censor it," he said softly.

Benny scampered back toward the truck, and Elizabeth walked slightly slower. "You know, I'm trying to teach him manners."

"Sorry," Brody said. "We're not much for manners around here."

Except that wasn't strictly true, because everybody had been so nice to her. Even Brody.

For all that he made her feel prickly inside.

"He won't scare him," Brody continued. "Too much."

She was thankful when they got into the truck that Benny had actually taken the center seat this time, and that meant she didn't have to sit so close to Brody. As it was, the cab felt small.

When they arrived back at the cabin, Benny scrambled out of the truck and went straight into the house, and Elizabeth lingered on the porch.

"Thanks for the dinner invitation, but… I really don't want to be a nuisance."

"Hey, you're new here. They say that you're supposed to get out and meet people and stuff when you move to a new place."

"Is that what they say?"

"I wouldn't know. I've never lived anywhere else."

She stared at him. He seemed so much worldlier than she could ever hope to be. He was a man whose whole demeanor exuded a kind of raw sexuality that made her extremely uncomfortable. That set her on edge and made her feel like she was too close to an open flame.

But he had lived here his entire life. In this little town, on this ranch.

"You don't know what to say to that?"

She felt her face get hot. "I don't know why, it just threw me off a little bit. I guess because you seem…" She tried to figure out how to say it without actually saying she had thought about *him* and *sexuality* in the same sentence. "Well traveled."

He laughed. "Is that a euphemism?" It had been. She hadn't really meant it to be, in quite that way, but it had been.

"No. I actually don't know how to do double entendre. It's not in my wheelhouse."

Except she felt like she might be flirting. And she didn't know how to do that either.

"That's a shame. If you want, I'm happy to teach you double entendre, because it is my second language."

She laughed, and it came out like a giggle, and she had no idea what was going on. "Right. Well. I will… I'll see you at dinner."

"See you at dinner."

It was clear, when she went back into the house and heard Benny mention Brody's name twenty times in about ten minutes, that her son had a serious case of hero worship on the pirate cowboy.

She was afraid he wasn't the only one.

CHAPTER FOUR

"I INVITED ELIZABETH to dinner," Brody said to Gus when he saw him again later that day. Gus was hunched over a computer, standing in the barn, obviously trying to work on those certification classes.

"Good," he said, the word more of a grunt.

"Her kid seems to like you," Lachlan said, a note of caution in his voice that Brody understood, given their conversation last night.

"He's a good kid," Brody said.

He thought about the things that he'd learned about her today. That her ex-husband was remarried, that he had other children.

It was impossible to tell what Elizabeth thought about that. It was impossible to tell what she thought about *anything*.

Except that she was attracted to him.

He could read that in her eyes. The way her lips parted when she looked at him. The way she blushed just a little when their gazes clashed. The way her breath quickened and…

Yeah. He could tell.

He wondered if she even knew that she was attracted to him. She had been flirting before she'd gone into the house, but he had a feeling that she hadn't *intended* to.

"How can you tell?" Lachlan asked. "He hasn't been here long enough to start killing small animals and prove that he's a bad seed."

Brody shrugged. "I assume all of 'em are good unless they prove otherwise."

"Interesting. I assume all kids are a pain in the ass until they prove otherwise," Gus said.

"It's a really good thing that you're about to be a father, and that you'll be giving therapy to a child, Angus," Lachlan said.

"I'm realistic," Gus said. "I'm not going to treat a kid like he's great, just because he showed up. I don't think that's a bad thing."

"Heads up, Benny is going to ask you about your scars." It seemed like a fair thing to warn his brother about.

Gus looked thoughtful. "Am I trying to scare him or…?"

"Just tell him the story," Brody said. "I mean, sans gory details. You don't have to tell him that our dad did it to you."

The whole subject was a tricky one for Brody.

Especially standing between these two brothers, who had gotten it so badly. Gus had earned their father's wrath that day because he had saved Lachlan from a hell of a beating. A beating that Brody was sure would've killed Lachlan.

And Brody was just on the sidelines of all that.

He'd always been too afraid to put a wrong foot out. Too afraid of being treated the way his brothers were, while feeling hideously guilty that he wasn't.

"His mother may not like that."

"She's been warned," he said.

"I'm glad that she responded to that ad," Gus said. "I don't know if this would've come together without her."

"Yeah. She seems great," Brody said. And he ignored Lachlan's look at him.

"So what else do we need to do to prep for Monday? That's when we have guests coming in, right?" Brody asked.

He was ready to have work piled on him. Give him something to do.

Work hard. Play hard.

He had to have one to have the other.

"As a matter of fact, Brody, I have a rock wall that I need finished."

"Perfect," Brody said.

He loved penance more than anything else. And if that penance might handle his unwanted sexual attraction to the hot single mom who had just moved onto the ranch, all the better.

All the better.

DINNER CAME AROUND a whole lot quicker than he was prepared for. He had taken a little bit of an Elizabeth break, and now it was time to see her again. It was handy that she always came with the kid as an accessory.

Plus, his whole family was around now.

Alaina had made about ten pizzas, and he marveled at the industriousness of his sister-in-law, even while heavily pregnant.

She had taken to her role on the ranch with gusto, and he had a feeling that Alaina, as the youngest of the Sullivans, just liked having something that she was in charge of.

Being Gus's wife suited her.

And it suited Gus too, which shocked Brody more than just about anything else. He would've said that Gus would never get married.

Actually, he would have said that none of the Mc-Clouds would ever get married, and now there were only two of them remaining who hadn't.

It was a weird-ass thing.

She had changed since their earlier encounter on the ranch. She had swapped her jeans—which had been a real visual delight, in his opinion—for a pair of navy blue wide-leg pants that were made of a very thin material, and if he was not mistaken, when she moved, it gave him a pretty intimate outline of her backside.

Not that he was looking.

He was officially not looking.

She sat down at the other end of the table, away from him, making conversation with the women and Gus. Talking particulars about the therapy program and the upcoming programming that they had on the schedule.

He could see that Benny's attention was wandering. Yeah. Well. Brody couldn't blame him.

He felt a strange moment of empathy for the kid. All by himself, around all this stuff he wasn't part of. Brody had grown up with a lot of brothers. He was still surrounded by them. But he knew what it was like to feel separate. To feel different. He wondered if Benny felt alone even when he was with his half siblings. They were part of something outside him. That was the thing. Even if his dad was great, and his stepmom was nice, and they tried to integrate him, Benny had come from another situation.

The empathy was getting a little uncomfortable now. Brody didn't traffic in fine emotions like that.

"My brother doesn't have video games, but I happen to know that he has some pretty great toys upstairs," Brody said. "He just got a lot of it out because he's having a baby soon."

"Boys don't have babies," Benny said.

"His wife… Whatever, kid. Anyway, do you want to go play with some army men or not?"

"I guess," he said.

"Is that okay?" He gestured to Benny, looking at Elizabeth. "Well, I guess I have to ask you too, Gus. Can he play with the army men?"

"Yeah," Gus said. "As long as he doesn't break them."

"You heard him. Just don't break the army men." He ushered the kid from the table and hustled up the stairs, hearing the smaller footsteps behind him.

"Right in here," he said, pushing open the door to what was going to be the nursery. This room had been their room when they were kids. He could remember, clearly, the bed that Gus had slept on in the corner, the trundle for Tag and Hunter, and the other for himself and Lachlan.

In hindsight, it was kind of a miracle they'd all had beds. It was difficult for him to imagine them now, with the opinions he had formed on his parents, shopping for children's furniture, and giving any kind of a shit about how the room was outfitted. But they'd had army men, he supposed.

That was the problem. Everything was a lot more…a lot more complicated than anybody liked to remember.

"These are great," Benny said, seeing the shelves filled with old toys.

Brody hadn't realized that Gus had saved so many. He'd kept all of them. And it was good stuff.

A strange weight settled on his chest as he looked around the room. Yeah. Childhood. That was supposed to be the easiest time of your life. The lightest time. It hadn't been the case for the McCloud boys.

And yet, there had been army men.

"You all right here, kid?" he asked.

He didn't really want to linger. He wasn't sure how Gus did it. How he lived in this house. Hell, he was going to put his kid in here.

Of course, Brody couldn't even imagine having a child, so he supposed the real thing was that Gus was light-years ahead of him in terms of emotional stability. Which was a strange thing. Because he never would've thought that about Gus.

He walked out of the bedroom, and left the door partly cracked, then started to walk down the hall.

He heard footsteps on the stairs, and stopped. It was Elizabeth.

She saw him, her blue eyes going wide, her breath hitching on a sharp intake. It made her breasts rise up and he could not help himself. He looked.

He realized then that they were in a very tight, enclosed space. Together. But his family was behind her back, and her son was behind his.

"Oh. Thank you. For…for getting him some toys, I was just going to look in on him."

"He's good," Brody said. "He's just sitting on the floor with the army men."

"It's a few weeks early for a Christmas miracle," she said. "He's playing with toys that aren't electronics."

"I weep for the youth of today," he said.

He took a step forward, as if he was going to go past her, at the same time she took a step toward the door, and it brought them into even closer proximity. He could smell her then. She smelled as delicate as she looked. And rich. Expensive.

He wondered what the scent was, he couldn't say that he'd ever smelled it before. Probably something the kind of women he normally hooked up with couldn't afford.

But she'd lived in an apartment.

Still, she had the look of a woman who had money. She exuded that.

She was an interesting collection of contradictions, was Elizabeth Colfax. And if he was the kind of man who wanted to find out more about a woman's contradictions, she would definitely be the one that he would want to learn more about.

But it wasn't *contradictions* Brody wanted to know about.

He let his eyes drop down again. Reinforcing that point. To her and to him.

But instead of getting mad, her breath seemed to catch and hold.

They had been standing there for too long. Too long for her to be anything other than lost in the same kind of thoughts he was.

The thing about being a guy who preferred a *random* hookup was that he didn't often experience *specific* chemistry. He was usually just looking for a woman who pushed his buttons in a general sense. One who wanted him, one who wanted the same things he did.

Never in all his life had chemistry come before that commonsense approach to casual sex.

This woman made no sense. None at all. His body

shouldn't be responding to her. And yet it was. There was a dark, sensual pull between them that superseded anything he'd ever felt before. It was specific. He could go out to Smokey's tonight and find a woman and hook up, scratch the generic sex itch, and as soon as he saw Elizabeth, he would be just as horny as he'd been before he got laid.

He knew it. Didn't have to have experienced it before to know it either. He just knew it.

He shifted slightly, and rested his hand on the wall just above her head, leaning in.

Her eyes went wide, and he saw a shiver of something that looked like interest and fear mingled together there.

Her eyes were just so blue.

And the look on her face...

"I'm going to go check on Benny," she said.

"Good," he said.

He shifted, moving away from her quickly, and headed down the stairs without looking back behind him to look at her ass in her flimsy pants. Because what had just happened was... He needed to go out to the bar.

"Hey," he said to Lachlan when he returned. "You want to go out?"

"Sure," Lachlan said.

He grabbed his coat, and he thought about telling Gus to give Elizabeth his regards, or something like that, but decided against it.

"Where are you guys going?" Hunter asked.

"Smokey's," Lachlan said.

"Why?"

"Don't ask questions you don't want the answer to, Hunt," Lachlan responded.

"It's Sunday night," Brody said. "The last gasp of the weekend."

"You have to get up for work tomorrow," Gus pointed out.

"I have to get up for work every day," he said. "I'm a rancher."

"Yes, but tomorrow we're starting the school stuff."

"I'm aware, Angus."

He followed Lachlan out the door, and the two of them made a beeline for their pickup trucks. They didn't ride together. That didn't work. Not if they were trying to hook up.

And that was the unspoken, obvious point of this trip.

It was a quick eight minutes from McCloud's Landing, down the dirt road to the highway that took them to Smokey's Tavern. His brother's headlights shone through his back window the whole trip, and when they killed their engines and got out of the trucks, he turned to Lachlan. "Next time, don't tailgate me."

Lach shrugged. "Next time, don't drive like a grandma."

"Hey."

"Sorry. That was offensive to grandmas everywhere."

He punched his brother on the shoulder, and the two of them walked through the door that led inside. It was a simple establishment, wood floors, a bar with metal stools that had cushioned red seats. A mixture of a fifties diner and a barn. An unholy car crash of the two, really.

It was packed out, in spite of the fact that it was a Sunday. Because there was nothing else to do in this whole area. And there were many people who lived in the mountains around these parts who came down to party nightly. It wasn't exactly a thriving singles scene, but "lucky them" women traveled to hit this bar. The kind that were after working men. Cowboys. A good time.

There was a passel of pretty women over by the juke-box, and he did his best to try and rouse some interest up inside of himself.

"Beer?" Lachlan asked.

"Sure," he said, walking over to a table in the corner. He would watch for a minute. See what he was in the mood for. It wasn't just about hair color or bra size or anything like that. He liked to get the feel for how a woman danced. If she was loud or quiet. The ringleader of the group or the wallflower.

All were valid.

What he was interested in was just dependent on his mood.

Lachlan returned a moment later with a beer.

"So, are you going to tell me what spurred the last-minute outing?"

"Nope."

"Does it have something to do with Elizabeth?"

"Where's your cute little shadow?" Brody pressed.

Lachlan scowled. "Don't talk about her like that."

"Well. It's a valid question."

"Sure," Lachlan said, his lip curled. "If you want to get punched in the face."

"I'm a few hits behind, Lach, you might as well clock me one." He let that joke sit between them. Sometimes, it was funny. Their dysfunctional childhood. The fact that their dad had never once hit him while he had used the others for a punching bag. And not just the kids. Their mother.

At least, before she'd run off and left them. She should have taken the other boys.

Should have left Brody alone.

Brody would've been fine.

"I'm not about to punch out my wingman. Her dad's not doing well," he said, looking down into his beer. "I should go over there…"

"Her dad's a nice guy," he said.

"Yeah," Lachlan agreed. "Never minded my ass hanging around. Most fathers would've been a little bit suspicious."

"And you two have really never…"

Lachlan's knuckles tightened around his beer. "Absolutely not. That is like asking if I've ever masturbated to a picture of the Virgin Mary."

Brody spit his beer out over the top of his glass. "Please. Don't ever put that image in my head. Ever."

"Well. You don't go asking questions like that. Charity is my friend. My best friend. And that is another reason she isn't here tonight. You may have noticed, but I don't like to include her in my bad behavior."

"Fair."

"I want her to respect me in the morning."

"Something you don't have to worry about with your hookups."

Lachlan smiled, but there wasn't a lot of humor there. "That's the best part about them."

He lifted a glass in salute, and Brody lifted his own and clinked it against the edge of his brother's.

"Who do you like?" Lachlan asked.

And he wondered for a second if he should feel guilty about this. About looking at this whole hookup lifestyle as a sporting event. Except… There wasn't much else to do here. And the sameness of his life was… Well, it was what it was. He had chosen to stay in Pyrite Falls. He had chosen to stay at Four Corners.

The bottom line was, he owed Gus. However much he gave his brother a hard time, he owed him. Gus had single-handedly saved Lachlan's life. Gus had taken care of them. He had been the oldest, and he had taken the worst of everything. And Brody had been passed over completely. For reasons he still couldn't understand. For reasons he would never understand. And he just… He had to stay. He had to stay and work off that debt. And there would be no amount of time that ever felt sufficient. Not really.

He could remember the conversation he'd had with Gus just a month or so ago. When Gus was screwing things up with Alaina, like a champ.

Gus had told him that not every scar was worn on your skin.

And that might be, but his brothers had scars outside, and the scars inside that came from someone who was supposed to care for you hurting you.

And he didn't have those scars.

"Haven't decided yet," he said.

There was a girl by the jukebox who was clearly the bubbly one of the group. Her giggle rose loud over the top of her friends', and every time she moved, she shimmied her shoulders and her breasts bounced. Which was interesting. He knew exactly what kind of lay she would be. Bouncy.

Fun, that was how he would've normally looked at it.

Then there was a woman scanning the bar, and her gaze had landed on Brody and Lachlan a couple of times. She was looking at them with some intensity. She was here to seduce somebody. He knew exactly how an evening with her in the sack would go, too.

She would attack whichever guy she ended up with.

She would definitely want to be on top.

Again, all fine. It just didn't fire up his blood. Not right now.

He sat there for a minute, his beer in his hand, the glass getting sweaty beneath his fingertips. He couldn't guess how Elizabeth would be in bed. She was strong-willed, but that wasn't the first thing that you saw when you looked at her. She was well put together, almost prim, but she was great with horses. She didn't shy away from hard work. She looked soft, but she was in athletic shape. At least, he assumed, because doing the kind of labor they did tended to build pretty good muscle tone.

He had observed some of that muscle tone when she'd been wearing those jeans earlier today. She definitely had toned thighs and a really good ass.

But he couldn't guess what she would want. If she'd want to be on top, if she would be a bouncy girl. Aggressive. Timid. Pretend that she needed him to be the aggressor.

"Are you here?" Lachlan asked.

"What?"

"You drifted off to somewhere, somewhere I couldn't follow you."

"Looking at our options," he said.

"The bouncy girl is cute," Lachlan said. "Or do you want the one who looks like she wants to tear some clothes off tonight?"

His brother had noticed the same two women he had. And they had the same assessments of those women. The thought made him feel vaguely unclean.

Maybe they needed to quit going out together.

"I haven't decided yet," Brody said.

"Does that mean I get first pick? Because I'm leaning toward the one who looks like she wants to take a bite out of somebody."

"By all means," Brody said. "Take the attacker."

"Good deal," Lachlan said, draining the rest of his beer before getting up. "See you later."

He got up and crossed the bar, and the whole group of women straightened as he started to get closer to them. But the woman he was aiming for took a step toward him, and Brody had to laugh. That was fate.

Well, as much fate as a one-night stand could be. Because that was all it would be. That was all it would ever be.

Of course, he always thought that was true for Tag. For Hunter. For Gus. Tag and Hunter because they had been serious manwhores on the same level that Lachlan and Brody still were. Gus because… He had always been withdrawn. His injuries had seen to that. He'd ended up with a face full of scars by the time he was thirteen. Not to say that women hadn't *liked* him back in his single days. They had. But it was definitely a certain kind of woman looking for a certain thing.

Gus had always played into that easily enough, but he definitely didn't go out on the town the way the rest of them did. He tended to withdraw. Go somewhere other than Pyrite Falls when he wanted to get laid.

And he'd ended up married to a fiery, bright woman quite a bit younger than him. Of course, Gus being Gus, it had started as a rescue mission when Alaina had gotten pregnant and the guy had run off. Gus had stepped right in there.

It was pretty obvious to Brody now that Gus had always had feelings for Alaina, and that was the perfect excuse for him to finally let himself make a move on it.

They were happy. They were in love.

All of it defied belief. And if he'd been asked two years ago if this was where his brothers would be, he would've said absolutely not.

Except for Lachlan. He watched as the woman trailed her fingertips up Lachlan's arm.

Yeah. Lachlan was exactly where Brody would have guessed. No learning. No growing. Same old, same old. Exactly like Brody.

So. Bubbly girl. Bubbly girl was the order of the day. She was cute. With dark corkscrew curls and a generous smile. And even more generous curves.

He decided it was time.

He downed the rest of his own beer and got up, and felt another ripple go through the group of women.

He supposed he should be happy to know that, even though he and Lachlan had been at this game for a long time, they were definitely still the two most desirable men in the room. It somehow didn't make him feel better.

He was still feeling a little bit long in the tooth for all of this.

A redhead darted around from the back of the group. A bottle redhead. He could spot that a mile away. He was all right with it, he could just tell.

But bouncy girl was quick. And she practically elbowed her friend, moving herself into the front.

"Howdy," he said. And he decided that he would let this little rivalry play itself out. He would decide who he was talking to in a second.

Except suddenly he felt tired. And when they both started talking, he felt exhausted. And not only that, he just wasn't all that interested. They were both hot.

He could take them both home. They might be into that. Find it forbidden and exciting. He probably should too.

He waited for that to feel exciting.

It didn't.

He could even map out how that would go, how he'd direct things and how it would end.

He was deeply bored.

He looked back over at his brother.

Lachlan was not suffering from malaise of any kind, and he was already halfway out the door with his woman. Brody waited. Waited until his brother was gone.

He wanted a beer. Or to go home.

The real problem was he kept thinking about Elizabeth. And exactly how she would be in bed. What it would be like to peel off that prim top she had been wearing. Floaty and white. Long-sleeved. Kind of like an angel. She was not his type. Not at all.

He didn't go in for that sort of thing. Understated. Restrained.

No. He didn't like that. He liked the woman standing in front of him. Bouncing. She was making it so obvious what she wanted. And so was her friend. And he could say yes, and have it if he wanted to. That was the entire point of coming out.

Except that moment in the hallway when he had breathed Elizabeth in, that expensive scent he couldn't place, that had been the hottest thing that had happened to him in his recent memory.

His stomach got tight just thinking about it. And he felt the blood begin to rush to his groin, and it had nothing to do with what was happening in front of him.

They were talking. He had no idea what they'd said. Because he was too busy thinking about where he'd rather be. And who he'd rather be with.

He was going to have to get a handle on this, because he was not hooking up with McCloud's Landing's newest employee.

"Can I buy you a drink?"

"Sure," she said, shaking her curls.

Bubbly girl was claiming it, so he went ahead and let her take his hand and he led her over to the bar. "Whatever the lady wants," he said.

It felt like reading from a script. It felt well-worn and obvious.

Lachlan hadn't bought his date a drink. But then, you didn't need to buy *that* girl a drink. Bouncy girls needed them. A little spoiling beforehand. It went a long way. Made them feel like it was a magical moment rather than something sordid, and it was very important, in his experience, to women like this, that it felt like they *mattered*, and he was paying attention.

Except he wasn't. But whatever. She didn't have to know that.

"Can I get a mojito?" she asked.

The bartender looked at him. "Make the lady a mojito, Jeb," he said.

And Jeb turned around, muttering something about it being *all gol dern fancy* around here these days. But Brody didn't care.

The drink was made pretty quickly, and the woman

sat down on the stool, shimmying her shoulders up to her ears as she took a sip from a straw.

"This is good," she said.

"Yeah. The drinks here are surprisingly good." Because looking at it, you would just think that they served piss water. But he didn't say that last part out loud.

"I'm Amanda," she said, smiling, her eyes glittering. She had enticing down to an art, he had to give her that.

"Brody," he said. "Nice to meet you."

Such a familiar dance.

The problem was, she could have been Amanda or Casey or Jocelyn. Redheaded, blonde, brunette. Bubbly, bouncy, or mean. It would've all been the same.

It wasn't her fault. None of it was. She was a nice enough girl, and she was very pretty. None of what he was feeling had anything to do with her.

He could take her home. They could have sex. It'd all function just right.

But it just made him feel… It made him feel a little bit dirty, and he couldn't remember the last time he'd felt like that over something this simple and straightforward. Or at least, something that *should* have been simple and straightforward.

"I have to go," he said. "But the mojito goes on my tab."

"What?" She looked confused.

"Don't think it's anything you did. Because it's not."

And then she laughed. She flat-out laughed. "Are you worried that some stranger declining to have sex with me is going to hurt my self-esteem?"

He blinked. "Well… I was a little worried about it."

"I'm a girl boss," she said. "It's going to take a lot more than the rejection of some random cowboy to make me feel bad about myself. Anyway. I like my consent enthusiastic. So if you aren't into it, there's no reason to go there."

He had misread this woman. And while she was certainly more interesting than she had been a minute ago, he still wasn't *that* kind of interested.

"Well," he said. "Good."

"And I can buy my own mojito."

All right. Maybe he was too old for this. Maybe he didn't know anything about *anything* anymore.

Weirdly, it felt good. Walking out of the bar by himself, with a setdown like that. Reminded him that he wasn't actually irresistible.

Turning her down actually had been the right thing to do. Because that was the problem. He'd only been thinking about himself. But then, he had a lot of practice with that. Pretty much other than family, he only ever thought about himself.

He was kind of a sad asshole.

He got into his truck and started the engine, pulled out of the driveway, and began the drive back to his cabin. And he couldn't remember the last time he'd gone out with the intent of bringing someone back home, and wound up alone.

It was still Elizabeth he saw in his mind's eye as he made the drive.

She was back at the ranch. So for some reason, it didn't actually feel like going home alone.

CHAPTER FIVE

SHE HAD TAKEN a bath, and now her skin was overheated. She slipped into a very soft, very sedate pair of pajamas, and climbed beneath the covers. The bed here was so soft. And it was just so quiet. It was nothing like staying in that apartment complex, where she could hear people walking around above her head until all hours. Where people often shouted in the parking lot over trivial matters that were apparently worthy of level-eleven volumes of shouting, no matter what time of day it was.

It was silent here. Sometimes, so quiet it scared her. Then, when it wasn't silent, it was crickets. And coyotes. Which was a little bit unsettling.

Listening to a whole pack of yodeling dogs made goose bumps break out across her skin.

And the reason she was currently examining all of this was that she was trying to avoid thinking of that moment in the hallway with Brody.

She closed her eyes, and she could see him. So close. Worse, she could smell him. That woodsy scent. Masculine and enticing. The way he had put his hand on the wall behind her. She hadn't felt trapped, not in a scary way. She had felt cocooned.

And then apparently he had gone out to hook up. At least, that was what his siblings had been talking about when she had come down the stairs from checking on

Benny. There was a whole raucous conversation happening about Lachlan and Brody, and the fact that they had renowned "luck" with women. That they were the biggest playboys in all of Pyrite Falls, at least now that Tag and Hunter had hung up their belt buckles.

It had made her stomach curdle.

She wondered if he was with a woman right now.

And what it must be like.

To be the focus of all that attention. She'd felt just a sliver of it in the hallway. And she had run away from it. Because she hadn't been able to handle it. Because the promise in his eyes… That was a promise that she was not able to keep.

She wasn't quite sure what to do with this. The fact that there was something between them seemed mutual. At least, it had been in that moment. But maybe that was just how he reacted when a woman was so obviously melting over him. It wasn't like she was subtle. She didn't have any experience with this.

She punched her pillow and growled. Thankful for the fact that she was exhausted.

Because sleep started to descend over her, and it came pretty easily.

But she dreamed. And not lightly. Vividly.

In her dreams, she could feel his hands on her skin. His mouth. The whiskers on his jaw scraping over her neck as he kissed down her body. In her sleep, she gasped. Arched her back up off the mattress. And in that dream, he put his hand between her legs.

And when she woke, it was with a jolt, her internal muscles pulsing, her orgasm screaming through her like a wild thing.

She had just… She had just come from a dream.

Her heart was thundering so hard, she thought she might be sick.

She looked at the clock and saw that it was 5:00 a.m., and she was going to have to get up in less than an hour anyway, to get Benny ready for school, and to get ready for the day, so she really might as well just get going.

Her legs were shaky. She got into the shower, because she was sweaty, and tried to rinse the memory of the dream off her skin.

She chose her clothing carefully. A pair of black breeches, a white tank top, and a navy blue jacket with gold buttons. The kind of thing she would often wear if she was showing. But it seemed appropriate for today, when she would actually be meeting with clients.

Not that she had any idea what *appropriate* was. Not at this point.

She made coffee, very strong coffee, and drank a little bit too much before she went to get Benny up.

He grumbled the whole time. But she managed to get some oatmeal in his system, and trundle him out the door in time to drive slowly over to the one-room schoolhouse.

Her heart rattled around like a caged bird when they approached the blue building.

There were kids pouring into the building, but there weren't any parents. She wondered if most of the children walked. There were quite a few of them Benny's age, and she was grateful for that.

A pretty, dark-haired woman was standing in the doorway, and Elizabeth got out of her car to greet her. "Hi," she said. "You must be Elizabeth. I'm Tala Everett." She looked down at Benny. "And you must be Benny. You can call me Mrs. Everett."

"This is the whole school?" Benny asked.

"Yes. And we go on a lot of adventures here. The school is so small we get to do a lot of special things. You're going to have a lot of fun."

"Thank you," Elizabeth said. "I don't know if he needs…"

"I have everything he needs. I'm so lucky that all the families here put so much into the schooling."

"That's… That's wonderful."

And she was feeling more and more at ease with all of it as the moments ticked by.

Because the teacher seemed so nice, and the school was quaint, and there were only a handful of children, all different ages, and she was confident that Benny would get just the right kind of attention here.

She knew that he was hesitant, and she understood that. New schools were never easy. When she'd been young she'd changed schools all the time. The hazards of foster care.

She blinked, and she did her best not to think too far back. There was no point to it. This was now. And she had Benny now. And he had her.

He always would.

Sure, things were a little more back-and-forth than she wanted, and it had really upset her at first that he was going to have to move between houses at all. But that was her own baggage. Her situation hadn't involved moving between two stable parents.

Stability mattered more than traditional family. She knew that well.

The only time she'd ever had real stability was when Denise Newton had taken her in for the last three years of high school.

She had been an older woman with no children, and had seen a TV spot about the crisis in the foster care system, and had taken Elizabeth in. She'd been the most steady influence Elizabeth had, other than Carter's mother.

Her death when Elizabeth had been nineteen had been devastating. But she was always grateful for the years she'd had with something like her own family. And maybe it had been part of what had spurred her to marry Carter and...

She was going to not think about that.

"You okay, Benny?" she asked, trying to look as upbeat as possible, and not at all nervous.

"Yeah," he said, shifting his backpack on his shoulders.

"Come on, Benny," said Mrs. Everett. "Let's go." And Benny followed the pretty young teacher into the building, with a cautious smile on his face.

Elizabeth felt...untethered. She was used to Benny being in school at this point, and given her busy schedule, she frankly looked forward to the school year at the end of every summer. But it had something to do with being in this new place. This new place that she had chosen. This new place that was better.

She took a deep breath, trying to shift the weight from her chest. The guilt.

She didn't know why the more distant past was on her mind right now. She had done a pretty good job of not obsessing about it. She'd had a full-on PTSD panic attack the first time she had walked into the apartment that she moved into after separating from Carter. It had reminded her too much of foster care.

Of being moved on when she wasn't ready.

Sometimes, going from somewhere nice to somewhere small and cramped and terrible. The good places had never lasted as long as she would've liked. They were like vacations, she'd tried to tell herself.

But her life with Carter wasn't supposed to be a vacation. It was supposed to be her *life*. Her real, permanent life. But it hadn't been. Any more than one of those lives that she'd stepped into during her time in care. She hated those thoughts. They made her feel as sad as she sounded. Reminded her too much of being that tragic little girl with a garbage bag.

She had decided during that panic attack that she was not going to think of her childhood. That who she was as an adult had nothing to do with that, no matter her change in circumstance. No matter that her marriage had ended when she didn't want it to. And no, she wouldn't have the money that she'd had as Carter's wife. But she wasn't destitute, and she could take care of herself. She had the skills that she had learned when she'd been with him—her experience with horses.

No one could take that from her.

She wasn't that girl anymore. And Benny wasn't like her either. She had *chosen* to be here to give them both a better life.

And they were going to have one. Right here.

She got back in her car and drove toward McCloud's Landing. She hadn't taken an entire tour of Four Corners yet, but she would have to do that soon. What she had seen of it was incredible. Beautiful. And she was fascinated by the way that it was run.

Her thoughts drifted—in spite of her best efforts to think of the mundane—to her dream about Brody.

Honestly, she would prefer childhood trauma to *that*.

At least she'd had enough therapy to begin to process her trauma.

She didn't know how to process subconscious sexual fantasies about Brody.

She rolled her shoulders back, trying to relax. When she pulled up to the barn, she could see movement inside, and her whole body went on alert. And then, the defensive. She got out, trying to steel herself. Thankfully, the movement inside was Gus.

"Good morning," he said.

"Morning," she returned.

"Looking forward to getting a start on today. Thank you," he said, "for all your expertise."

"No," she said. "Thank you. For the opportunity."

And she really did mean it. Because this had been the first real opportunity she'd seen to change her life since the divorce. And the only thing that she was sorry about now was that it had taken so long for her to figure something out.

So maybe all her thoughts about putting her past behind her hadn't really helped. She had gotten really good at ignoring the things about her life that made her uncomfortable.

But you made the decision to change it. So there's no reason to beat yourself up over not doing it sooner.

It was exactly what she would've told a client. But of course, these things were a lot harder to take on board herself. Which made her feel vaguely like a hypocrite. But, oh well. She hadn't gotten involved with therapy because she was perfect. It was because she knew how difficult it was to try and heal from something on your own.

And nobody should ever feel like they were alone.

Her first session with Loralee would be in less than

an hour, and she needed to get the horses prepared, along with her proposed plan. She had worked with women like Loralee before, but of course, everybody responded to trauma differently, and just because the situation might be similar didn't mean dealing with it would be identical. For weeklong intensives like this, the patient would often work with her, and continue to speak to their typical therapist via telehealth after different sessions.

That way, there was something new, something to help foster a breakthrough, but also something familiar.

She started to get out the different buckets that she would be using for this particular session, and some cards for labeling. And that was when she heard footsteps behind her. And just like she had known when he came to her door, she knew who it was without turning.

"Gus wanted me to assist," he said.

"Oh," she said. "I... I would actually prefer if you didn't."

Her heart gave a kick, and she told herself that what she was saying was about Loralee, and not about last night's dream.

"Really?"

"This woman is recovering from an abusive marriage, and I would rather not have a man in the space. Especially not until I figure out exactly where she's at mentally."

She expected pushback. He didn't give it. "She isn't due for another hour, is she?"

"Well, no..."

"So, let me help you with setup. Get the horses warmed up."

"I don't..."

"I know the horses. How many are you going to get out?"

"Three. This is just going to be to familiarize her with the method and the animals."

"We have three that are really chill with each other, I'll go get them."

He turned on his heel and went into the stables, and she could only stare after him. He wasn't going to listen to her, apparently. She went into the stables behind him. "I really do have this."

"I said it was fine."

"I said it was fine," she said.

He grinned, and her heart did something funny, but so did the rest of her body. And as he put his hand on the door to the paddock, she got a visceral image of his hands on her skin. That dream that she'd had last night moving to the forefront of her mind. And it left her speechless.

Her whole body felt like it had been lit on fire. She was… She was not okay.

And she wanted to say something to get rid of him, but she knew that that would only make things more obvious.

If only she were…

If only she were a more normal person. Someone who'd maybe had experience with dating. She hadn't been approachable in school. The only person who had shown any interest in her was Carter, and once that happened, she had latched herself on to him.

Her skin crawled, as she remembered her own pathetic gratefulness at him wanting to be with her.

There was so much dark stuff in that particular barrel, and it was best kept covered.

And when he led the horse out, his large hand moving over the animal's neck as he stroked him, then gave him a pat, her body jolted.

"Which other horses?"

"Strawberries," he said. "You already know her."

She went down to the pretty roan's stall and opened it up. While she did that, Brody got the third horse, and then they led them out to the arena. She took Strawberries off the lead rope, and Brody followed suit with the other two.

"That's Black Magic," he said pointing to the black horse with white socks. "And Carl."

"Carl?"

"Sometimes, simplicity is a good thing, Elizabeth," he said.

And the way he said her name, that vaguely mocking tone, lazy and laconic and unconcerned, did something to her.

"I'm all about simple," she said, watching the animals mill around the space.

"Really? You seem fussy."

"I'm not fussy," she said, blinking rapidly.

She didn't own a single article of clothing that she hadn't taken with her from her marriage. She had learned to live with little, and she had learned that early. He had no idea the level of simplicity that she could exist with.

And she could tell him. But she wasn't going to.

If she seemed…in any way smooth or sophisticated, even now, with only the things that she had taken away from her marriage, it was because she'd cultivated this image and she had done it with intent.

She had been so determined to match her husband,

to fit into their life, and she'd taken it with her when she left.

She didn't need to talk to him about it now. She didn't need to talk to him about it ever.

This was not the getting-to-know-Brody-McCloud hour. It was the getting-ready-to-see-her-first-patient hour.

"Okay," he said.

That did it. She turned around to face him. "You don't actually know me."

"You're right. I don't. But I've made some assumptions."

"Well, I've made some assumptions about you," she said.

"Really?" he countered. "Why don't you indulge me by telling me what those assumptions are?"

"Because I don't care what your assumptions are about me, so why should I tell you what I think about you?"

"It's enough to know that you think about me, Elizabeth. You don't need to give me details."

He was a shameless flirt. A shameless flirt who had, in all likelihood, had another woman in his bed last night, and he was acting like she was now the only woman in the world.

She wondered how many hearts he'd broken. Probably a lot of them.

At least Carter wasn't a heartbreaker. Not systemically.

Sure, he had broken her heart one time, but then he had gotten married, and he showed no signs of breaking Ashley's heart.

"You're a bad bet," she said. "Any woman would be an idiot to make it."

"That's why I encourage women to never bet on me. Other things, sure. But never bet on me."

"Well. Good to know that I was right about that."

"Definitely. You're probably right about everything. I'm not that interesting."

And the problem was, that was a lie. He was that interesting. She couldn't take her eyes off him, even while she insulted him.

"You went out last night to hook up."

"I did," he said, his expression grave.

Her stomach churned, and she hated herself for that. She was far more familiar with jealousy than she would like.

He looked great, but not at all apologetic, and she chose to just not ask him any follow-up questions.

"Don't you want to know how it went?" he pressed.

"I obviously don't," she bit out. "Or I would have asked."

"I didn't go home with anyone."

"I don't see why I would care about that." She kept her eyes on the horses, and her heart was thundering hard at the base of her throat.

"Yeah," he said, taking a step away from her. "I don't know why you would either."

And she wondered what he had thought about saying, because there had been something else. But he had thought better of it. And she should let him think better of it. She was going to allow him to think better of it.

And she ignored the crushing regret that she felt over that. Over that moment that had just passed. But this wasn't what she was here to do. Her attraction to him was entirely inconvenient, and anyway, even if he returned it, there was nothing that she could do about it.

She lived in a tiny cabin with Benny, she wasn't in the market for anything casual *or* serious. And she had a feeling that Brody was the kind of guy that didn't do serious at all. She wasn't experienced enough to really know that, but she sensed it.

The regret that she felt was that she couldn't…

That she couldn't have that dream.

Even just for a night.

The idea of it made goose bumps rise up on her arms, and she rubbed at them, trying to make them go away.

She didn't live the kind of life that made that possible. She wasn't the kind of person it was possible for, anyway. At least, she didn't think so.

"I'll get out of your hair," he said.

"Great."

And now it was time for her first therapy session, a good reminder of why she was here. She wasn't going to allow herself to get derailed.

CHAPTER SIX

HE HAD ALMOST made a move. Very close. But then he
had taken a step back, looked at her, looked at himself,
and asked himself what he was doing.

She wasn't a bar girl. She wasn't a woman out on
the town, looking for a good time. In fact, she couldn't
have made it clearer she wasn't looking for anything.
She was also a complication. She lived at the ranch,
she had a kid...

Well, for the first time in his life, he showed a little
bit of restraint. So he supposed he should be proud of
himself for that.

He wasn't, though. He didn't do "proud of himself."
It wasn't in his wheelhouse.

He was facilitating things today, not working with
any of the clients but making sure that everything was
set up when it needed to be, that the horses were taken
care of. It was easy work, honestly, and he found himself wishing that there was something physical he could
labor over to alleviate whatever it was Elizabeth was
doing to him.

But no matter how busy he tried to keep, accomplish-
ing other things, he just kept running into her.

And he happened to be right outside the main barn
when she pulled up with Benny, who roared out of the

car with a huge grin on his face. "We went for a hike for school," he said.

"Really?"

It was weird, having a kid be so happy to see him. To have the kid want to tell him about his day. He didn't even know him. But then, he supposed he had hooked him up with a chance to play with army men last night. So maybe Benny was just a fan because of that.

"Yeah, it was so cool. We identified different mushrooms. And one of the older kids told me that there were bears in the woods."

Elizabeth looked startled by that. "Bears?"

"There are bears in the city," Brody said. "Surely you must have figured there would be some out in the woods."

"Well. I don't really like the idea of him hiking around with bears for school."

"Doesn't seem any more dangerous than a lot of the other things that you can find in schools these days," he said.

She pulled her mouth into a line, and lifted a brow. She was going to go ahead and make her very best effort to not be charmed by him. Which just made him want to charm her. And he had just decided he wasn't going to do that.

"It's not as bad as I thought," Benny said, as if he was making a grave admission to his mother.

"Well," she said. "Good."

"It's fun to have older kids in the class. And the third-graders get to take care of the little first-graders. We made sure they stayed on the trail."

He could remember those days. They didn't have a teacher that was quite as nice as Tala Everett, in fact, she had been a pretty strict, old-school schoolmarm. But he'd liked his days in the schoolhouse. It had been a nice reprieve from the reality of his actual house.

He could remember being Benny's age, and feeling proud of taking care of the little kids. And definitely not feeling like he was one of the little kids.

"Did anybody put a frog in the teacher's desk today?"

Benny looked horrified by that. "Why would anyone do that?"

He laughed. "It's a prank."

"Benjamin Colfax, you will not put a frog in the teacher's desk."

"No," Brody said solemnly. "You really don't want to turn out like me. And that is the Brody McCloud path. You don't want to walk on it."

"Why not?" Benny asked.

"I… Because," Brody said.

He hadn't expected to get stumped by a child. Well, the truth was, he could tell him why, but it would be a longer, more complicated story than Benny would have patience for, and there would be details his mother wouldn't appreciate him sharing at all.

The kid shrugged and started skipping around in a circle, looking at imaginary markers on the ground, as if he was trying to hit each one.

"Do you have homework?" Elizabeth asked.

"No. Mrs. Everett said she doesn't give homework. She doesn't believe in it."

He saw Elizabeth mouth a prayer of what looked like thanks, and he definitely felt like he was looking into a window at a life that he didn't understand.

His parents had never cared if he had homework. Hell, his mom hadn't even stuck around.

"It's more work for me than it is for him," she said quietly. "Of course I have to openly support whatever the teacher chooses to do. But I really don't like fighting about fractions over dinner. I didn't care about them when I was in school. Caring about them on behalf of a cranky child is a bridge too far."

He chuckled. "I can't imagine caring about anything other than what I want to care about at a given moment."

"Kids have a way of doing that to you," she said.

It underscored an important difference between them. Something they should both pay attention to.

"Do we have trails here?" Benny asked.

"Yeah," Brody said. "Lots. Mostly we ride horses on them, but you can definitely hike on them."

"Can you show me?"

Elizabeth's eyes went wide. "You mean you want to do something other than play video games?"

"The trails around here are really cool," Benny said.

"Yeah," he said. He tried to rack his brain to think of a place that might be cool to take a kid. Immediately he thought of the caves. "There's a pretty quick hike that goes down toward the creek, and there's a couple of caves back in there. We used to go down there looking for gold nuggets."

"Can I see?"

"Yeah," he said, and then realized that Elizabeth was staring daggers at the side of his head. "If your mom says it's okay," he said.

"Supervised," she said.

"Well, you're welcome to come with us."

How was this happening? How had he gotten himself roped into this?

You roped yourself, dumbass.

"I'll have to change," she said, indicating the prim dressage attire that she was wearing. Those very tight breeches, and the tall black boots.

"Better hurry, we only have about an hour and a half left of daylight."

"I don't want to get stuck in a cave in the dark," she said.

"I'm not going to let you get stuck," he said.

"I'll meet you…"

"Just come back with us," Benny said.

Which was how he found himself sitting in the front seat of Elizabeth's car, being driven back to the cabin.

"Come on in," she said softly, when she turned the car off.

So he followed her and Benny into the house.

It had a distinctly more lived-in feel than even just a couple of days ago. Little boy's shoes, some toys on the floor, and a bowl of fruit on the counter.

"Where'd you get the fruit?" Which was maybe the dumbest question he'd ever asked anybody.

"Your sister-in-law brought it by. She said it came from her sisters."

"Oh yeah. The Sullivans have a big garden." That was underselling it. "I mean, actually it's huge. They're trying to get a store set up on the property. We've been working on it, weather permitting."

"So they're another family that has a stake in the ranch?"

"It is actually four separate ranches," he said. "Each family owns a plot, but we work cooperatively."

"And now the Sullivans have married into your family, and the Garretts are about to?"

"That is correct."

"Any chance of the Kings marrying in?"

He huffed a laugh. "Not unless big changes are on the horizon. Considering Arizona is the only woman, and she's married, and the rest of them are... Not my or Lachlan's type."

"I see," she said.

"Mom," Benny said. "Go change."

She startled. "Well, ask nicely," she said, before turning and walking down the hall and closing the door behind her. And he couldn't stop himself from wondering which article of clothing she was going to remove first.

He imagined the jacket coming off. Then her shirt. And then her hands would go around and unclasp her bra...

"I don't understand how grown-ups can stand around talking about fruit."

He looked at Benny. "Someday you will."

Because someday, there would be a woman that Benny thought was beautiful, even if he shouldn't think so much about how she was beautiful, and he would stand around and talk to that woman about anything, just so he could watch her lips move.

And he was back to thinking inappropriate thoughts.

Elizabeth came out of her bedroom dressed in jeans, hiking boots, and a sweater that conformed lovingly to her figure.

Damn, she was hot.

"We might as well walk," he said. "There's a trail that we can take from up here that'll lead us straight down there."

"Sure," she said, managing to look reluctant, even as she led the charge out the front door.

Benny quickly passed both of them up.

"You don't know where you're going, Ben," he said.

Benny slowed down then. And it was his turn to take the lead of this strange, ragtag crew.

He had chores to do. He didn't know why the hell he was doing this.

Don't you?

It was weird, the way he saw himself in the kid. They didn't have anything in common.

But there was something about that age. Something about…

"This way," he said.

The trail was mossy and rocky, and slightly slippery.

Benny slipped once, and Elizabeth reached out and grabbed hold of the back of his shirt. And a minute later, she went unsteady, and Brody grabbed hold of both of her arms, holding her upright, drawing her back against his chest.

"Careful," he said softly.

She looked up at him, and her pupils seemed to expand. "Yeah," she said, moving away from him. But slowly.

"You can never come down to these caves without an adult," Brody said, feeling suddenly afraid that he was showing the boy something he maybe shouldn't have. That was probably why Elizabeth had looked at him like that.

Like she was worried about the same thing. But of course she'd thought of all the potential consequences right away, and he hadn't.

"All right," Benny said.

But the kid said it so casually, he couldn't be entirely certain he was listening.

"I'm serious," Brody said.

"You better listen to Brody," Elizabeth said. "He's a pirate and a cowboy."

"I know he's not a pirate," Benny said, as if they were ridiculous.

"I'm hurt," Brody said. "I'm obviously a pirate."

"What exactly do you plunder?" Elizabeth asked, smiling at him.

"Well, that is a loaded question," he returned.

Her cheeks went pink, and she looked ahead quickly, like she knew and she was trying to hide it from him.

When they reached the bottom of the trail, the mud gave way to a rocky riverbank, the water rushing by.

"The cave is this way," he said, gesturing off to the left.

Benny did run ahead of them then, whooping and hollering as he went.

"This is so good for him," she said. "I was just feeling… I was feeling good today, but also…" She shook her head. "I don't know why I'm telling you this."

"Well, I don't know why I offered to show your kid a cave. But here we are."

They looked at each other for a moment. He felt like they were acknowledging that they were both acting a little bit out of character, and neither one of them knew quite what to do about it. Or if they even *should* do something about it.

"That means you can finish what you were going to tell me," he said.

"I was feeling guilty," she said. "I didn't have a very stable childhood. And I didn't want that for him." That surprised him. That she could have come from a background that was anything other than pristine. She just seemed…perfect. And he'd assumed that kind of class had to come from, well, the same type of class. She sighed. "Already having the two households… And now I've gone and moved him a few hours away from his dad. It's why he's so mad at me."

"How does his dad feel about it?"

"He's *furious* at me. The truth is… He's conveniently furious at me. Carter isn't as involved in Benny's life as he should be. His mom basically forces him to keep the terms of the custody agreement. If she didn't, Benny would spend every weekend with me. He's just mad at me, and wants to be mad at me. And I know that Carter thinks I'm making things unstable for Benny. But I haven't seen him this happy… Ever."

"I'm sorry," Brody said. "That he's like that."

"Yeah. Me too. He *wasn't*. But things change. People change. I… I'm trying to change. I'm trying to stop being a victim of my circumstances. I'm kind of an expert at that. Got divorced, didn't want to, moved into an apartment because it was what I could afford in proximity to Carter, and I wanted Benny to be involved in his life… Well, now I'm making a decision for myself, and I actually think it's a good one for him. There's a cave. He's about to explore a cave. And it scares me. But it's an adventure."

"Yeah," Brody said. "Every little boy needs adventure."

"I bet you didn't have any shortage of adventure growing up here."

"Yeah well… He didn't actually get a chance to ask my brother about his scars."

"No. I think he got distracted by the army men."

He felt right then like they were both back in the hallway. In that moment of obvious tension. Her breathing increased fractionally, her pulse pounding at the base of her throat. He wanted to press his lips to it. He wanted to take her in his arms and kiss her.

And then he remembered, they were walking toward a cave, and there was a child present.

"Well. If Gus had told the story, you would know a little bit more about our childhood."

"He was a boy when that happened?"

"Yeah. He got locked in a shed when it was on fire. Our dad set the fire. And locked him in there."

She stopped walking so abruptly that a spray of gravel shot up around her feet and hit him in the back of the leg. "What?"

"We had a lot of adventures here. They weren't all good ones."

"Brody, did he…? He was abusive?"

"Yeah," Brody said, tension building in his chest. He shouldn't have brought this up.

"Did he hurt you?"

"No," he said.

And he could feel the questions brewing inside her, but she didn't ask any of them.

He was glad of that, because he didn't have answers for them. Whatever they were, he didn't have answers.

He hated his dad.

And he didn't.

How the hell did you explain that? He couldn't. Not to himself. Not to his brothers. So he just didn't think on it much at all.

And he sure as hell didn't talk about it.

They rounded the corner and came up to the mouth of the cave, dark and yawning, and a little too like a portrait of Brody's soul for his liking.

"Whoa," Benny said. "Do you think there's a bear in there?"

"Probably not," Brody said. "Come on." He reached into his pocket and took out his keychain flashlight, and shined it around the mouth of the cave.

There was a small tunnel that went back pretty deep, but the main cavern was big, and fairly shallow, giving a sense that you were in a cave, without actually putting you in any danger of being lost or anything like that.

"So cool," Benny said, delighting in his words echoing off the cavern around them. "Did you ever find any gold in here?"

Places like this had been an escape from their father, and escape from the tension in the house. That had been gold, all on its own.

"No. But we had a good time looking for it. And sometimes that's the whole point."

CHAPTER SEVEN

SHE WAS STUCK on the cave adventure. Had been ever since it had happened. Hadn't stopped thinking about it since Brody walked them back up to the house and said goodbye without coming back inside.

He'd shared things about his life. Dark things. Deep things. She didn't know why. It made her want to know more.

Maybe it was something to do with him. Or maybe it was because this man, this stranger, seemed so much more interested in Benny than Carter had for a long time.

That thought immobilized her. She needed to get to her next appointment with Loralee, and she was frozen, standing there in the middle of the barn, completely undone by that realization.

She swallowed hard, then pressed forward. Loralee, a petite woman with dark hair, was standing in the center of the arena, waiting for Elizabeth.

"Good morning," Elizabeth said brightly. "How did your conversation with your therapist go after our session yesterday?"

"Oh, it went well," Loralee said, looking tentative. They had discussed what was going to happen today, and she had seemed nervous even as they walked through it.

Elizabeth knew that yesterday, she had done her session with Elizabeth, then had gone back to her cabin, to speak to her therapist, and then that she had been tasked with going and getting ingredients to make herself dinner. Whatever she wanted. And she wasn't supposed to worry about anything. Whether or not someone else liked it, whether or not it was healthy, nothing.

She was just supposed to focus on pleasing herself.

"And how was your dinner?"

"Oh. I ended up… This is going to sound really stupid, but I couldn't decide what I wanted. I was able to pick whatever I wanted, and I don't know how to do that. I…had a salad." She looked crestfallen.

"You don't have to feel bad about that. You just have to try again tonight."

"Maybe I need to make a short list before I go out."

"It gives us something else to work on. Not your short list, but your confidence in your own desires."

"That's the thing. I don't have any confidence in my own desires. My own desires landed me in my marriage."

That grazed Elizabeth close to the bone. "Don't be angry at yourself for that." She shook her head. "It isn't your fault that somebody took advantage of your feelings and lied to you about who they were."

"So my therapist keeps telling me. But it's a journey."

"Understandable," Elizabeth said.

"Okay. So, what exactly am I supposed to learn in this exercise?"

"You're just going to… You're going to bond with the horses. Gain confidence. Interacting with horses is a lot like interacting with other people. They pick up on your anxiety. And you need to build trust with them. Horses are prey, and they perceive us as predators."

"But they're… They're huge."

"Yes. That's true. But they think that you might be a danger to them, and they pay very close attention to your emotional state."

"So I have to be… Not nervous."

"You're not going to get it perfectly right the first time. That's okay. One thing you don't have to be here is perfect."

She looked relieved to hear that. Absolutely and completely. And Elizabeth wondered how long she had spent walking on eggshells, being convinced that she had to be perfect. Being convinced that everything she did had to be a certain kind of perfect.

Elizabeth couldn't fix everything. But hopefully she could give this woman her confidence back.

And who's going to give you yours?

She brushed that right off. It wasn't the same. She hadn't been abused. She didn't have any claim to that kind of trauma.

"All right. Let's get started."

She went to the adjoining paddock and opened the gate, which brought in the same three horses she had briefly introduced Loralee to yesterday.

The woman extended a shaking hand as the first horse trotted by her. And then she retracted her arm quickly.

"It's okay," Elizabeth said. "I promise."

The session went pretty well, and when the horses went back into the neighboring paddock, she turned to Loralee. "Now, remember, don't worry about anything you see as being a mistake. It's all just learning."

"I have a feeling I'm going to need a lot longer than a week here."

"Well, you can always come back. We never really finish with ourselves."

"I need to learn how to be as forgiving about myself as you seem to be."

"Well, I'm not that forgiving of myself," Elizabeth said. "I'm just working on me too."

"Elizabeth," Loralee said, looking at her. "Can I ask you…? You seem to be very intuitive about what it's like to start over."

"I'm a therapist," Elizabeth said.

"I know. But I have a therapist. I've had a lot of therapists. And there's just certain things they don't seem to quite get."

This woman was so guarded, so closed off, and Elizabeth could understand that. Elizabeth didn't work in traditional therapy settings, but even so, she typically adhered to the best practice of not sharing her own story with a client.

But she could tell Loralee needed something to grab on to. Something to make her trust.

People talking *at* her meant nothing. She needed to know Elizabeth understood what it meant to start over. That she knew what it was to be a woman alone, facing an uncertain future. A woman who had lost a piece of her identity and had to find her feet again, on her own.

"I got divorced six years ago," Elizabeth said.

Loralee's eyes crinkled at the edges. "You don't look old enough to have gotten divorced six years ago."

"I got married very young. And I didn't really know what I wanted. Much less how to carry on afterward. It's been a slow process of figuring out who I am."

A very slow process. One that wasn't even close to completion.

But then, having a child complicated everything. Because she had to orient her healing around him. Which was fine. It was just that she hadn't had alone time to figure herself out. To fix whatever she wanted for dinner or...

Unbidden, that Brody dream popped into her head again.

Right. Well. She hadn't had the chance to do that either.

The only man she'd ever been with was Carter. And she'd been celibate for six years.

Which was fine. She had never really thought of herself as a sexual person. As far as she was concerned, the best thing about sex was being close to someone that you loved.

She had spent her life moving from home to home, and the thing she had liked about being intimate with Carter was how close she had felt to him. How secure. Of course, then she had discovered that just because she felt a certain way didn't mean that another person felt the same. Didn't mean they were having the same experience.

So it didn't matter. Not really. If ever she fell in love again, she could explore that part of herself. But she didn't need to do it otherwise.

She might have had an orgasm dreaming about Brody, but the idea of deciding to have wild, torrid sex with him, only to find herself struggling to climax...

Well, that horrified her.

"And are you doing it? Figuring out who you are?" Loralee asked, looking at her hopefully.

"Yes. I'm trying. It's why I'm here too. To become a little bit more me."

"That's exactly what I need. To become a little bit more *me*. I've just been so afraid for so long it's taken all of these pieces of myself away."

"I've never been afraid. Not of my ex-husband. I can only imagine what you're going through as far as that's concerned. But I relate to being overwhelmed by possibilities and options."

"So what would you fix for dinner? If you could have anything," Loralee asked.

"I..." She found herself thinking of Benny's favorite. And had a difficult time thinking of her own. Then she thought of a pasta dish that she'd had at a restaurant years ago. Pasta that had been swirled in a Parmesan cheese wheel, with ham and peas in it. Benny would hate everything about it. But she had loved it.

"Pasta. With Parmesan."

"That does sound good," Loralee said.

"Yeah."

"Maybe you should fix that for yourself for dinner," Loralee said.

"Maybe I will."

Except she knew she wouldn't. In fact, she had just a little bit of time to go and hit the grocery store, and if they had them, she was going to get dinosaur-shaped chicken nuggets because Benny would like them.

And it was more important that she got something that Benny liked than making herself something that he wouldn't enjoy.

After Loralee left, she went to get the horses and put them back in their stables, so that she could feed them, and that was when Brody showed up.

"Gus's orders," he said.

"I don't need help." She was feeling raw, and she kind of wanted to be alone.

"You say that every time."

"Yeah. Well. It's true. I don't need help."

"And what would you say to your patient if she told you the same thing?"

"I'm not a patient." Except after that conversation, she was beginning to wonder.

But her circumstances were different.

All things considered, she was pretty well-adjusted.

He took the horses into the stall alongside her, and then went into an empty stall and grabbed a couple flakes of hay, chucking them into the enclosures.

"Did Benny get off okay for his second day of school?"

And that just about did her in. Because Carter hadn't texted her to ask about Benny's first couple of days of school. And this man had just asked. Like it was intuitive and easy. Like it was obvious that Benny was something she would want to talk about, because her whole world was oriented around him.

"Yes," she said, her throat tight.

"Good."

"Thank you. For taking Benny to see the cave yesterday."

"No problem. He's a good kid."

She knew that. She didn't need his opinion on the subject. But, she would be lying if she said that it didn't make her feel warm that he'd said it. "He is," she said. "For all that he's been through. He seems to be pretty well-adjusted."

"What do you mean, what he's been through?"

And there was something suddenly dangerous on his face, and she thought about what he had said about his own childhood. The things he'd said that happened to his brother.

"I don't mean anything like what you told me yesterday." She felt guilty. Making him think there had been abuse when in reality her life just hadn't been her perfect dream come true. Which seemed shallow by comparison. "I just never wanted him to be in a broken home."

Brody looked at her for a long moment. "Look. I'm not an expert on kids. Not even a little bit. But I've been in your cabin. I've watched you with Benny. Your home doesn't look broken to me. It looks like he has a great home with a mother who loves him very much."

"Thank you for saying that. It doesn't always…"

"I lived in a broken home. I lived in a broken home while my parents were together. It was still broken after they split up. But that wasn't what made it broken. I know what it actually feels like to live in a home like that."

He was sharing himself again. Giving her hints as to what he'd been through, and it made her want to know. She really didn't *want* to want to know more about this man. She didn't want to be curious about him. About what he'd been through to end up as…what he was.

She wasn't even sure what he was. She'd written him off as a beautiful, beautiful flirt. A man without substance.

He wasn't that.

He was gorgeous, but he wasn't insubstantial. No, he was deep. In a way that scared her.

A way that made her feel like if she wasn't careful she could get in over her head and drown.

She cleared her throat. "I never thought of it that way."

"I can't speak to the way his dad is…"

And she felt guilty again. Because Carter's behavior could not at all be compared to the kind of thing he had spoken of yesterday.

"Carter is… He's not bad." It annoyed her that she felt the need to defend him somewhat. Or at least not throw him under the bus entirely.

"Is he not?"

"Sometimes, it's easy for me to let myself think that he is," she said, sighing heavily. "That he's all bad. Of course I don't want Benny to spend any time with him. I want him all to myself all the time. I don't want to not have him with me. I don't want his life to be divided between two bedrooms. I don't want to share. And I also want Carter to spend more time with him. For Benny's sake. I want Benny to think I'm amazing and perfect, and I want him to take my side in what happened between me and his father. And at the same time, I want him to be able to hero worship his dad." She closed her eyes and tried to swallow. She was aware that she sounded insane. But she had never voiced these feelings to another person. And she didn't know why she was doing it to him.

This man who had occupied her dreams and made her feel things that she had never felt before. Things he didn't know about. Things he certainly hadn't gone out of his way to cause.

He had never even touched her.

He certainly hadn't asked for this.

Here she was. Spilling her guts. In a way that she hadn't known she needed to. She had really needed to, apparently.

Her life was so neatly compartmentalized. There

were horse people, and she talked to them about horses. There were some school moms, though she hadn't been that close to any of them. It was more that their kids had liked playing together, and that was bond enough. But they just talked about school things, kid things.

There was no one for her to talk with about these kinds of topics.

Carter had been her person.

Until he wasn't.

She had spent her entire high school experience with him, and then her early twenties, and she just hadn't had friends when all was said and done. He had been her world, and then her world had transformed into Benny. And there was no place for this. For these feelings. These complicated feelings.

"I didn't have a dad," she said, the words coming out all heavy and scratchy. "I want him to have his dad. But I'm also petty. And deeply human. And really quite flawed. You know, they don't make you pass any kind of a basic competency test before they give you a baby. You just get to have one, and then you have to raise him, and I don't always know what I'm doing. Especially when it comes to navigating divorce. I've been divorced with a child longer than I was married with one, and I'm still really bad at it."

"I'm sorry about that. About your dad. But you know, I had a dad, and he… he was pretty awful to my brothers. Having a dad doesn't always make it all better, all easy."

"I know that a bad dad is worse than no dad. And I've always been thankful that mine wasn't in my life, based on what I know about him." She wasn't ready to get into all the specifics of her upbringing. It wasn't traumatic in the way his was. It had certainly shaped her, and given her issues with certain things. But everyone's upbringing affected them, she wasn't unique. She'd had an unconventional life, not a bad one. But people heard "foster care" and they got weird. Right now, they were having a good conversation, and she didn't want him to get weird. "I don't know though. It's tough. It's all tough."

"Yeah. So… What happened? The divorce I mean."

"Right. I… You don't want to hear this. You came here to help with the horses, you did not come to get a rundown on the drama of my life."

"I want to hear it," he said, those gold-green eyes leveling on hers, and he looked interested. More interested in her—not what she knew about horses or equine therapy, nor her kid—than anyone had been in a long time.

"Dr. Brody is in session," he said, grinning. "You can vent all your troubles on me. And you don't have to be fair. I don't know him. He's not my dad."

That made her laugh. In spite of everything. "Fine. We got married young. We became parents very young. And I thought we were happy. I really did. I had never been happier, so why wouldn't I think that what we had was the epitome of joy? It felt like it to me. But… It wasn't. Not to him. Apparently. I found that out after he told me that he had met someone else. Not only had he met someone else, he had slept with that someone else. And she was pregnant. And he was in love with her. I was heartbroken."

Brody frowned, the expression of genuine concern on that handsome face enough to make her heart skip several beats. "Of course you were." He shook his head. "What an asshole."

That simple declaration really meant something to her. Petty though it might be. "That's what I thought too. We had a prenup, which meant that I didn't get anything. Not anything. And…" This was where she had to be honest about her own stubbornness. "He did offer a few things. I declined them. I took the child support, I didn't take spousal support. That's something I came to regret later. Because by being wounded and stubborn, I impacted on Benny's quality of life."

"Again, he seems perfectly happy and healthy to me."

"I know. It's just… We lived in a really small apartment. And if he wanted extravagant things, his dad had to buy them."

"That isn't actually a struggle, Elizabeth," he said, and if he had been anyone else, she would have been angry. But it was Brody, and he was just so handsome. "I understand that you feel guilty about it, because I think it's compulsory for parents to feel guilty about the things they've done and haven't done—not mine, of course, but normal parents—but you know, not having a new PlayStation and a big house isn't harmful to your kid. What's harmful is what my dad did. What's harmful is not being there, like my mom. You love him. He's taken care of. He doesn't go to bed hungry. He has a bed. You've done a lot for him. Don't be so hard on yourself."

No one had ever said that to her before. No one.

She looked up at him, and she thought that she might actually cry. She swallowed hard.

"Why are you being so nice to me?"

"I really don't know."

It was honest, that answer, she could tell. He looked mystified. Absolutely mystified.

Her heart was pounding so hard she felt dizzy, and she needed to get some space. Because this was too much. It was all too much.

She started to head toward the tack room, the lead rope and bridle, which she had just taken off one of the horses, in hand, and Brody came in behind her. She was about to tell him again that she didn't need any help, but when she turned around, he was right there. So close that his scent filled her again. Even closer than he had been in the hallway that evening.

He was so tall and broad, his Adam's apple bobbed up and down right in her line of sight and she could feel herself blushing. Could feel the heat rising in her face, and her whole body.

"Just brought the other lead rope and bridle," he said, turning to the wall and hanging both up on the pegs there.

And she moved to follow his lead, but then that put her right there... Right in front of him again.

She looked up, and there was something helpless that went through her.

If you could have anything for dinner... What would it be?

Right now, it wouldn't be food. And it wouldn't be dinner so much as dessert.

She felt lightheaded. Dizzy. Looking up at him...

She swallowed hard, and felt like her throat was lined with prickles.

You're not sexual, remember? You just like to be close.

Being close to Brody would be very, very nice.

You don't love him.

No. She didn't. She didn't even know him.

He listened to you.

She found herself moving nearer to him, and before she knew what she was doing, she extended her hand, and pressed it to his chest.

His movements were instantaneous and shocking. He covered her hand with his, pinning it there, a low growl in his throat. And she could feel his heart raging beneath her palm.

Then with his other hand, he grabbed her arm and brought her up against him, his eyes glittering with intensity.

And there was no space to wonder if he felt the same thing she did. This reckless heat that defied everything she had ever known about herself, all the things that she had just reiterated inside.

Then he leaned in, and his lips touched hers.

CHAPTER EIGHT

SHE WAS DIZZY. She thought she was going to collapse.

That woodsy scent of him filled her, his heat nearly overcoming her.

He was holding on to her, and if he hadn't been, she would've crumbled into a heap, right at his feet. She had only ever kissed one man in all her life. And this was different. So very different. His whiskers were rough, just like they'd been in her dreams, and his hold was stronger than she had known to imagine.

His grip was bruising as he held her there, and she found herself arching against him, leaning in, trying to find some way to alleviate the ache that was building inside of her.

The ache that had been building inside her since the first time she'd laid eyes on him months ago.

She had thought that he was the most beautiful man she'd ever seen, unequivocally, even then.

But she had never imagined that she would end up here.

In his arms.

And she hadn't imagined—even in her dreams— that it would be like this. She had never experienced anything like this. She didn't know that you could find something this incredible in something as simple as a kiss. Of course, this kiss couldn't be called anything like *simple*.

It was a full-body experience. Her heart was raging out of control, her breasts suddenly feeling heavy, her nipples going tight.

She was… She throbbed. Between her legs. She was wet there, instantly. Embarrassingly.

Except… She couldn't even be embarrassed, because she was just too hot. And she was driven by this.

His body was so hard, and he was so tall. And everything about him was different. Everything about this kiss was different than any of her previous experiences—all with only one other man.

This wasn't about closeness. It wasn't about comfort. It wasn't about being soothed by not being alone. This was about passion. About heat and fire, and the kind of desire that she'd never known existed inside of her.

She found herself clinging to his broad shoulders, then letting her hand slide down his chest, those muscles…

They were so…

She didn't have words for it. She didn't have words at all. She only had need. And there was no thought. No thought of the future, no thought of anything but how amazing it felt to have his mouth on hers.

He parted his lips, and slid his tongue inside for a taste. And she shivered. He growled, and pushed her against the wall. It was hard behind her, and he was equally hard in front of her, and when he arched his hips forward, and she could feel him… All of him… She nearly went up in flames.

She found herself moving her hands down lower,

over his flat, hard stomach, and down to the evidence of his desire.

She gasped when she grazed him with her fingertips. She hadn't gotten the full measure of him, but just that little exploratory touch was a revelation.

And she found herself doing something she would have never thought she would do. Not Elizabeth Colfax. Only been with one man, married at twenty, mother by twenty-one. Celibate for six years. *She* would never do this. She would certainly never put her hands on a man's belt and began to undo it with shaking fingers as if she might die if she couldn't get to what was behind it. But there she was. She got the belt undone, and then she went for the button on his jeans, before he jerked himself away.

"Hey," he said, his voice rough. "Take a breath."

She was dizzy. And then suddenly, she was humiliated.

She had just… And then he… He was the one who had presence of mind to do anything. To stop it.

She had been a stranger. A really horny stranger, acting like a sex-crazed beast.

She looked at him, at this faint slash of red that covered his cheekbones, at the way his chest rose and fell sharply. She could still see his arousal, pressed hard against the front of his jeans, his belt hanging open.

But he'd been able to stop.

And she hadn't been.

She still didn't want to. Her heart was thundering, and she was shaking. Shaking with unsatisfied desire.

"I don't want to take a breath," she said.

"Yeah, I don't really want to either, but I think that we maybe should."

"I… What are you, a prude?" And she was shocked to hear that come out of her mouth. Shocked that her embarrassment right now was making her feel mean. But it did. He had kissed her. She had kissed him. It was all a little bit muddled in her head who had started it, but it had happened. She hadn't kissed any man other than Carter, and now she had kissed Brody, and they had *really* kissed, and he was the one to break it off. She felt dismayed.

Dismayed was a completely understated word for what she felt. She felt demolished.

Like everything inside her had been bulldozed, everything that she had ever thought about herself, and it had all made room for… This need. This deep, fiery need, and he was acting like stopping was easy.

"No. I'm not. But you shared some pretty vulnerable stuff with me, and I'm afraid…" A muscle in his jaw jumped. "I don't want you to get the wrong idea."

"What?"

"I'm not a… I'm not a relationship guy."

She felt like the floor had been upended. She was actually getting a talk. From a very handsome man who thought she needed to know that he didn't want to marry her just because they had kissed. And in fairness, she had no real experience with dating.

She had fallen into a relationship. One that had turned into marriage and motherhood. And she had no actual experience with relationships outside that. She had never hooked up, she had never… Any of that. So it was surreal to an insane degree that this was happening to her at all. And that her heart was still pounding and that place between her thighs throbbed.

"I told you I had a really terrible experience with love and commitment. I'm not naïve."

"Sure. But I did think that I should probably put my cards on the table. You have Benny, and I respect that. That responsibility. He's a great kid. Also… You live here."

Then she was just ashamed, because this man had outlined all kinds of things that she should have thought of on her own. Things that she should have been conscious of. Aware of. Things that should have mattered a lot more to her than they did to him.

She was letting her body lead. And when had she ever done that in all of her life? If she wasn't so appalled, she might be kind of proud of herself. Or at least in awe of her own capacity for debauchery, heretofore undiscovered and unexplored.

"You're right." She took a step back from him. "You are… You're right. I got carried away. I think… You're an attractive man."

"I got carried away," he said. "And you are the sexiest damn woman I've ever seen."

She really wished he hadn't said that, because it made her throat go tight, made her stomach get tense. Made her hungry for him all over again.

How long had it been since she'd felt beautiful? Desireable? She'd been replaced by another woman and she might not linger on what that had done to her self-esteem, but the damage was there for sure.

He thought she was sexy.

"Well. I guess we can both agree that we can't get carried away again."

"Right. Agreed."

Suddenly, she just needed to get away from him. All

of the comfort that she had felt in his presence had vanished, and she needed to… To get her head on straight. To figure out what had happened, what she was thinking. Somehow she had a feeling it would take a lot more than a couple of hours between now and when she had to pick up Benny to figure it out.

THE SNOW FELT like insult to injury. It was early in the year to get this kind of snowfall, and Brody didn't care for it. Not at all. He didn't like snow. People said it was picturesque. Peaceful, beautiful. His brother Gus loved the snow. But Gus was a secret sap, and Brody wasn't anything of the kind.

It was cold, it was wet, and he wanted nothing to do with it ever, and there it was, sludging down and building up quickly. Little white flakes of freezing hell that were guaranteed to worm themselves down into his boots and make him cold and soggy long before he had to come in from the grind.

This time of year just wasn't his favorite. It got dark so early. And he didn't care for Christmas all that much. There was no point to it. It was just an interruption as far as he was concerned. They hadn't really celebrated it ever in his family. That would have been far too functional for the McClouds.

So basically, it was just a long dark slog as far as he was concerned. And when the sun started to shine back through and the first vestiges of life began to appear in the form of flowers pushing up through the ground, he gave thanks to whatever deity changed the seasons.

Snow.

He needed to cut some wood for his cabin. It was going to be freezing. Elizabeth was going to need some wood.

Yeah. The snow isn't your real problem.

Because then he thought of her. And his whole body went tight.

Yes. Maybe she was the problem. And that kiss.

He hadn't been able to help himself. She had been there and she had just looked so… She was beautiful. Which seemed insipid, actually. He kept thinking it. Over and over again. But it didn't capture what he felt when he looked at her. Which was something beyond appreciating her beauty.

Something that went right down deep. Something visceral and primal and…

Now there was snow in his boot. Dammit. That really pissed him off.

He growled and started to walk over to the wood-pile. "Hey Brody."

He turned around, and there was a kid. Walking… Literally in his footsteps. Literally in his footsteps in the snow. And if anything had ever terrified him in his life, it was what he was looking at right now.

If anything could have drawn a bigger line underneath what a mistake his kissing Elizabeth was, he couldn't think of what it might be.

"Kid," he said. "How you doing?"

"Good. It's snowing." As if he would obviously be good because of the snow. Kids, man.

"Yeah, you *would* like snow."

"Huh?"

"It's a fact. Kids like snow," he said.

"Yeah. Because snow is good."

Spoken like a little beast who didn't have to be outside longer than he wanted to, and who had a mom waiting back in the house to make him cocoa.

"What's good about it, then?" he asked. "Can you tell me?"

Benny looked at him like he was an idiot. "It's fun to play in."

"Maybe that's the problem," Brody said. "I have to work in it."

"What work are you doing?"

"I'm about to go chop some wood. For my place, and I figured that you and your mom might need some too."

"Can I help?"

He thought about what Elizabeth's face would do if she was standing there and heard him agree to let her son help him with a task that involved an axe.

He had a feeling that what followed would involve parts of his body and an axe, and he wasn't into that.

"Sure," he said, carefully. "I'll find something for you to do. Come with me."

The kid kept on walking, taking big leaps to plant each one of his footsteps into Brody's.

Brody had to turn away.

"Does your mom know where you are?" Brody asked.

"She told me to go outside and play because I was driving her crazy."

"Did she?" He wondered if Elizabeth was as foul tempered as he was. He was pretty mad at himself.

She'd had her hands on his belt buckle, clearly intent on getting his clothes off him. And he wondered if she would've gotten down to her knees in front of him if he would've let it go on for just a little bit longer.

Wondered if she would have…

He was standing in front of her kid.

And he had just told himself that it was a good thing that nothing had come of that.

A good thing that it had stopped.

It just didn't feel very good, when he felt irritable, and still really wanted her.

"Yeah. But I wanted to go out in the snow anyway."

"Because you like the snow."

"Yes," Benny said, continuing to speak to Brody as if he was thick.

"I bet you like Christmas too."

"That's another thing that *everybody* likes," Benny said with authority.

Brody lifted one eyebrow. "I assure you, they do not."

He stopped in front of the woodpile and grabbed the axe that was leaning up against the side of the shed. "Okay. We've got some logs to split."

"Can I use the axe?" The kid was keen and eager.

"No. Because your mom will kill me. Probably with the axe. And I don't want to go down like that." *Not without seeing her naked first.*

"She wouldn't really kill you." Benny sounded confident in this. But you could never really know your parents.

"I think you might underestimate her."

"What can I do?" Benny asked, practically hopping in place.

"You can bring me new logs, and then when I split them, grab the split pieces and put them over in the bed of the truck."

"Okay," Benny said, gamely running over to the woodpile and grabbing a piece of wood, hefting it in his little arms as best he could.

Brody grabbed hold of it with one hand, set it up on end on top of a big stump, and put an awl at the center of the top wedging it in a natural split in the madrone. Then he lifted the axe and brought it down swiftly, sending the two pieces of wood flying opposite directions.

"Wow," said Benny.

He was not used to garnering admiration for a simple ranching skill. Kids really were a trip.

"More," he said, gesturing toward the woodpile, and Benny scurried into action. He chuckled when the kid picked the next biggest piece of wood he could find and brought it over with great effort. And he relieved him of it with one hand yet again.

They continued on like this, him cutting wood, Benny collecting the pieces and putting them into the truck.

It was an old, borderline rusted-out pickup truck that they used for carting around less desirable things, things that you wouldn't want rattling around in your nicer truck. They always left the keys in it. If somebody wanted to steal it, they were welcome to it.

Finally, they had a neat pile, and it was a quick drive up to the cabin.

"You want to ride in the back?"

"Yeah," Benny said enthusiastically, climbing up on the tailgate.

"Here," he said. "Sit on the toolbox right up against the window."

The logs wouldn't roll that direction because of how they'd been stacked. The kid would be perfectly safe. It was funny, he'd spent a whole lot of time running around this place with no supervision. He and his brothers had driven this truck all around when they were way too young to be doing that, with all of them in the back. Of course, they had lived in the kind of environment where parents hadn't much cared what happened to them. Or had been the true and active danger to their children.

So really, no one had cared what they'd gotten up to.

But now in his advanced age—he was thirty-four, after all—he did think a little bit more about safety.

They got into the truck and he fired up the engine, started to drive forward, looking in the back to check on Benny. The kid looked thrilled. The snow was still falling, and it was freezing, his cheeks were pink, and he had a wide grin on his face. It was infectious. It made Brody smile too.

They rocked and rolled through speed bumps, but Brody took it slow, and kept the ride as smooth as possible, even while the truck pitched and swayed a little bit. He turned on the radio. It was filled with static, but he could still hear the twang of country music coming out over the questionable speakers.

And he cranked it up.

By the time they coasted into the cabin driveway, the snow was really coming down. And when he stopped in front of it, the door burst open.

"What exactly is going on?"

"You sent him outside," Brody said, looking at Elizabeth's extremely worried expression.

Seriously, the kid had no idea. She would kill him as soon as look at him if he did the wrong thing. He had the sense that he had done the wrong thing as far as she was concerned, and he was about to get a lecture.

Not death, though. There was a little bit of comfort in that.

"I see that. And you…found him?"

"I did," Brody said. "We cut some wood. And brought it to you, because you're going to need some in your woodstove, since it's snowing and very, very cold."

That seemed to lower her hackles some. "Oh. Well. That was nice. It was nice."

And then their eyes connected, and her cheeks went pink. And he knew that she was thinking about the kiss. The Lord knew he was.

Maybe that was why she was mad at him. A man could hope. Mad not because they had kissed, but because they had stopped. He had been questioning himself on that score ever since. But then there was the kid. And then there was… Brody. And everything he was.

"All right, Benny, now you have to help me carry it all up onto the porch."

Benny's grin slid off his face. "That's a lot of work," he said.

"Ranch life is a lot of work, kid. But we loaded the wood up, now we need to finish the task."

"That doesn't seem fair, though, because I did help load it up."

"First of all, life isn't fair. Second of all, an unfinished task means you may as well not have started. That would make loading the wood useless. Do you want to make all that work you did useless?"

"No," Benny grumbled, and climbed up the side of the pickup, and jumped down to the ground, rounding to the tailgate. Elizabeth gasped when he did it, but didn't freak out wholly.

Brody lowered the tailgate, and Benny started taking hold of pieces of wood.

"Why don't we make a stack right here beneath the

window, close to the door. That way it will be easy for your mom to get at it when she needs to start a fire. Or better still, easy for you to grab it while your mom does that."

There was still grumbling, but he was doing it.

Elizabeth looked over at him. "You're awfully authoritarian."

"I just think he ought to do some things for you. Is that authoritarian?"

"Well, I just…"

"You feel guilty, so you don't want to ask him to do anything. *I* don't feel guilty. Not about much of anything."

Damn, he was a really great liar. He could take his show on the road.

"Well, how nice for you," she said, rolling her eyes.

They looked at each other, and he could feel the heat arc and expand between them. "That's a perk of living for yourself. Not much point in guilt."

"Sounds potentially lonely."

They both paused to watch Benny dramatically grunt as he set down a couple of pieces of wood by the door.

He cleared his throat. "I find ways to keep the loneliness at bay."

Her breath caught, and he did his best not to fixate on it. On what she might be thinking. On just exactly what thoughts were going through her mind right now, and if they had anything to do with the kiss they'd shared.

Holy hell. He'd never once in all of his life fixated on a woman like this. Not even when he was a horny virgin. It had been about *sex* then. Not about a particular person.

Actually, it had been about sex in all the years since.

He'd never wanted one person like this, at the expense of any other woman, any other desire.

And here he was, overthinking a kiss. Playing it over and over in his mind. Wishing that had gone further. Hating himself for stopping it.

"I assume your anti-loneliness tactic has something to do with horses?"

"I don't like horses like that," he said, and he knew the grin that he gave her was wicked.

She flushed. "That wasn't what I was implying. Remember? Double entendre isn't my thing."

"And remember, I'm incapable of avoiding it."

"Yes. I do recall you saying something about that."

He shrugged. "When your home life is no fun at all, you learn to make your own fun."

Which he had done. It was one reason he had embraced alcohol and sex and every other indulgence he could find, like a needy child clinging to his mother. He hadn't had a mother. So he'd gone with debauchery.

That had been Lachlan's preferred form of dealing with things too. So the two of them had tested the bonds of propriety thoroughly since they were way too young to be doing the things they were doing.

As an older brother, Brody probably should have felt guilty about leading his younger brother down the wide path to perdition, but, when you'd been born into a particular sort of hell, it was tough to worry overmuch about damnation for drinking a whiskey.

Of course, you couldn't use fake IDs in a town like Pyrite Falls. Everybody knew who you were. But they had gotten pretty skilled at stealing the exact truck that he had just driven here with, with all the wood in the back, and traveling a few towns over.

"I imagine that is a valuable skill to have."

"It is. Look, life can be a…" He looked over at the kid. "A really mean person." Elizabeth laughed at him. But he continued anyway. "But, there are things you can do to make it a little bit better."

Like kissing beautiful women in tack rooms. But he didn't say that. Because he had been the one to cut it off. But he was just… He was worried. That was the thing. And he wasn't the kind of guy who went through life with a lot of worry. But he was worried about this. She didn't seem like the kind of woman who was used to casual physical relationships. And those were all he did.

Throw in the added complication of her living on the ranch, working for their family, depending on them, and being in the kind of position she was in, with her son, with issues with her ex-husband…

He just felt like she needed a lot more than he could give, and he was a bigger gamble than a woman like her would ever want to take. All for an hour of pleasure. A few hours of pleasure. Hell, maybe a dirty weekend.

Except, there couldn't even be a dirty weekend, because there was a kid. A kid who would be home *all day* on the weekend.

And Lord knew, he would make her scream so loud it would echo throughout that whole tiny house. There would be no way to cover it up.

Well, now he was lost in thought about how loud he would like to make her scream. He wondered if she was a screamer. She looked a little bit too sophisticated for that, but the way she had kissed him… The way she had let her hands move all over his body, the way she had been ready to undo the buckle on his jeans and…

He really needed to get his head on straight.

She was not a woman he could mess around with. She had been hurt and...

He didn't want to hurt her.

He really didn't.

"The town hall is tomorrow," he said, doing what he could to redirect the conversation. "You should come. You and Benny. All the kids go, and they play games. The grown-ups get drunk and dance around the fire, but you don't need to do either of those things."

"That sounds like a sacred ritual."

"I promise you it's not. Unless you know of any sacred rituals involving red Solo cups."

"I don't," she said, suppressing a smile.

"Great. Well. I'll see you there, then. I mean, maybe I'll see you before then." And he wasn't leaving now. What the hell was *happening*?

He was tripping over his words while talking to a woman. Which was not something that he could ever recall happening before in his life.

"Yeah. I'll look forward to that. Seeing how the ranch runs. I mean, in the broader sense."

"Good. Of course, it's going to be cold. But... There's the bonfire."

"Right."

"Am I done yet?" Benny called.

"I better help him," Brody said, moving into action and grabbing a whole pile out of the back of the truck and bringing it up to the front of the house. "There. That should keep you warm."

And he felt like she heard it, even though he didn't say it. That he would like to keep her warm.

After he had gotten her hot.

He needed to get a grip.

"Right. Thank you. I'll probably see you tomorrow."

"I'm sure you will."

And he turned and walked away from her, walked away from Benny, and got back into that rusted-out old truck, and played back scenes from his life through his mind. A reminder of who he was. A reminder that this was some kind of weird aberration that had nothing to do with anything he'd been before, anything he'd been through. That it was some strange part of him, some primal, testosterone-driven part of him that didn't remember that he was fucked-up beyond all reason. That part of him thought it was just fine that he was attracted to a super sexy single mother.

She had proven that she could reproduce. Yes. That was the issue. He was having some kind of biological crisis. It couldn't only be women who had biological-clock nonsense. It stood to reason. Propagation of the species and whatever bullshit.

But that was biology. And he was a man who very much knew who he was. He just had to stop forgetting.

CHAPTER NINE

ODDLY, SHE HADN'T seen Brody the following day, and now she was incredibly wound up about seeing him at the town hall meeting that evening. The town hall meeting—she had discovered—was something that all of the McClouds took very seriously. It was their chance to give an update on what was going on with the equine therapy, their chance to talk about any resources they might need, and their chance to give input on the other ventures happening at Four Corners.

They were an interesting bunch, the McClouds. Varying degrees of hard and occasionally difficult, but always well-meaning. Gus was gruff, but incredibly sweet with his wife, and he clearly cared about the people at the ranch more than just about anything.

Tag was a little bit more reserved, Hunter a charmer. Lachlan was very much the same.

And by all accounts, Brody was that same kind of charming flirt. And he had charmed her, against her will.

It was just… He didn't treat her the way that Lachlan did. Lachlan was always happy to give her a wink and a nod. The way that Lachlan talked to her felt generic. Like he could be speaking to anyone at any time, probably in a bar.

But that wasn't how Brody talked to her. And most notably, Brody included Benny. Her heart had jumped up into her throat when she had seen Benny sitting in the back of that pickup truck, but he had been fine. She had wanted to scold Brody for it. But… The way he had been with him…

He was firm. Kind of strict. Probably more than her and Carter ever were. But then, she and Carter were always trying to compete for who might be the real good guy in the scenario. The one that Benny actually wanted to spend time with.

Brody wasn't doing that.

And Benny had responded to it. It was amazing. She really needed to stop thinking about how Brody was different.

She needed to focus on all the ways that he was just like his brother. Far too handsome for his own good…

Well, her brain stalled out there. Because she thought of the kiss again. He wasn't just handsome. It was more than that.

He wasn't a sexy superhero, untouchable because he was fictional, and on a movie screen. He had been there. He had been very, very touchable, and she—in fact—had touched him.

It was difficult to believe. Sometimes, she could convince herself that it was actually just a product of her fevered imagination. The same one that had cooked up that fantasy dream that had made her actually…

She started singing. Off-key, while she drove herself and Benny over to the town hall. Because she needed to get her thoughts redirected, so even though she had a terrible voice, she thought maybe warbling about being a firework lighting the sky up would make her feel better.

"Mom," Benny said, covering his ears.

"I'm making a joyful noise," she said.

"It's bad," Benny said, but he laughed.

"I have my talents. Music might not be one of them, but I like it a lot."

"Keep practicing I guess," Benny said.

And she loved that he was still the age where he believed that "practice might make perfect" with anything. She was pretty certain that *practice* wasn't going to fix *tone deaf*, at least not without professional intervention, but she liked that he could still believe in that.

That he still believed in things.

He was good for her heart.

They drove all the way to a part of Four Corners she hadn't been to yet. Sullivan's Point. The little farmhouse off in the distance was beautiful, picturesque, and the barn, where all of the trucks were parked, was old, but warm and inviting. There was a big bonfire already, as promised, table set outside, laden with food, and gas heaters all around them, providing heat.

It was cold outside, and the snow from yesterday still hadn't melted in patches. But it looked like they did a great job of making the outdoors cozy here.

There was a whole passel of kids running around in the front and playing.

"You know them?"

"Yeah. It's all my friends from school."

"Well… You can play with them," she said.

And she felt like she had just physically taken a baby bird and flung it up toward the sky. And as she parked the car, and Benny unbuckled, tumbled out, and ran off, she knew a severe sense of loss.

Wow. You are overdramatic.

She was. But then, he was everything to her. He was the thing that had given her purpose when she had felt like there wasn't any. And as embarrassing as it was for her to admit now, she really had gone through a time when she hadn't felt like her life had much purpose. It was the heartbreak. And not just that, the way the rug felt pulled out from under her. Just when she had finally been beginning to trust in some good in the universe.

She'd been so happy. A young mother with a baby, handsome husband, a beautiful house...

She found herself distracted by Brody standing in the doorway of the barn. Like he had known that she'd arrived. How would he know that? There were people pulling in behind her, people walking around all over the place. Her arrival shouldn't be any more significant than that.

Except, he began to walk toward her. She knew that he was walking toward her. She knew that he saw her.

That realization felt more significant somehow.

He saw her.

It felt like more than she'd bargained for.

She got out of the car, and he closed the distance between them, his fingertips brushing the edge of his cowboy hat. "Howdy."

"Hi. I... Was I supposed to bring something?" She gestured to the tables full of food.

"No," he said. "You don't need to worry about that. You just get to enjoy the food. Come on in."

She looked back at Benny and the other kids.

"He's fine," he said. "Kids run wild here, it's what they do. He doesn't want to sit through the meeting."

So she walked inside with him, and she could feel everybody looking at her. It reminded her of a Western you might see on TV, set in the 1800s, like he had walked into a church and announced they were courting, just because he was standing next to her. That was what everyone's gazes felt like.

Which was fanciful. Beyond fanciful. Because Brody McCloud was certainly not making any declarations by walking into a barn with her.

"Let's find a place to sit. My family's over here."

She was surprised how many people were there. And Brody explained the different families, the staff, and everyone in between. "Sometimes, people from town just come," he said. "Because we try to keep these events jovial. And we have enough food to feed anyone who might need something. And enough company to make sure that nobody around is lonely."

That filled her with warmth.

The meeting itself was a fairly brief affair. Gus got up and talked about the first week running the ranch, and he gave a quick introduction to Elizabeth, who sat there feeling like the whole world really was looking at her.

But it all moved on quickly. Fia Sullivan got up next and talked about the inroads they were making with their farm store, and the Garrett and King families gave an update on their meat production. It was all interesting to somebody who had never been part of a working ranch.

Equestrian facilities were very familiar to her, but this was not.

"Well, I expect you're all done listening to us talk," one of the King brothers said. "So, time to go eat."

She had any number of people coming up to her and introducing themselves, talking to her, laughing with her. And that continued all through dinner. And the food was incredible. Various pies that she learned had been baked by the Sullivan sisters, with produce fresh from their garden. Rolls and loaves of bread, baked by Violet and Evelyn Garrett.

Meat grilled by Denver and Landry King.

Pasta salads, potato salad, macaroni and cheese, scalloped potatoes, basically every form of starch and mayonnaise that you could possibly imagine, all provided by the ranching families.

It was a feast. Even Benny ate everything on his plate, and didn't complain once about not liking something. It was a modern-day miracle. The kind she had never expected to witness in her lifetime.

And then the music started playing, and people began to congregate around the bonfire, where she knew there was alcohol. And it didn't take long for the dancing to begin.

"Do you dance?" Brody asked.

"No," she said, feeling horrified. "I don't dance. At all. Ever. Not once in my life."

"Oh, now that you've announced you're a virgin, I'm going to need to be your first," he said.

And she could tell the moment he realized that landed heavier at the center of her chest than he had intended it to. Not just her chest, everywhere. She suddenly throbbed between her thighs.

"I think you know that I'm not actually…"

"I meant a *dancing* virgin."

"Right. But, that's not what you call someone who has never danced."

"A dancing novice implies that you've *dabbled*. You just said you never had."

"I'm not dancing with you," she said.

"Sure you are," he said, extending his hand. And in

spite of herself… She took it. She had no idea what she was thinking, grabbing a hold of his hand like that. No idea why she was letting him lead her to the bonfire and take her hands, moving her in time with the music. He twirled her, then pulled her back against his body. And everything around them seemed to fade. Her chest got lighter, and she just…couldn't help but smile. She didn't worry about anything. Didn't think about anything. She couldn't remember the last time she had felt like this. Just… Happy. She couldn't remember the last time she'd really had fun.

There were floodlights mounted on the barn, and she looked over to see the kids running around in the grass, doing cartwheels, tagging each other, screeching.

It was just… Glorious.

Benny was out there having a good time and she was…

He spun her again, drawing her back against him, his gaze serious. "Elizabeth…"

"Brody?"

"Would you like to see the back side of the barn?"

She had no idea why she would want to see the back side of the barn.

She blinked. "Is it different than the front side of the barn?"

"Yes. Very different."

"Notable?"

"I think very notable."

"Okay…"

He took her hand and led her away from the bonfire, and she followed, because he had said he was showing her the back side of the barn, and that it was a notable back side to a barn, so why wouldn't she go with him?

But when they got around behind it, it was just dark, there was no one back there, and she had no idea what about it was so different. "How is this different than the front side?"

"Well, in the front of the barn, I have to keep a respectable distance between the two of us. And in the back of the barn, I can do this."

Then he leaned down, and pressed his mouth to hers. And the world caught fire.

CHAPTER TEN

HE WAS KISSING her again. And he knew that it was a really damned bad idea. And he didn't care. Not even a little bit. He couldn't care. He was lost to logic. Because he had been holding her in his arms, dancing around the bonfire, and she was just so soft. And even with the smell of the smoke, the burning wood, the alcohol, he could smell her. Flowers and vanilla and everything sweet and feminine and wonderful. Something that he suddenly felt starved for, and he had dragged her back here without thinking it through.

Liar. You thought it through. You just wanted to kiss her.

She wrapped her arms around his neck, clinging to him, as he gripped her chin and held her head steady, parting his lips and dipping his tongue deep, tasting her, the slick friction driving him crazy.

"I see," she panted. "I see how it's different."

"Dammit," he said, cursing because this was a lost cause and so was he. Cursing because he just needed her. He needed this woman. In ways that he couldn't articulate. In ways that he would never be able to understand.

Impossible ways.

It went beyond logic. It went beyond being horny. It was all about insane chemistry. It was like she was the only one who could give him this thing that he was dying for. Something that he couldn't go another moment without having. Something essential that he needed to bring into himself. That floral-vanilla-and-feminine softness.

Dammit all. But really, dammit all. He was such a lost fucking cause.

He pressed her up against the back side of that barn, and luxuriated in the feel of her full, glorious breasts pressed against his chest. That woman.

"You are something else," he growled, biting the side of her neck. She gasped, arching against him. And he just… Kept on kissing her. And he couldn't remember the last time he had kissed a woman, just kissed her. He didn't think he ever had. Just kissing. Enjoying the way that it amped up the fire between them. Needing the flame to rise higher.

Needing more.

But not being in a hurry to have it.

He thought that his chest was going to burst with the way his heart was beating. So hard, so fast. He thought that he was losing his mind.

Or at the very least, losing his sense of time. Of place.

She moved her hands down his back, and then back up, and he found his own hands wandering, moving down to cup her breasts. And she gasped. He slid his thumb across them, and even through the lightly padded bra, he could feel her nipples beading. Begging for his attention. He wanted to strip her naked. Right then and there. Wanted to take her top off, get his hands on her bare breasts. He wanted to unbutton her jeans, unzip them, stick his hand down into her panties, and feel if she was wet for him.

But they were just around the back of the barn. And he couldn't do that. No. Lord knew, he could not do that. He would get carried away, and the whole King family could be standing there next to them with their mouths open, and he wouldn't even know it. "Brody," she whispered, arching against him, and he flexed his hips forward, letting her feel what she did to him. Letting her feel just how hard he was.

And he was hoping that she was going to put her hands on him again. He wasn't disappointed. She reached between them, cupping his arousal through his jeans, moving her hand over him, taking in the shape of him.

"Oh Lord," she said, the sound reverent and a curse, all at the same time.

"You want that?"

His words came out thick, slurred, and he would love to say that it was all practiced dirty talk from years of hooking up, but that wasn't it at all. He just genuinely wanted to know if she wanted him. Because it mattered. It really mattered.

"Yes," she responded.

And suddenly, there was a raucous cheer somewhere around the barn, and music started playing. And that made her jump. Seemed to jar her back to the side of reality.

"Oh gosh," she said.

And the innocence of that exclamation, in light of what they had just been doing, made him smile.

"Yeah," he groaned. "I think I forgot myself."

"We were…"

"Making out," he said. "Like teenagers."

She started laughing. Helplessly. And she buried her face against his shoulder. "I don't know what's wrong with me."

"There's nothing wrong with you."

She lifted her head and he could see her eyes glittering, even in the darkness. "I think that's because you don't know me very well."

"No. That's not it."

"I don't do this," she said.

"You may not believe it, but neither do I."

"You're right, I don't believe it."

He sighed. Hard and heavy like his body. "No, what I do, Elizabeth, is hook up. I do not make out with women that *live* on my ranch."

"I imagine that proximity is not exactly ideal for you."

He laughed, but it was painful. "No. Like garlic to a vampire."

"But here you are," she said.

"Here I am."

"We should get back."

"We should. We really should."

"Benny might want to leave."

He nodded slowly. "Yeah. He might."

"I…"

"I'll tell you what. Let's not make any proclamations. I did that last time, and I ended up feeling and looking like a horse's ass." He leaned in and kissed her. Just light. Just briefly. "Let's see what happens."

He wasn't a man who just…saw what happened. He went out to hook up, and everyone knew the score. Sex was had and they went their separate ways. He didn't kiss a woman sweet and light, like it was the end of a church picnic.

He didn't leave things open-ended.

And yet.

Here he was.

She nodded. "I can do that."

Maybe they would cool off. Maybe nothi~~ would~~ come of it. He already knew that he was lying to himself, but he was okay with that. A person had to make compromises sometimes. "Okay. Should we…go back separately?"

"We could. If you think Benny might think something happened."

"Benny won't think a thing. But, I really, really value the job that I have at McCloud's Landing. And I don't want anything to cause problems."

"None of my brothers care at all what I do with who. And they certainly won't care what you do. We don't exactly have an HR department."

"No. I guess not." She closed her eyes for just a second, and the breeze kicked up, and in the light of the full moon, he could see her pale hair blowing around her face, framing it beautifully.

She really was stunning.

"Let's just walk back together, then."

He didn't hold her hand or anything like that, but they went around to the front side of the barn together, and Elizabeth separated from him pretty quickly, going to the knot of kids to find Benny. He was still playing.

So eventually, she went back to the bonfire with him, even though they didn't dance anymore.

He talked her into one drink, and they talked about the weather. And that was fine.

And when he got in his truck to head back to the ranch, he really wondered why the hell he was allowing this to happen.

And right before he fell asleep, it occurred to him, that he wasn't really allowing anything.

It was something out of his control.

He wasn't sure how he felt about that. But that was the thing about stuff that was outside your control. It didn't matter how you felt about it. It just was.

Maybe that was justification.

Yeah, it probably was. He was okay with that.

BENNY WAS SINGING about fireworks all the way to school the next morning, and Elizabeth was hypocritically irritated. She had no call to be, she had been caterwauling the same song last night.

Last night.

Before she had gone and disappeared behind the barn with Brody and kissed him like a desperate teenager.

Good thing she had a full schedule today, so nothing else crazy could happen.

Why is that a good thing?

Yeah, she was inconsistent, she didn't need her inner voice to tell her that. She had been mad that he hadn't continued their kiss, even when she'd stopped it, and now she was all jittery because something had happened.

She couldn't be pleased, and she didn't know the answer to that at all.

But she got Benny dropped off, and happily squared away at school, and then she went back to begin her next session with Loralee. It was their last one before Loralee would leave. And whether or not she came back was up to her. She knew from the meeting that things were going really well. That the boy with autism was growing in confidence and learning how to reach out to his parents for help. That the little girl with muscular dystrophy was loving the freedom provided her by riding the horses. And was thrilled with her new skill set. The confidence that she had gained was remarkable.

Loralee was still reserved. But, she had started getting better at choosing what she wanted for dinner.

And Elizabeth was happy for her there.

"I just wish I knew what I wanted the rest of my life to look like," Loralee said.

"You don't need to know what you want the rest of your life to look like. You're in a phase. We all go through phases. Maybe this isn't your favorite one, but it's a new one, and better than the one that you were stuck in."

"I guess so. Do you know what you want to do with the rest of your life?"

Elizabeth didn't even know what she wanted to do with the rest of her afternoon. Was raw and unsettled, utterly and completely at sea when it came to what was happening with her and Brody.

But maybe that was the key. What she had just said to Loralee. Maybe she took things too seriously. She was always trying to see ahead. To make sure that the decisions that she made were good. That they were the best for her, the best for Benny. Maybe it was all right if she made the decisions that were just about how she felt in the moment.

Justification?

Maybe.

"I think sometimes what we need to realize is that it's okay for us to be happy momentarily, even if we can't guarantee that we'll be able to hold on to it forever." Elizabeth hadn't realized that until the words came out of her mouth. That is what she was trying to do. Make sure that she never had anything good that she couldn't be absolutely certain she could maintain.

It was why she hadn't jumped into anything with a man—well, apart from the fact that she hadn't met one that she wanted to do anything with until Brody. The idea of love, a relationship, felt too unstable.

She'd had it with Carter, and it hadn't lasted. The happiness had been finite, and the idea of finite happiness made her stomach churn.

Because it reminded her way too much of being a foster child.

Finally landing in a good place. Finally getting something stable, and wonderful, and knowing that it would have an end date.

Even when she had gone to live with Denise, she had been three years away from being eighteen. And she had known that it was going to be transient.

Except, it had been for reasons she hadn't counted on. Denise had died.

That happiness had had an expiration date.

But maybe she had to accept that was life. Just life. And it wasn't necessarily a tragedy. It just was.

And maybe she needed to accept that there were certain things that were good for her no matter how long she had them. No matter how long they lasted.

"That's a really wise thing to say," Loralee said. "I think I take my happiness right now a little bit too seriously. Trying to do all the perfect things, trying to never get into a bad situation ever again..."

"Yeah I understand that all too well," she said. "But we aren't perfect. Just because we went through something difficult. We might have to go through other difficult things. It's just that we should hopefully be somewhat more equipped to deal with them."

"I hope so."

So did she. Because this felt like a revelation, and she was desperately concerned that all it was was justification for what she really wanted to do.

"I hope that you come back," she said to Loralee.

"I hope so too. Maybe in the new year. I feel like I have so much work left to do."

"We all do. It isn't just you. We all have a lot of work to do."

So maybe this was her lesson. Maybe this was what she needed. To just…

She started to walk around to the front of the barn. Brody should be here soon. He should be there to help her.

And there, just like clockwork, he was.

"I need help back at my house," she said, her voice sounding oddly loud, confident and assertive.

"At your house?"

"Yes," she said. "I can drive us there."

"Sure," he said.

He got into the car alongside her, and she took a deep breath. She hoped that she didn't chicken out. She really did.

She wanted to do something wild. She wanted to do something that made her happy now. She wanted to do something that felt good now.

She had always told herself stories. She wasn't that physical, she wasn't that sexual. She just liked being close. And at the very bottom of that was the idea she didn't deserve any more than she was being given freely by Carter.

She didn't deserve to critique his performance in the bedroom, or how it worked and didn't work for her, because she should just be grateful that he had shown her any interest in the first place.

That was how she had always lived her life. She couldn't ask for anything more from anybody, because she had to take what she was given.

She didn't deserve anything else.

Well, right now she wanted to abolish that completely. Absolutely destroy it. She deserved more. She did. She deserved everything.

And she was going to demand it.

Well, that probably wasn't true. She was probably just going to kiss him. And hope that he got the hint. If she had to after that, she would demand it, but she had a feeling that he would get what she was asking for. And, thank God.

When they got to the house she turned the car off, her hands shaking, then he got out of the vehicle when she did and led the way up the steps to her own house. She felt like that was a pretty good sign.

And once they were inside, he looked at her. "What did you need?"

And she did it. Threw herself at him. Threw herself into his arms, clasping her hands around the back of his neck. "Just you. Please."

"Well, thank God," he said, and his lips crashed down onto hers.

It was happening. He was kissing her, and they were alone. All alone in her house, with no one else about to interrupt them. They had time. And they had enough desire to light a fire in the woodstove with no effort at all. "Bedroom," she mumbled.

"Don't have to ask me twice."

He picked her up, like she weighed nothing, and walked them back to her bedroom, tossing her onto the bed, and he gripped the bottom of his shirt and wrenched it up over his head, and her mouth went dry.

He was, without a doubt, the most spectacular man she had ever seen. And for the first time, she was grateful that they didn't have the separation of a movie screen between them. Thankful that he wasn't some distant sexy superhero, but that he was a man, in front of her. Close enough to touch. To taste. And suddenly she wanted to do that. And she was not denying herself any good thing. Not anymore. So she got up onto her knees, leaned forward, and pressed her hands against his abs, licking him, from just above his belly button up to his nipple.

And he gasped, jerking sharply as she did.

"Was that bad?"

"No. Put your tongue anywhere you want."

"Everywhere," she said. "I want to put it everywhere."

"I am okay with that."

He wrapped his arm around her waist and lifted her up, bringing her lips against his again, and she arched restlessly, wishing that she were naked so that she could feel his skin against hers. As if he had heard that mental entreaty, he grabbed her shirt and tore it off, unhooking her bra and throwing it down onto the floor.

"My fantasies did not do you justice," he growled, his large hands moving to cup her bare breasts, his thumbs rough as he skimmed them over her nipples.

She had never really thought her nipples were all that sensitive. But it turned out they were. An arrow of pleasure shot itself between her thighs, and she was surprised she was able to stay upright. It was probably only because he had his arm wrapped around her waist, otherwise she would have tipped over.

Her hands moved down to his belt buckle, and she undid it as quickly as possible, not all that quick with unsteady fingers. She unfastened the button on his jeans, unzipped them, and before she could lose her nerve, pushed her fingers down beneath his underwear. He was hot, and hard, and as suspected from her tour of him through his jeans last night—huge. Her internal muscles clenched tight, imagining him inside of her.

She wanted him so much.

She had never wanted anyone like this before.

She was on fire with it. The need for him. The need for this.

She didn't know herself.

But it struck her then that it might not be because the ability to feel this was new. It was just because she hadn't *known* about it before. Because she had been a girl who had fallen into a relationship with a boy that had been defined by something else. And this was about her. It wasn't about pleasing him. She hoped he enjoyed it. Judging by the feel of him, hot and heavy in her hands, he was definitely on board with what was going on. But what she cared about was what she wanted.

She wanted him.

She wanted to take this moment out of time to be wild. To follow the desires that she felt raging through her.

And suddenly, she found herself being picked up by her hips and laid down firmly on the center of the mattress. Stripped bare.

And he growled, his eyes appraising her closely. And if she had been worried about what he thought, she might be embarrassed.

But there was no time to feel embarrassed. And she just… She just didn't feel embarrassed. Because his masculine appreciation was apparent. It couldn't be denied.

She found herself letting her knees fall open, letting him see her.

She had no idea where that had come from. That urge, that impulse, and the bravery to follow through with it. But it was there. Part of her. She was struck then to discover that she contained such multitudes. That she had only been with one man, and hadn't had sex for six years. Did her best not to think about any of it, but also contained *this*. This deeply exciting well of desire that drove her. Pushed her. And the curiosity within her to wish to explore this. To push boundaries. These beautiful boundaries. She hadn't felt like a woman…

Ever.

The word whispered through her, a truth she had been looking for.

It would be easy to say that being a mother had subsumed her identity, but that wouldn't be true. She had never identified as a woman, independent and free all on her own. She had defined her stability by her relationship with Carter, which was why it had been so difficult to lose him.

They didn't share this wild attraction. They didn't share a deep, abiding love that made her ache whenever she thought of him. She hadn't been heartbroken to lose him, not in that sense.

It was something else.

It was security. It was the thing that made her matter.

Because if Carter Colfax loved her, then maybe she wasn't just a foster child that no one had wanted to keep.

But then he hadn't wanted to keep her, and she had scrambled to find another source of identity, and that had been being Benny's mother. It had mattered so much to her. And it was a good thing. A wonderful thing. A beautiful thing. She loved her son.

But she didn't know who she was, standing on her own. In this moment that was just her and Brody, a man she owed nothing to, a man she wanted nothing from— apart from his body—it was all about the woman who she wanted to be. Who did she want to be in this moment?

Brave and bold, wanton because she could be. Desired and lusted after, because she was beautiful. Not anybody's project, not anybody's object of pity.

She wanted to be wholly herself, comfortable in her own skin, and separate from any other piece of her identity. At least, now. Not someone's ex-wife. Not someone's mother. Not someone's discarded daughter.

But Elizabeth. Completely herself.

He looked at her, the glint in his eyes getting wicked as he leaned forward, hooked his arms under her thighs and dragged her toward him. "I've been thinking about this."

And then he buried his head between her legs and started to lick her.

She screamed. Short, sharp, and shocked.

Because she had never. *They* had never. It had never been...

She couldn't even follow that thought all the way through to its logical conclusion, all she could do was clutch his hair, arch her hips against his mouth, pray that he never stopped.

Never.

It was slick and hot and streaked through her like lightning. This need. It was everything. A symphony of desire that she had never known her body could play. She had thought she was the problem. It wasn't her.

It wasn't her.

Whether or not she was going to come wasn't even a concern.

She was honestly concerned she would come too soon and embarrass herself.

That's men, she reminded herself.

Women can come as often as they want to.

Not her. Never before. One and done, if she was lucky.

But then her internal monologue was interrupted yet again when he pushed two fingers inside of her, continuing to devour her like an insatiable beast.

She gasped and rocked her hips faster against his mouth, luxuriating in the moment. In the feeling. She wanted… She needed…

And then she broke apart. Shattered like a thin glass windowpane, all that she was, disintegrating.

"Brody," she called out. "Brody."

And then she needed him to stop because she was too sensitive. It was too much. But he kept on going, kept on devouring her like she was the rarest of delicacies and he was a starving man.

She reached her peak again, bracing herself by flattening her palms against the mattress, trying to keep from dissolving.

He lifted his head, and smiled.

It was the single most erotic thing she had ever seen.

Him in that position, right between her legs, grinning at her, the acknowledgment of what he'd just done so clear.

"That was as good as I thought. Better."

"You really…" But she couldn't quite make her mouth form words, because she had lost her mind utterly and completely, and she couldn't seem to find it again. She melted into the mattress, laying her head back, and throwing her arm over her eyes. And then she felt him, looming above her. She moved her arm. And he grinned, before dipping down to kiss her.

"You are so sexy," he said. "I've been fantasizing about getting you out of your clothes since the first moment I saw you. So prim and proper, and damn, I wanted to mess you up."

She shivered, and impossibly, she felt desire rising inside of her again. There was no way. There was no way that she could have another orgasm after the two that had just taken her by storm.

And then suddenly, a bereft look crossed his expression. "I don't have a condom."

Relief surged through her. "I'm on the pill," she said. "And I haven't been with anybody in a very long time."

"I always use condoms," he said.

And she knew it wasn't a refusal, but a promise he was safe too.

"Great."

She would have said yes to him no matter what he'd said just then. She realized that wasn't responsible. But she didn't feel responsible. Not now. The hot, sexy cowboy that was taking her to bed in the middle of the afternoon was not about responsibility.

This was about making the sexiest mistake she had ever even considered making in her entire life. She was boneless, she was replete with desire, and yet she wanted him again. Wanted him more. Wanted everything. She needed him inside of her. Now.

"Please," she said, the plea coming out as a sob.

He shrugged his jeans off, and what she saw was the most beautiful sight she'd ever beheld. His whole body was a work of art. Sculptured muscle and just the right amount of dark hair. His chest was well defined, his waist narrow, his abs…

She had not thought that men were like this outside the movies. She really hadn't. And she had Captain America in bed with her.

Then there was his… His everything. She did not know they came that big.

She gave thanks that she wasn't a silly young virgin, because she knew what to do with a body like that. She might not have the experience, but she knew what the desire inside of her meant. She knew why she was slick between her legs, and why she felt hollow. She needed him. She needed that. Right now.

He positioned himself above her, and she felt the blunt head of his arousal at the entrance to her body. Then he thrust home. Hard.

She gasped. Because he was really big, and it had been a while. And then it just all felt… So, so good. And any concerns she had about whether or not she would be able to climax again were banished. Those concerns were lost in the great expanse of her need for him.

And then he began to move, slow and measured at first, going in deep before almost pulling all the way out. And she wanted to cry out and beg him not to. Not to leave her, but then he would slam back home, and everything just felt right.

She lifted her hips, moaning, and it was like it snapped a thread of control that had been holding him back. Suddenly his hands gripped her hips hard, blunt fingertips digging into her skin. His rhythm fractured, his movements becoming hard, rough, and she reveled in it. In him. He wasn't treating her like a sweet thing. Like a broken thing. He wasn't treating her like a project.

The cords in his neck were standing out, his teeth clenched tight, and she could see that it was taking everything that he had to maintain even a fraction of control. Because of her.

This wasn't like sex as she knew it. This fraught, brilliant thing that had sharp edges and bright beautiful magic, all rolled into one. She wrapped her legs around his waist, lifting her hips with each one of his thrusts. An animal-sounding moan filled the room, and it took a while for her to realize it was coming from her. And she wasn't embarrassed.

He lowered his head, ran the flat of his tongue over one of her nipples, and she whimpered with need.

He gave a shout, his movements becoming harder, more erratic, each one taking her closer to the peak. And then, she shattered. Her climax was different this time, deeper. She gripped him tight, pulling him into her. And that was when he found his own peak. His groan was more of a growl as he spilled himself inside of her, pulsing heavily within, as his muscles trembled.

And for the rest of her days, she would be in awe of the fact that she had made such a large, beautiful man shake like he was going to come apart.

And when it was over, he collapsed, rolling to the side, a gruff, masculine sound of pleasure escaping him.

She lay on her back, panting. Trying to catch her breath. Completely unable to do it. And then she looked at the clock.

"Oh *shit*," she said, mobilizing, rolling out of the bed.

"What?" He sounded sleepy. Dazed.

And suddenly everything they had done was no longer covered by the hazy focus of arousal. Suddenly, it all seemed very sharp. Very clear.

And it was time to pick Benny up from school. She was going to be late, because she had been having sex in the middle of the afternoon. Mother of the Year. Really. Great going.

"I have to… Benny is out of school."

"I can call somebody and see if they're nearby, and maybe they can grab him and…"

"No," she said. "I have to get him. He is my child. I can't send somebody else to get him because I was having… Because I was…"

"You were having sex," he said.

She groaned and covered her face.

"You don't need to be embarrassed," he said.

"But I am," she said. "I am. And I need to get dressed. Holy hell."

"Elizabeth," he said, reaching out and grabbing her arm. "Don't feel bad about what happened."

"I haven't… I have never… I have not been with anybody since my… It's been six years."

"Six years. *Six fucking years.*"

"Yes," she said. "Can you please stop looking at me like I'm a freak?"

"I'm not looking at you like you're a freak. I just can't believe… I literally can't… That was the hottest… I have never…"

And she realized that he was also not quite fully able to complete his sentences, so at least that made two of them.

"I really have to go," she said.

"I've never done that," he said.

"What?" All she could think about was the way he had put his head between her legs and feasted on her. And somehow, she could not imagine that that was the thing he'd never done before.

"I've never had sex without wearing a condom. I've never taken that chance. Even if the woman told me she was on the pill. Just... Always figure doubling up was the best idea. I've never been inside of somebody without a barrier."

He seemed shocked that he was making the admission, and it seemed a little bit raw. And she couldn't quite believe he'd shared that either. Or that it mattered.

"Oh. *Oh*. Why did you...?"

"I mean, desperation, partly. I wanted you so bad that I couldn't wait. And I thought it was worth it. You're worth it."

He looked a little bit dumbfounded, and she was quite certain that no man had ever looked dumbfounded over her.

And certainly no one had ever said she was worth... Anything. And maybe she shouldn't be flattered that there was a guy telling her she was worth having sex with without a condom, because she was an idiot, and she understood that men had notoriously low standards when it came to sex. But she just... She just did feel something. And it felt good. She felt wanted. Desired. Beautiful. In her clothes that were six years old and not even her. Out of them.

"I really have to go." She gathered up her clothes.

"You okay?"

"I'm… I'm good. I am. I can't… I have to go. I'll call you."

She dressed quickly, and ran out of the cabin.

She needed to get her thoughts in order before she tried to talk to him. Too bad she had no idea what that looked like. No idea what it would mean.

Just focus on the drive to school. Just focus on Benny.

But after all that. After finally finding herself. After feeling so much pleasure, being so grounded in her own body…

She wanted to think a little bit about herself too. And maybe she could do both.

CHAPTER ELEVEN

HE JUST FELT so good. So good. He couldn't remember the last time sex had made him feel like this. If ever.

She had been… And she had tasted… And he was…

I'll call you.

"Damn," he said to himself as he walked up the front porch to his brother Lachlan's cabin.

He could tell by the truck in the driveway that Charity was already there. And then another truck pulled in. Hunter and Elsie.

It was going to be a full house tonight.

He had been tempted to hang out at home, just in case, but Elizabeth had never been to his place, and honestly, he was sure that she wasn't going to get in touch with him tonight. Not with Benny home. Normally, he would love to have an interruption like that so quickly after sex. Hell, it would be the best thing he could even think of. Not having to have a conversation because the woman had to go. So damn satisfying.

Except the problem was he wanted to talk to her. He wanted to make sure she was feeling all right. Wanted to make sure she had enjoyed it. Wanted to make sure that… Hell, he wanted to put her in that big bathtub he knew was in the house and wash her hair.

God Almighty…

He pushed the door open, at the same time Elsie and

Hunter tumbled out of their truck. "Hey," Elsie said, grinning.

"Hey yourself, little sister."

"Don't call me that," she said wrinkling her nose.

"Why not? I'm collecting all these sisters lately."

"Yeah, but I already had brothers. And I didn't need more."

He heard a loud cackle from inside the house. Lachlan. "Too bad for you," he said, "because you're stuck with us."

"You guys are the worst," she said.

"Or are we the best?" Brody asked.

"For sure, the best," Hunter said, smiling.

Hunter and Elsie were carrying platters of food.

And he suddenly felt like a little bit of a jerk that he hadn't brought any snacks to poker night.

But he'd been busy. Definitely thinking about other things. Charity was in the kitchen, cheerfully baking cookies.

Really, Lach did have it made.

"Looks great," he said, pulling up a chair and sitting down.

"You seem like you're in a good mood," Lachlan said, eyeing him speculatively.

"I am just really thrilled with the work that we're doing here at the ranch," Brody said with an absolutely straight face. "It feels good to give back."

"Yeah, I don't think you care about that at all," Lachlan said.

"You don't know me."

"Oh, I know you," Lachlan said. "Unfortunately for me."

"You're such a jerk," Charity said.

"Hey," Lachlan said. "You are supposed to unquestionably be *Team Me*."

Charity's already innocent face somehow softened, her eyes going rounder. "Why is that?"

"Because I have been your best friend for years."

She sharpened. "Right. And I have spent all those years stitching you up, and pulling you out of scrapes. So you tell me exactly what I owe you?"

"Harsh," Hunter said. "I like it."

"Poor Lachlan," said Elsie, shaking her head.

"What? Poor Lachlan because we're so mean to him?"

"No," Elsie grinned. "Poor Lachlan. Because he's him."

And that got a good laugh out of everybody.

"Where are Nelly and Tag?" Lach asked.

"Went down to visit Nelly's mom," Hunter said.

"Where's Gus?" Brody asked.

"I find it best not to ask where Gus and Alaina are when they decline to show their faces at things like this."

"They're a whole thing," Elsie said, waving her hand.

"As if the two of us aren't," Hunter said.

Brody didn't have any inclination to think about what manner of whole thing his siblings were with their significant others. He was happy for their healing. But he did not need to know the details.

"All right," he said. "Enough chitchat. I'm ready to win some money."

"Very bold," Charity said.

The funny thing was, Charity typically took them all to the cleaners. He was certain it was because she looked so sweet. It was just hard to believe that when it came to poker she was a vicious, sharp-toothed animal.

His brothers and Elsie sat down at the table, and Charity a moment later, with the freshly baked cookies.

Beer and cookies might seem a strange combination, but it had become nostalgic for him. That was the thing. Their childhood had really sucked. Like, just really sucked. And one of the things that was so great about being adults was they had built something different. Something better.

Poker nights and cookies and beer. Gus's really terrible frozen pizza and dinners in his cluttered house, back before Alaina had moved in. They still had dinner there, but they didn't have frozen pizza or clutter.

Alaina was opposed to both.

But they were the building blocks of the better part of his life.

And it occurred to him then that he would add sex with Elizabeth Colfax as one of the good building blocks.

One of those nice things that he had gotten later almost as an apology gift from God.

"All right, five card stud, aces wild," Charity declared, suddenly looking serious as she dragged the stack of cards toward herself. She shuffled like a pro and then started to flick them around the table.

"She counts cards," Lachlan grumbled, as he swept his hand forward and slid the cards back toward him.

"Well, you're the one that invites her." Hunter said that, but they all knew Charity was just a fixture.

Even if Lachlan didn't invite her, she would show up. And they would invite her if he didn't.

They weren't the warmest family. It wasn't like welcoming people into their dysfunctional fold was normal for them. But Charity had sort of cheerfully wiggled in under the fence and become inevitable.

Play started, and they'd done their first round of bids when Hunter looked at him across the table.

"What did you end up doing this week with the guests?" Hunter asked.

"Not really anything. I was more facilitator."

"Yeah," he nodded. "That seems like something you'd be more into."

"What does that mean?"

Hunter gave him a strange look. "I don't know. Don't think too deeply about it, bro."

"He doesn't think too deeply about anything," Lachlan said.

"No. I want to know what that means."

"You aren't really a people person. Unless the *people* are women you want to sleep with."

Brody frowned. "That isn't true."

"He's been very friendly to Elizabeth," Elsie pointed out.

"My point stands," Hunter said.

Brody really wanted to be indignant, and wanted to argue, but given that he had slept with Elizabeth just that afternoon, he didn't exactly have a leg to stand on. Not that they knew that.

But it was not why he'd been nice to her. Not at all. He'd been nice to her because she was… And… Well.

I'll call you.

But she hadn't yet.

And for the first time he wondered if she meant it the way *he* sometimes did.

Which meant…

She didn't mean it at all.

"I like work," he said. "In that way you're right. I would rather do the labor. So. I guess point taken."

Except he was pissed now. And he took it as a personal mission to take all their money for the next three rounds of poker. And he did.

And at that point he realized he was going to have to walk back to his place tonight because he was actually kind of drunk.

"You're sure in a mood," Hunter commented.

He growled. "You put me there. I was in a great mood when I got here."

Brothers. Especially little brothers. And Hunter was *the fucking worst.* At least, Lachlan was still his partner in crime.

Your partner in crime? Because you're so into hooking up these days?

Just with Elizabeth.

Hell. She hadn't even texted him. Not a single text. No missed calls.

He had known that. He had known that she wasn't going to contact him.

Holy fuck. He was worried about a woman calling him. He had never in his life wanted a woman to call him. He wanted her to not remember his number. Or to not ask for it. Or just not give it to her. Which was usually what he did.

And here he was, acting like the teenager he had never been wishing that this woman would reach out.

"I need some air," he said, going out onto the front porch. Because he was a little bit tipsy, and he needed to sober up. He would get some air, go back inside, play another round of poker and eat about five more cookies. And that would help soak it all up.

He heard footsteps behind him. Hunter.

"I'm sorry," he said. "I obviously scratched against something that you weren't ready to deal with."

"What do you mean something I wasn't ready to deal with? You just said what you said, and I disagreed. But then I figured out what you meant. That's all. It's not a big deal."

"There's always a distance with you, Brody. That's what I meant."

He stared at Hunter. Hard.

"Just say what you mean," he said.

"Childhood was different for you."

He knew they thought that. Hell, *he* thought it. He didn't know why it hurt to hear Hunter say it out loud. Didn't know why it hurt at all when it was something he also believed.

It was just something that he hoped they didn't believe. And that was kind of it. He hoped that it was like that. But apparently it was. Like he had suspected. For a while.

"It isn't your fault," Hunter said.

"I know that," Brody responded.

It wasn't his fault, maybe. But he'd always figured there was a reason for it. There had to be. What made one kid inherently special to a psychopath? That was the question he didn't know the answer to. Never would.

"But you don't…let anyone in. It doesn't have to be like that."

"Lachlan and I are close," Brody said.

"Look, I'm not trying to be a dick. I wasn't close to everybody for a long time because I blamed myself for Mom leaving. Because I was special to her and I… I felt like I was the reason she had to stay, Brody. Stay to get used like a punching bag, and I told her to leave. I told her I would be okay. Look what happened to Gus."

"We all know what happened to Gus." The words felt dragged from Brody.

Yeah, he knew what had happened to Gus. Gus had gotten it the worst.

Worse than anyone.

Gus had nearly died at the hands of their father.

But their dad had hurt all of them. All but Brody.

Whatever Hunter said, they had that same trauma in common. And Brody?

Brody had been loved by that man. And it made everything in his soul feel sick and twisted.

Hunter was brave. For telling their mother to leave. For sharing his story now.

But Brody just couldn't share his.

"I couldn't deal with what I thought my part in it was. So I'm just saying I'm not accusing you of anything, or trying to be mean, I'm just… I'm not really any different. Or haven't been."

"And what made you want to have a heart-to-heart with me tonight?" Brody asked.

"I don't know. I just made a comment. I wasn't exactly prepared for this. I don't have my thoughts all lined out. And I don't have them all together. All I know is that things have been so much better for me since. And since Gus and I actually had a talk about what happened all that time ago. We tend to want to sit on things, us McClouds."

"Because there's nothing to talk about," Brody said. "The thing is, we were all there, Hunter. We were all there. We saw Dad's rages. And I saw him choose to take a swing at you, or Lachlan, or Gus, instead of me.

We were all there. There's no use talking about it. It isn't going to change it. All we can do is work the land now. Make you better now. And you are getting married, because you're an idiot, but Lachlan and I can continue to have anonymous sex and stay out as late as we want."

Hunter cleared his throat and looked off the porch, as if he could see anything out in the darkness. Brody had a feeling Hunter just didn't want to look at him. "There's no cure in anonymous sex. I just hope you know that."

"I'm not looking to be cured. I'm just looking to have as good of a time on this miserable rock as I possibly can. I look at it this way," he said, figuring he would give him a little bit of honesty related to what he had been thinking only a few minutes earlier. "We have a shitty, crumbling foundation. And you can only do so much with that. But every so often we get some pretty damned good building blocks. I want to build off those. So I take the good things, but I don't need to go examining the bad. And I sure as hell don't need to try and change it. Because nothing will change it. Nothing ever changes. It just is. And then you die."

"Cheerful."

Brody shrugged. "I never said I was. I think I'm realistic. About what life has to offer."

"So what about Gus and Alaina? Tag, Nelly, me and Elsie?"

"I'm happy for you. But I never figured I would go looking for that."

"You like Elizabeth, though." It wasn't a question. His asshole brother thought he just knew.

Sadly, he was right.

"Elizabeth is hot as hell," he said. "Didn't you notice?"

"She isn't my type," Hunter said.

"Well. That's bullshit. I know you love Elsie, but I've known you too long to buy into that. You have never had a *type*. You just like women."

Hunter laughed. "Fine. She's hot. I'm just not sure she's as hot as you think she is."

Brody frowned. "Which means?"

"I'm just saying I think you have a special thing with her."

"By that *special thing*, do you mean I want to bang her?"

"Do you?"

"Already did, bro." He regretted that. Dammit, he regretted that. Cheapening today.

He regretted it hard-core, that he had taken what had happened between himself and Elizabeth and used it to distance Hunter. To be flippant.

Hunter made a disgusted sound. "For God's sake, Brody. She has a kid."

"I know. I like the kid."

Hunter's eyes widened. "Oh. So, is this like…more than sex?"

"It was not more than sex. It was sex. That's it. I like her, I respect her. It's not mutually exclusive to the sex. It doesn't mean I'm never going to talk to her again. But now the sex is done. So… I'm good."

Hunter chuckled. "Just real good. Never need to do it again."

Brody nodded. "Never again."

"Great. Because she is a huge asset to the ranch, so if you could not chase her off, that would be awesome."

"I don't chase women off with sex. I'm *good* at it."

"How many beers have you had?"

"Three."

He wasn't drunk on beer. He was a little bit slurred from beer, but he was drunk on Elizabeth. But he didn't need Hunter to know that. And in fact, he wanted to stop talking about her. Because it was making him feel weird. Was making his chest feel too tight.

"Just… We can talk about things. I guess that was the whole point. Of the comment that didn't actually have a point until you forced there to be a point," Hunter said.

"Yeah. Sure."

"You're such a dick," Hunter said, shaking his head.

"So are you."

"You want to come back inside?"

"Yeah. I need more cookies."

"No more beer," Hunter warned.

"I will have a beer if I want," Brody said.

And he checked his phone ten more times over the next couple of poker games. And she still didn't call.

CHAPTER TWELVE

THEY HAD A new crop of clients coming Monday, but it was the weekend, so Elizabeth was off, and it had snowed again, which meant that Benny was outside tromping around in the snow, and she actually had a little bit of quiet time.

She fielded a text from Carter, who acted put out by about the fact that Benny couldn't just come over this weekend.

"Were you actually going to take him?" She asked out loud, only to herself, as she typed instead: We'll figure something out.

She was determined not to be mean.

She was also determined to hide in her house, because she was embarrassed about facing Brody.

Brody.

She couldn't even think straight when she thought about that man. He had done things to her that...

It made her hot even now.

And she was trying to draw a line under it and accept the fact that it was only going to be the one time.

It could only be the one time. And that was good. It was fine. It was fine because she didn't need to have sex with him again. The mystery was solved. The mystery was well and truly revealed, *nakedly.* Yeah. She had seen it all.

And so had he. And put his mouth on it all.
Oh Lord.

We are going to have to figure something out, came the terse response from Carter. Okay, she didn't know if it was terse, since she was reading it, but it felt terse in her heart.

I know.

It's too far away for me to just go get him for the weekend.

Three hours was not that far.

If you feel that way, I'm sorry. But the judge deemed it an acceptable distance for us to move.

I'm actually not trying to have a fight with you.

"Well, you suck at it." Again, said out loud while she typed: We'll figure it out, just maybe not right now.

She put her phone away. She didn't need to sit on it just to receive texts from Carter.

She suddenly heard excited moving, and she looked outside and saw Benny prancing around enthusiastically.

And then she saw why.

It was Brody.

Her heart clenched.

Benny had a bad case of hero worship for Brody, and it really scared her. Bad.

What about the hero worship you feel for him?

Yeah. But she more worshipped the abilities that he had with his mouth.

That made her face heat.

She went to the door and opened it.

"To what do I owe the pleasure?"

"Well," Brody said, fixing her with a look that felt intimate. "I thought you might text me before now."

Had he? Had he thought she might text him and ask him to come over? She wouldn't have been *opposed* to that. The guy was smoking hot and...

And she was not going to have sex with him with her son down the hall. It just wasn't going to happen.

"I was busy," she said.

"Yeah. Me too. Really busy. Playing poker. My brother's friend Charity took all my money."

Her lips twitched. "Sorry about your newly impoverished status."

"It's okay. The only mouth I have to feed is my own. I'll weather the storm."

"Doesn't answer the question of why you're here today," she pointed out.

"Well, Christmas is coming up. Just a little over two weeks. I couldn't help but notice that you don't have a Christmas tree."

She had brought a box of Christmas ornaments with her. Shoved it in the hall closet. She had done her best to make holidays spectacular for Benny. So she had a treasure trove of decorations. She just hadn't gotten around to doing anything yet this year.

"Well. Yes. I suppose we do need a Christmas tree. Is there a lot we can go buy one at?"

He laughed. Laughed at her. "No. I was thinking we would go hunt one out upon one of the trails."

"Tree hunting!" Benny said, leaping around like an excited frog.

"Yeah, it's so terrible here, huh, Benny?" she asked.

Benny looked at her and tried to force his mouth into a flat line. "I didn't say I liked it."

"But you can't really say that you don't," Brody said.

"Well." Benny's eyebrows were comedically angry. "There are more places to play."

"Priorities well and truly in order," Brody said. "You game for the tree hunt?"

"Benny," she said. "Go inside and get a hat and gloves."

Benny obeyed, scrambling up the front steps and going into the house. He closed the door behind him, and she stood on the porch with the steps between them.

"Kids are mean," Brody said. "I didn't really realize that."

"Yes. They are. Parenting is thankless and often terrible. And I wouldn't trade it for anything. I love that kid. And he drives me insane. But that's kind of the way it is."

"Well. Good to know. And not sorry I am firmly team: no kids for me ever." For some reason, that made her stomach feel hollow.

But it wasn't her business, and she had no right to have feelings about his life choices. So she'd just move on.

"And his dad drives me insane, but I don't have to deal with him anymore."

"What's going on with his dad?"

"He was just complaining to me about not getting to see Benny this weekend. But he doesn't take all of his weekends. He never has. He definitely could drive down here and get him if he wanted to."

"I'm sorry. That must be tough."

"It is. Thank you."

"I'm going to let you in on a little secret."

"What's that?"

"I don't really care about the fact that you don't have a Christmas tree. I just wanted to see you."

Her breath rushed out of her lungs in a wash. "Really?"

"I can't stop thinking about you. I was not very happy that you didn't call." His eyes leveled with hers and she couldn't breathe. "You said you would call me."

"I can't... I can't. It's too much. I... Benny is in the next room and..."

"I didn't need a booty call, Elizabeth. I just wanted to know you were okay. You left really abruptly and I didn't get a chance to make sure you were fine with everything that happened. And you said you'd call."

"I'm fine with it," she said. "I'm more than fine with it. You don't need to..."

Benny chose that moment to come roaring back out of the house, scrambling straight for the pickup truck. He took the middle seat, and Elizabeth was actually sorry about it. Brody drove them to the edge of the ranch, where things became wild, and they got out. He grabbed a hatchet and they started walking down the path. Benny bounced ahead, and Elizabeth saw every slippery rock as a potential slipping hazard and fought the urge to tell him to be careful every two seconds. She knew it only drove him crazy. She was trying really hard to give him space. Because space was what he seemed to like best about this place.

"Did you always get your trees in the woods?" she asked, desperate to make conversation about the things so they wouldn't end up in silence and get consumed by the tension arcing between them.

"Us? No. Hell no. In fact, we don't do Christmas trees. We don't really do Christmas. I don't know. I feel like at one point maybe we kind of did? When we were little. But I don't really remember it."

The way that he shrugged his shoulders made her think that he was lying.

"You don't remember?"

He cleared his throat. Short and sharp. And as they kept on walking through the trees, the pines looming overhead, dusted white, the sky crystal blue and clear all of a sudden, while the air stayed so cold their breath escaped in clouds, she was sure he was done talking.

But then he spoke. "All right. I remember one Christmas. And things didn't go quite perfect and my dad was an absolute bear about it. He made everybody suffer. I think after that, it was just… Easier to not."

She recognized that he was being vague on purpose. "What happened?"

He fixed a stare at her. "It's not a good story. I don't think you want to hear it."

"You don't need to protect me from anything."

He didn't know, of course. About her past. About how things had started out for her. Because she hadn't told him.

He thought that she was soft and that she came from a background she didn't come from, because of how she presented herself. She knew that. She knew how she looked. How she came across, and what people thought about her. Because she had cultivated that image on purpose.

"He just… He didn't like things that disrupted the

daily routine, so he didn't like holidays or any fuss like that. And he liked things being perfect."

"What happened?"

"She burned dinner. On Christmas Eve. He went to the Christmas tree and burned everyone's presents. Except mine."

"Oh."

"Yeah. I shared mine," he said quickly. "I didn't keep them."

It was clear he needed to say that, that he needed her to know that. How sad that he felt like he had to save the day when his dad had ruined it.

"Brody…" she said slowly. "It wouldn't have mattered what you did. You were a child."

"But I did. I shared them." She could see that that was really important to him. To make it very clear that he had done his best to restore the balance.

"That was nice of you," she said.

In that moment, for some reason, she tried to think of how she would talk to Benny. How you talked to a kid that had bought into some kind of alternate reality. You didn't just tell them they were wrong. Or that it wasn't real, not when their feelings were very real. You couldn't do that. You had to listen to them.

"It wasn't extra nice. I mean…it was the least I could do. There's not much you can do with your siblings' toys all getting burned."

"I'm sorry that you went through that."

Her birth mother hadn't been cruel. From what Elizabeth could remember of her, she had just been neglectful. The times that she had gone back to be with her, they'd been mostly marked by long stretches of time in a room that was mostly empty, a mattress on the floor, and gnawing hunger.

It wasn't this trauma. It wasn't. But she did understand…

That ache. The one that came from not having what everyone else took for granted.

"I spent my whole childhood in foster care," she said.

He stopped. Just stopped. She could feel his gaze on her, hard. "What?"

"Yeah. I was in foster care until I aged out of the system. I went back to my birth mother occasionally. But by the time I was eight or nine… That stopped. I don't know what happened to her. It's kind of fuzzy. Lost in all the transitions. I wish I could say I was sad. But I wasn't, really. I had lived with so many people all the time that going back to her didn't really feel different. And she always seemed overwhelmed, not happy to have me. There wasn't food. That was really hard."

"Well…" He seemed at a loss. "I mean… Isn't foster care just a really awful system?"

"It can be. I'm not going to say that it was ideal, or that it wasn't hard. Having to move around all the time. But I learned that there are adults that you can trust in the world. And I got to watch a lot of different mothers with their children. I learned a lot from them. There was this family… The Allreds. They had like nine children. And a rotation of foster kids. And everything was so organized." She smiled. "They always had tons of food in this giant pantry. It felt like a party all the time at their house. We had to go to church on Sunday, but I didn't really mind that. It was something they did as a family, and it just seemed really special. I still keep in touch with my foster sisters, particularly. They send me

Christmas cards. They all have a lot of kids themselves now. They're…family. Even though they aren't family."

"Oh."

"It's not the same as having stability all the time, but it's… I had a good experience. I mean… The people that I lived with were good people, but every time I had to move it was really hard. And sometimes it was a family like the Allreds, and sometimes it was lonely. Or a more transitional house or a group facility for a little while, and that was really lonely. I didn't like that. It's the moving around. When you wished you could stay. Or staying longer in a place you just didn't fit. I mean, that's kind of a thing. Even if they're nice people, sometimes you don't fit."

"So how did you meet your husband?"

"High school. I was living with this family, the Johnsons, and they had a really nice house. They live in this great neighborhood. They were a short-term placement, and I knew it. I was only there for a couple of months, but that was why I got enrolled in that high school. And I was allowed to keep going there, even though it was really far from the next couple of places I was placed in. I met him freshman year. And I just couldn't believe that he… That he *liked* me. All my life, all through school, people whispered about the fact that I was a foster kid." She tried to smile again, but it felt harder. "And it is *different*. I never felt like I could invite anyone over for a sleepover—and that wouldn't have necessarily been true with some of the families I was with, but the house wasn't mine. The parents weren't mine. It never felt like… *Mine*. During sophomore year I got taken in by a woman named Denise Newton. And that was where I stayed until I was eighteen. It was the longest I was ever with anyone."

"Just one lady?"

"Yes. She was in her seventies. And she took in older kids sometimes. I was the last one. An only child for the years I was with her. It was so different than what I was used to. She used to work at the high school, she was a librarian. And she really believed that it was important for kids to have stability during those years when often they had the *least* amount of stability, because people tend to want to take care of small children." She could feel emotion pressing against the back of her eyes and she blinked it away. "Anyway. She was great. She gave me a lot."

"Do you still keep in touch with her?"

Her chest clenched. "She died when I was nineteen. She was probably the closest thing that I had to an actual mother figure."

"I'm sorry."

"It's okay. I had… I had my mother-in-law. Well, the woman who would become my mother-in-law. Denise's death really pushed me into wanting to marry Carter. Because he was the other stable thing that I had. I just didn't want to lose him. I loved him. I mean, I really loved him too, it wasn't just stability. I really did love him. Or it was what I understood of love."

Stability. Being *kept*.

That for her, had been love. The epitome of it.

"I would never have any idea, looking at you, that…"

"That I ever had a struggle in my life?" She laughed. "That is by design, Brody."

This time she couldn't smile. This was the most honest she had ever been with anybody. Including Carter.

Carter knew she was a foster kid, because she had been one when they'd met. So she hadn't told him about the Allreds. Or the Johnsons. She hadn't told him that she remembered the way Sue Allred organized the snacks in her pantry and made weekly meal plans, and Elizabeth had filed it away to use in her own household. She'd never told Carter that she had liked the way Natalie Johnson talked to her about her problems, like she was a person.

Never talking down to her or moralizing.

How when Elizabeth and Carter had started dating, she had taken Elizabeth aside and told her that she needed to make sure she practiced safe sex, because there was nothing worse than having a baby you weren't ready for. Because it was what put kids in foster care. And that if she wanted to have sex, it was her choice, and she would get her whatever birth control she needed.

She hadn't had sex with Carter for another year after that, but she had let Natalie drive her to a clinic to get some birth control.

She had a network of women in her life who had taught her how to be a functional person. Told her the secrets she'd need to survive. It had helped piece her together into the woman that she was. Little bits from each of them. Truth be told, she couldn't remember the name of every household she passed through. Couldn't remember all the details. But she was certain that she had taken something with her from each one. Even if she couldn't get a clear image of it.

But she had kept all that to herself. They just hadn't talked. They had met, and they had experienced all of high school together. They had their first times together.

But they'd never talked about issues. About what they really wanted, because she had just been so grateful and happy to have him.

"I thought that Carter wanting to be with me was too good to be true. And then it turned out it was." Her throat got tight. It still hurt. Not the divorce. It wasn't about being heartbroken still. It was hurt for that girl she'd been. Who had believed in Carter above all else, and had thought nothing could break her fairytale. She might hurt for the girl she'd been forever. "I thought there's no way this guy, this handsome, rich guy likes me. That he loves me. Even when we got married, I just kept thinking it was a dream. It didn't matter that at that point we had been together for five years. It still felt like a dream."

"Did you love him?" Brody asked. "Or were you grateful to him?"

She laughed, she couldn't help it. Because somehow he had zeroed in on something that she had always felt somewhere inside of her, that she had never put words to.

"I would say that then I didn't know the difference. And really, for me there was no practical difference. He was stability in a way that I'd never experienced before. He's still the longest relationship I've ever had. I mean, except for Benny now. But the years that I had with Carter…outstrip any family, any parental figure, anything. So yeah. For me… There wasn't really a difference. Love and gratitude were mixed. And he gave me Benny. So I suppose the feelings that I have for him now are a lot the same as they always were. Except he *bugs* me. Like, bugs the hell out of me. And I'm okay admitting that now."

"Did he bug you then?"

"No, actually." She shook her head. "It's amazing how much more annoying someone is after they abandon you."

"What about this tree?" Benny shouted from way up ahead on the trail, pointing dramatically at a massive pine tree.

"That's too big," she said.

"It doesn't look big."

"It is," Brody said. "Let me show you." He walked up to where Benny was and stood next to the tree, which went a couple of feet over his head. "I'm six foot three, kiddo. Your ceilings are probably seven feet tall. And that tree has to be nine feet."

"Oh."

"They look smaller because they're outside surrounded by trees that are twenty and thirty and fifty feet tall. It's deceptive."

"What about that one?"

Benny pointed ahead at a smaller tree off the trail that was in a little clearing.

"That's great," Brody said.

He walked up with the hatchet.

"Give me an assist, Ben."

Benny looked delighted.

And suddenly she was just a whole jumble of feelings. Watching Brody show Benny how to cut down the Christmas tree.

She knew that she would work here for... Well, she didn't even know how long she would work here for. Hopefully, years. Maybe Brody would be in Benny's life all that time. She hated the idea of Benny losing this. It was funny, because Brody definitely didn't seem like the kind of guy who had set out to become any kind of father figure.

And even thinking it made her feel uncomfortable.

But she felt like he had taught Benny more lessons in the last week and a half than Carter had taught Benny in eight years.

They brought the tree down with ease, and Brody hefted it up over his shoulder, the movement fluid, drawing her attention to his muscles.

Damn, his muscles. And now she had seen them without clothes on at all, and she was even more into him.

Grateful or in love?

It was funny, because she didn't just feel gratitude for Brody. She felt like she had been entitled to what happened between them. Which was different because with Carter she had felt like she owed him. Everything had been mixed-up and messed up because she didn't have a good relationship, a healthy relationship with her own self.

"All right, you have to help me carry it," Brody said, gesturing toward the top end of the tree, which was still on the ground.

Benny went around to the other end, and picked it up, though it was clear to Elizabeth that Brody was doing the heavy lifting.

"Do you need help?" she asked from her position on the trail.

"Absolutely not."

"Are you trying to spare me heavy lifting because I'm a woman?" She was asking just to see what he would say.

"No. We're doing it because you do enough for everybody else."

It had been worth it. Worth that reaction.

It made her heart feel warm. It made her feel warm.

They carried the tree all the way down the trail, and then Brody hefted it into the back of the truck.

"Can I ride in the back?" Benny asked.

She felt nervousness twist up her stomach. "Okay," she said. Because really, it was safe. They were just going a little ways across the property, and she knew that Brody would go slow.

And she liked what was happening here. She liked to see what was happening with Benny. So she wanted to continue to encourage it.

Benny hopped into the back of the truck, next to the tree, and Brody got into the cab and closed the door. She followed suit.

He looked over at her. "I will drive at a snail's pace."

"Thank you," she said. "I couldn't be less cool than you."

"I'm a pirate cowboy," he said. "Everyone is less cool than me."

"I have yet to see evidence of your piracy."

"Did you want me to dress like a pirate?"

The exchange felt electric. Loaded. A welcome change from the heaviness of their previous conversation.

"I don't think I'm into that."

His lips curved into a very wicked grin. "You don't know if you don't try."

"I don't have time to try."

"I get that."

Silence fell in the cab, and the only sound was the wheels on the gravel.

"Life is just really complicated."

"I also get that."

And now she was sort of breaking up with the most handsome man she had ever seen. Which made her feel like her world was turning upside down again. Because she had never thought that she would be the one to walk away.

The old her couldn't have done that.

She didn't really want to do it now. But there was no way that it could end well. And she already liked him way more than she wanted to. And he was bound up in her work here, and there was Benny. Benny idolized him. Just loved him. And she could see a point where that would become complicated. Where there were expectations. Where there were things that would make him reluctant to connect with Benny, because it would seem like promises being made. And he had been clear about the fact that promises couldn't be made, and she got it.

"It was really nice, though," she whispered. "I didn't know that my body could do that. So thank you."

"You didn't know your body could do what?"

"Oh, do I really have to say it?"

"Yes," he said, looking at her for a second, his expression far too amused. "You do need to say it, because you introduced it."

"That isn't fair. You're impossible," she huffed.

"Yes. It's been said many times. I am a serious pain in the ass, Elizabeth, and I am well aware of that. You're not going to shame me into letting this go."

"Usually, I barely have one orgasm during sex. Multiples are off the table."

"Really?" He let his arm drape over the back of the seat, one wrist propped over the steering wheel, and he looked so cocky, it did something to her insides.

"And I've never… Carter never… You went…"

"I went down on you?"

"Yes."

"Holy hell. He'd never... Seriously. What the hell is wrong with that guy?"

Her face was flaming hot, she really didn't know how to have a frank discussion like this. And here she was in the middle of it.

You didn't know how to do a lot of things before Brody, though, and now you're just doing them. So there's that. You're just doing it, even though you don't know how, and that's really something.

That made her chest feel lighter. Made the tightness there ease. Maybe it was a terrible thing that they'd done this. And that they couldn't keep doing it. It had been a lesson. A good lesson. And everything was ending amicably. They would still be friends. Because that's what this was. A friendship.

She had not moved here expecting to have this.

This easy companionship with this man. He had bothered her at first because she had been attracted to him, and she had figured that out. Figured out what they could do with this. She'd had sex with him, and she wasn't ashamed. And she didn't feel prickly around him, or like she had to avoid him anymore.

That meant that it was the natural conclusion. The opportunity to step forward into a friendship.

Yes. Friendship.

"I think there was something wrong with us," she said. "As a couple. We were too young to understand what we actually needed out of a romantic relationship. And it's hard. Because he gets it with someone else. And I don't mean that because I'm jealous. I mean that because it hooked into my insecurities for a long time.

I thought it was me. But I think it was us. And it still bothers me the way that it rebounds on Benny. Because, of course, it's easier for him to mostly compartmentalize and focus on his family. And then he gets touchy with me about… About the fact that I can't live in limbo to serve him. To bring him his son when he wants him, keep him close at hand, and… Sorry. It always turns into that drama."

"It's the thing that you deal with every day. I'm not surprised that it comes up a lot."

He was just so understanding. She hadn't known men could be like that.

She hadn't known that anyone could be like that. She couldn't remember the last time she'd been able to talk to somebody and not be afraid of what they would think when she revealed the details of her life. Of herself. And she didn't feel like she was confessing shortcomings when she talked to Brody.

They pulled into the cabin, and he put the truck in Park. She heard Benny hop down, and Brody got out. "I'll go help him with the tree."

Her phone buzzed in her pocket. It wasn't the text. It was Carter. And he was actually calling her.

She answered. "Hello?"

"Hi. I thought that we should talk."

"Why? We never talk."

"I know."

It was a metaphor for their entire relationship. They hadn't talked anymore. They hadn't talked until it was too late. Until he was going off to marry another woman. Until he had gotten that other woman pregnant. And then they had talked. When the only talking left to be done was him telling her that they were over.

"So why are we talking now, Carter?" she pressed.

"I had an informal meeting with the judge this morning."

"You can do that without me?"

"I can, because you aren't here."

"Yes. But the judge knows that. I can certainly be on a phone call and…"

"There will be a phone call later," Carter said. "I just wanted to give you a heads-up. I'm asking that Benny come back home for Christmas break."

"What?"

"We share holidays," he said. "It's pretty normal."

"But not… Not like this. We both usually get some time on Christmas. And you don't get *all* of Christmas break. You've never wanted that."

"It's not going to be realistic for us to do every weekend when you live so far away. So I think we're going to have to work something out with school holidays."

"I'm three hours away," she said. "*Three hours*. Not three days. You act like it's insurmountable." And the anger she usually held back started to bubble up, spill out. "But then, you did that when we lived twenty-five minutes away. You don't always take your weekends. Why are you acting bitter about it now?"

"Because it bothers me now," he bit out. "Because… I was young and really stupid when we split up, Elizabeth. And I didn't know how to manage a blended family. But it's not two different families, or my real family and Benny. *Benny* is my family. I didn't know how to handle that, because it was inconsistent. And because I was still learning how to be a husband and father." He sighed. Heavy and tortured in a way she'd never heard him, and it forced her to acknowledge that she just didn't know Carter anymore. "Which I admit I didn't know how to do when I was with you. But I've been sitting with this, and how I want to change, and for a long time I just didn't think I could. And then when you moved... I realized I was really going to have to make an effort. I wasn't just going to slip into doing better with Benny, I was going to have...to do something."

"Did your mom put you up to this?" She felt crispy and raw, all at the same time, her heart beating too hard. Like it might burst out of her chest.

"No," he said. "I've realized how much of his childhood I've missed because I didn't want things to be..."

"Admit it. You didn't want to have a fractured, weird family like the one that I came from. You didn't want anything less than traditional, but that's what you got yourself into."

"Yes," he said, his tone hard. "It was snobbery. Over something that *I* created. Like I didn't want to acknowledge that I had an ex-wife and a kid somewhere else. I admit that. Because it is...my biggest failure, Elizabeth. The way I treated you. I was a bad husband. I was a bad person. Everything about what I did...it was wrong. So yeah, seeing you reminded me. Custody arrangements reminded me of it. I wanted to put it behind me, and I couldn't. I've realized I have to accept it. That I have the ability to fail someone, to fail myself, this badly. And the only way to begin to fix it is to fix my relationship with Benny."

And she couldn't hate him. That was the problem. It was hard, and she didn't like it, but he wasn't trying to push the blame off onto her. He never had, and it was almost worse. Because it made it impossible for her to just write him off, to tell herself that Benny would be better off if he didn't have him in his life.

Benny *loved* him. That was the bottom line. Benny loved his dad.

And even though Carter didn't take care of Benny or love him in the same way that Elizabeth did, he did. She knew that Benny needed him. That he wanted him around.

"Please don't take him from me for Christmas, Carter," she whispered. "We just got a Christmas tree."

"School doesn't get out for another week. You can do a Christmas thing."

"Carter…"

"You know we're going to have to do something. I'm going to have to have him for summer, or at least part of it…"

"I hate this. I hate that you still get to hurt me even though I don't love you anymore."

I hate that I still have to have you in my life.

I hate that I just can't be over it.

They weren't different. That was what hurt right now. She actually wanted the same thing he did. Not to escape a failure on her part, but to escape him. She didn't want their failed marriage lingering in her rearview mirror any more than he did, but it had to because they'd made a child together.

A child they both loved.

A child she wanted all to herself. But she couldn't have him all to herself.

Right now, she understood Carter better than she ever had. But she hated him a little bit too.

"I'm going to oppose it," she said.

"I thought that you probably would. But I wanted to

call and explain myself. I'll send you details for a conference call. Should be Monday."

"You didn't even check on my work schedule."

"Sorry. Is your work more important than this?"

It wasn't. And she knew that Gus would help her rearrange her schedule however she needed to. It was just not fair at all that she was expected to. It outraged her. Like the rest of this.

"You know nothing is more important than this."

"Great. Well, I'll send you the details. I'll talk to you later, Elizabeth."

And when she hung up the phone, she let out an unholy, angry growl that reverberated inside the cab. And both Benny and Brody looked her direction.

She stepped out of the truck. "It's fine," she said.

Benny seemed perfectly happy with that statement. Brody, she could tell, was not.

Benny was hopping around in the snow, not paying attention to them anymore at all. Brody brought the tree up onto the porch, and she made her way up to where he was.

"And what happened?"

"That was my ex-husband. He wants Benny to come for all of Christmas break."

"That doesn't seem fair," he said.

"I didn't think so either. Except he hasn't seen him for a while, and I think…"

"Are you trying to make yourself feel better?"

"I don't really have a choice, do I? If the judge decides that it's fair, because I moved…"

"Christmas means a lot to you, doesn't it?"

She wanted to shy away from the grave understanding on his face. It was too sweet, and she felt too raw.

"I just try really hard to give him happy holidays because…"

"And you try to give them to yourself too," he said. "I get that."

"You don't care about Christmas, do you?"

"Not really."

"Thank you for this. I'm going to decorate the tree with him tonight and… It might be the Christmas that I get to spend with him."

"Hey. It doesn't have to be Christmas Day. You can make Christmas whatever day you want. I mean, maybe that's the kind of freethinking that comes with having a terrible childhood. I don't have a lot of sacred days."

"Thank you." And she still wanted to cry.

"Let's get the tree inside," he said.

He opened up the door and carried it into the living room. She went down the hall and got her box of Christmas ornaments and her tree stand out of the closet. Brody took care of setting it up. She marveled at how easy it all was for him. She was usually the one wrestling with the tree and trying to screw it into the stand, and it was always too heavy for her, and it was really annoying.

It was really nice to have a man around, frankly. As regressive as that might seem.

But he was stronger than her physically, and that was quite handy.

"I have some spiced cider in the fridge," she said.

"You have cider?"

"Yeah. I'll heat it up. We can decorate the tree." And she realized that she was maybe stepping over some invisible line. "I mean, you did help."

"I don't know that I'll help decorate, but I'll drink some cider."

She went to the fridge and got the bottle out, and poured the contents into a pan on the stove. It was pre-made, she had not done it herself, but she did add an extra cinnamon stick.

Tears started slipping down her cheeks. She was being so dramatic. It was just… It was just not fair. Because Carter was doing what she had hoped that he would do, but it was a terrible time for him to do it. And he had given voice to a bunch of things that she had been worried about, but if he was dealing with them, how could she be angry about them?

She heard Brody walk up behind her, and he came to stand next to her, his big hands on the counter. He didn't touch her, but he was close. "You're not okay?"

"I'm being dramatic, because we aren't even talking to the judge until Monday."

"You're not being dramatic."

"It's just… He's ashamed of me. That's the thing. I was a foster kid that he married, and now I've forced him into the situation where he has a broken home. Because he couldn't love me enough."

"Did he say that?" Brody asked, his eyes sharp.

"No. But he said that he spent the last six years in denial over the fact that he has a broken home, essentially. And that we have to be a blended family, and it was simpler for him to just not be that."

"He sounds like a dick, Elizabeth."

"Yeah. I mean he kind of is. He justified having an affair and getting another woman pregnant, and all of that. But most of the terrible things he did are in the past. And he's just been kind of benign and I've gotten used to it. Even though the things that he does definitely hurt Benny sometimes, it's still left me with the most control, and now… I feel like I'm losing some of that control. I feel guilty because… Don't I want Benny to have a relationship with his dad?"

Brody shrugged. "Maybe you don't. Maybe that's one thing he's right about. It would be easier if you didn't have to blend. If he was just gone. If you didn't have to put up with him."

It was just so practically, baldly stated and she loved it. That he said it like it didn't make her a monster. That he said it like it made perfect sense.

And it gave her space to push against it. To be reasonable.

She appreciated that too.

"I thought that. But it just isn't how it works. He was such a huge part of my life and… He has to continue being part of my life because of Benny. I have to figure out how to deal with that."

"Maybe that's why my mom just left. If she'd taken us with… She'd have had to deal with my dad still."

Something inside of her went cold. "Your mom just left?"

"Yeah. I was about ten. She'd had enough. I don't blame her. My dad was such a monster, Elizabeth." There was something strange about the way he said that, like it was practiced. That his dad was a monster. An agreed-upon term that encompassed all sorts of actions, which were clearly a lot more complicated. A lot more terrifying.

"She didn't take you with her?"

He shook his head. "It would never have been me if she'd taken one of us. If she took somebody, it would've been Hunter. He was…her favorite. Or maybe she'd have taken Lach. I mean you aren't supposed to have favorites maybe." His gaze went remote when he said that. "But Hunter would have been hers. He told her to go. And leave him. Is it not the bravest damn thing you've ever heard? A little boy telling his mom to go, and that he'll be okay."

"That poor little thing."

"I know. And things just got worse after that. That's when... Gus. Anyway. Obviously, it isn't the same situation. Your ex is inconvenient, but he's not dangerous. Right?"

"Yes. Right."

"So it's different. But I'm just saying... I think the compromise part must be really tough. I sure as hell don't know how to do it. Instead, I just opted to not really have much in the way of relationships. I have my brothers. So, you know, compromises are at a minimum, because we all just kind of leave each other alone to do whatever needs doing. I don't know. It's a long-winded way of saying I think what you're doing is really hard. And I can't say that I understand anything but the fact that it hurts. I'm also really terrible at offering people comfort. I've done it pretty much zero times in my whole life."

She had a feeling he was lying about that. Because she knew about his brothers. And she knew that he had shared those toys. And she knew it was why he didn't like Christmas. Or even want to try to make a new version of the holiday for himself. But he was here. For the cider.

"I'll get you a cup," she said.

And she reached up into the cabinet and took down a simple, white cup that had come with the place. She ladled some steaming hot liquid out of the pan and handed it to him.

"Thanks," he said.

She poured herself some and looked out the window at Benny who was still playing with the snow. "He doesn't actually like decorating the Christmas tree," she said. "I find that very annoying. I had images of decorating for the holidays with my kids when I was young and didn't have a stable family."

"You thought about having kids?"

"All the time." It made her smile, remembering that. How simple it seemed then. "That was what I wanted. To be a wife, to be a mother. You have to understand, for me, having a real, permanent family was the biggest goal. Because I never had one. Not consistently. Not one that I stayed with. I thought that Carter and I would have a few kids by now. And they would help me decorate the Christmas tree, and we would listen to Christmas music and it would be warm and happy, and every time I've ever tried to make Benny help me decorate Christmas cookies or decorate the tree, it dissolves quickly. Granted he *likes* decorating the Christmas cookies, but mostly he just puts a glob of frosting on them and eats them. So there's no point actually coloring all the frostings and putting out a bunch of different candy."

"Sorry. I'm Team Benny on this one. I will watch you decorate the tree, though, and if you would like to have me over to decorate cookies, I can promise that I will eat them faster than you can get them done."

She bent down and opened up the box, and started to take out a roll of Christmas lights.

"I can do that," he said.

He stood up and grabbed the end of the lights and reached effortlessly up to the top, resting them on the branches before beginning to wind them around the tree. Another thing that was much easier for him than it was for her. It usually ended with her sweaty. And instead of watching him, and the play of his biceps and his other muscles while he completed the task, she decided to open up the other ornaments in the box.

There was the little box containing everything that Benny had made at school. Handprints, puzzle-piece picture frames, pretzel picture frames. Macaroni picture frames. Preschool, kindergarten, first grade, second grade. He hadn't made anything for third yet.

Those ones went on first. And then she filled in with the prettier, sparkly ornaments. Honestly, she was always torn with the desire to do a themed tree that was perfect and matching. Then she immediately felt guilty, because obviously, it was more important to have ornaments up with Benny's picture on them than it was to have an aesthetically perfect tree. Still, she was only human, and she supposed if that was one of her only real weaknesses, it wasn't terrible.

Just then, her eyes met Brody's, and she realized that he was, in fact, one of her other weaknesses. Big time.

Friends. Just friends.

Benny came into the house, his cheeks red. He opened the door too hard, and it hit the wall. She flinched. "Benny, please be careful. We don't own the house. And even if we did own the house, I don't want to fix a hole in the wall."

"I know how to fix a hole in the wall," Brody said.

"Remember, the thing about how I'm trying to teach him manners?"

"Sorry. Manners really aren't my strong suit." Except they were. He wasn't even half as feral as he pretended to be.

"Can I have some cider?" Benny asked.

"How did you know there was cider?" Elizabeth asked.

"I could smell it."

"Benny..." She didn't want to introduce something that would maybe fall through, but she felt anxious, and she wanted to know if Benny was at least okay with leaving for Christmas. As much as all of this was upsetting, it would almost make her feel better if she knew that he wanted to go.

Part of her wondered if she should wait until they were alone, but she didn't want to wait. Because maybe he'd say no and she could call Carter right now and tell him. Carter wasn't a monster. He'd let Benny stay if Benny wanted to.

"What?"

She started to go and get some cider from the pan on the stove, but Brody beat her to it, having finished with the Christmas lights.

She turned back to Benny. "Would you be interested in spending Christmas with Dad?"

"Oh. Yeah!" Benny said. "Him and Ashley always go out in the snow."

There was literally snow outside here.

"Yeah. I know that Christmas in that house is really beautiful." She tried to sound neutral but upbeat, if that was a thing.

It had been her house once upon a time. She knew how beautiful it was when it was decorated.

"Dad wants you to come for all of Christmas break," she said quickly.

"Really? He really wants me to come and stay for two weeks?" Benny looked…in awe. And happy. So happy.

It killed her.

He hadn't stayed away from her that long, ever.

He hadn't stayed with his dad that long, ever.

He clearly wanted to. Was hungry to.

And it didn't matter what she wanted. Not when she could see so clearly what Benny wanted.

She wasn't a monster either.

She knew right then that they didn't need to have a phone call with the judge. Benny was excited because it was something new. It was something different. And it crushed her a little bit.

"Can you stay with him for a second?"

"Sure," Brody said.

"I'll be right back." She stepped out onto the porch, and she closed her eyes. It was two weeks. And yes, it was Christmas. Yes, it felt sacred. But Benny's happiness was the most important thing to her, and if he had not wanted to go for Christmas, she would've fought tooth and nail to make sure that he could stay with her. But of course he did. Because it wasn't just his dad, it was his siblings. She felt completely disconnected from Carter's children, and why wouldn't she?

But Benny didn't. They were his brothers and sister. It would be a full house with rambunctious children, and why wouldn't he want to be there?

It just… It made sense. And it was fair, and she couldn't see standing in the way of it. She didn't need to make it personal, she didn't need to make it about her.

She pulled out her phone, and hit Carter's name out of her recent calls. "Hello?"

"Hi," she said. "Benny wants to come. We don't need to talk to a judge."

"Elizabeth…"

"I mean, we will, to make sure that we have a real agreement in place for how things are going to work when I'm here, because I don't need to be doing this all the time. I prefer it when we can keep the hassle between the two of us to a minimum."

"Right."

"But for this… He can go. He can go for Christmas break. But you have to come and pick him up, you have to have him back a full day before school starts, and you have to… You have to see it through, Carter. You can't decide that it's going to be too busy, you can't…"

"Hey," he said. "I promise. It was my idea."

"Don't you understand that I'm afraid for him? I just… I'm always afraid that you're ashamed of him."

"I'm not ashamed of him, Elizabeth. I'm ashamed of myself. He reminds me of that."

She sat with that for a moment. She could hardly take it in.

"You're ashamed of yourself?" she asked.

"I love Ashley. Don't… It's just there was no excuse for me to do things the way that I did. He reminds me that I broke us up."

He *had*. She would never have left him. Not ever. She also knew that there had been other issues in their marriage, issues that she would never have ever approached. Because she just wanted to be married. She didn't care if it was a blissfully happy marriage, just having the marriage had been blissful to her. For her, a successful marriage was one that didn't end. For her… That was what mattered.

And she wasn't entirely sure that it had been the path to the greatest and brightest happiness for herself or Carter. But things might've been simpler.

And since the two of them often struggled with the complications of arrangements... If she ever wished that things could go back to the way they were, that was really what she was fantasizing about. The simplicity that came with being in one household was it. Not being with Carter.

"Well, you have to get over that," she said. "Because it did happen, and it wasn't his fault. We got married too young."

"Yes. We did."

"Only time can fix that. The fact that we were kids trying to handle a very adult situation."

"We aren't kids anymore," Carter said.

"No. We aren't. So consider this a grown-up olive branch. As long as things go well."

"Right. Well. I'll be there to pick him up... When exactly does he get out of school?"

"December twenty-second."

"Wow. They really push it right up to the line these days."

"I imagine it's true for your other children too."

"Ashley knows all that stuff." She could hear him wince on the other end of the phone. "Yeah. That's another thing I should probably get a little bit on top of, right?"

"That is your and Ashley's problem. And not mine." And thank God. She might do it all alone, but she didn't expect someone else to share that sort of thing, so she couldn't be disappointed by it.

"I'll be there to pick him up December twenty-second, then. I'll keep you updated on the timeframe."

"Great. I'll see you then."

She hung up, her chest a tangle of complicated feelings. Because she had come here and it had felt a little bit like a bubble. Separate from that other life that she had left behind, and now that life she'd left behind was coming here.

She went back inside, and Brody was looking at her. She chose to just focus on Benny. "Dad is going to be here December twenty-second to pick you up. And you'll be back after New Year's."

Saying it made it more real. Made it burn a little bit.

"Awesome," Benny said.

Yeah. Brody was right. Benny not getting everything he wanted definitely wasn't a struggle, but it was certainly difficult when your ex-husband had a much nicer house, and way more extravagant Christmases than you had.

Maybe the real issue was that it wasn't a struggle for him.

It was a struggle for *her*.

It hurt *her*.

The thought made her chest feel bruised, but she did her best to breathe past it.

"Now," she said. "Let's decorate the tree."

"I'm going to take off. You and Benny have fun with your tree."

"Thank you for your help," she said.

"No problem."

And she knew that he was leaving to give her some space. To give her time with Benny since she had just committed to not having any around Christmas. But honestly, after all the heavy lifting he had done, she wished he had stayed to do a little bit more. Because she needed somebody to lean on right now. But it was just her and Benny. So she had to be the strong one. Even though she didn't feel like it.

CHAPTER THIRTEEN

DECEMBER TWENTY-SECOND. The date stuck in Brody's head. He couldn't really do much about it. It just kept rattling around in there. And he had a bad feeling that he knew why. Because Benny was going to be gone, and one of the barriers between him and Elizabeth being together...

No. It wasn't a good idea. Even if they were going to have the supervision of a child to worry about.

But that day was today, and he didn't know what time Carter was coming to pick Benny up, only that it was happening.

At the staff meeting that morning, Gus gave Elizabeth a list of assignments, and in spite of his brain telling him not to, Brody ended up interjecting. "She can have the day off, right? I mean, surely we can cover some things if we need to."

"I don't need the day off," she said.

She looked glassy-eyed though. And like she might need the day, so she could spend the time with Benny.

"It's the last day before this crop of people goes home," Gus said. "Then it's Christmas break for everybody."

"Yes, and on Christmas break Benny isn't going to be here," he said.

"Brody," Elizabeth said, looking stern. "It's fine. I can do my job. And I don't need you to interject."

Shit. He'd overstepped on this one. But he wanted to do something. He wanted to take that tired, worn look off her face and he wanted to smooth out all her concerns. He wanted to carry some of her burdens, dammit.

Except now he'd clearly made her angrier, and that wasn't his intent at all.

"I didn't realize," Gus said.

"I don't need special treatment," Elizabeth said fiercely.

"It's not special treatment," he insisted.

"It definitely feels like it is," she said.

"All right," Gus said. "If you're sure."

"I'm sure." She downed her coffee, and left the barn.

Benny wasn't in there. Brody'd noticed Elizabeth had gotten a lot more comfortable with letting Benny play in the general area, rather than needing him to be around her at all times.

"And what was that?" Gus asked.

"Nothing. I just know that she was upset about Benny leaving, so I wanted to say something. Because I knew she was never going to ask for herself."

"And what's going on with you and her?"

"Good Lord, Gus, you're like a nosy old lady now that you have a wife."

"Yeah. But, I'm nosy for good reason. You don't just stick your oar in, Brody. It's not really your thing."

This was the second time in just a couple of weeks that one of his brothers had tried to tell him how he was.

It wasn't less annoying coming from Gus than it was from Hunter.

Well. No, it was less annoying coming from Gus, because at least he was older.

Hunter was the baby. And he would always be the most annoying.

"Nothing is going on. She's my friend," he said.

"She's your friend. Because you have so many of those?"

"I have some," he said. "Though it may surprise you."

"It's not a bad surprise," Gus said. "It's just remarkable."

"I guess."

"You seem to be a little bit different these last couple of weeks. By which I mean not hungover half of the mornings you show up to work."

"Maybe I'm just getting old," Brody said.

"Well, I myself am out to pasture, so you're definitely halfway there."

"What do you need me to do today, Gus?"

"Oh, I have a whole lot of the kind of maintenance you just love. So whether you're being honest with me or not about your feelings, you have a chance to work out a lot of aggression."

"Perfect."

Gus hadn't been kidding. The work had been physical, and it had been intense. And Brody really didn't mind.

At about two thirty, he was walking up from the gully, where he'd been digging postholes for a fence that Gus wanted to put in, when he heard the sound of tires on the gravel, and knew that somebody was here.

He looked up and saw a big black SUV that reminded him of Feds pull into the ranch.

There was a guy behind the wheel, a woman with red hair, and he couldn't tell if there was anyone in the back because the windows were too darkly tinted.

This, he supposed, was Carter.

The SUV stopped, because clearly the guy didn't really know where he was going.

He rolled down his window. "I'm looking for Elizabeth Colfax?"

What struck Brody the most was how young the guy was. Well, probably Elizabeth's age. And he knew she wasn't quite thirty yet. He had kind of a soft face, a little bit round, even though he wasn't overweight or anything. Light brown hair pushed off his forehead. And he was wearing a sport coat, like this was a fancy dinner or something.

"Yeah," he said. "I'll walk you on up to her place. It's a dirt road, and it's not far."

He began to walk ahead of the giant vehicle, and if the guy was frustrated because he was going slow, well, all the better.

The little cabin came into view, and he stepped to the side, gesturing forward. He knew that he didn't have to continue following the SUV. He knew that he didn't have to be there for this. Except… He wanted to be.

As soon as the car stopped in front of the cabin, the front door crashed open, and Benny came running out with a giant duffel bag over his shoulder that pitched ahead of him, and knocked him off his balance. But of course, Benny being Benny, he wasn't deterred by that at all. "Dad," he exploded.

The guy got out of the car, and scooped Benny up in a hug. And to his credit, he looked genuinely happy to see his kid.

It made Brody feel conflicted, because mostly he just wanted to punch this guy in the face because he had hurt Elizabeth. Bad. In his mind, in his heart, that was unforgiveable.

He'd hurt her in the past and he had the power to hurt her now, because their son was between them.

But the guy clearly loved Benny. And Benny loved him.

So he supposed punching him unprovoked wasn't on the table.

Elizabeth came out of the house, her expression schooled into something flat.

The redheaded woman got out of the car then, her sleek hair tied back in a knot. And the back doors to the SUV opened, and the three kids tumbled out.

"Sorry," the woman said. "I guess we're kind of invading you. But they really want to see where Benny lives."

"Right. No. That's not a problem," Elizabeth said. "Hi, Ashley."

"Hello."

It wasn't frosty, not really. It wasn't warm either. It was just a neutral kind of acceptance Brody didn't think he'd ever seen before.

And Brody thought this was the perfect chance for him to insert himself into the mix.

"Have fun, Ben," he said.

"Thanks, Brody," Benny said, looking like Brody had handed him five bucks by calling him such a grown-up name in front of everyone. "Brody is a cowboy. And a pirate."

"A pirate," Carter repeated.

"Yeah," Brody answered, grinning as slowly as possible, because he just knew that him grinning at nothing in particular would make a guy like this mad.

He might not be able to punch him. But he could needle him.

"I'm Carter," he said, sticking out his hand.

"Brody. Brody McCloud. Part owner of the ranch." He stuck his hand out and shook it. Maybe a little bit more firmly than necessary. Carter seemed to take it as a challenge and squeezed his back.

He dropped his hand to the side and turned to the redhead. "Ashley," she said. "Ashley Colfax."

Oh. Of course the woman had the same last name as Elizabeth.

Because it was *Carter's* last name.

Brody didn't like that *at all*, even though he had no right to dislike it.

"Good to meet you," he said, tipping his hat rather than taking the ten steps it would take to go shake her hand. The kids had piled into the house, but the adults were standing around outside.

It was clear that Ashley and Carter felt no need to see the house that Benny lived in.

"Yeah," Elizabeth said. "This is the place. And... Down there is where we do the work."

"It's lovely," Ashley said. "It's huge. It takes like ten minutes to get back here off of the road."

"Each parcel of land is 13,000 acres," Brody supplied. "Been in the family for generations."

"Was that those early you-can-have-as-much-land-as-a-man-can-walk-in-a-day rules? Or piracy?" Carter asked, laughing at his own joke.

"You know," Brody said, "I'm not really sure."

Elizabeth suppressed a laugh when he said that.

"Everything's going good here?" Carter asked.

"Yes," Elizabeth said. "It's great. As you can see.

Adorable house, beautiful scenery. Couldn't ask for better. Benny has tons of room to play. It's really… Really something. The school is a little one-room building that kind of sits between the different ranches, and there are quite a lot of kids there."

"He told me a little bit when we had our phone calls," Carter said, clearly unwilling to let her think that he was completely out of the loop.

"I don't know what's taking them so long," Ashley said.

It had been like five minutes.

"I can go get them," Elizabeth said.

She ducked into the house, leaving Brody out there with Ashley and Carter. They really were a well-matched couple, and he could see how Elizabeth had fit into that life. But even though she still dressed the part, there was just something a lot more vibrant about her.

It was almost like she tried to hide it. Hide it behind a façade a lot like theirs. Because she had spent a long time trying to fit in that world, he supposed.

"So, you're her…boss?" Carter asked.

"Her friend," Brody said.

And he could see Carter's jaw firm up.

Oh yeah.

That guy knew a little masculine competition when he saw it. Brody had a feeling, though, that his reaction wasn't really about Elizabeth so much as it was about Benny.

Or, hell, maybe it was about Elizabeth. She said that she hadn't been with anyone since her divorce. It was probably really comfortable for a guy like him to have moved on but have his ex-wife just hanging around being Mother of the Year and nothing else. Yeah, he imagined that on some level, Carter enjoyed that.

Carter, he couldn't help but notice, was about four inches shorter than he was.

Petty, maybe. But, just true. Other men didn't like how tall Brody was. They took it as a threat.

Good.

Elizabeth returned a second later with Benny and the other three kids, two of whom were identical.

"Super cool," one of the boys said.

"Yeah," said the other one.

And they all began to run toward the SUV.

"Wait," Elizabeth said. "I need a hug." Then Benny threw his arms around her. And Elizabeth bent down and kissed him on the top of the head. "I love you," she said. "Have the merriest Christmas ever."

"Thanks, Mom," he said.

He wiggled out of her hold, and he imagined it was probably some kind of a miracle that he had submitted himself to that much maternal affection. And there was something suddenly...

Strange about watching this. Benny leaving his mother.

Elizabeth looked so sad watching him go, and he was just getting in an SUV with his biological father to have a really nice Christmas.

He was going to be gone for two weeks.

Had Brody's mother looked sad when she'd walked out of their house? Knowing that she would be gone forever? Or had she just gone away and never looked back?

It was a strange thought. He so rarely allowed himself to ponder any of that.

She was putting on a brave face. He could tell.

And when the SUV pulled away, she waved broadly, putting on brave gestures too.

She was a champ.

"Elizabeth," he said, when the SUV was out of sight.

"I'd actually like to be alone for a little bit," she said, forcing a smile.

"All right."

And he turned and walked away, because it was what she had asked him to do. But he spent the rest of the afternoon regretting it.

CHAPTER FOURTEEN

"You want to go out?" Lachlan asked.

Brody thought about it. He really did. He didn't know what he was doing. The whole thing with the Christmas tree, and hanging out with Elizabeth like that. He didn't like the way it made him feel. He didn't like how he'd felt seeing her face as she'd watched Benny leave. He didn't like how he'd felt watching Benny leave. Like his chest was full of cement. He didn't know what he was doing. That was the thing.

"Yeah," he said. "Sure."

"Great. Let's plan to meet at Smokey's around eight?"

"Sounds good to me."

The usual thing. Drive separate vehicles, don't drink too much, because the goal isn't to drink, it's to meet women.

Except, there was only one woman that he was interested in right now. And he didn't know how long that was going to last. It was completely inconvenient. He didn't want to deal with this. Didn't want to. Didn't want to be fixated on someone he couldn't have. Because that was the bottom line. He couldn't have her. It was… It was an absolutely impossible situation. Because she was the kind of woman who needed a man that could provide stability. He could support somebody financially, that wasn't the issue. It was the damn *being-a-husband-and-father thing*.

He was the last person who could get involved in that.

So he went back to his place. And he figured going out was the best thing to do. So he prepared for that. Took a shower, changed his clothes.

And then he found himself texting Elizabeth.

Have you ever been to Smokey's?

It took five minutes for her to respond.

I don't even know what that is.

Local bar.

No.

Want to go out?

It took a long time for that response to come through too.

I guess I might as well.

Great. I'll be by to pick you up at about 7:50.

You go out that late? That's usually when I put my pajamas on.

The bar doesn't even get hopping until ten.

Maybe this is an exercise in futility. It was. He knew that. He still wanted to meet her.

He didn't warn Lachlan. Which he knew wasn't the best move. But he did it anyway. Because he was past the point of making good decisions. There would be other people from Four Corners at the bar tonight, he was sure that. And for some reason, inviting her made him revise what he had chosen to wear. He stripped off his T-shirt and found a black button-down shirt, put it on with his jeans.

There. He looked a little bit more like he might match up to her now. Not that it was a date. He was just taking her to the bar so that she could see it. He pulled up to her cabin, and the door opened and she rushed outside, almost like she was afraid of what would happen if he had come up those stairs.

She didn't have her shield. Not anymore.

She was wearing a completely respectable dress that fell just above the knee and didn't conform overmuch to her curves. But the problem was, he had seen everything beneath that dress. And even if it wasn't for quite as long as he wanted to see it, he had. And he felt... Well, he felt a lot of things about it. The problem was, he hadn't gotten his fill of her.

He didn't know what it would take to get that.

He really didn't know.

He got out of the truck, because even though she was on her way to him, it was the thing to do. He rounded to the passenger side and opened the door for her. "You look nice," he said.

She looked up at him, her eyes going round. "Thank you. You... You look nice."

"Thank you."

And it was like the air between them had frozen, holding them in place. And there was a moment where he could see leaning in and kissing her. Taking over both of their better senses and walking her up the stairs back into that house. Even though he knew that was what she had been avoiding. Yeah, he sure as hell knew. But if he kissed her, she wouldn't resist. If he kissed her, she would say yes. Because whatever might be logical or real or reasonable, they wanted each other.

But he didn't take that direction. He didn't go that route.

He didn't, because it just wasn't the right thing to do. Not right now.

And she got into the truck and the moment passed. He took a breath. Then he rounded to the other side, got in, and started the engine.

"It's just in town. You've been to town. There isn't much to it."

"Yeah. As far as I can tell, ice cream, a diner... The bar, and then, of course, the grocery store. Which is mostly bait and tackle."

"Not wrong," he said.

"You get most of your food off the ranch, don't you?"

"We have the resources for it. We're hoping to make the ranch a little bit of a destination for that kind of thing. We can sell our own beef in the farm store the Sullivan girls are opening. Mostly, because we're such a huge operation, the Garrets and the Kings sell their stuff to grocery stores farther afield. We're big enough that we can actually go use the USDA weigh station, all of that. Some of the smaller outfits... It isn't worth it. It's expensive to haul your animals all the way over there."

"Yeah. I don't know anything about any of that."

"It's a whole thing."

"But you've always been horses at McCloud, right?"

"Always. Hunter is passionate about the breeding program. That's still his pet project. Me, I just like to work. I don't really care what it is. I do a lot of the construction jobs, the repair jobs. Jack-of-all-trades, master of none. That kind of thing."

"I don't know that I'd go so far as to say you're a master of none…"

The air around them sharpened. "Now, Elizabeth, you told me that you didn't speak double entendre, but if I am not mistaken, that was some great dirty talk."

"I really wasn't trying to. But I guess it was."

She sneaked a look at him from the corner of her eye. He kept his eyes on the road. To the best of his ability.

"It's so weird to be going out. Even when I don't have Benny back at home… I guess it isn't my home anymore. But I mean, back in real life. It's not my real life. That's where we used to be. Even then, it isn't like I went out because he was gone. And now, here I am, exploring the bustling nightlife of Pyrite Falls."

"You are going to be sorely disappointed if you think the nightlife is bustling."

"You go out, though," she said, and he could hear the euphemism in that too.

"Yeah. I do. But I live here. And… I'm not a relationship guy, as we've established."

"You're a sex guy, though," she said.

She surprised him when she was bold. He didn't know why. Because in spite of her smooth appearance, he'd learned she was no shrinking violet. The woman who had weathered the heartbreak that she had, the disappointment. The woman who had moved from home

MAISEY YATES   227

to home as a child. Of course she was tough. Strong. Of course she wasn't afraid. Of course, even though she was reserved in some ways, she was also bold. Why wouldn't she be? She'd had to forge her own way, and she had damn well done it.

He could only be in awe of her.

"Yeah," he said. "I am."

"Hence the bustling-nightlife stuff."

"I guess so. I mean, it's a great way to forge flimsy relationships based on lust and alcohol, and that tends to be my speed."

"Noted."

"Hey, you shouldn't knock it till you've tried it."

"I just don't know how to do it," she said. "And I'm not sure that I could, even if I did. Or that I would want to. My only experience with that kind of thing is… Getting in too deep too fast. Well. Then, there's you. But I suppose that's where it's best left as a one-off."

"Yeah," he said. "That was my thought."

His body disagreed. Vehemently.

Thankfully, right then they pulled up to the front of Smokey's Tavern, which was hopping, because it was getting to be close to the holidays, and people tended to get real sad this time of year, so the alcohol consumption tended to go up. Also, a lot of people's mother-in-laws were probably in town, and they were avoiding them by sitting on the barstools and drinking beers, rather than hanging out at home.

No one could be blamed for that.

"This looks rustic," she said.

"It's Pyrite Falls, Lizzie, everything is rustic." He didn't know where that had come from, and she looked stricken when he said it.

"Elizabeth," she said.

"Sorry."

It wasn't just that she didn't like it, he could see that. It was something more. He wondered if Carter had called her that. That douchebag.

He went around to the passenger side of the truck again, but she was out before he could open the door for her, and then she was walking inside without waiting for him. He caught up to her, holding the door open. "You can't get rid of me that easily."

When he walked inside, the first person he noticed was his brother.

And Lachlan looked at him with an expression on his face that put Brody in the mind of someone who'd been slapped with a mackerel.

He put his hand on Elizabeth's back, and realized he probably shouldn't have done that. But it was too late. He guided her over to where Lachlan sat. "Hey," he said. "I brought Elizabeth with me. She hasn't been here before."

Lachlan arched a brow. "Really."

"Benny is gone. For Christmas break. So it was a good time for her to go out and see the nightlife."

"Which I'm told is bustling," she said.

The bar was packed full of people. You couldn't say it wasn't *bustling*.

It was the damn season, after all, and people had to have their ways of coping.

There were a lot of women there, as usual. Girls dressed up in dresses with shockingly short hems and long sleeves. He liked that look. He always had. But still, no one appealed in the same way that Elizabeth did. Nobody could.

"What would you like to drink?"

"You don't have to buy me a drink."

"I would like to," he said.

"I don't think you should buy me a drink. I think you should buy a drink for one of those women over there. Because they're who you came for. Right?"

He was tempted to say yes. Because after all, that was who he had come for. At least, in theory. Or historically. But truth be told, hooking up tonight had never seemed feasible. And he had brought her for a reason.

"No. They're not why I'm here. Actually, I wasn't really all that into coming out tonight until I thought of inviting you. So. I would like to buy you a drink."

"But why? Because we just talked about the fact that it had to be..." She looked quickly at Lachlan, who was occupied talking to a woman who had just approached him.

"Yeah," he said. "I know what I said. Does that mean that I can't want to be here with you?"

"I suppose not," she said.

"What'll you have?"

"I guess... I don't know. I don't really drink beer. Can you recommend something?"

"Sure. I'll get you one on tap."

"Let me rephrase. I don't know beer at all, so that doesn't even mean anything to me."

"All right. I'll just get you what I'm having." But of course, he revised what he was going to get, making sure to choose something a little bit milder so that it wouldn't be too intense of a taste for her. He brought them back and set them on Lachlan's table. He pulled up an extra chair, and gestured for Elizabeth to have a seat.

At least ten women came over to chat Lachlan up,

and he and Elizabeth didn't really make much conversation. Rather, she just looked at everything happening around them. There was one near brawl, quite a bit of bad line dancing, a lot of people hooking up. Some people taking off their wedding rings.

"People come from other towns," he said, "for that reason."

"That's... Distasteful," she said.

"People are distasteful," he said. "But the fact of the matter is, there's a lot of small towns around here, and if you want a little infidelity, you've got to go a few towns over. Otherwise somebody's going to be on the phone to your wife in five minutes. I mean, you run the risk of that, even coming here. Because you might be over here at the same time one of your wife's friends is over here trying to get lucky."

"This seems complicated."

"It is. I've always kept it easy by not ever being married."

"Yes. Well. That is a lot easier."

"You want to dance?" He didn't know where that had come from. He didn't typically dance. He would, because sometimes a man had to do what a man had to do to get a girl interested in going home with him. Some of them needed the full deal. A hamburger, dance, and then sex.

But he just wanted to dance with her again, like they'd done at the Town Hall. Because he knew now it had been six years since she'd been with another man, so he wondered now if, until their dance, it had been six years since anyone had danced with her. He wondered if that ass Carter had ever taken her to dance at all. If he'd really appreciated what he had with her.

Somebody strong and beautiful and soft all at once.

She was unlike any woman he had ever known. Unlike any person he had ever known, and he was just sure that her dickhead husband had never had a clue what he had. He was stuck on the fact that he had a broken family. That things didn't look normal. Probably in the same way that he was stuck on Elizabeth being from an unconventional background, not realizing that it had made her who she was.

"Oh, I don't need to…"

"It doesn't all have to be about need. Sometimes, it can be about want."

He reached out his hand, and she had to stare at him for a moment before she took it slowly. Lachlan cast a glance at him as he led Elizabeth out to the dance floor.

Mind your own business.

He mouthed that back to his brother.

Who looked away and busied himself weeding through the selection of women who were vying for his attention. Lachlan should be thrilled. Brody taking himself out of the equation for the night meant the bar was his oyster.

He noticed Denver, Justice and Landry King in the corner. Daughtry wasn't here, but he was the only brother with a job off the ranch. A State Trooper, Daughtry was more straight and narrow than his brothers. The brothers? Not at all. And when they separated from the wall, Lachlan's competition was engaged.

There were suddenly half a dozen women headed their direction.

He shook his head.

"Well, it's good for Lachlan to have a little bit of a challenge."

"Oh?"

"The Kings."

He directed her gaze toward the door.

"Right. They are… Something."

He suspected she meant *handsome*. They weren't really Brody's type, but women definitely seemed to like them.

"Yeah. Well. Don't even think about it. Those guys are trouble."

"Again. Pirate cowboy. How are you not trouble?"

"Oh, me too. But I'm trouble you've already gotten in." She laughed, and he pulled her up against his body, moving her in time with the music. "You could've done better, quite frankly," he said, his voice husky.

"Really?"

"Yeah. There's some nice guys around here. Sadly, I'm not one of them."

"You say things like that, and yet you always seem pretty nice to me."

"Don't let that fool you."

"You mean don't let your actions fool me? My experience is that when a man tells you he's nice repeatedly, that's the real red flag."

"Damn. I didn't think you had dated all that much."

"I haven't. But I do live in the world. So I've observed a few things here and there."

"I actually think it's pretty amazing, everything that you've been through. And how… Not cynical you are."

"I'm cynical," she said. "Not all the way through. The thing is, I have to believe that there's goodness in the world, because I'm raising a child that's going to grow up in it. I have to hope that there are good things out there for him. Better things. I can't write off the entirety of humanity, because my son has to go out and live among it. It's kept me from drowning in my own hard feelings too much."

"Makes sense."

Maybe it was more than that. Maybe it had to do with the fact that she had someone else to live for.

Brody had sunken right into selfishness. Because his primary concern was himself. His own comfort. Yet. He was kind of a selfish bastard. If his family knew...

He had grown up sometimes feeling like it was Tag, Lach, Hunter, Gus...and him. Separate. On his own. And if they knew...if they knew what he'd done, that would confirm it.

He clenched his teeth and shut that off.

He was with Elizabeth. And he definitely didn't need to spoil anything by thinking about his father.

Yeah. Definitely not.

The song picked up tempo, and he used his only really good dance move and spun her out, then back into his body. "I'm a one-trick pony. So I hope you enjoyed that."

"I did," she said, smiling.

So at least there was that. At least he'd given her something to smile about. He didn't know why he cared about that so much with her. But he did. He really did. She was just really special and he didn't think anyone had ever treated her like she was. Not to the degree he thought she should be. And something about that felt wrong to him. Especially having grown up being treated like he was special. That he somehow mattered more than his brothers did, or whatever the hell. And feeling like he shouldn't be treated that way at all. And there was Elizabeth… Not getting even a fraction of what she deserved.

And he couldn't help himself. Not even if he tried. But the truth of the matter was, he wasn't trying. He had asked her out, and it was kind of a date. And he wanted to dance with her because he wanted to. Not just because it was what she deserved.

And he didn't want to be one and done, even though it was supposed to be. Even though he'd spent all evening telling himself it had to be.

Benny was gone. For two weeks. They had a chance to do what they wanted to with those two weeks. It made it neat. Gave it a cutoff. Made it something that felt manageable. Made something that seemed doable.

Made it something that maybe they could handle.

So he gave in.

And he kissed her. Right there on the dance floor, right in front of everybody.

They were all consumed in their own potential hookups. And he didn't care even if they did stare. But they wouldn't. Because everybody was out for themselves tonight.

And it turned out so was he.

Except… He was out for her too. And that made it feel different.

Because it wasn't just about hooking up. It was about her. Because she mattered, not just physical pleasure. Not just scratching an itch. That was how it had been. It was how it had been since he had first met her. And he couldn't fight it anymore.

He just couldn't.

She moaned, her body going soft against his as he consumed her lips, drank from them. Took what he'd been fantasizing about, ever since that last time they were together, and amplified it. Made his desire a beast that he could hardly keep a handle on.

He wanted her. He wanted her so damned bad.

And he wanted her to know that. Wanted everybody in the room to know that she was a desirable woman. That all the men in here should be mad that it wasn't her they were going home with. Because she was incredible. She deserved for people to know that.

He sure did. Down to his bones.

He wrapped his arm around her waist, cupped her cheek with his hand.

And he was getting hard. Could hardly control himself. Right there in Smokey's bar, and he really should get a grip. Except the only thing he wanted to get a grip on was her.

He couldn't help it. She was everything he'd ever fantasized about, and a whole hell of a lot of things he hadn't known to fantasize about.

She was singular. There had never been another person in his life that affected him the way that she did.

He just admired her. All that strength. All the everything.

He pulled away from her, and she was breathing hard, her lips swollen from the kiss.

"Brody..."

"Tell me you don't want to," he whispered, his voice rough.

"I can't do that. Because I do want to. It's just that I shouldn't."

"Yeah. I know. But you *should* be with your son for Christmas, and the man who married you *should* have understood you. *Should* have wanted to stay with you.

And my dad shouldn't have been such a dick. So here we are, saddled with a whole lot of things that shouldn't be. Saddled with a whole lot of bullshit. So we can have something that we want. Because I really, really want you, and I tried to talk myself out of it. I'm trying to be logical. I don't have any logic where you're concerned Elizabeth. But I do have two weeks. Two weeks."

Her breath seemed to escape her body in a rush. "Yes. Yes. We can… Take me home?"

"Finally."

He turned and looked at his brother, who was definitely staring at them. And gave him a wave.

Because he was going home with Elizabeth Colfax. Thank the good Lord.

CHAPTER FIFTEEN

IT WAS A MISTAKE. She knew that it was a mistake. She was already a whole lot more attached to him than she should be. Already a lot more attached to him then she had ever intended to be. And now she was going to sleep with him again. Maybe a lot of agains.

But she was just so sad. She had been ever since Benny left, and she was trying to be logical about all of it but she just was having a really hard time.

Brody was gorgeous, and he made her want to feel, not think. He made her want to escape the dead zone that was her heart at the moment because everything just felt so difficult. He was the kind of hard she wanted. Hot and muscular and burning for her.

She needed that. Because today had felt like one long rejection, and even if it wasn't, this, this man being drawn to her, wanting her, needing her, that meant something. It meant so much. It meant more than she could ever put into words.

"Brody…" She said his name as soon as they exited the tavern, and then she found herself getting pressed up against the side of the building as he kissed her. And it was so hot and wild and unlike anything she had ever experienced. She had never made out with a man in public. They had gone around the back of the barn that time, and that had been the closest she'd ever come. But they were just a few feet from the door, and he was plundering her mouth without any shame. Owning what they were about to do.

And it made her feel giddy. Free.

How much of her life had she spent folding in on herself? Making herself smaller. Making herself acceptable, because that was what you had to do when every situation in your life had been based on someone else allowing you there because of their good graces.

That was foster care. Even when it was good. Somebody was benevolent, so they were letting you live with them. That had been what it felt like the entire time she was with a man that she had thought was too good for her. The entire time. That she had to be on her best behavior, that she had to do the right thing. The best things. That she always had to dress a certain way and talk a certain way and act a certain way, and that she could never betray where she had come from.

This was low-class behavior.

Her mother-in-law would call it that for sure. Carter probably would too. Ashley would probably, literally, clutch her pearls.

There was a time when Elizabeth would have also, but not so much because it shocked her. Because she thought that clutching her pearls was what she was supposed to do.

Frankly, she felt sorry for Ashley, who wouldn't know what this was like.

Right now Elizabeth didn't have to care. She wasn't responsible for another human being for an entire two weeks. All she was responsible for was her own self. She could cook whatever she wanted. Eat whatever she wanted. Have dessert.

And tonight, Brody was going to be her dessert. For the next two weeks, she was going to indulge in him like he was a carton of ice cream.

The perfect place to drown her feelings.

She was so here for it.

And so she let him kiss her like that, in full view of everybody, felt his erection as he pressed against her, hard and glorious, and the memory of it made her shiver.

Yes. She wanted him. She wanted this.

More than anything.

She wrapped her arms around his neck, and pressed her breasts hard against his chest, arching into him.

He groaned, his hand sliding down her back, down to cup her ass.

"I can't wait," he said.

"You can't wait?"

It was cold outside, but she was hot because of him.

"Come on, get in the truck."

"The truck?"

"Yes," he said.

They got in and started the engine, and he didn't drive them back toward the ranch, rather he took a dirt road right next to the tavern, and drove up just a little ways, before going into the thick of the trees.

He reached into the back of the truck and pulled out a bunch of blankets. "Come on."

"What?"

She got out of the truck, and went around to the back. He dropped the tailgate down, and piled the blankets back in it.

"It is freezing," she said.

"That's with the blankets are for."

"Please tell me they're clean blankets," she said.

"Scout's honor. I have not touched anyone else since you arrived at this ranch."

"You've brought women here, though," she said.

"I don't remember," he said. "I mean, I have. But I don't remember it. I can't think of anything right now. Anything but you."

And then she decided to go ahead and ignore the truth of any of it. Maybe he meant that, maybe he didn't. Maybe he said that to every woman he put in the back of his pickup truck, but she wanted to be here. Wanted to be here with him.

It was dark. And she had kind of wanted to see him. But this wasn't going to be just one time. Two weeks. They had two weeks.

She sat on the blankets, and he knelt next to her, kissing her, reaching around and undoing the zipper on her dress. It fell away from her body, the night air biting into her skin. It was cold enough for snow. Suddenly, she didn't really care. Logic wasn't leading this train. Not remotely.

He leaned in and kissed her neck. And she shivered. "I want you so much," he whispered.

And she was hot then. She had never done this. Sex in the back of the truck. Sex in any vehicle. She had never been wild for anyone before. And Carter had certainly never been wild for her. Not like this. She undid the top button on his shirt. Then the next one. And the next one. Her only complaint about the choice of venue was that she couldn't see him all that well.

You will. When you do it again.

That gave her the encouragement to take it slow. To take her time. She moved her fingertips over his chest, down his stomach, and she felt him sucking a sharp breath when she made it to the waistband of his jeans.

She pushed his shirt off his shoulders, and while he went to work on his jeans and boots, she got rid of her shoes, her underwear. She shivered again, and he pulled her up against the whole length of his body. She wrapped her legs around his waist, as he brought her over the top of him, and lay back flat on the blankets. She let her head fall back, her hair touching the middle of her back, his hands moving up and down her spine, his thumbs brushing her hipbones, teasing just around the edges of where she ached for him the most.

He moved his hands up to cup her breasts, teasing her nipples. It felt so good. He felt so good. She could hardly stand it.

She had often thought that she might die a death by a thousand cuts. Little indignities and humilities that she had suffered all throughout her life. But it had never once occurred to her that she might die of pleasure.

Brody McCloud made a case for that.

She lowered her head and kissed him, kissed his chest, kissed down his stomach. She made it down to the thick length of his arousal and desire arced through her. She had never done this before.

The reality was, her sex life with Carter just hadn't been very adventurous. They'd known what they'd known, and that was about it. And...

She had never felt overly invested in experimenting with him.

Because that just hadn't been the focus of the relationship for her.

She skimmed her lips over his hard shaft, and he cursed, pushing his fingers through her hair. She took the broad tip of him into her mouth, and then sucked him in deep.

She was surprised how much it turned her on. His own response, the helpless groan that came from him, the way that he held tight to her hair. But also just... Him. The way he smelled, the way he tasted. She wanted everything. Absolutely everything. She worked him like that, bringing her hands in when her jaw began to ache, pleasuring him until he was swearing, until his hold on her hair was punishingly tight.

"Not yet," he said, pulling her away from him and drawing her up his body. "Not like that. Not like that."

"Well, *someday* like that."

"Sure. We have two weeks. But that's not how I need you right now."

He positioned her over the blunt head of his arousal, and she rocked her hips back, sinking down slowly onto him, taking him inside of her inch by inch.

She let her head fall back, and she looked up at the stars, at the crisp white moon, everything so clear and bright and cold. The silhouettes of the pines an inky black against the velvet blue of that winter sky.

And Brody filled her. As the cold air filled her lungs.

She gripped his shoulders as she started to move her hips in rhythm with her desire.

She wanted this man. So much. And she was having him.

She was suddenly wholly in her body. In the moment.

Whatever else happened today didn't matter. Only this. Only the way he made her feel. Only the way he amped up the desire in her. Because he did. And it was beautiful. Perfect. Just like him. She rode him until her thigh muscles started to shake, until her orgasm rolled through her like a thunderclap. Then he growled, holding on to her tightly, flipping their positions and laying her down on the soft blankets, positioning himself between her legs and thrusting back inside.

He went hard. Fast. She couldn't catch her breath. It was glorious. The only sound was them and that clear quiet wilderness. Their need. Their desire. As if it was the only thing that mattered on earth. As if it was the only thing that was real. And everything else was a dream.

She felt a climax begin to build inside of her again. And she held on to his forearms, her fingernails digging into his skin as he roared out his release, the same moment she found hers.

"Brody," she said, his name making it real. His name a spell. An incantation to keep the moment going. To make sure she didn't have to be outside it.

She desperately didn't want to lose this. Lose him. She desperately wanted it all. Everything. Everything.

He shifted, pulling one of the fuzzy blankets over the top of them, and holding her against him, kissing her head.

"We can't fall asleep out here," she mumbled. "Oh gosh. I would be a headline. 'Single mom gets freaky in the backwoods and freezes to death after illicit romp.'"

"Would that be the headline?"

"Yes. Whenever possible, women are *mothers* in headlines."

"Why do you suppose that is?"

"I don't know. To make it matter more? To make people feel bad? In this case, it would be to make my actions all the more shocking. I clearly should never have done anything so irresponsible, since I have a child."

"Well. For the next two weeks the only person you have to please is you. I promise I won't let you freeze to death."

"I appreciate that."

"I try to be a considerate lover."

"Keeping me from freezing to death really is expanding things."

Her heart was beating so hard, like it was trying to jump out of her chest. She loved it. Loved this.

She held on to him for a moment, her hands pressed against his chest as their breathing returned to normal.

Then he kissed her on the top of the head, and sat them both up. "We better hunt for clothes, or we really are going to become a cautionary tale."

She put her underwear back on. Put the dress back on. And for the first time in six years, the dress didn't feel... Like her. Her clothes didn't feel like they belonged to her. Which was crazy. Because of course they did. They were the only things she'd had for six years. And they had been so much a part of her identity. That woman who looked sophisticated and classic, and rich. Even though she wasn't any of those things.

They didn't fit her now. Not now. Not the woman who'd had crazy sex in the back of a pickup truck with Brody McCloud.

He'd called her Lizzie.

She pushed that away.

He got dressed too, and they got back in the truck. He settled a blanket over her lap as he started the engine.

She snuggled into it.

"Will you come back to my place?"

"Yes," he said, without hesitation.

She had a feeling that was momentous for him. But

she didn't ask about it. Instead she thought she'd give something to him.

"I took these clothes. In the divorce. And I have taken really good care of them, because there's no way that I could ever afford to buy clothes this nice again."

"Oh."

"What?"

"It just explains some things."

"Like what?"

"Why they don't really look like you. I made a lot of assumptions about you, based on those clothes. But I don't think… They're not really you, are they?"

"No. I wanted to be… I wanted to be something different than what I was. My…"

Tears gathered in her eyes. She didn't know why she was telling him this. Didn't know why she was even mentioning it at all, except he had called her Lizzie.

"My name isn't Elizabeth."

"What?"

"Well, that isn't true. It *is*. You know, you can change your name to anything. And when you get married, your name doesn't just *change*. You have to change it, and it seemed like a good time for me to change my first name too. Because I'd been going by *Elizabeth* for a long time."

"What was your name then?"

"Lizzie. Just Lizzie. No Elizabeth. But it sounded so… Sounded like the name a teenager might give to her kid. Which is exactly what it was. It wasn't a real name. Not to me. It just made me feel different. Of course, most people assumed it was a nickname. But there were lots of times when grown-ups would ask me if it was short for Elizabeth, and I'd have to say no.

And see how mystified they were by that. Because it's usually a nickname."

"Yeah. But that doesn't mean there's anything wrong with it. It doesn't mean there was ever anything wrong with you."

"I don't see how that can be true," she said. "Because it sure feels like there is. It sure feels like there always has been. Things got a lot easier for me when I became Elizabeth Colfax. And not Lizzie Barton."

"Is that why you kept his name?"

"No. I kept his name so that I would have the same last name as Benny. But I realized when Ashley introduced herself to you the other day just how weird it is. I don't especially like being connected to them. Not because they're awful. They aren't. Just because… You know, it's all those connections. I don't think I have my own life, Brody. I really don't."

"Can I call you Lizzie?"

"Sometimes," she said, her chest getting tight.

"I'll call you that. And nobody else will. So there you go. That's your own life. Something no one even knows about. The name no one else is allowed to use. And you like it, because when I say it, I'll be making you come."

She throbbed between her legs. She couldn't help it. How did he make her feel things in her heart, and in intimate places, all at the same time?

Because they're all intimate places. That's how.

That was a sobering thought, and one she didn't particularly want to latch on to.

"Let's go home, Lizzie."

And she was glad to hear him say that.

CHAPTER SIXTEEN

WHEN HE WOKE UP, the ceiling was unfamiliar. And he could honestly say that had never happened before.

He did not spend the night with women. They didn't spend the night with him. It had never happened. But they'd gone back to Elizabeth's—Lizzie's—cabin, and he'd spent the whole night making love to her in that bed. And then he'd fallen asleep, holding her close to his body, listening to her heartbeat until sleep had taken him too.

Hell.

He got up and looked around the room. He grimaced when he saw his jeans. It was sweatpants o'clock. But, he hadn't brought anything with him, so it couldn't be helped. He put his jeans on and went out into the kitchen and started a pot of coffee. Then he hunted through the fridge, took out some eggs and bacon, and set them on the counter. It didn't take long for him to hunt down basic biscuit ingredients. He was a grown-ass man. He knew how to throw together a biscuit. He had lived by himself for a lot of years.

He put the biscuit dough together, made little balls from them and popped them into the oven, then started scrambling eggs, a dish towel draped over his shoulder. He was whistling, because he was in a great mood, because he'd had sex so many times last night he'd lost count. And what man wouldn't be in a good mood about that?

And sure, it had something to do with her. Of course it did. It couldn't be all about her, then not be about her. It was definitely about her. She was everything.

That reverberated uncomfortably in his chest as he whisked the eggs and poured them into the frying pan.

The bacon was sizzling away on the back burner, and Elizabeth came out wearing a fluffy white bathrobe, her blond hair a complete disaster.

"Is that bacon?"

"Yes ma'am," he said.

She stood there staring at him. "Did I have so much sex that my brain is short-circuiting and I'm having insane pornographic fantasies during the day now?"

"How is this pornographic?" he asked. "I'm just shirtless."

"You're cooking breakfast. I could have an orgasm just thinking about that."

"I'm happy to watch."

"How about you watch me over coffee instead?"

"I mean, I'd rather watch you come, but whatever."

She turned pink and walked over to the cabinet where the mugs were.

She took out two. And poured two cups.

She handed one to him. Then she leaned against the counter and continued to watch him cook. The oven timer dinged, and he went over and pulled out the biscuits.

"You did not make biscuits," she said.

"I did. I've lived alone for a long time, and I don't believe in starving."

"But you just… Made biscuits. Even I just buy a can."

"What do you mean, *even you*? That sounds sexist, Elizabeth. And frankly I'm shocked."

"I don't think you are," she said.

"You're right. I'm not. Not even a little bit."

And suddenly, her blue eyes looked misty. "I just can't… I can't remember the last time somebody cooked me breakfast."

"Well, it was my pleasure."

And he meant it. All the way down to his soul. He meant it.

She took a sip of coffee and sighed, and he watched as her eyes lingered on the Christmas tree.

"Did you do Christmas with him yet?"

She shook her head. "I thought I'd wait and see what Carter got him for Christmas. Is that petty?"

He shrugged. "Does it matter if it is?"

"For the first time in years, thanks to McCloud's, I can actually spend big on Christmas, and Carter took him, so…"

"You're going to make sure that you get him the best gift. Makes sense to me."

"It isn't honorable."

"Who cares? I mean, seriously, who cares? You aren't going to tell Benny that's what you're doing. And it isn't the only reason you want to get him a nice present."

She wrinkled her nose. "No. Of course not. Of course it isn't."

By the time breakfast was completely ready, they were both on their second cups of coffee. Sitting around the tiny table in the space between the kitchen and living room. It was a strange kind of intimacy he had never engaged in before. Mornings. He didn't do them. Never had. And this was something even more different, because it was more than an awkward see-you-later.

More than he had imagined a morning with a woman could be. It was companionable. Which was a really strange thing. But it was… Nice.

Or maybe that was the bacon. It was tough to say.

"Do you have any plans for the rest of this…time?" he asked.

"No," she said. "It turns out I don't actually have a life. I mean, not outside those regular things that I do. Work. Benny. I'm either busy being an equine therapist or I'm busy being a mother. I don't know what I'm going to do, being not busy."

She took a sip of coffee. "We can't just have sex," she said.

But it was almost question.

"I mean… We could," he said.

"I think at a certain point it becomes a chafing issue, Brody. Though I'm not an expert."

"Chafing. Please. That feels like an alarming lack of faith in my skill level."

"Far be it for me to impugn your masculinity. Which I am happy to report is healthy. Extremely healthy."

"Well. Glad you realize that."

"I had this conversation with a friend. I mean, I told her that she should cook dinner for herself. Whatever she wanted. And she had such a hard time with that, because thinking around the restrictions that had been imposed on her life by her ex-husband were difficult, even though she wasn't with him anymore. I don't know how to think around the restrictions that I've put on my own life. The things that I let myself do. The things that I let myself be…"

"I don't know," he said. "Sounds like life to me. In that… We all put limits on ourselves, don't we? It's what makes you not a giant asshole. My dad didn't have any limits on himself as far as I can tell. He did whatever he wanted, hurt whoever he wanted… He was just… I've always put limits on myself. I work when I'm feeling restless and… Go out when it's time to do that." And he put limits on the interactions that he had with women… Except this one. Right now.

It had a time limit though. He didn't even have to impose one. He didn't have to worry about it. Because Benny would be back just after New Year's, and everything would end organically. This was it. This was the chance. And yeah, maybe after that, they could have some other school breaks. But it would probably be easier to just let it go. After they had this time.

Made perfect sense to him.

"Well, since you're skeptical about the sex-all-day thing… We could go do something."

Also, she could do things without him. He didn't know why he was inserting himself into this.

"Like?"

"There's a town about an hour and a half away. Copper Ridge? They do a big Christmas thing every year. I've never been, because obviously I hate that kind of thing."

"You hate that kind of thing, but you're inviting me to go?"

"If you want to. Because somebody ought to take you to do something, Elizabeth. That's just how I feel about it."

"Are you taking me on a date?"

"I think we went on a date last night," he said.

"Yes," she said. "You bought me one beer and I put out spectacularly."

"But I made you breakfast. And now I'm offering to take you to a cute and very lame—in my opinion—town. So I think it evens out."

"Yeah. Okay. Because this is... This is make-believe, right? Like... Maybe this is what I would be doing if my life were different. Maybe I would've had a series of sexy cowboys in my bed, and dive bars, and cute Christmas events."

"Maybe."

"All right. Let's do it."

"I better go get some new clothes."

"I'll be ready in an hour."

"Sounds good."

THE HOUR GAVE her time to catch her breath and to take a shower by herself, even though she thought about Brody the whole time. Every time a voice in her head asked her what the heck they were doing, she shoved it aside. This was just... It didn't need to be anything. That was her problem. She was always trying to start new initiatives, make declarations, start as she meant to go on and things like that. It didn't have to be that. This could just be what was happening right now. And it didn't have to mean anything more, and it didn't have to be anything more. It could just be a day in Copper Ridge. It could just be a night of sex.

And maybe another night of sex. Because she certainly didn't intend to *not* sleep with him again. She was in the house by herself, so why wouldn't she? Seemed perfectly reasonable to her.

It genuinely did. She got out of the shower and blow-dried her hair as quickly as possible and looked woefully at her closet, which wasn't fulfilling her needs at the moment. But she found a navy blue dress, some heavy leggings, and a red plaid coat. She put on red lipstick to match and felt a little bit edgier than she did sometimes. And she welcomed that. Because she felt different. And she was ready for different. She was ready to stopped clinging to that old life. Because that's what it was. Clinging to that old life.

She sighed heavily, and took one last look in the mirror before heading back to the living room. Where she stared out the window waiting for Brody to come back. When he did, he was in black jeans, a black wool coat, and a black cowboy hat, and the sight of him looking like an outlaw made her stomach do tricks.

He was just so damn sexy.

She had never obsessed over the sexiness of a man before in her entire life.

He was glorious.

Something new and different. A gift. An indulgence, and at the same time… He could never be anything quite so simplistic. Because that implied that she had control over him, and she didn't. Brody was his own man. Brody called the shots. Pretty unequivocally.

The man undid her.

The smell of his skin, whatever soap he used, spicy and masculine and enticing. What she wanted to do was bury her face in his chest and tell him to forget it. Forget the cute small town, forget her concerns about chafing. You only live once. She would rather go down in flames in the end.

Except, better sense prevailed, and she decided they needed to do something other than sleep together.

"You ready?"

"Almost."

She leaned in, stretched up on her toes and kissed him on the mouth.

He moaned, and the sound was intoxicating. Sent a shiver through her entire body.

"Yes. Now I'm ready."

"Super glad we decided to go out," he said.

They walked to his truck and got inside.

"It's out toward the coast. Right on the ocean. Really pretty."

"Oh. That's even more exciting," she said.

"Yeah, the Garrets have kin over there. That's where Wolf met his wife. You haven't met Wolf yet, not formally, I don't think."

"I don't think so. I would definitely remember meeting somebody named Wolf."

"Yeah. People tend to remember him. Women especially."

"Well now, Brody. I'd say you sound a little bit possessive there."

She didn't know what pushed her to say that. Normally, she would be too insecure to say something like that. She was a woman whose husband had left her for another woman. Who had gotten that other woman pregnant. She hadn't had the highest sense of self-esteem for the past few years.

"Hell yeah," Brody said, and it thrilled her down to

her toes. "If Wolf weren't happily married I wouldn't let him within a ten-mile radius of you."

"That's extremely unenlightened."

"I never claimed to be. Though I have to say, I've never been particularly possessive before."

"I make you feel possessive?"

"Whatever this is… For as long as it is… It's different."

Her breath hitched, her heart speeding up.

"Yes," she agreed, looking out the window as they pulled off the dirt road onto the main highway.

The road to Copper Ridge was beautiful. The dense trees and the ferns beneath them were dusted with ice and snow, which faded as they made their way toward the coast, where the weather was just a little bit milder. They made easy conversation, this time not about groundbreaking things, like her real name or his father. Just about little things, like favorite desserts and foods, but she realized that there were deep truths underlying those topics as well. Because neither of them had had a traditional family, and the things they enjoyed were revealing. From her particular delight in real orange juice instead of powdered juice or Kool-Aid, to the chocolate chip cookies that his brother's friend Charity made.

"I can still remember that first time I had a cookie like that," he said. "Fresh-baked and warm, right out of the oven. I think I was twenty-five."

"Really? You never had a homemade cookie before then?"

"No. Back then, we didn't do the town hall meetings or anything like that. Back then, things between the families had grown pretty contentious. So during our childhoods… We didn't share things the way that we do now. Hell, now I get baked goods more often than I should."

"It must've been very different here, the generation before you guys."

"Very different. A hell of a lot of narcissists were running this place. And now… Well, there's the Kings. And their whole thing. I wouldn't say anybody is particularly close to them, and they tend to be more insular than the rest of us. But… It's still better. Still different. We take care of each other. We are family. All of us."

"I love that. Especially as somebody who had spare little family growing up. I've depended on other definitions of *family*. Extended family. I've depended on different ways that you can build something good. Even off of a foundation that isn't."

He shrugged. "I guess that's what we do."

"People are kind of amazing," she said softly. "We do just keep hoping. We do just keep trying."

He cleared his throat. "Yes."

Right then, they pulled off the highway and turned onto a narrower street. And she could see the ocean, out to the left, gray and vast. And before them was the most adorable town she'd ever seen. The buildings bright white and merry cranberry colors. Lights and greenery all over the place. There was a big banner strung across the street that proudly proclaimed Victorian Christmas Weekends every weekend until Christmas. There were carolers walking down the street wearing period dress, and she rolled down the window so that she could hear them singing "God Rest Ye Merry Gentlemen." The wind was cold and biting, but milder than it had been inland. The air was damp with that salty tang that let you know you were near the sea. She let her head fall back against the seat, and she smiled.

Of all the things she had imagined for herself this Christmas, this wasn't one of them. But it was a lot better than she had thought it would be. A lot better than she had thought it could be.

She spotted a bakery, and was instantly interested in that.

"I think we should go get some cookies," she said.

He grinned. "Let's see if I can find some parking."

It proved to be pretty difficult to find a place to park, and they had to go against the curb all the way down at the end of Main Street. The town was bustling, full of people enjoying the carolers, the roasted chestnuts, the free apple cider.

And as they got out of the truck and started down the street, she had this wonderful realization that nobody there knew who they were. Nobody knew anything about her past, nobody knew that Brody wasn't the kind of guy that was ever going to offer a commitment. Nobody knew that they weren't together. Nobody knew that all they were doing was passing time in bed.

And this beautiful man, who stood out on this crowded street of people, could've been hers. As far as anyone here knew.

This was a moment out of time. A chance to get lost in fantasy.

Her heart clenched.

You know better than that.

She did. But was it so bad if underlying the fantasy, she kept it real? That she was real with herself about the fact that this would come to an end? She knew that it would. It would never be forever. Because it was always going to be too good to be real.

She wasn't the kind of girl who got this life.

She had things. Wonderful things. The house at McCloud's Landing. The job.

And Benny, most of all. The chance to be a mother when she had never really gotten to have one.

The chance to have family when she had been denied that in so many other ways in her life.

It might not be conventional, but she had. It wasn't that she didn't have a wonderful life filled with brilliant things. It was just...

For a while when she had been young, she had fantasized that a man could really love her. Forever.

It didn't matter that Carter hadn't been her fantasy. She could accept that now. She had liked Carter so much. She had a crush on him. She had loved him as much as she could have then, with everything she knew.

But she hadn't really understood what she wanted from a sexual partner, from a life partner, from a husband, from the father of her child.

And while Carter was fine, with the perspective she had now, he wouldn't be the top pick in any of those arenas. Too bad, since he was Benny's father, and nothing could be done about that. But as for the rest... She didn't want it back. She honestly hadn't, ever since they had divorced. She had wanted certain things back. The simplicity, the house, the horses. But not him. Just the things that he represented, and that was what she realized right then.

He'd been a symbol. And that was all. Brody wasn't a symbol. He was the only man she wanted. He was the man she wanted to be walking down the street with.

She was proud to be walking with him. So just for the moment, she wanted to pretend. And why not? This moment was like a snow globe. Safely ensconced in a magical world. Nothing outside it. Nothing that could touch it.

Once they stepped outside the bounds of it, reality would creep back in. But for now, it didn't have to.

And it was like he read her mind, because suddenly he clasped his big, warm hand around hers. And they were holding hands like they were a real couple. Not just a couple of people having sex. She looked up at him, and he caught her eye, before looking away for a moment. She smiled, even though he wasn't looking at her anymore.

They walked into the bakery, and the smell of sugar and butter filled her nose, and she smiled even wider. And there were cookies. Fresh-baked chocolate chip cookies.

"I think you need some," she said.

"I have a favorite cookie," he said. "Maybe I need to try some pie."

"Okay. Fair. May I pose the question—why not cookies and pie?"

"Listen to your girlfriend," the redheaded woman behind the counter said.

"I suppose I will," Brody replied.

She knew that he was just playing along. Knew that he was just doing his best not to make it weird. She didn't care. It made her feel like she was floating.

They sat down in the little shop with three pieces of pie and a little bag full of cookies that they were saving for later. "Which one is best?"

"So far," he said, "as I've only tried one, the caramel apple."

She snagged a bite and moaned. "That is good." Then she quickly took a piece of the pumpkin pie.

"I thought the pie was mine," he said.

"No. We're sharing."

"This is why I like being alone," he said. "I don't like to share."

"You'll share with me," she said smiling.

They finished eating and continued on down the street, Brody holding her hand still, and her holding the cookies.

There was a little boutique, and she couldn't resist stopping inside, considering she had a yearning for some new clothes. She grabbed a sweaterdress, and a couple of other things, and Brody milled around awkwardly at the front.

"Have you ever waited while a woman has gone clothes shopping before?"

"Not a once," he said.

"Well. Enjoy. Just be grateful I didn't ask you to hold my purse."

"Hey," he said. "I'll do it. I don't mind holding your purse."

"You can just hold the cookies," she said.

She was just about to duck into the changing room when she saw a little rack with lingerie right next to them.

A little thrill shot through her system.

She had never really done lingerie before. Hadn't actually seen the point of it. Of undressing just to go get dressed up into new underwear, and coming back out and it… It had always seemed very self-conscious.

But just then, she didn't care about the logistics. It wasn't about that. It was about trying to channel feelings about herself, her body, her sexuality, that she'd never had before.

About it being hers, about her body being sufficient to turn a guy on. Yeah. She liked that thought. She grabbed a white lace nightgown, and a red bodysuit.

She ducked into the dressing room and examined the flimsy garment. She was thinking it looked like way too much trouble when she saw that the bottom… Well, the… It just wasn't there. It was completely open.

Her face went hot. But hey, that was one way to solve an undressing problem when things were heated.

She took the perfectly acceptable sweaterdress, a pair of sweater leggings and an oversize black top, and a rather sexy black dress, and held them over the top of the lingerie before heading to the front of the store to check out.

Fortunately, he didn't seem to notice what all she had gotten.

"Thank you," she said.

"No problem."

He took a shopping bag from her hands. "I'm full-service."

The way he grinned at her was so wicked that it made that place between her legs throb. "Well, I already knew that," she said.

"But did you know that also extended to pack mule duties?"

"That's news," she said, feeling breathless.

She picked up a few other things. Some Christmas decorations and some items for her kitchen.

And Brody carried all of it. By the late afternoon,

they were ready for lunch and stopped at a little stand right on the beach for some fish-and-chips. They piled her shopping bags on the top of a picnic table and sat across from each other, him making liberal use of her tartar sauce, and her using half the bottle of malt vinegar on the fish.

There was a strange, faraway look on his face all of a sudden as he looked past her out to the ocean.

"What?"

"Nothing. It's... I never leave McCloud's. I mean, not that I never have. It's just..."

"What?"

"I don't actually think you want to hear this."

"You don't get to decide what I want to hear."

"It doesn't speak well of me."

"I don't care," she said. "I didn't think we were worried about things like that. I thought we just said things. Because whatever this is... It is what it is, right? And I can't go on forever. You don't need to impress me. The same as I don't need to impress you. Unless the rules change, in which case I'm going to feel awfully embarrassed."

The corner of his mouth hitched. Then he let out a breath.

"I go out of town sometimes to hit different Western bars. Hook up. Stuff like that. I guess, especially when I was in my twenties, you could call some of the stuff I did... A bender. Get drunk, hop beds, don't remember what happened, don't remember anyone's name, barely even remember your own name. That kind of thing. But I can't remember the last time I went somewhere just to be there. And I wasn't drunk, and I wasn't trying to forget something."

Her chest felt sore.

"Really? That's the only reason you've ever traveled?"

He was quiet for a beat. "Yes. The only reason. Mostly, I just work. Hard labor kind of exhausts the demons right out of you. There's something cathartic about that. Ten-dollar word. I bet you didn't think I knew that one. Just goes to show you, you can get a pretty good education in that little one-room schoolhouse."

"I appreciate that," she said.

She stole a French fry out of his basket. He took one out of hers.

"Today was fun," he said.

It was such a simple admission. And one she had a feeling meant a lot.

"When was the last time you got to know anyone?"

"I can't even remember. Not really getting to know them. Nothing real." He cleared his throat. "Anyway. Don't tell my brothers that I enjoyed the day in the cutesy little town, please? Because they will spend the rest of my life making me pay for that."

"Scout's honor," she said.

For all of his beauty, for all of his easy manner, she sensed a profound sadness in Brody. She didn't know why she hadn't been insightful enough to see it right away. Because now… She couldn't not see it. There was a heaviness that he carried, and it ate at her. And he had done so much for her. From cooking her breakfast to bringing her here. Carrying her bags. Giving her multiple orgasms. Restoring her confidence in herself. It… It hadn't even occurred to her to do something for him. Because she was on a journey of self-discovery, and she was loving it. But Brody wasn't an inanimate object that she could buy like a sweaterdress to symbolize a new lease on life. Brody was a man. And he was bringing his own baggage to this equation. And there were aspects of it that were new to him too. Maybe not the sex in the back of a pickup truck, but the talking. The connecting. Doing things just for the sake of doing them.

He worked. And he played his way to oblivion.

But she sensed that Brody McCloud had never just… lived. He'd never just existed. He'd never just sat and felt comfortable with who he was.

She had the feeling that he… That he might not like himself very much. When she looked at him, she saw the most amazing, beautiful, wonderful man she had ever known…

That is getting a little bit deep, Elizabeth.

Yeah. It was.

Maybe she needed to walk that back, but she knew it would end. She did.

So what was wrong with acknowledging that he was wonderful? He certainly wouldn't do it.

She remembered his Christmas story. That heart-wrenching, horrible Christmas story. His father burning all of the gifts.

What must it have been like? To be the one who didn't get that kind of abuse, but who must feel marked by it, all the same?

There were a lot of different kinds of abuse. She knew it well, not just because of her job as a therapist, but because of her time spent in foster care. She had met children who were neglected—like her. The kind of benign lack of care that could lead easily to death, even though it wasn't a thoughtful, active cruelty. She had seen kids scarred by physical abuse. Kids that had been worn down by ugly words. And she knew… She knew that it all left a distinct pattern of scars. If not on your skin, beneath it. And that everybody healed from it differently. Or didn't, as the case may be. She knew that Brody had scars. He might not wear them on his skin, but they were there.

She wanted to do something for him. She wanted to do something to help fix him.

She just wished she knew how.

"We might want to start heading back," he said. "The road is bound to get a little bit slippery tonight. It's supposed to get down to freezing over in Pyrite Falls."

"Okay," she said. "Let's head back, then."

They gathered up their trash and threw it in the nearby can, some lingering seagulls looking disappointed that there weren't any leftovers for them.

Then they walked all the way down the street to where they had parked.

The carolers were singing "Hark the Herald Angels Sing," and she started humming, and carried it on until they were in the truck, headed back down the road.

"I don't know that song," he said.

"Really?"

"No. I know a couple of Christmas songs. But not really…"

"Oh. I know a lot. From school, mostly. And Christmas specials. And the Allreds used to take us to church."

"Yeah. I never went to church. My mom had a rosary, and some stuff with saints? She was kind of into that. But… No. We never went to church. My dad would've caught on fire before he ever made it in the door."

"My dad's in prison," she said. "At least, that's what

my caseworker told me one time. Vehicular manslaughter. He was driving under the influence and he hit a pedestrian. It was just one of the many things that he did that hurt people. At least, that's my understanding. It happened really soon after I was born. I think my parents only lived together for a couple of months of my life. Things went downhill for my mom after that. She quit being able to take care of me. She was really young. Seventeen, maybe? Somewhere around there. That was what the caseworker told me. She tried. For a while."

She looked out the window.

"And when she didn't try?"

"She forgot to feed me. Or… Stay home with me? I guess used to just leave me. It was when she started staying away for a couple of days at a time that the neighbors noticed. I got removed from her care for the first time when I was four months old. And I went back and forth for years."

"I'm sorry."

"There's a lot of different ways to hurt people," she said. "They don't all require fists. Or fire."

He didn't say anything. The only sound was the tires on the road.

He knew she was right. Because he had secrets… secrets that would hurt his brothers. More than fire ever could. Elizabeth had shared so much of herself. And it all revealed her to be even more of what he already believed her to be.

Brave and humble and perfect.

His secrets weren't like that.

She wouldn't peel back his layers to find a better man. She'd just find a mess.

She went back to humming Christmas songs.

And that was mostly it for the rest of the drive.

Brody decided to go back to his place that night. Because he didn't figure spending the night with her tonight was a great idea. But he was regretting that.

He was wishing… He was wishing that he'd stayed with her, but it was ten thirty, and he knew it was damn well too late to be headed over, because it would look like a booty call. And it would've been.

She had been confused when he'd told her he'd have dinner at his place.

He felt like a dick.

No *ifs*, *ands*, or *butts* about it.

He got in his truck and drove over to Smokey's. Not because he was going to hook up. But because he was keeping himself from driving over to Elizabeth's.

The place was packed out. December twenty-third malaise filled the air.

Filled with all kinds of people who didn't want to deal with the holidays, including his brother.

Charity was also there, though, looking frail and pale.

"Hey," Brody said, pulling out a chair and sitting down next to them. "You okay?"

"I spent all day at the ER with my dad," she said. "I just don't know how much longer he's going to last."

Brody knew that Charity's father was the only parent she had.

That their relationship was extremely close.

He couldn't imagine what it was like to have a good parent like that, and be on the verge of losing them. He and Lachlan might not have parents to speak of, really, but that didn't mean he dismissed the connection that other people had with theirs.

"I'm sorry."

"I'm just exhausted. Dad has to spend the night in the hospital, and I couldn't bear being there anymore. Plus I had to go back and do a checkup on one of dad's patients."

Lachlan touched Charity's shoulder. "I took her out for a commiseration beer."

"Well. Well deserved. I'll buy you one if you end up wanting another."

"Where's your girl at?" Lachlan asked.

Charity looked interested in that statement.

Brody tried to look innocent. "Don't know what you're talking about."

"Oh," Lach said, tapping his chin and feigning like he was trying to solve a math problem. "The woman you left with last night? Who also happens to work at our ranch?"

"I know who you mean. I object to the label."

"So you're going to tell me that nothing happened."

"I'm not going to tell you that. But I'm not going to tell you anything, in point of fact, because it's none of your business."

"And where were you today?" Lachlan asked.

"Again. None of your business. But also not a big deal. I took Elizabeth down to see Copper Ridge."

An expression of wistfulness crossed Charity's face. "It's always so pretty every Christmas."

"Yeah. Beautiful. And a real snooze fest."

He felt like a jerk. Because it had not been a snooze fest. Nothing with Elizabeth was. It couldn't be.

"And yet you did it anyway." Lachlan looked at him. "I think you've got it bad."

"Got what bad?"

"I think you've got feelings for her." Lachlan lifted his beer and held it out toward him. "You're the latest McCloud to fall." He tipped his beer back and took a drink.

"No," he said, the denial coming out swift and intense. "Not at all. She's hot, and I like her. But it isn't like that."

"Sure it's not. Except it looks exactly like that."

"I don't have that kind of shit in me, Lach. It isn't my thing."

"Why not?"

"What do you mean, why not?"

"I mean why not? I know why *we're* messed up." And he knew just what Lachlan meant. Lachlan, Tag, Hunter, and Gus. Not Brody. Because they were them. And he was separate. "We spent all of our lives getting used as dad's punching bags. But what the hell is your problem, Brody?"

He'd always felt it. But it shocked him to hear Lachlan say it so forcefully, when he never had before. "I've had stitches more times than I can count," Lachlan said. "Broken bones that never got healed. Shit. I'm like a walking catalog of minor injuries. And you... You don't have a scar on you. Why the hell can't you just get over it? Gus has a wife. *Dad lit him on fire*."

"Saving your ass," Brody pointed out.

Charity moved, and it was almost like she put her body between Lachlan and Brody. And Brody was under no illusion that she was protecting *him*. Not even remotely. It was all Lachlan that she was standing in front of. It was only Lachlan that she cared about.

"It isn't Lachlan's fault that your dad went after him," Charity said. "He was a kid."

"I know that. But he's acting like I chose to not get my ass beat. I mean, I wouldn't have chosen to get my ass beat. But no one asked."

"I'm just saying. You have the luxury of being a little bit less screwed up. Do something with it."

"Where is this coming from? Because you were in total agreement with me about single mothers just a couple of weeks ago."

"Because I didn't realize… Look at you. With her. You can't let it go. If you could let it go, you would have. So what? You're going to pretend that nothing is happening just because… Because why?"

"Because something is *wrong with me*," Brody said, and he didn't know he was going to say that until the words came out of his mouth. He hadn't known that he felt that.

He didn't know what to say. Clearly, Lachlan didn't either.

Or Charity.

It just got all quiet.

"What?" Lachlan asked finally.

"I don't know, Lachlan. I don't know. But something is. And I just want to keep my head down, and keep doing my work on the ranch, and keep going out on the weekends until…"

"Until you die?"

"Until I *fucking die*. Are you happy? Does that make you happy? Do you feel like you understand now what I want and where I'm coming from?"

"No. I don't understand. I don't understand you, Brody."

"Well, good thing you don't have to. Because I didn't ask. I didn't ask for this little intervention. I didn't ask for your opinion. I didn't ask to get taken to task over the fact that I didn't get abused. I didn't… I didn't do anything. I didn't."

Lachlan suddenly looked regretful. "I know you didn't. I know… Dammit. I'm sorry. I just…"

"Don't fight," Charity said, pleading. "Your lives were a mess, and being mean to each other about it isn't going to fix it."

He knew that was true. He was afraid that nothing would fix it. Not a damn thing.

Something is wrong with me.

He hadn't realized that he thought that until he said those words.

"I need another drink."

"Feel free to get plastered," Lachlan said. "I'm already designated driving this one," he said, gesturing to Charity. "I'll just take you both home, and you can get the pickup later."

And he decided that was a damn good idea. He was going to go ahead and get plastered, because it was better than having feelings.

He was all right with letting the water between him and his brother flow under the bridge.

Something is wrong with me.

What he didn't want to do was keep thinking about the words that he'd said. What he didn't want to do was keep thinking at all.

It was just too much. It was all too much.

And by the time he'd stumbled back to his bed and crashed down on top of the mattress, he was glad that he'd gone to the bar instead of going to see Elizabeth. Because oblivion was what he wanted. And it was never oblivion with her. Things were sharper, clearer. More.

And he didn't want that.

He wanted it fuzzy. He wanted it confusing. He wanted to not remember.

And he remembered every single day that he'd ever seen Elizabeth Colfax.

Bright and sharp and clear and burned into his mind.

And that just wasn't what he wanted. Not ever.

"Good morning, sleeping beauty."

Brody felt like someone was hitting his temple with a pickax. And as soft and sweet as the voice he currently heard was, it was making the headache worse.

And then there was a sharp jingling sound next to his head. "The fuck?"

"Your brother drove me to get your truck this morning," the voice said.

He turned over and squinted against the light.

"Lizzie?"

"I'll let you get away with that, Brody McCloud. But only you."

"Merry Christmas Eve," he said, the inside of his mouth feeling like it was lined with fur.

"Yes. Merry Christmas Eve to you too, you absolute disaster."

"I'm sorry," he said, sitting up. He realized he was naked. And he pressed the sheets to his lap, not because he was embarrassed, but because it didn't feel polite to expose her to him without being sure that she wanted to be exposed. It was morning. Hangover aside, he had a condition.

"It's nothing I haven't seen before, Brody," she said.

She had her Mom Voice on. Dammit. Why was that hot?

"Yeah, I know," he mumbled.

"Do you have chores to do today?"

"Yeah," he said.

"Great. You have chores to do and I've got a couple of things to do as well."

"What things do you have to get done?"

"That's for me to know, Brody. Sober up. I'll see you later."

CHAPTER SEVENTEEN

SHE HAD SENSED that something was going on with him by the time they had parted yesterday, and clearly it was a get-rip-roaring-drunk something.

Lachlan had come to her place this morning and told her what happened last night, then he'd driven her back to Smokey's to get Brody's truck.

"I was a little bit of a dick to him last night," Lachlan said.

She wanted to ask him why the hell he had been mean to Brody.

But she hadn't done that. Instead, she had just listened.

"And he drank a lot, so I have a feeling he has a really terrible hangover," he continued.

"Well."

"I don't know what his deal is. He's impossible to talk to," Lachlan said. "Not that I'm any better... But he's always been..."

"Yeah. I know." She didn't have a very hard time talking to Brody at all. But one thing she had been certain of from the beginning was that their talking wasn't something normal for him.

She drove his truck straight back to his place, and let herself in, waking him up. And now it was time for her to hatch part of her plan.

She was driving to Mapleton to get a big haul of groceries and a few presents.

She would go to the sports-and-outdoor store and look for something there. Granted, she didn't know what he had, but when she had talked to Lachlan about presents, he had informed her that a man could never have too many knives. And that bullets always made a great gift.

She had found it best not to argue. She was just grateful to have ideas.

She went to the grocery store and got all the fixings for Christmas dinner. Since she was in town, she stopped and bought some more clothes. She was systematically replacing all of the things that she had brought with her from her marriage to Carter. All of the things that she had brought from her old life. It seemed like the best thing to do.

Then she went to the outdoor store, where she wandered endlessly down the aisles until a woman wearing camouflage took pity on her and directed her to a few things.

She left with a knife that had blades you could swap in and out of the handle, and several boxes of ammunition for a few different kinds of guns, which the woman assured her would work for the sort of guns a rancher was most likely to have. Maybe Elizabeth had been bamboozled. But, she felt accomplished. And right now that was what mattered.

SHE DROVE BACK to Four Corners, and set about making a batch of cookies. Chocolate chip cookies. And yes, she knew that he already had a favorite one. That his brother's friend Charity made them, but she wanted to make him cookies. Because she still thought it was outrageous that he had never had a fresh-baked cookie until he was twenty-five years old, and she felt like the man could use several different favorite cookie recipes, all things considered.

When they were just about done, she texted him.

She had cider brewing on the stove, homemade this time, and Christmas music playing. There were presents under the tree.

And this wasn't just for her. Some replacement because Benny was gone. It was for Brody.

Of course, maybe he did something with his family. But she had a feeling he didn't. Not based on what he had told her.

She waited for a response to her text. And waited. And then suddenly, there was a knock at the door. She let out a sigh of relief, and smiled. That seemed like him.

She got up, and went and opened the door. "You could've texted," she said.

"Yeah. I could have. But I started a few and didn't really know what to say. Since you saw me hungover this morning. Undoubtedly, not my finest moment."

"That's okay. I feel like you've seen a couple moments of mine that weren't exactly my finest."

"Do you mean sad, because your son went to spend Christmas with your ex-husband? Because that isn't nearly as ignoble as being hungover because you went out drinking with your brother and got into a fight with him."

"Maybe not. But there's not much point in comparing battle scars, is there?"

"I guess not."

"The point is we just all have them."

"I guess we do."

"Brody… Merry Christmas."

He stepped into her house and looked around. "White Christmas" was playing over a speaker on the counter, and the Christmas tree was glimmering even more beautifully than it ever had before.

"I want to make you a big Christmas dinner tomorrow. And tonight, there's cookies and cider. And there's presents for tomorrow morning. I'm going to make you breakfast."

"I…"

"And tonight sex. Lots of sex."

"Okay," he said.

"You look a little bit shell-shocked."

"I'm not sure what I did to deserve this."

"Just… Everything since I've met you."

"Including the hangover?"

"Okay. Maybe everything except last night. But, that's a minor experience in the grand scheme of things."

"I guess so."

"Now we're going to be merry," she said.

"Is that what's going to happen?" he asked.

"Yes. It's what's going to happen."

"Typically, I don't like being told what to do."

"Well, typically, I don't go around demanding what I want. But in this case… I'm going to."

"Doesn't sound like much of this is for you."

"I love cookies."

"Anything else?"

"Sex. With you."

"I'd like to hear more about that."

"Cider and cookies first."

He grimaced. "Now they feel like a punishment."

"It's called delaying gratification. What do you know about that?"

He looked at her, for too long. "Way too much."

She actually believed that.

"Well, a little more won't hurt you."

"I guess we'll find out anyway," he said.

"Yes," she said.

She brought a mug to him, filled with steaming liquid, and a plate with warm cookies. "I can't believe nobody ever makes you these."

"I told you. Lachlan's friend bakes cookies."

"This is Charity, right? The cute vet?"

He frowned. "I mean, I guess. *Cute* in the way that a doll is or something."

"She's cute," Elizabeth said. "And she isn't making cookies for you. She's making them for Lachlan."

"She makes them for all of us."

Elizabeth shook her head. "Trust me. They're for him."

"What…? You mean, like… She's making them *for* him?"

"Yes, Brody," she said, speaking very slowly. "Because she likes him."

"Because they're friends."

She rolled her eyes. "I think she *likes* him."

"They aren't in fourth grade," he said. "And she's engaged."

"What?" Elizabeth looked genuinely shocked by that.

"I know. I know." Brody shook his head. "It's…the weirdest thing to me, but they're friends. Though it's like… I don't know, *more* somehow, but not in the way

I always thought. She protects him, like a feral creature. I thought she was going to take a chunk out of me at the bar."

"What happened with you and Lachlan last night?"

"It was stupid," he said.

"It couldn't have been that stupid. He knew that you were upset, and he came to see me this morning."

"He was probably looking for me."

"You know, I don't think he was. I think he knew that you wouldn't be at my place." She didn't even bother to pretend to be irritated that Lachlan clearly knew that they were sleeping together. She had a feeling that Brody and Lachlan couldn't keep much from each other, even if they tried.

It was funny. They were the last two McCloud brothers who were single. And she had a feeling their experience of their childhood couldn't have been more different. But they were both wounded by it.

"He was mad at me. About… He just brought up some stuff from the past. Stuff about my dad. About me not…"

"Did he say something to you about you not getting hit?"

His expression went hard. Any goodwill she had felt for Lachlan a moment ago was gone.

"He isn't wrong," Brody said.

"No, Brody, he is. He doesn't get to tell you how your childhood should have made you feel. Any more than anyone gets to tell me how mine should have made me feel. People have always treated me like I was damaged. And I have issues, I do. But people cared about me. Enough adults showed up and showed me that there were good people in the world, and that made all the difference to me. Did you have that? Did you have one person show up and show you that you are worthy?"

He looked lost. Right in that moment. Like the lost boy he must have been back then, and everything in her ached.

His throat worked, and he looked away from her.

"My dad," he said.

That stunned her speechless. She just stood there, holding her own mug of cider and staring.

He looked back at her, and there was something defiant in his expression now.

"Yeah. My dad showed me that I was worth something. My dad taught me how to ride a horse. Taught me how to lasso a calf. Taught me how to shoot and skin a deer and pound a nail. So yeah. Lachlan and I had different experiences. I had a different experience."

"Do you ever get to talk about that?"

He shook his head. "There's no point. What he did to them… It's unforgivable. So I don't think about that stuff. I don't think about it. It doesn't matter."

"It did matter though, didn't it?"

"I don't want to talk about this. I really don't. I didn't want to talk about it when Lachlan brought it up, and I don't want to talk about it now."

"Okay. We don't need to."

He looked up at her. "That's it?"

"You said you didn't want to, Brody. I'm here if you do. We had a pretty easy time talking about everything. I told you my stuff. You didn't run away. I'm not going to, either, because you're telling me that your feelings are more complicated than anybody has given you permission for them to be."

"I don't need anybody's permission to do anything," he said.

"Of course you don't. And I didn't say you did."

"I know you didn't say that. I'm just… Thank you for the cookies. I appreciate the spirit. And I will consider them the first cookies ever baked for me."

She could tell that he was trying to put a Band-Aid on all of it. And maybe he was right to do that. What was the point in playing these games? What was the point of trying to get to the truth when there just wasn't time for that? What was the point?

She really did wonder. Maybe there wasn't a reason. It was just that she… She knew a certain kind of closeness. But it wasn't this. She had told him things about herself she had never told anybody. She had shared her fears, her insecurities. She told him exactly why she had been vulnerable to falling into a relationship, the things that she had thought. These small, mean issues that she always felt so embarrassed about. And he had just accepted it. He had taught her that somebody could accept it. He had made her feel like she could accept it more. Like she could accept herself more.

She wanted to give him something. Something that looked even a little bit like that. Was that not reasonable? *It seems like it ought to be.*

But it could also be just cider and cookies and an evening spent not being so lonely. An evening spent making each other feel good. Why couldn't it be that?

You're trying to make something "forever." And you know you can't do that. You know you can't force it.

She repeated that to herself. Repeated it to herself because it was that important.

She needed to understand. And she needed to listen.

Because she had already done this overly attached thing. She had already misconstrued something romantic for something permanent.

It wasn't wrong to believe that "forever" existed. She refused to believe that it was. She had found a kind of forever with Benny. That forever family that she'd always wanted. She didn't have to project that onto a man.

"These are delicious," he said.

She took a sip of her cider and sat on the couch directly beside him. She snuggled against him, and looked at the tree. It was beautiful.

"I always dreamed of making my own Christmas," she said. Because she couldn't help herself.

He didn't need to share with her, but there was something healing about her being able to say all these hidden things in her heart that she had never been able to speak out loud before. To know that the man that she said them to was going to want to see her naked later, and he wouldn't stop wanting her just because he knew... Because he knew her.

Because he knew she wasn't fancy Elizabeth Colfax. Because he knew the name was borrowed, and so were her clothes. Bought with money that was never hers.

Yeah. He knew that.

He knew that, and he was here anyway. "I saw so many different Christmas traditions growing up," she said. "Different holiday traditions. I loved all of them. I thought they were all beautiful. I love seeing the way it brought families together. Families of all kinds. No matter their faith, no matter their traditions... They were all wonderful, because they were nothing like what I had ever seen before. But I always wondered what kind of Christmas *I* would make. I had two Christmases with

Benny while married to Carter. And I imagined those being the foundation. The traditions that I would have for the rest of my life. In the house, with that man, with all the children that we would have. And then it was gone. I did my best to make new traditions. But I'm always trying to do that." She had realized this about herself recently, and now she was saying it out loud. "I'm always trying to make the one thing that will last forever. And this Christmas isn't going to be like any other Christmas. I'm okay with that. I'm okay with looking back on this, and having this as a memory. And not something that happens every year."

"I've never thought of things that way. Traditions and ongoing things, and one-time things… The only thing I've ever really counted on is that life will bite you in the ass. In familiar and unfamiliar ways, randomly all the time."

She laughed. "I mean, you're not wrong. I might be a little more satisfied with the state of affairs if I learned that level of acceptance."

"I don't know that it's acceptance. It's kind of pessimistic."

"Fatalistic, maybe."

"Maybe."

"It's hard to be fatalistic sitting in front of a Christmas tree this pretty."

"I don't know about that. I think I can be fatalistic anywhere I want to be."

"Now, that's optimism."

He laughed. "Did you get Benny's presents?"

"No, Brody. Those are your presents."

He looked at her, his expression sharp. "What?"

"Those are your presents. I got them for you. But you

can't open them yet. Because it's only Christmas Eve. You have to open them Christmas morning."

"That doesn't seem fair."

"Well. I have something you can open tonight."

She got up off the couch, set her mug of cider down, then gripped the hem of the new sweaterdress and pulled it up over her head.

He couldn't breathe. He couldn't think. And everything that had happened in the last hour just dissolved. All the difficulty, all the stinking conversations, all the tough admissions and memories he preferred not to have.

Because she was standing in front of him in a red bodysuit that resurrected his very dead Christmas cheer.

It was lace, see-through, and there were straps, and it was a complicated thing of beauty, crisscrossing over that pale skin. He wanted to…

He wanted to tear it off her. Like a caveman. Like…

He was short-circuiting.

In all his days, he had not thought that the prim woman who he met all those weeks ago would be able to send him into this kind of a tailspin. Not in a million years. Not in a hundred million years. He had been certain that she was a prude. He had been certain that she was stuffy…

And right now, standing before him, she was a siren. And if she was going to lure him to his death, then he was going willingly. Because he had never seen anything more beautiful in all of his life, and he had never wanted anything like he wanted Elizabeth Colfax right now.

Lizzie.

His Lizzie. Because he was the only one who was allowed to call her that.

So he did.

"Lizzie," he said, the name coming out a growl.

She arched her back, and the breath left his body in a gust.

He could hardly breathe past his desire.

The curve of her breasts, the way he could see the shadow of her nipples through that fabric…

"Please tell me that didn't come from your ex-husband."

"No. It came from Copper Ridge. You were very nice to me, hanging out in that store while I shopped… It made me want to do something nice for you too."

"That is very, very nice," he agreed.

And he didn't even care that it was being presented as a reward. A little bit transactional. She said it light, she said it flirty. And hell, it made it really dirty, and he was 100 percent okay with that game.

All for him.

Yeah. He liked it. He liked it a lot. His reward.

For that Victorian Christmas nonsense.

She shifted slightly, and he could see… Holy hell. There was no fabric between her legs.

He felt like he might be dying. Then and there. And he never wanted to get laid in front of a Christmas tree, but it was quickly becoming a serious fantasy for him.

She grinned, and moved toward him, then she straddled his lap on the couch, leaning in and kissing him on the mouth.

He growled, pushing his fingers through her hair, kissing her deep and wild, licking into her mouth as he did.

She moaned, rolling her hips forward, her center

making contact with the rigid length of his arousal through his jeans.

He had never been so hot for it. Never been so hot for any woman… Ever.

But that had been true from the beginning. He had wanted her and no one else from the moment he had first set eyes on her. And he hadn't been able to make himself want anyone else no matter how hard he tried.

He just wanted her.

And it was more than sex. More than chemistry. It was that thing that made him want to move mountains for her. It was that thing that made him want to *talk* to her.

That thing that made him want to *listen*.

What a strange damned experience that was.

The thing that made her story almost more important than his own, which was what made it easy to finally… Tell bits of his.

He couldn't have explained it before this moment. As if the brush of her mouth on his in the way that she ignited his blood brought clarity to him that he'd never experienced before.

Somehow.

Even while good sense and reason were being blotted out. Even while he could scarcely breathe, let alone think.

He didn't think there was any oxygen getting to his brain.

He pushed his fingers between her legs and discovered that she was wet for him.

He groaned, let his head fall back and began to stroke her, moving his fingers through her slick folds, before pushing them deep inside of her.

She moaned, letting her head fall back, resting her breasts forward, and he tilted his chin up and licked her through the thin fabric of the garment she was wearing, before biting down gently on her nipple.

She gasped, her hips rocking in time with the movement of his fingers.

"What a gift you are. What a gift you were all along. And that husband of yours was too damn stupid to see it. What an idiot. His misfortune… That's my gain."

She whimpered as he continued to suck her nipples through that fabric, while he worked his fingers in and out of her body, while she moved her hips and moaned, begging him for more. He was happy to give her more. He was happy to give her whatever she needed.

He pushed the flimsy cups on the garment to the side, baring her breasts, leaving the rest of the red lace in place. He had no intention of undressing her altogether. It was too beautifully filthy to look at her like this. His partially unwrapped gift.

And it reminded him, that's what it was. That's what she was. A gift.

She smoothed her hands over his chest, kissed him deep and hard on the mouth, then wrenched his shirt up over his head.

Shaking fingers worked his belt buckle, and she freed him from his underwear before settling herself over the blunt head of his erection. She began to slide down onto him slowly, and it was too much. It was just too damned much. He stood, one arm around her waist, bracing her as he walked them to the Christmas tree and laid them down underneath it. He positioned himself between her legs and thrust home. Hard. Those colored Christmas lights painting her skin, the glitter from the golden ornaments reflecting lights over the top of that.

And the sound of their pleasure drowned out the Christmas music, and he couldn't tell anymore if it was sacred or sacrilege, or some mix of both.

But then, he'd never been able to tell. Not in his life. What was good. What was bad.

What made him good or bad.

Because he didn't have an answer. To which it was.

He knew one thing, though. He knew that he wanted her, and right now, he had her.

And that was enough. It had to be enough. Because it was all he damn well had.

The fierce pleasure of her body closed around his, the deep satisfaction of being buried inside her. Of listening to her cries of pleasure even as he sought his own.

He had that.

And it was good.

She was good. He was certain of that. Of all the things in this world he couldn't make sense of, he knew this for sure.

She whimpered, and he reached down and pinched her nipple, and he felt her climax ripple around him. And he chased his own, unable to hold back. Unable to stop himself.

"Lizzie," he said, the name fractured on his lips, fractured in his soul, a jagged mirror reflecting pieces of himself that he wasn't ready to see.

But he needed her all the same.

Even if he wasn't ready.

That was the problem. He wasn't ready for her.

He didn't think he ever would be.

But here they were.

Here they were.

He lay with her under the tree. Looking up into those lights and dark green branches. Something he imagined kids did. Kids who didn't have ogres for fathers and absentee mothers. Kids who hadn't been in foster care and never felt like the home they were in wasn't theirs.

Kids who were comfortable. Secure and safe.

Except, nothing about him felt childlike at the moment.

He was glad of that. And as he drifted off to sleep beneath the Christmas tree, he thought this was probably a singular moment. To feel thoroughly debauched and thoroughly innocent, all at once.

And he thought it was probably only Elizabeth who could ever make him feel that.

He was looking forward to Christmas.

He couldn't remember ever thinking that before.

He fell asleep with his lips curved into a smile.

CHAPTER EIGHTEEN

SHE WOKE UP EARLY, with Brody still tangled around her. On the floor, of all things.

She was half out of that wild outfit that she had worn for him last night. It made her feel so confident. So... Not her. And it had been wonderful.

And then somewhere, midway through making love to him, she realized she did feel like herself. The self that was emerging through this whole affair. Much more confident. Sexual. A woman designed to feel pleasure, not just serve other people. Who actually enjoyed her body.

It was a gift. He was a gift.

Smiling to herself she stumbled into the bedroom and found some pajamas more suitable to Christmas morning.

Except then she went out into the living room and saw him lying there, no shirt, his jeans undone, exactly the way he had left them last night.

She licked her lips. He was so beautiful. And right about now, he looked like her Christmas present. Undressed and under the tree.

She smiled to herself, and set about making some coffee.

As soon as it started brewing, she heard him stir.

"Merry Christmas, Brody," she said.

"Merry Christmas," he mumbled, dragging his hand

over his face, the sound of his skin against his whiskers intimate, sending a shiver through her body.

"Did you sleep well?"

"I did. But I have a feeling my back is going to hurt like a son-of-a-bitch today."

"Well. Probably. Sleeping on the floor was maybe not the best idea."

"No," he said.

"Does your family have plans for the day?"

"Gus will go to the Sullivans'. Hunter will go to the Garretts'. I imagine Tag and Nelly will go spend the day with her mother."

"So everybody else's families are a little more into the holidays than yours?"

"Yeah. The Garretts… They had a pretty dysfunctional upbringing, but I guess Sawyer and Wolf worked really hard to keep things light for Elsie. Hunter's wife, you know."

"Yeah. I know. And Gus's wife?"

"She has all sisters. The Sullivans. You saw them at the town hall. They make everything, cook all kinds of stuff. They love a big celebration. Their parents are… Kind of problematic, but they aren't horrible. They all still speak—though the parents never come back to the ranch. Alaina certainly has her issues with them, but it's not anything like our family."

"Right. Well… Lachlan and Charity are invited to have some food."

"That might be good. Her dad has been pretty sick. Maybe he can come?"

"I'd love that. When you text him, I'm going to start turkey and mashed potatoes and stuffing. All the things that I normally make for Benny."

"Sounds good."

"Two o'clock, probably."

"Okay," he said.

"But first you need to open your presents from me."

"I still can't believe you got me presents. And what the hell are they?"

"You're going to have to open them and find out."

"How do I do this?"

"Well, usually I have Benny sit on the floor, and I hand him his presents. But since you're not my child, we can do it however you want."

He laughed. "Okay. I can appreciate that."

"Except... Here. This one first. Because it's lame."

She handed him the smallest present. He unwrapped the end of it. "Bullets," he said.

"A very nice woman in camo assured me that you cannot have too many of these."

"She's not wrong. Hey," he said, grabbing the next box, which was identical. He shook it. "I'm going to go out on a limb and guess these are more bullets."

"Correct."

He opened six ammunition boxes in all.

"Can you use them?" she asked.

"I can. Thank you."

There was another box, and she handed it to him.

He opened it up. She couldn't wait for him to figure out what it was. "It's a knife. But has, like, different kinds of blades you can put on it. Like a saw, and that hook thingy. It's really cool. And utilitarian. It's like a really big-boy Swiss Army knife."

He laughed. "Okay. This is really cool. I love it. And..." Suddenly his smile faded. "I..."

"What?"

"I cannot remember the last time anybody got me a present."

Except she could tell from something in his eyes that he did remember the last time someone had gotten him a present. And it wasn't a good memory.

"It's a good thing, right?"

"It's a good thing," he said. "Thank you. Thank you for this. I haven't… Done Christmas morning. And you know what… I know it's not going to be a tradition every year. But this is always going to be Christmas to me. This is what it will mean. This is how I'll remember it."

She blushed. "Good. I'm…" She leaned in and kissed him. Just kissed him. Not in a way that it was leading up to anything, not overly sexual, just to let him know that she was there.

He texted his family while she cooked breakfast, and her heart felt tender.

Then, after she got the turkey in the oven, they went to her room, and finally made use of the bathtub.

Which was sexier than any fantasy she'd ever had before.

But she had to cut it short, because she had more food to make.

At two o'clock, Lachlan, Charity and Charity's father, Albert, arrived. Charity was holding a large Tupperware container filled with cookies.

"I don't know if you have dessert, but I wanted to make sure I brought something," she said.

"Perfect," Elizabeth said. "We cannot have too much in the way of treats."

Charity was such a sweet-looking woman, with long blond hair and floral dresses. She looked like she was part of another era, or maybe just a storybook. Elizabeth set the cozy table, and placed the turkey and all the sides out. She didn't know these people very well. Well. Except for Brody. Who she knew better than she knew just about anybody. And it was a different kind of Christmas. But there was something sort of wonderful about it.

She wondered how Benny was doing. She wanted to call him, but she also didn't want to disrupt the day. And in that way, it was good that she had distractions.

"Very kind of you to have us over," Albert said.

He had a gentle, slightly distracted manner about him. There was something sort of fragile about the way his hands moved. He had on an old-fashioned newsboy cap and a tweed jacket, and Elizabeth thought then if she could have chosen a father, it might have been him.

"It's my pleasure," she said. "My son is away for Christmas."

"That must be difficult," he said.

He reached across the table and patted Charity's hand. "I've never had to share her. She's the best veterinary assistant I could have asked for."

"Dad raised me by himself," Charity said.

It was a surprise, to know that Charity had been raised entirely by a man. She was so soft and feminine.

"I didn't do so bad, did I?" he asked. The question was so earnest it made Elizabeth's heart hurt.

"You did great, Dad."

"I have a very extensive insect collection. Fascinating creatures." The segue was abrupt, yet not unpleasant. "But of course you don't do veterinary work on insects, which is perhaps why I find them so interesting."

"Why don't you tell her about the animals you do work on," Charity prompted.

They spent time talking about his years as a veterinarian to the area. How he always made house calls, and how he knew everyone within a fifty-mile radius.

"And you're a veterinarian too?" she asked Charity.

She knew that, but she hadn't ever talked to Charity about it.

"Yes. I went to school in Virginia."

"Worst years of my life," Lachlan said.

It was clear that Charity was universally adored.

After dinner, Lachlan and Brody began to clear the table, then went to do the dishes. Albert began to nod off on one of the chairs next to the fireplace.

And she and Charity sat at the table with mugs of cider.

"Thank you for doing this," Charity said. "If you hadn't… We probably wouldn't have done anything today. Dad and I just would've had a quiet meal at home. It's nice to give him something like this."

"He seems sweet," she said.

"He is," Charity said.

"Maybe next year…"

Charity suddenly got a sad look on her face. "I have a feeling next year will look different."

She hadn't realized it was that serious.

"Oh. I'm sorry I…"

She shook her head. "Dad would say being sorry is impractical. I thought… I thought there would be more time. But after… He had a bit of a scare the other night and we went to the hospital and it isn't good news. But this… It's a real Christmas. A warm, family-feeling Christmas."

It was. Even though it wasn't her ideal Christmas, it was warm. And it did feel like family.

"Your fiancé?" Elizabeth asked. But she noticed Charity didn't have a ring.

"Oh, Byron lives in Virginia. I met him at school. It's…not a great time of year to travel."

"And what would Lachlan have done?"

"I don't know," Charity said. "He might've made his way over to my place. He might've gone out. I don't know which side of him to expect sometimes. And I certainly can't tell him what to do."

"They're just like that," Elizabeth said, looking down at her hands.

"The McClouds?"

"Specifically, those two McClouds," she said.

"Things have been difficult for them," Charity said.
"I know."

"You and Brody are…close," Charity said.

"I don't know about that. Well. I guess so."

There was really no point hiding the truth. She didn't have the energy to do it. And Charity was far too canny, anyway.

"I've known Lachlan since he was sixteen years old. I still don't always know what he's thinking. I worry about him. He's as unforgiving to himself as his father used to be."

"Whoever said time heals all wounds hadn't seen some of the injuries that can be inflicted on people," Elizabeth said. "I really do believe in healing, but you have to seek treatment."

Charity smiled. "Well. That is very true. And some men are too hardheaded to do anything half so sensible. They'd rather rub dirt in it and pretend it isn't there."

Of course, Elizabeth could be that way too. Always pushing ahead, not being fully honest or aware of the things that she was dealing with.

She had transformed her identity into being there for someone else, rather than doing work on herself. Had created a facade that she always hoped no one would see through.

She was working on that now. She really was. Because of Brody.

"And some men just pretend they don't have a wound at all," Elizabeth said, thinking of Brody.

"Lachlan is my best friend," Charity said. "But even I don't know everything they've been through. I know… I know it was different for Brody."

"No one is that sympathetic to him," Elizabeth said.

"I don't know if the McClouds are all that familiar with sympathy. Or care of any kind. It was…brutal here for them."

"For Brody too," Elizabeth said, feeling insistent.

"I know." Charity drained the rest of her cider and looked over at her father. "I should probably get him home."

Lachlan and Brody had just finished up in the kitchen.

"Lachlan," she said, "we should go."

"Sure," Lachlan said.

"Thank you again," Charity said.

"Yeah. Thanks."

It was dark outside, and when Elizabeth opened the door for everyone, she realized that it was snowing, the twilight making the snow glow blue.

It was beautiful out there. Perfect and silent. Like Christmas ought to be. Or so the song said.

There was something holy about it.

She closed the door and turned, looking at Brody. "Merry Christmas, Brody," she said.

"You keep saying that."

"I know. Because I want you to feel it."

"I don't know that Christmas is ever going to mean all that much to me. But it was a nice day."

"I'm glad."

"Do you have any more presents for me?" he asked.

And she thought of the other bit of lingerie that she had bought. "I just might."

"Good. Because I have to tell you... Having presents I don't have to share is probably my favorite part of the whole thing."

She felt the same way. She just wished that it were true.

Because she did have to share him. With his demons. And she didn't know if there was any way around that. She really didn't.

HE SHOULDN'T LET them sink into this. It wasn't smart. And he knew it. But he was basically living at her place. It was stupid as hell.

He should have kept a better line drawn around all of it. He really should have kept a better line drawn around Christmas.

Christmas had been...

Well. If he could've imagined a perfect Christmas, that would've been it. It was just that he didn't think Christmas was perfect. Because it reminded him of too many things. Too many awful things.

It had snowed buckets that day, and in the two days since.

And he shouldn't be lying in bed way past work time with Elizabeth right now either. Another on the long list of things he shouldn't be doing.

He was, though. Naked and wrapped around her in her bed. Having gone from never having shared a bed with a woman for the entire night to having done it every night possible except that one when he'd gone and indulged his hangover.

"You know what I think we ought to do," he said, not really thinking the words through before they came out of his mouth, all rusty from sleep.

"If you say sex…"

"I mean, I'm always going to say that. But I was thinking a sleigh ride."

"A sleigh ride? Who's doing sleigh rides after Christmas?"

"Me. Brody McCloud."

"You don't have a sleigh."

"I assure you that I do."

"No way."

"I do. With a harness. With bells on."

"I bet you look cute in that," she said.

"Oh, Lizzie, you really do want me to play dress-up, don't you? I'll get a pirate costume one of these days."

Except they knew that there were only about five days left until "one of these days" wouldn't come anymore. Because it was going to be New Year's, and then Benny would come home, and that was it.

"Yes. A pirate costume with a black mask, and above all else, I want you to say…'as you wish.'"

"I think that's a whole different fantasy."

"I have a lot of them since hopping into bed with you."

"I think you had them before that."

"Since meeting you," she said. "But do you really have a sleigh?"

"Yes. I would never joke about something this serious."

He didn't know why they had one on the ranch, only that they did. Stashed away in one of the back barns, covered by a tarp.

It was like a kids' fantasy, so obviously—obviously—their dad had never taken them out in it even once. He'd driven it as an adult, just because, but it wasn't something they got out routinely. Once or twice to delight some of the ranch kids, but that was it. It had been years since they'd done anything with it.

She got dressed up in that same plaid coat and some leggings and a sweater, and he put on his warmest, weathered boots, jeans, and a coat. And gloves. They had to have gloves.

Then he led her down to the barn where the sleigh was stashed.

When he uncovered it, she gasped.

"That's like a movie," she said, moving close to the vehicle, running her hands over some of the carvings on the ornately painted wood.

"It is. I don't know where the hell my dad got it, because it doesn't seem like he would own anything beautiful, but it's been here for a long time. I imagine it predates him. It's about the only thing that makes sense."

"I feel like I should have an extraordinary fur coat," she said. "Or a ball gown."

"The fur would keep you warm. The gown, not so much."

He went to the stalls and fetched two horses that were big and strong, well able to pull the sleigh, and Elizabeth helped him get them into their harnesses. Which did indeed have bells. He hadn't been kidding.

They climbed into the sleigh, and he snapped the reins, moving the team forward.

And she laughed. So free and easy, and the sound did something to him. That sound that was just pure joy, with none of the worry that she so often seemed to carry. And he had done that. It was extraordinary. Knowing that. Because he had never felt like he'd made a single situation easier in all of his life. And here he was, making her laugh. It felt like something. Felt like the wind.

They took the sleigh across the snowy expanse of fields that stretched out as far as they could see, to the base of the mountain.

The sky was moody and gray, and swirls of snow began to fall all around them, Elizabeth's nose and cheeks turning pink.

This was so different. This moment. She was carefree. And it was like... All that other stuff that stood in the way of being with her. Her baggage, Benny...

That made him feel guilty. Being Benny's mother made up a huge part of who she was. And he was really fond of the kid. It was just... They could just have fun like *this* if it wasn't for him.

You mean if it wasn't for you. That's the actual issue.

Well. Maybe. But it was complicated. She didn't have any idea.

He gritted his teeth and urged the team on.

For once, she was in the moment, and he was stuck in his head. He rode her over to the end of the field, where there was a lookout point that revealed the snowy river below, the rocks on the banks capped in white, the trees lightly frosted.

"It's beautiful," she said. "For all that I moved around all the time, my life was pretty small. Mostly, the Portland metro area. Once a little farther outside of it. I never dreamed I'd live in the country. But I wanted to. I dreamed a whole lot of things, and it took until the last few months for me to really realize that if I wanted something I was going to have to make it happen. And if it felt difficult, I was going to have to become the kind of person who could do it. I think that's the hardest thing. Realizing that you have to change in order to have something that you want."

He gritted his teeth. "Yeah. I mean… You really did a lot. It's amazing."

"So have you. You've all done so much. It's incredible. The way that you banded together with your brothers to make this place possible is nothing short of incredible. Especially given the example that you had."

"Hey. It's not…"

"I'm serious. I get why things are hard for you with your brothers sometimes. I get why it's difficult, but they're wrong about you. They shouldn't act like they know what it's like to be you when they don't. They might think they had it worse than you, but they didn't… They don't get to decide how growing up like that made you feel. I know you all love each other, but they've got that wrong."

"I might agree with you," he said. "If I wasn't a liar."

She looked at him, her eyes widening, and he realized that he'd gone and said it.

He hadn't meant to. He didn't actually want to have

this conversation. He never wanted to have it with anybody. Ever.

But she was giving him something no one else ever had. She was sitting there treating him like he was one of the wounded. Like his pain was important. Like he wasn't separate from his brothers, and she had no idea.

"A liar? About what?"

"The only thing that makes me acceptable to them is that I'm on their side about Dad. Even though he didn't treat me the way that they did, I disowned him the way that they did. We don't know where he is. He's a monster. We all hate him."

"Sure," she said.

"I have a hard time with it, though," he said, the words a big angry ball in his chest as he let out a hard breath. "I do know where he is."

"Brody…"

"Because I've seen him. After Gus ran him off the ranch… After Gus told him he better never show his face around here again… He got in touch with me. And I went to see him, Lizzie. So you see, the thing is… They're right about me. I'm not on their team, and I never was. I wanted to be. But I was too hungry for that thing that only my dad could give me. I was too hungry to be… Loved. And for whatever reason, whatever twisted reason, he loved me. And I just couldn't turn away from it. I told you, he taught me things. He made me feel important. And it was like… Sometimes, it was like I could pretend he was two different people. That a switch would flip when he was around the other boys and…"

The words got stuck in his throat. He could hardly breathe.

"I lived a double life, Elizabeth." He didn't deserve to call her Lizzie, not right now. "I'd go have a beer with my old man sometimes and then come home and sit across the dinner table and look Gus right in the scarred face."

"It's all bad," she said. "That he made you feel like that, that he ever played you off of them, that he ever hurt them… You're not the bad guy. You can't be."

"Now, that's not fair. Because you know what it's like to come out of a dysfunctional situation. And everything you've done as an adult… That's to your credit, right?"

"I don't…"

"And you were willing to give me credit for everything that we've done ever since taking over the ranch. But I can't have credit and no blame. That isn't how it works. As an adult, I made the decision to keep in touch with him for a while, even after Gus ran him off. And I… I him loaned him money, Elizabeth."

"Why?"

"He needed it. He needed an operation, and I took money away from the ranch to give it to him. And I told Gus that I spent it on a truck. I did, but not all of it. I lied to him. I basically laundered money out from under my own brother to help our dad."

"When was this?"

"Oh, more than ten years ago now. That was the last time. It was the last time I saw him, because I couldn't bear it anymore. And…you know it wasn't even the guilt, really. It was realizing my dad wanted money and not a relationship with me, not really. And then… that it hurts me to know that makes me think I'm even more messed up. What's wrong with me?"

"Have you ever heard of Stockholm syndrome, Brody?"

"Yes. I am familiar. But I don't need you trying to diagnose me with anything, when the fact of the matter is… It's just all a mess. Inside of me, and I can't make it not one. I hate him. With everything that I have. And I love him. I never wanted anything more than I wanted my dad to be proud of me. To love me. Even though I could see the things that he did, and I could see that his idea of what was okay wasn't. So why the hell do I want that man to be proud of me? It doesn't make any sense. It doesn't. It never has. And I know that. Down to my bones, I know it, but it still is. Just like I know that he's trash, and I still couldn't throw him out like the garbage that he was."

"Because you aren't a sociopath, Brody. Just because he feels nothing, doesn't mean you have to. He's your father, and it's actually not wrong for you to feel something for him. What's wrong is what he did to all of you. It isn't that I don't love my mom. Or… Maybe I love the symbol of what I wish a mother could be. And I've taken that symbol and turned it into something… I don't know."

"Your mother didn't hurt people. Not like that. Like you said, there are a lot of different kinds of abuse, but the way my father did it… It has a lot of victims."

"I understand that. But you're one of them."

"Sure. It doesn't… If Gus knew… What they think about me would be pretty set in stone. We had this distance between us… And there's no way to get across it. Because the way we were raised was just too different."

"Seems to me you were boiled in pots on the same

stove. Might've been different burners, but it was the same fire."

"I just don't… I'm not the hero that you think I am. And you know what? It's real tempting to let you think that I am. Because I like the way you look at me. And I like the way that… Benny seems to think I'm pretty great. So it would be better to let you just keep on believing that. But I'm a coward. That's the bottom line. I wanted that relationship with my dad, and I kept it. I was afraid of what would happen if I didn't keep it. I didn't know who I would be. Because I was the one that Seamus McCloud loved. And I didn't want to lose that."

And much to his surprise, she looped her arm through his and rested her head on his shoulder. "I'm sorry, it doesn't make me hate you. If that's what you were trying to do."

"Can you see how messed up it is?"

"Yes. It's totally messed up. And maybe if I was your brothers, I would be mad at you. But I'm not your brothers. I'm somebody who has also gone through some difficult things. Who knows what it's like to try and make the best of a complex situation that nobody would choose. I know what it's like to be…" She sighed. "Please try to understand what I'm saying is the way that I mean it, and not how it could come across. I'm tied to Carter, even though I don't want to be. We have a common love. We made a person together. I would love to be done with him, and never see him again, not because I hate him so much, just because… He feels like a mistake that I made when I was a kid. I haven't thought I was in love with him since I was twenty-three years old. It seems unfair to continue to have to negotiate having him in my life. But I do. I know what it's like to be tangled around somebody whether you want to be or not. I get that it's very different. But then... I also have a mother I haven't seen since I was six, who didn't treat me particularly well. And whose love I wanted all the same. Who I wanted desperately to be with and desperately to escape all at once." She shook her head. "No. The problem is, I just understand how imperfect these things can be. And how we don't get to control the way that we feel about them."

He had never talked to anybody about his family situation before. Not people outside the family. It was so strange to have her opinion. And have it be so definitively... For him.

"My brothers..."

"Are great. But they're not the ones I know. So, I'm going to go ahead and put my bias firmly in your corner."

"That doesn't seem fair."

"This kind of thing isn't fair." She pressed her forehead to his, her breath a cloud in the cold air. "You're my favorite, Brody McCloud. Maybe that isn't fair, but it's how it is."

Her favorite.

He knew what it was to be the favorite. The favorite of a psychopath. He couldn't say that he liked it. But this was Elizabeth. Lizzie.

And being her favorite felt different. Even if it shouldn't.

He closed the distance between them and kissed her, luxuriating in the feel of her soft mouth against his. Just kissed her.

Because it felt good to have someone sit with him. Because it felt good to have someone listen.

And everything in his chest was heavy, a jumble of

things that he didn't want to untangle, and someday
he'd have to…

*Or you won't. Because this holiday will come to an
end, and it doesn't have a bearing on the rest of your
life. Because it's just a holiday. That's all it is.*

A vacation from being alone.

Because haven't you had enough?

They kissed out there in the snow, sitting in the
sleigh, the achingly beautiful wilderness stretching on
around them in silent glory, the pine trees cloaked in
white winter coats, every sound dampened by the snow.

He could hear his heartbeat, he was sure of it.

Something wild and new, and terrifying, beginning
to take root in him. Like a flower trying to grow beneath the surface of all the ice.

Just like that.

But the problem was, the ice would eventually win.
And it wouldn't be strong enough to break through.
Because of course it wouldn't be. Because that was the
kind of thing reserved for the miraculous, and miraculous was one thing his life had never been.

He wanted fiercely in that moment. An image that
he couldn't quite hold steady in his mind, a feeling that
he couldn't find a name for. He wanted. But there was
no purpose to it. No point. And in the end, it would be
nothing more than that frozen-over wasteland.

"Ready to head back home?" She asked the question gently, softly. She meant her place, and it wasn't
his home. He shouldn't go back with her, come to that.
He should start to put some distance between them,
because when it ended, it was going to feel like having
a limb separated from his body, because he had gotten
too used to this, and it wasn't right.

But instead he cracked the reins and began to turn the large sleigh, skimming over the snow. "Yeah. Let's go home."

Because there was one thing he was good at, it was living a lie. He'd done it for more than ten years now.

So what was one more?

Except the dark, thrilling thing that he realized as they hurtled back toward the house was that she knew his lies now.

And he was terrified that she would look inside of him and see all the rest. Before he'd even had a chance to identify them. More than anything.

And that scared him most of all.

CHAPTER NINETEEN

NEW YEAR'S EVE, the McClouds apparently did have a celebration. Because it was something that involved fireworks and drinking. And it seemed they were all very much for fireworks and drinking.

And bonfires.

Unlike at the town hall meeting, this bonfire would be set up at McCloud's Landing. Down by the river bank. It was nearest to Hunter's house, which was situated right there so that he could fish, so he said.

They brought out coolers filled with beer, platters of cake and a passel of what looked to be legally questionable fireworks.

"Totally on the up-and-up," Lachlan said.

"Yeah," Tag said. "Some guy sells them on the side of the road."

"I don't think that makes them legal," Nelly said.

"Don't go throwing around all those fancy college words," Tag said. "I'm not as well-read as you."

"I'm pretty sure that you understand that word."

"Never assume, darling," he said.

"My mother was your teacher," Nelly pointed out. "I know she taught you better than that."

Everyone was down there, including the whole Garrett family, who Elizabeth hadn't gotten a chance to meet yet. She met Sawyer and his wife, Evelyn, Wolf and his wife, Violet. And their children. Cute babies that made her heart ache for a stage of parenthood that she had passed a long time ago.

She hadn't even thought about having more kids since she and Carter had gotten divorced. It was something she had let go of completely. But there was something about this that made her ovaries ache, and she didn't like it. She knew it had to do with the combination of the cute babies and Brody.

What a pain in the rear.

She did not need that. She did not need to go getting sentimental over all of this. Over him.

But his declaration about not having children from the other day still echoed inside of her. She understood that it hurt him, what he'd done. Even if she couldn't fully understand why. It was more about how his brothers would feel, she did get that. But she sensed another worry beneath it, and she just couldn't quite figure out where it came from.

That poor man.

He was tortured with it.

But then he'd taken her back home and he'd made love to her like it was the only thing he'd ever wanted to do, after kissing her like he had all the time in the world out there in that field.

But the problem was, she just… She loved him.

That was the problem. His pain was her pain. What he wanted, she wanted. This place… She cared about it. Because it was his. And it felt a little bit like hers, and part of her wanted to make it theirs.

He put her needs above his own, he prioritized her pleasure.

He was a strong and steady influence for Benny.

He was broken, yes.

Not shattered beyond all repair.

And she knew better than anyone there was nothing wrong with broken. When you were dropped right at the beginning of your life, it was impossible to come away without some damage. She knew that. She also knew that she still mattered, even with all of it. She also knew that she deserved to be happy. It had been the realization that she'd been having this whole time. And it wasn't about trying to make a good thing last forever.

No. It wasn't that. She had thought she was in love before. She hadn't been. She could see clearly now the holes in that. All the ways that it had never been love. All the ways that it had never been, when she had so desperately wanted it to be.

But now there was this. Now there was him.

And she had never known that love could take this kind of shape, so she knew she hadn't fashioned it out of thin air. It wasn't a fantasy, it was something wondrous.

Beginning and end.

"Would you like a drink?" Evelyn Garrett offered her a choice between champagne and sparkling cider. Elizabeth opted for the champagne. She didn't have anyone to be responsible for tonight, so there was no reason to be... Responsible. It was a couple of days without Benny. He'd had a great Christmas, and he'd taken joy in showing her all of his loot over a video call. She missed him. She was ready for their separation to end. A video call a day would never be enough.

But it meant she and Brody would end too. And that she wasn't ready for at all.

It will end unless you do something about it.

Unless you stop coasting through life, and start asking for what you want.

"Champagne," she said.

"Great," Evelyn said, pouring her a generous glass. And then she poured herself some too. "I'm finally not pregnant or breastfeeding, so I will indulge myself."

"That is reason to celebrate," Elizabeth said. Which seemed funny, given what she had just been thinking about. That brief, wistful fantasy of having Brody's baby.

The idea made her stomach clench tight.

"You have a son, right?" Evelyn asked.

"Yes. He's with his dad for the holidays."

"I hope you've been enjoying your time off."

She couldn't help it, her gaze drifted to Brody. "Yes. Definitely."

"I'm sure they're keeping you busy over here."

Thankfully, Evelyn hadn't seemed to pick up on what she was thinking.

"Yes. Definitely," she repeated. She took a sip of the champagne. Brody was drinking a beer, talking and laughing with his brothers, and you would never know that he was the same man who had spilled all those dark thoughts on her, out in the sleigh.

A man who felt separate. Who felt alone. Who couldn't trust his own feelings.

That made her ache. Because… She understood that. She had felt for a long time like she couldn't trust her own feelings. Because she had picked wrong with Carter, because she had been wrong about love then, she couldn't go and make any more claims for herself. That was ridiculous. She had grown and changed and seen more of the world. She knew more. She could trust herself. It was okay

She trusted that she really did love Brody McCloud. And it didn't matter how long she'd known him, or how long she hadn't. It didn't matter whether it would last forever.

It was a beautiful thing to be able to love him. It felt right to realize that on New Year's Eve. To know that no matter what, this was the right thing.

He deserved to be loved. And she deserved to let herself do it.

He wasn't a resolution, or an easy dream.

He was a man. With all the complications that he came with. He wasn't easy, and she…

Well, it was simple to think she never would've picked him. Except the thing was, she had never intended to pick anybody. Because she had been too scared to do something like that. She just wasn't scared now.

Okay, maybe that was a lie. She knew a little bit of anxiety. It was difficult not to. But she wasn't so much concerned about the outcome. Not now.

Not worried about making something that looked perfect.

Maybe… Maybe she could just love him. And maybe she didn't need to worry about whether or not he would marry her or be a father to Benny. Maybe it would work to have him in her life in whatever way he could handle it.

And maybe it would grow. Or maybe it wouldn't. She wouldn't know for sure. Not unless she tried.

She took another sip of champagne.

"I moved here from New York," Evelyn said, and

when she did, Elizabeth took note of the other woman's accent.

"That's a big move," Elizabeth said. "It felt like a big change coming from Portland."

"I've never regretted it," Evelyn said. "Sure, I've missed a few things. Cupcake ATMs and being able to go buy whatever I want at whatever hour I want it. That isn't real life, you know? This… Here… I found somebody that I love. And that's real life."

Evelyn was right. This was real life. The beauty, the worry, the uncertainty. The loving. It was real life.

She loved Benny, but she couldn't be with him all the time. Loving him meant being okay with this distance. Even though it hurt. Loving him meant that she had to let him have the best relationship with his father that he could have. She couldn't force Carter to do things differently, she could just let him be the father that he was. The father he wanted to be.

And do her best to be there for Benny if he became disillusioned with that, if it hurt him… And maybe it wouldn't. Maybe what Carter gave him would always feel like enough. Because he had so much support from Elizabeth at home.

And maybe loving Brody would have to be the same. Allowing him to have distance if he needed it. Because something in her knew… Well, if she told him this… He would think that she was making demands, and that would freak him out.

"I think I might be realizing the same thing," she said. "The work here that Gus is doing on the ranch… I love being part of it. My son loves it here. He loves the school. And there's Brody…"

"Ah," Evelyn said. "He is a handsome devil. Emphasis on devil."

"Yeah. I've heard that. I haven't seen much of the devil, though. Maybe just a pirate cowboy."

"What?" Evelyn laughed.

"Nothing. It's just amazing what can happen when you decide you're going to make your life into what you want it to be, rather than sitting back and accepting what other people did to you."

Evelyn nodded. "And that, I relate to. That's a story for another time. But someday, I'll tell you how I caught my best friend having sex with my fiancé on a desk in our office building, and answered a mail-order-bride ad to come out here. Well. I guess I did just tell you. That's the tale."

"Wow."

"Sometimes, the impossibly painful exists to get you on the road you were always meant to be on."

"That's true," she said, her voice scratchy now. "That is very, very true."

She walked over to where Brody was, and stood close to him. He looked over at her, his mouth kicking up into a grin. "Hey. You having a good time?"

"I have champagne. I can't complain."

She was introduced to Sawyer and Wolf, and smiled, unsure if she should touch Brody or not.

He put his hand on her lower back, and that answered the question for her. It made her cheeks get hot. No one said anything, but she had a feeling that his brothers had already guessed that something was going on between them.

Something that, as far as he knew, was going to end

in two days. Something she wasn't going to let happen. Or at least, something she was going to challenge.

She had never fought for what she wanted before. Because before, she had been conditioned to believe she just needed to be grateful. Grateful for the crumbs that she had been handed. It wasn't up to her to fight for anything. She wasn't worth that.

At least, that was what she believed. And she did now. Not now. Now she was ready. For a battle, and for a compromise. For a life that didn't look perfect, but was happy.

And… She had that anyway. No matter what. Because she had Benny.

She would like to have Brody too. In whatever capacity she could.

They hung out by the bonfire, and at a certain point, the men started on the fireworks. They shot up into the sky over the river, sending glimmering sparks down over the surface of the water.

It was magical, this. It wasn't polished, it wasn't classy or… Any of the things that she had once thought might remove the pain of her childhood. Any of the things she'd thought at one time would've made her feel whole. Would have made her feel acceptable. No. It wasn't any of those things. But it was real. And it was the place that she had chosen to be. And somehow it fit her.

But maybe that came back down to what Evelyn had said earlier.

It fit because there was love.

It fit because she loved Brody McCloud. And that was really all that mattered.

They began the countdown to midnight, and she was

exhilarated when Brody grabbed hold of her, and kissed her when they got to "one." It didn't matter that it was temporary in his mind. He was all right, staking his claim. Already okay with making it public. So maybe… Just maybe, he was more in line with her thinking than she had given him credit for.

The kiss made her head spin. And when they parted, he looked at her. "Happy New Year."

"I love you."

CHAPTER TWENTY

THE WORDS ECHOED in his head. Echoed in his soul. He couldn't remember the last time anyone had said them to him.

Liar.

He could remember. He didn't want to. He didn't like the memory. He didn't like the person who'd said them. He didn't want to love the person who'd said them.

Nobody else had heard. And everybody except Lachlan and Charity had been too busy kissing to even really notice that he had kissed Elizabeth. Much less listen in on the conversation.

"I…"

"You don't have to say anything," she said.

"Okay," he said.

Somewhere in there, the words "you have the right to remain silent" floated around his brain.

He figured maybe he should.

"Will you come back to my place tonight?"

It was a bad idea. Except… Why? This was the thing he had been worried about. Well. Kind of. And now she'd said it, so he couldn't keep it from happening.

Benny was coming back in two days. So maybe… Maybe it was best to just…

"All right."

"Good."

They said their goodbyes, and left the party right around when everybody else dispersed. They got into the truck and didn't say anything as they drove back to her place.

Her place, which felt as familiar as his own. Where he had taken to stashing clothes and a toothbrush. He'd moved in. Hell. He hadn't really admitted that until now. Her place was nicer, a little newer than the one he stayed in on the property. It made sense to be here.

It was dark in the house, and before she could move to turn on any lights, he pulled her into his arms and kissed her.

Selfish bastard.

She loved him.

She loved him, and that broke something inside him.

He should tell her he couldn't do this. He should tell her he could never be her husband, could never be Benny's stepdad. Couldn't live in this cute little place and plan for the future. He should tell her there was something wrong with him.

But instead, he kissed her. Because he wanted her. Instead, he kissed her, because feeling loved felt so damned good, and that had always been his weakness.

Except this time… This time he was hurting the person who loved him. By not being good enough to tell her what they couldn't be. What they couldn't have.

He tried to tell himself that she knew. She had to know. Because they had met, and she knew about the jagged, messed-up pieces inside of him already. So she had to understand. She just had to. But he was too much of a coward to say anything. He kissed her anyway. In the dark, in the quiet, in the first moments of the new year. With the end of all that they were looming.

He kissed her.

He drank that love in, because he needed it. Because he wanted it. Because he would never in all his days want a damn thing more.

She had always been too beautiful for him. Too soft. *That isn't fair. She's not just that.*

No. She was strong, and she had been through too much. Foster care all of her life, with no one ever adopting her. Only the woman who had taken her in for the last few years of high school and then died. And that husband of hers…

People had handled her so badly.

He couldn't be trusted with her love. Not when it had already been so misused.

And he still wasn't strong enough to turn her away. Not now. Even though he should. Dammit, he should. But he just couldn't. Evidence of why he couldn't accept this. Because he was weak. It was so clear. So apparent. And even as he called it what it was, he couldn't stop himself from wanting more from her. From demanding more.

Their clothes came off easily. Because that part had always been so easy.

And he lifted her up off the ground, wrapped her legs around his waist and walked them both down the hall, laid her down on her bed, all soft and beautiful and everything she was. And he kissed her. Every inch of her. Until she was moaning. He could give her this. He was good at it. He could make her desperate with desire for him. He could do that.

There might be a lot of things that he couldn't do. He regretted every single one of them. But he could do this.

He could take this beautiful, untouchable creature and touch her everywhere. Could make her cry out her need.

Could make her forget. Everything but the moment. And she loved him.

What a piss-poor offering this was. To a woman who loved him.

But it was what he had.

He kissed his way down her body, and feasted on that place between her legs. Until she was whimpering, arching up off the bed. Until he was confident that it would be this sensation burned into her whenever she thought of arousal. Whenever she thought of need.

That she would never forget him. No matter who came next.

Because there would be some man. Some man who had been raised in a perfect suburban home, who didn't have all this disaster rolling around inside of him. And maybe he would even move her away. To a house with a white picket fence. And he would give her everything that she deserved. But he couldn't give her this. Only Brody could give her this.

Because one thing he knew. No man would ever want her as much as he did.

When she was shaking, begging, he moved between her thighs and thrust inside her.

She gasped, arching against him, and he lost himself. He gave himself up to the wild abandon of his need, his rhythm uncontrolled as he surrendered to the beast roaring through him.

She cried out his name, he shouted hers, and he knew without a doubt that there would never be a moment that he moved past this. If he couldn't get over his childhood to be with her, then he would never get over her.

He would never want to go out. Hooking up would never mean anything. It would never feel like anything.

Not when he'd had this. Not when he'd had Christmas with Elizabeth.

No. Nothing would ever mean a damn thing after that.

He lay next to her, breathing hard. And he didn't say a thing. But neither did she. She curled up against him, her hand on his chest, and just for a minute, he imagined this. Imagined it as forever. Imagined it as something possible.

Just for a minute. Because he could only hold on to it for that long. Because after that... After that, he slipped into the abyss of his own soul. And was reminded of everything he'd ever done wrong.

And was reminded that it was impossible.

CHAPTER TWENTY-ONE

He was gone when she woke up in the morning, and she wasn't really surprised.

All of his things were gone. The toothbrush, his clothes. He hadn't told her that he didn't love her.

He'd just looked away.

Because Brody was good at that. She already knew that. Brody was good at it, because this was what he did. He slept with people, and then he left them. Under the cover of darkness, no doubt. And for a minute, she just sat there, holding her sheet to her chest, giving in to the feeling that the mattress was sucking her down into the floor, deep into a chasm of despair.

She loved him. And he'd left her.

He'd damn well left her, just like everyone else, except at least Carter had explained to her why he was leaving. At least, there had been another woman. At least—

No. There was no one else for Brody. Nothing but his own demons, and some deep truth down in the center of who he was that he didn't want to get into. That he didn't want to acknowledge. She could chase after him. But she'd said her piece. She loved him. She hadn't asked anything of him. And she had told herself that she would accept whatever he was ready to take.

So maybe he wasn't ready to take any of it. Maybe he needed some time.

She was going to have to trust that her love was enough. And that in the end, Brody would come back to her, because he felt the same way. That very thought was terrifying, because it required a level of trust in her own self that she wasn't sure she could find. In her own appeal, and her own importance.

Should, except one thing had been true about her and Brody from the beginning. They hadn't been able to stay away from each other even though the whole situation was improbable. They hadn't.

So it would have to be true now. It just would. She had no distractions. Not today.

She had to just sit in her own sadness. She couldn't retreat behind being Benny's mom. She couldn't retreat into her job because they were still on a break.

She just had to sit with this.

And hope.

It was by far the hardest thing that Elizabeth had ever done.

BRODY FELT BROKEN. And that was a new experience. He'd felt that way a whole lot of times in his life. But this was the first time he felt like he was maybe able to do something about it, and just wasn't. It was some bullshit. And he didn't know how to get past it.

That was the problem. He didn't know how to fix it. Not any of it.

Not himself, not...

He sighed heavily and walked up to the door of his brother's house. Because it had to be Gus. Gus was the one he'd betrayed the worst with his actions.

Gus who had borne the brunt of it. Gus who had cared for them.

It was his wife, Alaina, who opened the door.

"Hey Brody," she said, hand on her baby bump, her expression confused.

"Is Gus around?"

"Yeah. He's having coffee."

"Great. I just… I need to talk to him."

"Yes," she said, stepping out of his way. He went past her and saw his brother sitting at the dining room table.

"Good morning," Brody said.

"Clearly not. Or you wouldn't be here. Coffee?" Gus asked.

It was such a strange thing, to look at his brother, his scarred face, evidence of the abuse that he had suffered, sitting in their childhood home. With a wife. With a baby on the way.

Put together in a way that Brody just wasn't. And the thing was, Lachlan had a point. Why couldn't Brody seem to sort through all of it? Why, when they were the ones who had suffered in a way that he didn't? And maybe, maybe it was the lying. And maybe there would be no way for him to sort it all out. Maybe he could never be fixed. But part of him really wanted to try right now.

Part of him wanted to try to make sense of all of this.

"So Elizabeth said she loves me," Brody said.

"Yet you don't look happy," Gus said. "Sit. Have coffee."

He found himself doing what Gus said, because it was a habit. Listening to his older brother.

Maybe that was why he was here.

He poured himself some black coffee and then sat down across from Gus. "Of course I'm not happy about it."

"I mean, I get it. Kind of. I was thrilled when Alaina

said she loved me. I didn't say it back, though. That was kind of the big hang-up there."

"Well, I relate to you. I'm not... Look, who doesn't want a beautiful woman to love them? But the problem is, she's got a kid. And she needs all this stuff. She was in foster care, and... I can't be the perfect rescuer for her. She deserves that. She deserves..."

"I learned something being a married man, Brody. Women don't like it when you tell them what they deserve."

"Well. I didn't tell her. I didn't actually talk to her."

"Pansy ass," Gus huffed.

"I don't want to hurt her, Gus. It's the last thing I want to do, and that's the problem. She's been married before. She thought she was in love. She thought she was in love, and that guy abused it. What if I do the same? What if there's something wrong with me?"

"Why would you think that?"

"You tell me, Gus. You tell me. What makes a man like our dad *love* somebody? What makes him...? There has to be something fundamentally twisted in me, doesn't there? Because in the same way that he looked at all of you and just... Hated you... He loved me. What the fuck must be wrong with me?"

"Oh. So now we're responsible for the way Dad treated us?"

"No. Hell no. That isn't what I meant."

"You didn't make Dad love you, any more than I made him set me on fire, Brody. That's bullshit. That's an excuse."

He had to tell him. He had to.

"No. It's just... It's not the same. I... Gus, I know where Dad is."

Gus got still. Silent, his hands rested flat on the table, his lips pressed into a firm line. "You, what?"

"I know where Dad is. I've seen him. Lots of times, actually."

"You've seen him?"

"It's been a long while, but yeah. I found him, after he left, and I... I'd go visit him sometimes. Make sure he wasn't drinking himself into an early grave by...having a drink or two with him at the bar and driving him home. I paid... Remember ten years ago when I said I bought a truck? I didn't. I lied to you. I mean, I did buy a truck. But I only spent about half the money on that."

"I just thought you got a really bad deal," Gus said. "I remember that truck. It was kind of a piece of shit."

"It was. It surely was. Because I used the rest of the money to pay for a surgery that he needed."

Gus looked...at a loss. And it made Brody feel worse than he'd ever imagined it could. "You took our money, and you paid to do something to heal that bastard?"

"Yeah," Brody said. "I did. Because that's how much I wanted someone to love me. I made a really dumb decision, I betrayed you, and..."

Gus set his elbows on the table and tented his fingers, resting his chin on the tips of them. He was silent for a long moment.

"I'm not gonna lie to you, Brody. I can't understand. I... I'd kill Dad as soon as look at him. I sure as hell wouldn't save him."

"I don't blame you for that. I kept that from you, and it's been killing me. Because all the things that you guys think of me... I guess you're right. I guess you are right. I... I was always in the middle. I knew that what he did to you was wrong, but I wanted so much to have Dad

the way that I did, that I didn't oppose him. And then…
And then later, I didn't cut him off."

"I'm not mad at you," Gus said, after a pause.

"You just said you couldn't understand," Brody said.

"And I don't. Because I think about that man, and I
see the bastard that tried to kill me. But I'm not mad at
you. Because the thing is, he screwed all of us up. Deep.
So badly. We didn't even have a chance. And you know
what, as messed up as it is, it probably says good things
about you that when you love someone, it's not all that
easy to stop. That you're not an asshole who would've
left him to die."

"Maybe it means I don't love the rest of you enough."

"Bullshit. Here you are. Working with me. Here you
are, every day. Here you are in my kitchen telling me
all this even though it kills you."

"This is the problem. The way that I feel… The way
that I've loved people… I don't know how to do it right.
I don't know how it looks when it isn't twisted. I don't
know how it looks when it isn't a mess. How do I ask
her to be part of that? To be part of me?"

"It seems to me she's the one that's doing the asking. And this goes back to what I was saying. You can't
tell a woman what she wants. You can't tell a woman
what she can handle. They don't like it. Ask Alaina. She
just about took my eyes out over that. I don't need you
to be the same messed up that I am, Brody. That's the
bottom line. You don't need to want to kill somebody.
Even on my behalf."

"I do hate him," Brody said. "It's just…"

"That's the thing. We didn't really have much of a
chance. Who showed us what love was? We had each
other. And it wasn't perfect. Because how could it be?

We are a product of where we came from. But I met a woman who loves me. And that taught me some things. It changed things. Loving her has changed *me*. I understand myself, the world, in a way that I didn't. And because of that, I think I'll be a pretty good father. At least, I hope I will be. The same as I think you'll be a good stepfather to Benny."

"Getting ahead of yourself," Brody said.

"Yeah. I know. But that was going to be your next excuse. If I know one thing, it's that if you wait until you feel like you're good enough, you'll make excuses until the end of time. But if you just… If you just let it go, if you just have to decide that the world is a damned miserable place. Or at least, it can be. And if you have the opportunity to seize some happiness in it than you damn well should."

"Why?"

"What do you mean, why?"

"Just… Why me?"

"You have to stop making it all about you. I don't know what answer you're looking for, Brody. That you're uniquely special or uniquely cursed, but you seem to want to be *something*."

Gus shifted, lifting his coffee mug to his lips for a thoughtful moment before continuing. "Here's what you are, an idiot who found a woman brave enough to love him. So what do you do with that? You're the only one who can answer that question. You're the only one who gets to decide what kind of happy you're going to be. Is it Dad? Does he get to decide? I decided no. That asshole doesn't get to have a thing to do with whether or not I'm happy. He scarred up my face… But he didn't get to decide whether or not I was worthy of love. He doesn't get to do that to you either. He doesn't get to determine what love is. Not for you. You get to decide. Just like you get to decide what your life looks like. We didn't get to control any of that." And suddenly, Gus's breath left in a gust. "And you know what…? You spent a long time trying to hold on to love. Just that little, broken kind that you got. That's pretty brave. Why not make use of it? Be brave enough to be happy. Be brave enough to have a better kind of love."

His brother's words scraped his poor battered soul raw.

"And if I'm broken?"

"Fix your damn self."

And he knew that he was staring down a crossroads. He'd done it before. And with all the shame inside of him, he had gone and met with his father, let him manipulate him, let him beg him for money. He'd given it to him. It had been a decision made with a whole lot of shame and a whole lot of fear. But he realized that deciding to make something with Elizabeth… That was the opposite.

And that was how you knew.

He realized that then. Plain as day. That was how you knew it was real.

"I have to go," he said.

"Good. Get your ass out of here and go make a smart decision."

"I will. I sure as hell will."

He left his brother's house, and he didn't even bother to get in his truck. He ran. Ran to Elizabeth's house.

He ran to his future.

CHAPTER TWENTY-TWO

WHEN SHE HEARD the intense knock on the door, she knew it was him. Of course she did.

She went and answered it, even though she didn't really want to.

"Brody…"

"I have something to say," he said.

"I… Well… Say it, I guess."

She didn't know if she should be bracing herself for a blow. For a big letdown. For him to tell her exactly why it wasn't going to work. Exactly why he didn't love her. Or why he *couldn't* love her. She didn't want to hear it. She wanted to stop him. And yet. She felt like she owed him a chance to say his piece. And she felt… Brave enough.

Strong enough. To take whatever came her way. Whatever.

Happened.

"It's taken me a while… Like thirty-four years… To sort through what the hell love is. And whether or not I wanted it. Or whether or not I hate it. Whether my dad loving me meant there was something wrong with me. And it all got so twisted in me, and I was afraid that if I tried with you… What I gave you was going to be wrong. That it was going to be some cracked, messed-up version of what you deserve. But I went to talk to Gus this morning. And I realized something. I realized that trying to get my dad to keep on loving me… It made me crazy. It made me anxious. It made me ashamed. And nothing with you ever makes me feel that way. That's how I know it's real. Because there's no room for any of that when I think of you. When I think of how I feel for you. I don't know how to be a husband, Lizzie. I don't. I'm not a fancy guy with a fancy house… I never thought about being a father. And shit, you need a guy that's going to be a good father figure. That's even harder than being a biological dad, isn't it? Because I've got to figure out how to be there, and not overstep. I've got to figure out how to strike a perfect balance when… I've never found balance in my life at all."

Every word out of his mouth took her breath away. Every word healed the cracks inside her.

Made her hope.

Oh, how she hoped.

It hurt. But it was good.

"Brody… You… Just be you. That's the man that I fell in love with. Everything that you've been from the moment that we met."

"But my track record is terrible," he said. "I've never been in a relationship, I've never even thought about what it would be like to get married…"

"It doesn't matter. I knew Carter for years. And I trusted him. I trusted that he would be with me, based on knowing him. But we didn't know each other, because we didn't even know ourselves. And that's one of the craziest things about being with you. It's taught me about me. I know myself better now for having been with you. And that's a miracle. You made me understand all these pieces of myself. You… You made me okay with being me. Not just Carter's ex-wife or Benny's mom. Or a foster kid that nobody wanted. I told you that I loved you with no expectations, Brody, not because I didn't think you could live up to them, but because I was okay with not having what I wanted right away. Because I just felt… It isn't a weird, insecure love that makes me feel worse about myself. It makes me feel better. It makes me feel stronger. It makes me feel like I'm worthy of all kinds of things."

"You want to marry me?"

"Yes. I do."

"Can I call you Lizzie?"

"Forever."

"Are you going to end up having to keep his last name? Because it's okay if you have to. I understand why you did. I understand that it was for… That it was for Benny."

"Yes. It was for Benny. But you know… I was clinging to something with that. To this ideal. The need to pretend that my old dream wasn't broken. I didn't want to be broken. And I didn't want my family to be. But it won't be. It's not. It might not be what I dreamed of but, my dream wasn't as good as this reality. Because it was just a picture. Nothing more. This is more than a picture. It's life. It's deep. And I wouldn't have it any other way. So even though Benny will always be Benny Colfax, it doesn't make him less my son if I am Lizzie McCloud. Elizabeth. I still want to be Elizabeth. I need something nice for my business cards."

He laughed. "That's fine with me. I never… I never thought I could do this. I never thought anyone would love me."

"I do. I love you, Brody McCloud. Everything you are."

"I love you too."

"Thank you for making me the best version of myself."

"Me too," he said. "Me too."

"Benny won't be back until tomorrow. You know what that means?"

"We can have sex all day," he said.

"You can have half the day. Now we have a wedding to plan. Because I can't live in sin with you, I have an example to set. But I also can't *not* sin with you. So that means this has to be quick."

"In the aid of not sinning, I will make a binder and plan that wedding better than you've ever seen a wedding planned, and I'll do it in record time."

"I have absolutely no doubt."

"And then, when Benny gets back… I have an idea."

ELIZABETH WAS VIBRATING with nerves. And excitement. Benny was coming back today, and Brody had been gone for most of the afternoon.

He had a plan, he hadn't let her in on the details of that plan. But… She knew that he wanted to have a man-to-man talk with Benny.

She saw Carter's black SUV rolling up the road, and right behind him was Brody's beat-up pickup truck.

Her heart lifted at the sight of both.

She couldn't believe it. And it didn't feel too good to be true. It felt right. It felt like life. It didn't need to be perfect from this day on. It just needed to have Brody and Benny. It just needed to be… This.

And she had every confidence that it would be. Because she didn't feel like she didn't deserve it. She felt like enough.

And so did all of this.

The SUV parked right up in front of her cabin, at the same time Brody rolled up in his truck. And when she looked through the windshield, she thought...

What?

Brody was wearing a black mask.

Over his eyes.

And then he got out of the truck and it all became clear. Black from head to toe, with black gloves and black boots.

He was dressed as a pirate.

Then Benny scrambled out of the SUV. "Brody!"

"Benny," Brody said.

"Benny!" And then Benny looked away from Brody, and at her, and the smile that lit his face filled her with joy.

He went running toward her, and she scooped him up into her arms, twirling him in a circle. "I'm so glad you're home."

"Me too. It was too long," he said. "Dad said next time I could just come for Christmas and go home after if I want to."

"Very reasonable of your dad."

The door opened, and Carter got out. "Hey Elizabeth," he said.

"Did you have a good Christmas?" she asked.

"Yeah," he said. "We did. It was great. Benny has a bunch of stuff in the back of the... I was just going to get it. Am I missing something?"

"Definitely," Brody said, not taking his eyes off Elizabeth. "You're definitely missing something."

Carter went around to the back of the SUV. Opened it up and took out Benny's backpack, and several more bags full of presents.

"I'll see you later," Carter said after he had left the bags on the porch. "Love you, Benny," he said, reaching out and giving Benny a hug.

"I love you too, Dad."

And that was why she knew it was worth it. No matter how much it hurt when he was gone. No matter how hard it was. It was worth it because he loved his dad.

And love was an everexpanding thing. It didn't have to be small or selfish. And it didn't take. His loving Carter didn't take any love from her.

Love just grew. And she could find it in her to… To love Carter as the father of her son.

To not be so hurt.

Because she wasn't missing anything. She wasn't wistful anymore that they had to share custody. That they didn't share a household. Because how could she be?

She had been trying to fit herself into a space that she didn't fit in.

"You look different," Carter said, stopping and looking at her for a moment.

"Yeah. I am. I'm sure I'll be talking to you a little later today."

"Okay…" He looked like he wanted to ask questions, but also like he realized it wasn't his place to ask those questions.

To give him some credit.

"See you."

"Yeah," he said.

And then he got in his SUV and drove away, leaving her with Benny, and the pirate.

"You might be wondering why I am dressed so nicely," Brody said to Benny.

"That wasn't exactly it."

"Well. I dressed in my best pirate gear because I have a question to ask you."

"Okay," Benny said.

"Ben, I would really like to marry your mom," Brody said. "But I wanted to talk to you about it first. Because you've been with her, the two of you, for a lot of years. I love her, and I want to be with her. And I want you to understand that. That I want to be with her because I love her. Because I know you love your mom a lot. And I want you to be sure that my intentions are honorable. Even though I am a pirate."

"What?" Benny asked, his eyes going wide. "You want to marry my mom?"

"Yeah. I think…a big part of that for you to think about is that it would make me your stepdad. I know you have a dad, and that he means a lot to you. That you love him. You just had Christmas with him. I'm not trying to take his place. I'm gonna make a lot of promises to your mom when I marry her. And I owe you promises too. I'll be there for you. Answer your questions. Probably make you do chores you don't like. I won't make you call me dad, because you have one. But… Basically, what I want to do is fill in whatever needs filling in. And we both want to take care of your mom."

"Yeah," Benny said.

"Is that okay with you?"

"What if it's not?" Benny asked.

"I'm going to marry your mom anyway. You heard the part about how I love her, right?"

"Yeah…"

"But I just want to know what I'm working with," Brody said. "Because I'll work as hard as I can to prove to you that I deserve to marry her. And to earn your respect. A man can't just demand it. He's got to show he's worthy. Especially when he's a pirate cowboy."

"Yeah," Benny said. "You can marry my mom. You're a pretty cool guy."

"Thanks, Ben," Brody said. "That means a lot to me."

Elizabeth couldn't help it. She started to cry. Because he was perfect. He hadn't asked an eight-year-old's permission. Because a grown man shouldn't. He'd been perfect. Authoritative, and respectful. And she just loved him. Plus, he was really hot in the pirate outfit.

"And now I suppose I have something to formally ask you," he said, turning to Elizabeth.

Her heart leaped up into her throat.

"Brody…"

"I went to a little jewelry store in Gold Valley after I found the costume." He pulled the ring box out of his pocket and got down on one knee. "Elizabeth… Lizzie… Will you marry me?"

"Yes," she said, flinging herself into his arms. "Yes."

He took the ring out of the box, and pried open her grip so that he could take her hand in his and put the ring on her finger.

It was the most beautiful ring she had ever seen. The most beautiful moment. This was her family. Her perfect, whole family. And there was nothing broken about it.

She kissed him, and then he groaned.

"What do you need from me, Lizzie? Just tell me, and I'll give it to you."

"I don't need anything special, it turns out. All I really need is for you to love me."

He smiled. That wicked smile that she loved so much. "As you wish."

EPILOGUE

THEY MARRIED QUICKLY, and by the following Christmas, they had a brand-new house built and completed at McCloud's Landing. By the next Christmas, they had added a girl to their family. And two Christmases later, another one.

Benny didn't even complain about being surrounded by sisters.

He was the best big brother. Elizabeth was so happy to finally get to appreciate that. She had always felt disconnected from that when it came to Carter and Ashley's kids.

But she got to watch him with her and Brody's little girls, and it filled her with so much pride she could hardly stand it.

As for Benny and Brody... Ben. She could never remember to call him Ben. Well, sometimes they butted heads. Brody was stricter than Carter. Brody also took on the heavy lifting of fatherhood, because Ben was with him more of the time. Ben didn't call him dad, but Elizabeth knew that he was a father to Ben in every way that counted. Ben still loved Carter, of course he did, and thought of him as his dad, but... Brody was a pirate cowboy. And in that sense... Carter would never be quite as cool.

And… Well, Brody was taller.

A little tougher, just a little bit more of everything. And if that made Elizabeth feel smug… She tried not to show it. Not all the time, anyway.

She could never have imagined this when she had first come to Pyrite Falls all those years ago. But it was… It was better than anything. It really was. Better than that ideal perfection so many other people had. And if perfection had to break in order for her to have true happiness, she would go back and choose to break it every single time.

They were having their first Christmas, which was the Christmas they had a week before the actual holiday, because it let them celebrate with Ben, and they were gathered around the Christmas tree, the girls getting to open one present, while Ben opened all of his from her and Brody, the Christmas tree lit up merrily behind him.

"How are you doing, Lizzie?" Brody asked, smiling at her as they watched Ben excitedly open up the fishing pole that Brody had chosen for him a couple of weeks ago.

"I'm doing just perfect, Brody. Just perfect."

"I told you. When I think of Christmas, I'll always think of that Christmas we spent back at the small house. Under the tree…"

Her face got red. "Don't talk about that right now."

"Why? No one else knows what happened."

But she did. She'd never forget.

"I love you."

"I love you too."

It was amazing how much she loved Christmas now.

But… She also didn't need to cling to it as the most magical, as the only chance for this kind of joy. With Brody, she felt this kind of joy every day. And that was worth celebrating all year long.

* * * * *

WILD NIGHT COWBOY

CHAPTER ONE

SHAYNA CLARKE KNEW one thing. She couldn't go on like this.

She looked down at the valley below, from where she stood on the viewpoint. The trees were a blanket of green, jagged bottle brushes layered one over the other in an endless patchwork. There was a line where the trees frayed and became red, charred, twisted. The evidence that remained of a wildfire three years ago.

This land, this stalwart land where she'd grown up, found peace, comfort and tranquility for all of her life, had changed more than she had in the past few years.

She had always found peace out here.

Her father was the pastor of the oldest church in Mapleton—both in terms of the age of the building and the average age of the congregation. And while she sat in church every Sunday to hear her father's gentle word, the wilderness had always been her true church.

She took a deep breath, of the pine, the earth, the way the sun baked them both and mixed them together.

Out here she felt wild, when in truth, her staid floral dresses were turning her into wallpaper.

She could feel herself fading into the peeling paint of the Mapleton Episcopal Church. And she didn't much care for it.

She also didn't know how to change.

She didn't really think she was allowed to. She was Shayna Clarke, pastor's daughter, and everyone in the church loved her. And also reminded her often that she was a good girl. It never felt like a compliment, but more of a warning in many ways.

Her father had done such a nice thing adopting her, he deserved the good girl she was.

She was his reward for his good deeds.

The expectation that she be a reflection of his parenting, his teachings, and also an emblem for why charity was so important, weighed on her.

It always had.

She knew how to dream. In her mind, she was as wild everywhere as she was here on the mountain. In her fantasies, she knew exactly what she wanted. How to find the sort of man who set her body and soul on fire. How to touch him. How to ask him to touch her.

In reality, she was so entrenched in her role in this small town she felt nearly trapped by it. If she hated it, it would be easy. She could simply break out of the mold and leave all the shattered pieces behind.

But she didn't hate it.

She loved so many things about her life.

She didn't know how to be the Shayna she was in her head—the Shayna who read erotic romance and wanted a man who did the things she had found in those books—with the Shayna she was during the day.

A church secretary who loved the work she did in the community.

Her father had adopted her when he'd been fifty. Never married, with no children, he'd taken her in when he'd found out about a congregant whose great granddaughter had needed someone to take her baby.

Shayna loved her father. And she loved the quiet life she lived with him. Or at least, she had.

Until she'd begun to feel like the quiet was stifling her. Smothering her.

She could pinpoint the moment it had hit.

She'd been in the grocery store, buying a fiber drink for her father, and she had run into ten geriatric members of the church and she'd had lovely conversations with them.

Shayna had also seen two people closer in age to her from a distance, and one of them had been a man, a reasonably attractive man named Michael who she knew from high school, and who she'd had nothing to say to.

Nothing at all.

It was realizing that her life was so out of step that had sent her into a spiral. Well, that and her looming twenty-fifth birthday. Because twenty had slid into twenty-five with her barely noticing, and she had realized that twenty-five would slide into thirty with no actual changes.

Unless she made them.

She knew how to make a quilt, and a loaf of bread, and some very good cookies.

She didn't know how to make changes.

She knew how to dream about freedom. She didn't know how to take it.

She'd been cautioned against being out here right now, out in the woods, because the rumor had been that Zane Fox was back.

She could only barely remember Zane Fox, and the Fox family. He was at least ten years older than her, so she'd been very young when he was arrested out in front of the church, though she could remember it.

She could remember looking out the church window, seeing him bent over the hood of a police car. She could remember thinking of a wolf at the zoo. Her dad had just taken her to Portland and to the zoo. She'd been devastated by the sight of such a beautiful animal in a cage, and seeing Zane in handcuffs...had been like that.

So strange how it lingered in her memory like that.

She turned away from the view and shrugged her backpack higher up onto her shoulders as she continued down the trail.

And for some reason she felt drawn away from the rocky edge. She generally liked to walk so that she could see down below the whole time—the closest thing to risk-seeking behavior she ever engaged in—but right now she found herself drawn into the trees. Maybe because it was warm.

But either way, she followed that still, quiet voice in her soul. She didn't always think it was God, but given her upbringing, she did sometimes wonder. And she was a little afraid to ignore it when she felt a strong pull toward something.

So away she went, down the winding trail that led into the dark dense of the trees. It was rocky and uneven, but beautiful, silent there in a way it hadn't been beneath the wide expanse of sky. She could hear branches shifting, birds fluttering.

She paused and listened.

And then she continued on. And stopped.

There, right there, was a cabin. Sheltered by the trees and from the sun. It was dilapidated. To the point of looking abandoned. She hadn't realized that anything here was private land, and she knew she was trespassing now. And yet she stood, still, unable to move.

This felt like something. The verge of adventure maybe.

And all her fantasies rose up and tangled with that possibility.

Zane Fox.

His name whispered through her, across her soul, and then she heard heavy footsteps.

"What are you doing here?"

She turned sharply, and her heart leapt up into her throat.

It was him.

She could remember. Those blue eyes. But she'd had no idea how big he was. She only came to the middle of his chest, and when he took a step toward her, she felt like she was being swallowed by him.

His face had scars on it, a day's worth of dark beard. He looked wild, and yet he smelled clean. Like the forest.

He was the kind of man she could find in one of her books. The kind of man her mind conjured up for her late at night.

The kind of man who would know just how to hold her—firm like she wanted it.

Her sexual fantasies had an edge no one would believe. Well, first of all, no one would believe good girl Shayna Clarke *had* sexual fantasies. Much less that she fantasized about being dominated. That pain and pleasure tangled together in her mind. That she sometimes touched herself with one hand while digging her fingernails into her thigh with the other. Chasing an edge that was hard to find on her own.

That what she liked most of all about men wasn't a handsome face, but all that strength.

That she felt a deep desire to feel that strength against her own softness. To be held down. Restrained.

Zane could do all of those things.

The thought made her feel thrilled and panicked at once, because this was reality, not the safety of her mind, and she wondered if the mountain air and thoughts of freedom were making her giddy.

The reality was, she was a virgin who should want safety, softness and a man she knew well her first time.

Instead, she wanted a hard, controlling man who would take charge of it all. Who would push her. See what she could handle. She wanted a dominant man, and she knew that.

She'd started reading romances when she'd found them in boxes donated to church charity sales, and it was always the large, commanding men who captured her imagination.

She looked around her small town and she didn't see those men. Maybe that was the biggest reason she'd always felt stuck.

She knew her fantasies. So well. She knew what she wanted.

She'd never found it.

Right now she felt like she'd run squarely into it.

"I'm…hiking," she said softly.

"Not here you shouldn't be, this is Fox land."

"I didn't know."

"You better run, Little Red," he said, his tone nearly mocking.

"I…"

"You heard me. It doesn't do you any good to be here. Run away, Little Red, before you get eaten."

And then she suddenly felt it. The peril, rather than

the soft edge of fantasy she'd been tempted to embrace. She was alone in the woods with a large man who was rumored to be dangerous. He'd been arrested, tried and convicted for armed robbery years ago.

He'd served jail time, everyone in town knew it, for a crime he'd certainly committed.

And he was giving her the chance to run. Telling her to run.

So she did. She ran.

She stumbled and her backpack came loose and fell away from her shoulders and she didn't care. She left it behind as she ran, her feet pounding on the ground as she fled.

And when she reached her car, breathless, her heart pounding, sweat dripping down her forehead, her whole body trembling, she realized that it was the most exhilarating thing that had ever happened to her in her entire life.

SHE'D BEEN FAR too pretty. And too soft.

He knew who she was.

The preacher's daughter.

That man had been good to Zane back then, and he could remember the wide-eyed little redhead he'd towed along on those charity visits back in the day.

He'd scared her on purpose. He liked to be left alone.

He'd only come back here because a fool would turn down free property, and while Zane Fox had been many things in his life, he wasn't a fool now.

The place was hardly habitable, and it brought back bad memories. Of fists and screaming, and illegal stills. Of his mother weeping, and going away and never coming back. Of his brothers, who were probably all dead now, and his father, who was definitely dead.

This wasn't a happy place.

There were so many ghosts, he had half a mind to sell it, after he got something habitable built. Right now, while the land could fetch a decent enough price, it wasn't going to sell for what he'd like it to. So he'd been working on a new dwelling for the last few months. Building a house on your own wasn't the most fun task, but Zane never expected life to be fun.

Life, in his experience, cut sharp and deep and mean.

And was very little else but teeth and claws.

She was soft.

Yes, she was soft, and that was why he'd told her to run.

He didn't touch soft things.

He liked women who were as hard as he was. Though that came with its own issues. Especially back when he'd been on parole and the girls he'd hooked up with had kept stashes of coke and heroin around.

Ever since he'd come back to Mapleton, though, he'd been more of a hermit, finding something new and interesting in the solitude.

Of course seeing her had made him very aware that he'd had the sort of solitude that left him hard and aching for a woman.

He hadn't been celibate in a long time, mostly because he'd had five years of enforced celibacy and he was deeply uninterested in continuing on in that vein. So he prioritized sex. And food he liked. Because he knew what it was like to not be able to choose to have those things. And he knew what it was like to not be able to choose your own clothes, and your own TV shows.

He'd lived that for five long years.

So now he chose it all, and he reveled in it, and he didn't feel guilty about a damned thing.

He'd also spent these years learning a trade. He'd gotten into construction, and then he'd gotten into being a contractor, and during that time he'd learned a lot about real estate and what sold and for how much. From there he'd begun investing in property, and he'd seen the inheritance of the Fox land on his father's death—in prison of course—as a chance to reclaim his whole sordid childhood.

But then of course he'd decided to build it all himself, and it had turned into a penance of a strange kind that he hadn't anticipated.

Or maybe it was more of an exorcism. But his reaction to the preacher's girl proved to him he had a lot more demons than he liked to admit.

He bent down and picked up her backpack. And was hit by the scent of soap and wildflowers. Damn.

He kept it held tightly in his hand as he walked back toward the cabin. If she came back for it, she could have it.

But he had a feeling he'd effectively scared her off, and he wouldn't be seeing Little Red again.

Which was just fine by him.

Because he would be tempted to eat her up.

CHAPTER TWO

SHE DREAMED OF HIM.

And when she woke up, she was sweaty and throbbing.

She had always been outraged when people had scoffed at sexy books and acted like the women reading them couldn't distinguish between fantasy and reality. And here she was, letting her fantasies bleed into reality.

He was dangerous. And yet she'd dreamed of him. Big and rough, and over her, kissing her, his lips hot and intense on her skin as he...

She put her hand over her mouth and sat there in bed, her knees drawn up to her chest, her heart pounding.

She should have sex dreams about Michael. Who was safe and anodyne and a known entity and not a source of gossip.

She shouldn't have sex dreams at all, because she'd never even been kissed.

But that wasn't how she was built.

Part of her...part of her had sort of hoped...thought that maybe fantasy was only fantasy, and someday she would go on a date with a man like Michael and she would be okay with...*normal*.

But Michael didn't make her burn. Zane Fox did.

But she wasn't an idiot. A dream was a dream. A book was a book. A fantasy was a fantasy.

He wasn't a fantasy object. He wasn't the hero in a romance novel. She had to remember that and not totally romanticize him.

Well.

That dream hadn't been *romantic*.

She felt flushed all over again.

She got up and looked outside. There was rose-colored light spilling over the top of the mountains and it was going to be a gloriously warm summer day. The kind of day she would normally go and have a hike on.

He had her backpack.

Maybe she should go and get it.

Or maybe you should listen when the scary man makes it clear that he's scary, and stay away.

Little Red.

It was funny he should call her that since she'd seen him and thought of a wolf all those years ago.

Funny, but more in the sense that it was unsettling than it being a joke.

She found herself putting on her shorts, her T-shirt and her hiking boots, and found herself getting into her car and driving the fifteen minutes back to the trailhead.

By the time she got there it was about six-thirty in the morning, and surely he wouldn't be up and about then.

You want to see him.

Why?

She argued with herself all the way up the trail, and she found herself standing on the edge of the woods again, staring inside, and now the tragedy was she knew what she'd find there.

And so she couldn't claim to be uncertain about why she felt drawn into the forest.

It was him.

Or my backpack.

But she couldn't shake off the erotic dream.

Or the fact that she was just so desperately bored. And that seeing him—and dreaming about him after—was the most exciting thing she'd ever experienced.

So she kept on walking.

And when she got into the trees, she saw movement, and froze. And just then, she saw him. Striding up the path across from her, toward the little cabin.

He was naked.

His hair was wet, and she couldn't see...the details of him because he was turned to the side and moving at a good clip, but she could see enough.

He was muscular, with ink on his skin. He looked like the kind of dangerous man she'd always wanted. The kind who would never want her.

He looked rough. He looked brutal. Would he be?

Her brain got all tripped up with thoughts like that, because she shouldn't want it. But she did. And always had. Did she have to start slow when she knew she wanted it all?

Her heart was pounding so hard she thought she might faint. She held absolutely still because surely he wouldn't see her if she did.

But then he stopped. And looked through the trees, and she knew the exact moment he saw her.

Because he smiled.

Slow and dangerous.

Showing his teeth.

The better to eat you with.

He didn't say that, but she heard it all the same. Heard it echo in her soul.

Across her whole body.

He turned to face her fully and her heart leapt into her throat. His body was sculpted and tattooed, hair covering his chest, as dark as the hair on his head.

And then....

She sucked in a sharp breath. And again, she ran.

And ran and ran.

Not from Zane. From herself.

HE STOOD THERE in the clearing for a long moment. He'd been down at the river having a bath, which was his custom here, and he hadn't expected to have a visitor, let alone that one. And damn, his body had responded.

She'd been looking, that was for certain, and she hadn't done a great job of disguising that. Not that she'd tried.

She'd stared openly, but not frankly in the way most women in his experience did. She'd looked shocked.

And then she'd run.

Well, nice to know his naked ass was that scary.

He charged into the house and grabbed his clothes, which he'd laundered down in the creek yesterday and had set out to dry. It was a mission keeping clean out here, but he did it. He couldn't stand to live in squalor. The house might be rustic, but he'd made it clean and functional. There was no running water but he'd made a clean space with gravity-flow facilities, and he liked to bathe in the creek, so it all worked for him.

He had a clean, neat bedroom and a nice new bed he'd bought and had brought in. He had electricity running on solar panels and on a backup solar generator. Things worked pretty well, in his estimation, and he didn't plan on being here come winter.

He had some work to do today, so he didn't have time to think about Little Red and her hungry, wide eyes.

He had to get a move on.

CHAPTER THREE

SHE HAD ANOTHER dream about him that night. Now she could fully imagine his body. His muscles.

She had a very vivid imagination because it was far too easy for her to feel what it would be like to have him touch her. What his rough hands might be like against her soft skin.

He would have rough hands. She knew it.

She baked bread. All day. And she did her best not to think of him, and she tried to remind herself that her dream was just a dream, and it wasn't him. It was a fake man her subconscious had created.

He wasn't the real Zane Fox and he had nothing to do with the real Zane Fox, and she needed to remember that.

She baked a batch of cookies and she packed the bread and cookies away. Then she got into her car and drove to the widow Martin's house, one loaf of bread and a few cookies for her. She delivered three loaves to elderly congregants and when she had done so, felt like perhaps her good deeds had washed her clean of her transgressions. Of her fantasies.

But she could still see them too vividly. And she found herself with half a dozen cookies and two loaves left over, and then found herself at the trailhead again.

She was wearing a dress. And her shoes weren't practical to walk up there, not now.

And yet, she got out of the car and found herself carrying a basket and wandering down that familiar trail in her red floral dress.

She stumbled on the rocks and kept on going, gritting her teeth. This was insanity, and yet here she was.

It was late in the day, so he wouldn't be naked.

Maybe.

Maybe he wouldn't even be there, which wouldn't help her retrieve her backpack, but she could leave the bread as a peace offering.

So she went on, cursing the rocks without using profanity and trying to keep her thoughts from churning back to her fantasies, or her memory of his naked body.

She arrived at the cabin and didn't see any movement, and she seriously considered running. Like hell, in fact.

Which was the closest she came to profanity even in her own head.

But she didn't.

Because she was boring and she was tired of being boring. Because she was stagnant and she was sick of that too. Because the last three days she'd felt alive, and she wanted to keep on feeling that.

So she pressed forward to the cabin, and on a deep breath, she knocked.

She didn't hear anything.

She was almost relieved. At least that was what she told herself the feeling of the air in her lungs evaporating was. Relief.

Not disappointment. Because disappointment would be ridiculous.

She set her basket down on the threshold and turned away, trying to hide her disappointment even from herself.

But when she was only about ten paces away from the door, she heard him.

The door opened, and then he spoke.

"Well, well, there you are, Little Red. And I don't think you're looking for grandma's house."

SHE WAS BACK, the little idiot. Zane would never hurt a woman, he would never and had never forced himself on one. He'd never coerced a woman, even. If she didn't want to, he didn't want to.

And given the experiences he'd had in his life, he was absolutely opposed.

She wasn't in danger because he'd *make* her do a damned thing.

She was in danger because he was almost certain she felt the same electric pull that he did. He also had a feeling it would be too much for her. And that if they touched, neither of them would be able to resist.

She was in a dress today, delicate and sweet, and if anything was revealing of who she was, that was it.

It was ludicrous. All of it.

And he should have let her walk away, but he hadn't.

He'd always been bad at resisting temptation.

She turned, her gray eyes looking luminous. "No. I was looking for my backpack."

"Oh, were you?"

"Yes."

"Not me?"

She cleared her throat, looking admirably brave. "Well, I believe you have my backpack, so by that very token, yes, I was looking for you. But in aid of getting my backpack returned to me."

"Must be a special backpack."

She shook her head. "Not really, it's just mine."

"I can understand that." He regarded her for a long moment. "Come on in, Little Red."

He could see her debate that.

"I'm Shayna," she said.

"Pastor Clarke's girl, right?"

She looked a little surprised. "Yes. And you're Zane Fox."

He grinned. A warning, not a welcome. "Guilty as charged. On more than one count, in fact."

"I know who you are," she said. "I remember you getting arrested in front of the church."

That stuck in his gut. He didn't like it. He'd come to terms with a lot of the things in his life, from the indignant to the criminal, but he didn't like she'd seen him bent over a cop car.

"You must have been knee high to a flea back then," he said, stepping out of the doorway and sweeping his arm to the side so she'd go in.

"I was eight."

"I see."

"But I remember it. And I remember feeling so sorry…"

He cut her off. "Don't feel sorry for me, Little Red. I did the crime."

She seemed to ponder that. "I wondered."

"I did. I held up a liquor store with my father. I held a gun the same as he did."

"You were what…eighteen?"

He didn't see the point in following her down that path. She was looking to absolve him because of his age. But that wasn't an excuse. "When you were eight did you know bad men got arrested?"

"Yes."

"Did you know stealing was wrong and robbing liquor stores was bad?"

"Yes," she said.

"So there you have it. No excuses."

She shrugged his words right off. "My dad is a pastor, right and wrong are kind of his thing. Wasn't yours a career criminal?"

"He was. Emphasis on *was*. He's dead now."

She nodded slowly. "I'm sorry."

"I'm mostly sorry for the worms he's poisoning while he goes back to the dust. The man was toxic, through and through."

If she was shocked by his crass statement, she didn't show it. "I've heard about him."

"I imagine in the same breath you heard about me."

She didn't deny it. "Do you have my backpack?"

"Just a second."

He went out of the living room, back into the bedroom. There were only two rooms in the cabin. The living room and kitchen area, and the bedroom. And he took her backpack off the chair in the bedroom and walked back out into the tiny living space.

"Here you go, Little Red."

"Thank you," she said.

"What's in the basket?" he asked, gesturing toward her.

"Oh. Bread. And cookies. I thought you might be in need." She looked around the space. "I'm surprised by how the place looks inside. It's a bit…"

"Cleaner than you thought?"

"And newer."

"I learned to do construction when I got out of prison.

That's a practical skill. I know how to fix things. Good with my hands."

He didn't imagine it. She turned pink. Bright pink. From her cheeks down her neck, a color that vanished beneath the neckline of her dress.

If he wasn't mistaken, her response to him was a bit carnal.

But then, she'd seen him naked coming up from the creek, and she was back. To get her backpack, yes, but also with bread.

Don't let your imagination run away with you.

Except, he wasn't a man who did that. Not ever.

He didn't get caught up or swept away. He was firmly planted in reality, and the reality was, this woman was looking at him and turning pink, and she was back in his house when she didn't need to be, and she'd brought him bread.

"So you'd say…you'd say you changed your life?" she said.

"Do I rob liquor stores anymore? Is that your real question?"

She shook her head. "It isn't."

"Then maybe you should make your real question clear."

She looked surreptitiously around the room, like she was checking the place out, but he had a feeling she was just avoiding eye contact. There was something on her mind, that was for sure, and it wasn't backpacks or bread.

"You changed your life," she said. "And I don't know how to do that. I'm stuck."

"I imagine you aren't stuck in a life of crime."

She shook her head. "Worse. I'm boring."

He laughed. "Oh honey, there's a lot of shit that's worse than boring. If you'd been to prison, you'd know that."

"Okay, that's fair. But I still want to know how to be different."

He shrugged. "You be different. I don't know why I'm giving life advice to a little girl in a red dress who looks like she just escaped the local nunnery."

It was a mean thing to say and he could see that he'd gotten her good. But why worry about that? She should leave. And if he had to poke her a bit to get her to go, that was all the same to him.

She set the basket down on the counter.

"I did *not* escape a nunnery. I am not a child. I am not just the preacher's daughter. I am not boring, not on purpose. I just… I just…"

And then she did something wholly unexpected.

Right then, Little Red flung herself across the space, and against his chest, and then she stretched up on her toes and kissed him.

CHAPTER FOUR

SHE HAD NO idea what on earth she was doing. He was as unyielding as stone against her mouth, but he was hot.

Not stone. Not a mountain.

A man.

She shook with her need, her need to be new, her need to be different. Her need to touch him.

She had never kissed a man in her life and now she was kissing a stranger. A man she didn't know at all. A man she only knew *bad* things about.

But the house was clean and new, and he hadn't made a move toward her. Not when he'd been naked and not now. He'd never once actually made her feel threatened.

He'd invaded her dreams. And maybe this was absolutely, utterly foolish. But she'd never been foolish in her life.

She'd been taught to revere sex as something sacred. Something that shouldn't be done casually and yet part of her had always believed she needed to have something softer to introduce her to it. The truth was, she knew what turned her on. Didn't it make more sense to pursue what she actually wanted? Rather than testing it out in a way she didn't?

She wanted him. She'd never wanted a real flesh-and-blood man before. They'd always been figments of her imagination, tailored to her every imagined need.

He was all those things, made flesh.

It wasn't foolish. It wasn't even impetuous.

She'd dreamed of him. Of this.

It was…glorious.

He didn't move for another beat, and then when he did, he was pure energy. With one hand he cupped her chin and with the other, he clamped his fingers around her wrists and walked her back against the wall of the cabin before drawing them up over her head and pinning them fast.

The dominant motion thrilled her.

How had he known?

That this was her secret, shameful fantasy.

Not a gauzy romantic wedding night. Not lovemaking. But a man who would handle her roughly. Dominate her. A man who would make her feel small and fragile, who would consume her. Overwhelm her.

How did he know?

It was perfect. And perhaps she should be terrified. She should certainly be ashamed. The world might have moved to a place where sex positivity reigned, but in her own life, it was all much more mystifying, not discussed, and hushed to the point of being a secret. And most especially, she had never known what to do with these desires. These ones that existed outside of romance altogether, and took up space somewhere much more carnal.

"Is this what you're after?" he growled. He dragged his forefinger along her jawline, and it was rough. Just like she had fantasized. Just like she had imagined. And even though he held her fast, even though there was the illusion that she was trapped, he was asking.

She knew that she could tell him no and she would be able to leave if she wished.

"Yes," she gasped.

"I didn't take you for a naughty girl," he said. "I guess I was wrong."

Was she? Was she *naughty*? Wicked? She didn't feel bad about it, and she supposed that she should. She supposed that she should feel hideously ashamed, and yet the characterization lit her on fire.

"You kept on coming back, tempting fate. I should've known that this was what you were after. And it *is* what you're after, isn't it? A good rough fuck. Because you should know that I don't do anything else."

She nodded, unable to speak. She didn't have words. None at all. Where would they come from? She was out of her depth, and yet, she found there was nowhere else she wanted to be. This man was the encapsulation of something that she hadn't even been able to put words to only a few days ago. The restlessness.

This was her fantasy.

She didn't know Zane Fox, not really. And perhaps what she was doing was foolish, and yet...

Wasn't she entitled to something foolish?

He made it very clear what and who he was, she was not going into it with any illusions. Didn't that matter? Wasn't that *all* that mattered?

"I know what it is," she said. "That's how I want it."

His lips curved into a smile, dangerous and feral. He cupped her jaw again, his hold tight, and then he slid his hand down to encircle her throat.

"You're beautiful," he said, the words gentle, as was his hold, but there was something so possessive about it. Something that spoke of his strength, and it sent a flood of pleasure radiating out from between her thighs.

She let her head fall back against the wall, licking her lips, her breath unsteady. She was so aroused she was in pain. This was more than her dreams. Of course it was. Because he was actually touching her. He was right there, rock-solid wall of hot, hard man. He was glorious. Perfect.

Beautiful, but not in a shiny, polished way. Not in that easy, handsome way that Michael was. Or in the way any man she'd ever known was.

No. He was like the mountains. Unyielding, and wild.

And she wanted to be overtaken by it. By him.

"I don't… I'm not quite sure what to do." She looked up from beneath her lashes, and she watched as his jaw went granite.

Perhaps she shouldn't have admitted to being so inexperienced. But it was the truth. Either he would be compelled by it or not. She had been told before, by the sewing circle at the church, that men were ravenous creatures seeking to devour the innocent.

She was an innocent. And she was ready to be devoured, so she had to hope that Zane Fox was as debaucherous a character as he had been made out to be.

"What do you want?" he asked, his voice rough. Desperate.

Had she made him desperate?

"For you to show me. To show me what I want. Show me what you want. I want you to… I want you to be in charge."

A light sparked in his eye. "I see." And then his lips curved into a smile. "That's a game you like?"

She nodded. She was unwilling to verbalize the fact

that she had never actually played it before. Either he realized or he didn't. Maybe he assumed she was being coy. And that was just fine by her. If it got her what she wanted, if it made him take the lead, she was happy with it. She just wasn't going to be playing the part of vixen because she didn't know how to do that.

Keeping the hand on her throat, he released his hold on her wrists with his other hand, and let it drift down to her curves, down her hip, beneath her dress and up to her hip. He pushed his hand beneath her white cotton panties and gripped her ass, hard. Then he moved it, and gave her a smack. It was slightly hindered by the wall, but it left a sting that was satisfying.

"Yes," she whispered.

"Well, today is turning out a little different than I thought it would. I didn't think that I would be getting baked bread." He moved his hand around to the front of her underwear, and pushed his fingers down beneath the fabric, stroking her slick flesh. She cried out. "And I definitely didn't think I'd be getting fresh-baked cookies."

She was trembling, his rough, wicked fingers playing havoc over her heated flesh as she began to rock her hips in time with his strokes. "Naughty girl."

It turned her on, the roughness in his voice. His obvious pleasure in her wickedness. She had been good all of her life, so having him, this man who was so obviously bad, dangerous, tell her she was *naughty* lit her up from the inside out.

He pushed a finger inside of her and she let her head fall back, gasped as he worked her, moving his thumb in a determined circle at the sensitized bud there, as he penetrated her slowly, watching her face as he did.

She found herself unable to look away from him.

She waited for the shame. For shame that surpassed pleasure, because she was letting a man touch her intimately, and she had never done such a thing before.

But the shame didn't come. Only excitement.

It was so much more like her fantasies than she'd thought it could be. She was wild here. Full of need. She wasn't a fool.

She had known herself.

He kept on pleasuring her, as he undid the buttons on her dress and let it fall open, as he slipped it off her shoulders and let it fall down to the ground.

He looked at the simple bra, and she was shocked by the heat that she saw there in his eyes.

She wasn't dressed to seduce anyone. And yet she could see that he was seduced.

He unhooked her bra, let it fall free, and she wasn't ashamed. Still.

"Look at those. Damn. You are pretty."

He lowered his head, and sucked one nipple into his mouth. She arched her back off the wall, pleasure flooding her. He moved his hand in rhythm with his tongue, his lips, and she felt desire building inside of her. Felt the promise of an orgasm beginning to bloom.

She was familiar with her body, and what gave her pleasure.

But she hadn't fully been prepared for *him*. While she might understand what the crescendo of pleasure was leading to, she hadn't fully anticipated how intense it would be to receive this kind of pleasure from another person.

Suddenly, she started trembling everywhere, and her orgasm broke over her. She clung to his shoulders, moving her hips against his hand, restlessly trying to soothe the ache deep within her.

"Zane," she panted.

"I like it when you say my name," he said, lifting his head and looking at her, directly in the eyes. He reached around and cupped the back of her head, kissed her hard as he pushed his fingers through her hair and held her fast, guiding her movements as he did so. He kissed her deep.

And she began to tremble more.

It was *shocking*. The idea that she could be this turned on this quickly.

But soon, she was on the verge again, from his kiss. From the deep slide of his tongue against hers.

It was so glorious.

"Bed," he said, the word a short, decisive command, but there was no doubt about the fact that it was a command.

She nodded and, wearing nothing but her underwear, took the walk to the bedroom. She could feel his eyes on her. It was a power move, this. Giving her orders, watching her fulfill them. He liked it, and so did she.

He shut the bedroom door, even though there was no need, not out here. But there was something erotic about it. Something decisive. He moved over to the nightstand, every motion methodical. He opened the drawer, and he took out a box of condoms. Her breath was coming in short, hard bursts again, her heart beating so hard she thought it might go through her chest.

"Panties," he said. "Off."

He was still fully clothed, but she'd said that she wanted to take orders, wanted to please him, so she knew that she had to obey. She took them off slowly, and far from being embarrassed, she was aroused by watching his face as she revealed the entirety of her body to him.

"Well, Little Red," he said. "Good thing my mouth is all the better to eat you with."

She shivered. And he moved to her, wrapping his arm around her waist, and moving his hand slowly down her back. Down to her rear again.

Then he lowered himself to his knees, roughly parting her thighs and angling his mouth to center over the most intimate part of her. He licked her, deep. It was so hot, so arousing and shocking, that she cried out, steadying herself on his shoulders. He took her leg and draped it around him, opening her to him, as he began to lick deeper and deeper into her body.

All she could do was cling to him, trying to brace herself. Trying to do anything to keep from melting into a puddle. To keep from collapsing entirely.

He pushed two fingers inside of her, the stretch foreign, and slightly painful.

He growled as he held her fast over his mouth, going deeper, harder.

And she shattered again, completely unable to believe that he had managed to call a second peak of pleasure from her body like this. With such efficiency. With such ruthlessness.

And then she found herself being picked up off the ground and laid on the bed.

"Spread your legs."

She obeyed him, lying there with her thighs parted, completely open to him. Completely bare.

"Good," he said. He took his shirt off, and it took her breath away. He was even better looking than she had realized from far away yesterday. His body even more muscular, more sculpted. She could see the tattoos now. A dragon that wrapped all the way around his midsection. Smoke curling up his shoulder.

A wave done in a similar style, reaching up past his hipbone.

He undid the buckle on his jeans, undid the button, the zipper. Then took them down along with his underwear, and boots. He was completely naked. And she could see that the ink on his leg began down at his knee and extended upward. She also saw that…

He was quite a bit bigger than she had anticipated. Again, she wasn't totally naive. She'd seen pictures of naked men. Aroused naked man. But she thought that men who were featured in such photographs were bound to be much more generously endowed than other men. He exceeded them.

But she didn't feel fear. A pulse quickened in anticipation deep within her core. It was a good thing that she liked pain.

At least, she always had when she was in control of it.

But here, she wasn't.

Rather than frightening her, it thrilled her.

She had never wanted the control.

When he looked at her, he licked his lips, and the eroticism of the moment overtook everything. Her good sense, if she had any. She wasn't sure that she did.

Because here she was, laid out naked in bed in front of a stranger like she was a snack.

And loving it.

She arched her back, up off the bed, her hips bowing up to him, in anticipation.

"You'll get it," he said. "Be patient."

He picked up the condom box and opened it. It was notable to her that it hadn't been opened yet. He took a packet out, separated it from the strip and tore it open. He rolled the latex over his length, and gave himself a couple of slow, firm strokes for good measure. He was teasing her.

He joined her on the bed, lifting her thigh up and draping it over his hip as he positioned himself at the entrance to her body. She forgot to be afraid.

He thrust into her in one smooth movement, and she cried out in pain and pleasure. She was blinded by both, the exquisite tearing sensation vibrating through her, her jaw, her teeth. Everywhere. All the way down to her toes. She was consumed with the push and pull of it. Too full and not full enough. Overstimulated, and yet how could it ever be enough. He looked at her, his blue eyes a little bit wild. More than a little bit feral.

"Good," she said. "So good."

He growled, gripping her chin and holding her face steady, pressing his forehead against hers as he began to thrust inside, hard and fast. He gave no quarter. He had realized her inexperience, but he hadn't backed down. Because he knew. And it was that that made her want to fly off the bed in a million pieces. Exhilarated.

He *understood*.

She'd never been able to share this with anyone. She didn't have words for it. She had been too embarrassed. She'd never been close enough to anyone.

But he knew. He wasn't a stranger, not now.

He knew her better than she knew herself.

It hurt, but she liked it. It was too much, but she wanted it.

He wasn't treating her like she was fragile.

Not like she was innocent, like she needed to be talked down to.

He saw her.

Stroke after stroke, he filled her, pleasure ramping up inside of her again.

He was so big and thick and glorious.

She turned her neck, and he bit her.

The clamp of his teeth down on her sensitive skin pushed her over the edge. She cried out, her internal muscles pulsing around him, drawing him deeper.

It was a cataclysm inside of her. A whole tsunami of need. Like that wave on his hip had come up to eclipse them both.

And then he followed, a low growl signaling his release, as his thrusts became fractured, hard and furious before he let out one last long slow roar.

He pulsed deep within her, and aftershocks spread throughout her body.

"You really are a bad girl," he said.

"Am I?"

He got up and moved away from her. "You might've told me that you were a virgin."

"Why?"

"Because it's fucking hot."

She felt color stain her cheeks, pleasure flooding her. "Is it?"

"Yes. I might've liked to know that I was the first man to be inside of your body. I got a little kick out of that."

"You wouldn't have been more gentle with me?"

"Why? Did you need me to be?"

She shook her head. "No. I didn't want you to be at all. That's why I didn't say anything."

"Of course not. You told me to give you what I wanted. And so I did."

"Thank you." She looked at the wall behind him, her head swimming. "That was what I needed."

"Rough sex with a stranger?"

She nodded. Decisively. "Yes. It was. I might've been a virgin, but I'm not an idiot. I know it turns me on."

"And none of the boys in town did it for you?"

That was an interesting way of looking at it. Because she had been convinced that it was something to do with a defect in her. But the truth was, she never got close enough to any of the men in town because they didn't turn her on.

"Yes. That is exactly it. I knew none of them could give that to me. Whether because they don't have it in them or because I'm Pastor Clarke's daughter. Nobody wants to defile me and then have to look at my father from the front pew on Sunday."

"Lots of eligible men at your church?"

She couldn't help herself. She laughed. "No. That's more of a metaphor than anything else. But they all know who my dad is."

"Yes. I know how that goes." He looked her over. "Come on. Let's go down to the creek."

"Why?"

"To get you cleaned up. To get me cleaned up. I don't have running water in this place."

"Oh. Of course. That makes sense."

"Come on. There's nobody up here. At least not usually. I have had a little redheaded intruder the last few days."

"Well. You had my backpack."

"I did. Good thing you came back for it."

She nodded slowly. She should leave. She should get dressed and go and sit in her shame. Because she should feel ashamed. Any minute now, the buzz from the sex would wear off, and she would realize that she had done something terrible. But it wasn't washing over her, and frankly, she didn't want to go.

So instead, she followed him, completely naked, out into the sunshine.

CHAPTER FIVE

HE COULDN'T HELP but stare at her ass as they walked out the door. She stopped. "I don't actually know the way to the river."

Well. That meant he wasn't going to be able to stare at her the whole way down.

What a pity.

"Follow me."

He felt… Well, he felt better than he had for a long time, and he had no doubt that he shouldn't. He should probably be concerned for his immortal soul. But then, that ship had probably sailed a long time ago. Deflowering the pastor's daughter—and enjoying it—was probably not even chiefest among the things that would keep him out of heaven.

She seemed worth it, though.

She was something wholly and utterly outside of his experience. When he'd gone to prison, he'd only had sex a handful of times. He'd been young. He'd had a few years of celibacy and when he'd gotten out, he'd found he liked a certain kind of woman. A woman with a lot of experience.

He'd never been with a virgin before.

He hadn't lied to her. It was hot.

The possessive feeling that washed over him was intoxicating.

She was *his*.

She'd never been anybody else's.

Power surged through his veins.

Yeah. That was fucking perfect.

The creek was a short walk away, and it flowed slowly. It was the perfect place for a dip, in his opinion. She looked a little bit less certain. He picked her up, and held her close to his chest and walked them both into the water. She wrapped her arms around his neck and looked at him, her gaze luminous and questioning.

"I take care of what's mine." He hadn't meant to say that quite so definitively. She was a stranger to him. And he had nothing to offer her.

He never even considered keeping a woman. Never considered keeping anyone. His family was a long line of assholes. Every branch on his family tree was full of mistletoe. Poison that dragged the whole thing down.

He'd never wanted to bring anybody else into that.

But she was soft, and beautiful, and he couldn't imagine not seeing her again, and with the way that he controlled his life in the years since he'd gotten out of prison, he didn't even fully know how to imagine a scenario where he didn't get what he wanted. Where he was deprived forever, because he simply didn't do deprivation. Not anymore. He sluiced water over her pale curves, letting the droplets roll down her breasts. He watched as her pale pink nipples tightened in the cold. Damn, she was beautiful.

And he realized he didn't know anything about her. Nothing apart from her name.

And for the first time in his recent memory, he wanted to know something about another person.

"Whatever happened to your mother?"

"Oh," she said. "I don't have one. Well. I mean I do. In the way that all creatures do. But I don't have one in any way beyond the biological. I don't know who my biological father is at all, but my father, the pastor who adopted me, is the only parent that I have."

"I see."

"It's one reason that my life has been the way that it has been. I'm an only child, with an older father, and I've always had the community around me. But I... Don't get me wrong. I love my life. Many things about it. But sometimes I feel invisible. Sometimes I feel like part of a person. You know, it's the funniest thing, when you're adopted you're often expected to be very grateful. And I am, I suppose. But it's almost as if your life is never fully yours. So many other people project their expectations onto you. Not my father. It's the hazard of living in a small town. The hazard of being the daughter of someone who is so beloved."

"Sounds fucked-up."

She blushed. Prettily. She had gotten excited by his language when they'd been making love. But in this context, it seemed to embarrass her a little bit, and he found that charming.

It made him want to give her things. Pieces of himself he'd never given anyone.

"I suppose," she said. "But it's also my life, and I don't really know anything different."

"I don't know anything different than the life that I had, and I know enough to know that it wasn't functional or normal. My mother left when I was fifteen. And it was for the best. Because she was high on meth all the time and my dad would get mad about her sampling the product that he was supposed to sell. And then he hit her. Yeah. It was better that she wasn't here."

"Your dad cooked meth?" she asked.

"Yep. Thank God not in the cabin or it wouldn't have been habitable. That's hard to get out. You know, that's the reason that we got put away for so long after the robbery. There was a substantial amount of meth in the getaway car. And that, I had nothing to do with. I will admit the part that I played in the whole thing. But the drugs… That was never me. I saw enough to know to stay away from that shit. It's a good thing too, because in prison… Contraband goes around, believe me, it's tempting. To escape for a little while. And when I got out, it wasn't much better. The memories… Prison was actually better in a lot of ways. I got an education, at least. Before that, I didn't even have a high school diploma. Yeah, I learned a thing or two in there. I'm not even mad."

She looked like she didn't know what to say to that. It seemed fair. He hadn't known quite what to do with the gift of her virginity. She'd given him her first. He was giving a first by sharing.

"You ever known anybody that's gone to prison before?" he asked.

She shook her head. "No. What do the tattoos mean?"

He looked over and touched the dragon on his shoulder. "It meant I thought it looked cool, and a guy on the inside knew how to do it."

"They don't look like prison tattoos."

"I thought you said you didn't know anyone who'd gone to prison."

"I've seen TV."

"I had them touched up after. Do you judge me?"

He didn't know why, but it was important to know.

"No. One thing I'll say about my dad is that he is the least judgmental person on the planet. You know, I don't really feel like I have to behave because of him. He has always made it very clear that my life is my own, and he will love me no matter what."

"Even if he finds out you're depraved?"

She laughed, and wiggled out of his arms. "This feels like a dream. You know, I have a lot of dreams. Sexy ones. I've been dreaming about you the last two nights."

"You're bolder than I expected you to be."

"I think mostly because it still doesn't feel real. This is who I am in my head, it's just I've never been brave enough to be this person outside of my head. Here with you, it all feels the same somehow. Or maybe it's just because I was so tired. So *damned* tired of being good all the time."

He remembered how she was bad for him. And he felt himself getting hard again, in spite of the cold water.

She was a novelty. He didn't know what it took for novelty to wear off. It hadn't felt like a novelty after prison. It had felt like an aching, angry need to glut. This wasn't that. It was something else. Something different.

"What would you say if I told you I was thinking I needed to have you again?"

"I'd say yes," she said.

He picked her up out of the river and carried her back to the cabin, brought her back to the bed and showed her more. He made her cry out his name over and over again. Until they were both spent. Until she dozed, draped over his chest, the remaining impressions of his fingerprints turning the sides of her hips purple. It was the prettiest thing he'd ever seen.

When it started to get dark outside, she stirred. "Oh no," she said. "I really do have to go."

"Why?"

"Because. I usually go and cook my dad dinner on Fridays. He'll be expecting me."

Her cheeks turned pink, like she was a little embarrassed to be thinking of her dad right now. And fair enough.

"All right then, better get on."

She nodded, and started to collect her clothes.

And when she was gone, his house felt…empty. He went and took a can of soup out of the cabinet, then heated it on the stovetop. He took out one of the loaves of bread she'd given him and cut some slices, dipping them into the soup.

And his house felt empty.

It was the weirdest damned thing. He hadn't remembered the woman existed until three days ago and now his house felt empty without her.

CHAPTER SIX

SHE'D SOMEHOW MANAGED to find something to talk about with her dad through dinner, but it had been hard. She kept replaying what had happened earlier. Over and over again.

How had that…happened? Who was she?

That woman who had flung herself into his arms and kissed him. Who had bathed in the river after and then gone back to his bed…

Memories flashed through her mind. Of the second time. When he'd bent her over and showed her what it was like from behind. When he'd staked his claim on her that way, branding her with his iron hold, with the thickness of his arousal as he thrust into her.

She stayed up late baking because she could think of nothing else. Fiction and fantasy no longer felt like a haven when she was so utterly consumed with the reality of him.

How overwhelming he was.

She was still grappling with the brutality of what she'd done to herself the next day when she went out to deliver goodies. This was her life, and it was her life still. Church mouse, basically. Church secretary, really.

Sex hadn't changed that.

And yet it had changed *her*.

Changed everything.

Zane hadn't asked her to come back, and there was church in the morning. She didn't have dinner with her dad on Saturdays because he spent Saturday in prayer and had to go over his notes. So she could disappear for a whole evening and never be missed.

But it seemed risky. It seemed foolish.

She told herself that all the way back to the cabin. This time she had a huge picnic hamper, with a roast chicken, dinner rolls, potato salad and green beans. She really hoped he hadn't decided to have a party and use the rest of the condoms without her, because she didn't have enough food for a party and it really would be awkward.

He opened the door before she knocked. Then he wrapped his arm around her waist and drew her inside, setting the hamper down on the floor before bringing her flush to his body and kissing her like he was starving.

She smiled against his lips. Because it was okay that she had come back.

He was clearly glad to see her.

He pushed her up against the wall, and he reached into his back pocket, taking his wallet out. He produced a condom from the wallet and freed himself from his jeans. When she realized what was going to happen, she gripped his shoulders, bracing herself for the impact of him. Though nothing could truly prepare her.

He gripped her hips and pushed her dress up, swept her underwear aside and thrust into her. She was pinned between his chest and the wall, and caught between need and fear. So sharp and keen that she didn't know which would cut her deepest.

She never wanted him to stop.

But she was afraid. So afraid of how much this already meant.

She clung to him, and she found that she didn't want to let go. Like this man, his grip, his intensity, everything he was, was holding her to the earth. It shouldn't be that way. It didn't seem possible. It was dangerous, that was what it was.

Inviting the big bad wolf to eat you.

They told children fairy tales for a reason. They were meant to be warnings. *Little Red Riding Hood* was a metaphor for not talking to strange men in the woods— or anywhere. But she'd done more than talk to him. Just days in, and she felt like he was an essential piece of who she was.

Need gathered low within her and she fought it. She didn't want to be done, not yet. She knew he could make her climax more than once, but this wasn't one of those moments, she could sense it, even having as little experience as she did. This was meant to be quick. Hard and fast and taking her over the edge.

She focused her world on him. His touch. The slide of his hardness within her.

Yes.

Zane.

And it was his name, echoing through her like a promise, that made her unravel. That made her cry out in ecstasy.

Zane.

He went right after her, roaring out his pleasure as he pulsed deep inside her.

Zane.

He held her there, between him and the wall, for a

breath. And she felt it, hot and powerful on her neck. She wanted more. She wanted him.

It was the more that scared her. The certainty. The depth of it.

She clung to him because if she didn't, she feared she would detach from the earth completely.

How had she not realized that one of the best things about being invisible, wallpaper Shayna was that she always knew who she was?

She was anchored by it—usually. So certain of what would happen tomorrow—usually. And how she would respond—usually.

But she'd stepped off the trail, metaphorically as well as literally, and it hadn't just taken her to a new place, it had taken her to being a new person. And she didn't know what this person would do tomorrow, or any other day. She had no idea at all.

He moved away from her on a gust of breath and she found herself sagging against the wall, breathless and spent.

"Thank you for bringing dinner," he said.

His voice was rough, so she knew he wasn't entirely over what they'd just done, but he was putting his clothes to rights and she dimly realized he'd moved away from her to discard the protection that he'd used.

"Oh. Right. Of course."

She wasn't sure she was hungry for dinner. Not anymore.

"I didn't expect to see you again," he said.

And that statement, the vaguely hopeful note in his voice, the underlying vulnerability of it, reverberated within her like a struck chord on the church's piano.

"I was hardly going to give you my virginity and never return, not my style."

"I couldn't have guessed what your style would be," he said, a slight grin tugging at the corner of his lips.

"Me either, I guess. But I know now." And that realization made her feel more certain, not less.

Maybe she was still just Shayna Clarke, but she acted in a different way because she'd done different things. Maybe what she dreamed about wasn't a part of a whole separate person, but maybe this was simply who she was when given the chance?

It was a strange thought, and one that grounded her without him holding her there, all on its own, which was some sort of miracle from where she was standing.

"I'll dish up," she said, softly.

"No," he said. "I will. You can go get yourself together."

She didn't take offense to that. He wasn't calling her a mess, and she knew it. He was giving her a minute to herself.

She took it.

She slipped into the bedroom and put her clothes back into their place. She smoothed her hair down and took a couple of deep breaths. He didn't have any mirrors in the house. Not as far as she could tell and maybe that shouldn't be shocking. He didn't seem like the kind of man who was at all vain about his appearance.

But even so.

It was slightly inconvenient for her. Maybe he'd get them someday. Maybe some other woman would look into them. She had no idea what he imagined for his future, what he wanted. Because he was a stranger and that was the issue with having sex with a stranger.

She didn't know what this meant. If it was something he often did.

Well, she was the one who'd come to him.

The one who'd kissed him.

So it was maybe safe to say that unless women found themselves wandering the woods and flinging themselves into his arms on a Tuesday, he didn't do this specific thing often.

So that was a comfort, she found, even if she didn't want to know why.

She emerged from the bedroom to find that there were two plates of food made, and laid out on the small wooden table in the corner of the living area.

"Thank you," she said.

"I've never had anyone around for dinner," he said.

He took a seat at the table and she followed suit, taking her position across from him.

"In this place?"

He shrugged. "Ever. You might find it shocking but a lot of people don't necessarily want to have a meal with an ex-con."

"Oh."

"Well, they would. Everyone likes a free meal, I guess. It's only that I've never seen fit to engage in this kind of hospitality."

"Do you not have friends?" she asked, realizing it sounded sort of desperate and pitying. Which wasn't her goal. But she felt slightly desperate. And pitying.

"I have a few. They just aren't come-round-to-dinner friends."

"What kind of friends are they?"

"People I met in prison."

"Oh."

He smiled. "Not exclusively. I also have some friends from my construction days."

"Oh, okay."

"That makes you feel better."

"It isn't about feeling better, I just… I'm not sure sometimes if you're teasing me."

"I guess if you'd have told me about your life I would have felt the same way. I wouldn't have believed in twenty-five-year-old virgins who were flitting around mountainsides, but who also had vivid enough sexual fantasies that they'd jump a guy in the woods that they had chemistry with."

"You make it sound a little more wild than it is." Her face went hot.

"It's as wild as it gets, Shayna."

He said her name and it made her feel warm.

"Well, I'm not used to being wild."

"I get that."

They were silent for a moment, regarding each other across the table.

"So. Your dad used to cook meth."

He laughed. And she found herself laughing too. Because this was ridiculous, and so were they, sitting here in this cabin, when he'd been inside her a few minutes ago, and they didn't even really know each other. Except they did.

Except he was the only one who knew what she fantasized about. The only one who knew what she really wanted. At least, like this. He was the only one who knew how unhappy she was with her life.

So much so that this detour seemed…about right.

"Yes," he said. "My dad did used to cook meth. He also made moonshine, which in light of the meth sounds more like a quirk than some hard-edged criminal behavior."

"Well, yes."

"Your dad is a preacher."

"Yes, he is. All he ever wanted to do was serve the community. He grew up in a poor town off the freeway in Northern California. He served in a few different communities there, was at a few different churches. He landed here back in the eighties."

"Ah, the eighties. I was born in those."

"Ancient," she said, her lips twitching.

"Nineties kid."

"Yes. Though not really. I didn't really do pop culture. And it wasn't that my dad was overprotective, he just wasn't into it. I really liked my childhood. It was different, but it didn't need to be like anyone else's to feel happy. It's only that now…well, the last few months, since my birthday, I've been feeling like my life is stagnant. I haven't always felt that way. I've been happy working at the church and doing community service. I've been happy living here. But I realized there was nothing marking the time. And my whole life was going to slip away. My dad… He was like that, I think. I think he meant to get married and have children. But he never did. He just settled into his life and before he knew it he was fifty and he'd forgotten to do some of the things he'd always intended to do."

"That's a different kind of life," he said, his voice low. "Must be kind of nice. I felt like I'd lived ten lives by the time I was eighteen. By the time my arrest hit. You know, I figured I'd be dead by the time I was your age. Instead I was two years out of jail and figuring out

what that looked like. There was at least some struc-
ture in there."

"Was it…horrible?"

He shrugged. "My life was a war zone before I went
in there. It was rough and there were rules to learn. But
I'm good at avoiding the wrath of abusers. I did it all my
life. I know how to bait a fight when I'm in the mood
to do that, but I can also stay clear of it if I want. I read
a lot, in prison. Got my GED."

She felt a small surge of…pride. "That's really great."

"I didn't take the chance for granted. I actually didn't
want to be my dad, not ever. But I was also tangled up
in his world, and in his morals. Which weren't good,
not at all. It jarred me, the arrest, because I realized if
I didn't change, it would be the first of many. I didn't
think I was like my dad. I judged my dad." He let out
a rough-sounding breath. "I still do, if I'm honest. But
I've seen how it can be when you slide from the life
you were raised in right into a life of crime. I can see
how that works, I can see how you feel like you know
the whole world and how it works by the time you're
eighteen because you've been living rough, living to
survive. I wouldn't say it gave me sympathy for the
devil. But it did make me realize at some point I had
to make a choice that was my own. It wasn't enough to
be superior and just think… I'm better than that guy.
I had to decide."

She nodded slowly. "I think that's amazing."

"Well, don't go thinking I'm too amazing. I'm just a
white-trash idiot from the mountains who decided to be
less of an idiot, because I got put in a cell long enough
to take a break from my life and make better choices."

She rested her chin on her hands. "But that's true of

everyone. I made the easy choices until a different one was in front of me. Until I fully realized I had to decide. And the only reason I was coasting along in an easy, 'good' life was because it was the one I was born into. We all make choices. You were starting from a much different place than I was."

"That is the truth," he said.

It was getting late and she knew she should go, but she didn't want to.

So when he cleared the dishes away and then took her hand and led her to the bedroom…she let him.

CHAPTER SEVEN

THE SUN CAME up and shone through the window, gold and pretty, and tangled through her red hair. She was like the sunrise, right in his bed. He couldn't remember the last time he'd spent the night with a woman. Maybe he had, in those blurry years after prison when he'd been fueled by desperation. But it hadn't been this.

What a jarring, weird-ass thing to have it be in this house.

This house that, until now, had been the site of nothing more than pain and bad memories.

But now there was Shayna, and he truly didn't know what to do with that. With this person who came here to be with him, and simply for no other reason. Unless this was an upgraded version of charity for her.

Dinner and sex.

He hoped not. Because when he'd shared with her it had been real. The furthest thing from charity. It was the most he'd ever given another person and he wanted to think it was the same for her.

It was strange. She was very sweet, and she was innocent. He believed that. But she was also hungry. Maybe those two things weren't incompatible.

They couldn't be, because she contained them both. And she did it well.

She stirred and stretched, the blankets falling below

her breasts, and his body stirred and stretched in response.

She opened her eyes, and there in the sunlight he saw that her eyes weren't simply gray. They were flecked with blue and silver. The sky and the sea. All right there.

"Good morning," she said.

"Good morning."

He kissed her forehead, and wondered what the hell kind of man he was pretending to be, kissing her forehead like that and smiling down at her. He wasn't a relationship sort of guy. He never had been.

He'd never had the chance.

He went and made some coffee using a tin pot on the stove and then brought a mug back for her into the bedroom.

She sat up, the blankets clutched to her chest in a belated display of modesty.

"I've seen all that," he said, leaning against the door frame and sipping his coffee slowly. "Hell, honey, I've *licked* all that."

She turned red, and he loved it.

"Well. Sure."

"You're cute. Do you know that?" he asked.

She smiled and looked down. "No. I don't. I've always felt like I was horribly, terribly plain."

"Who made you feel that way?"

"I'm invisible," she said. "Wallpaper. Nothing special or pretty. No one ever wanted me, or was interested in me or anything like that."

"Or maybe they were afraid of your father. If not the preacher one, the heavenly father one. I don't worry much about all that and even I probably would have been deterred if you hadn't flung yourself into my arms." He shifted his weight, staring at her. "Or maybe, Shayna, there was never anyone who deserved to know you. Maybe there was no one you wanted to share with, because they couldn't give you what you needed and you knew it. You knew yourself better than most people who've been having sex for years. Maybe you had the good sense to know the people around you weren't what you needed."

She shrugged. "Well. Maybe."

"No *maybe* about it. It certainly isn't because you aren't pretty, Shayna."

She looked like she had to think about that. And hard. "I guess I've never given a lot of thought to my looks either way."

"Liar."

She took a sip of coffee. "This is a bit much for such an early hour, Zane. But okay. I maybe wished that I was beautiful sometimes."

"Tell me about it. You said you had a lot of fantasies. Tell me about them." His body went sharp and hard with interest.

"Um. Well, I've never really talked about them before. But I read a lot of…books that fire up the imagination."

"Smut?"

She sniffed. "I wouldn't call them that, no. But I've always been fascinated by the idea of being swept off my feet. Of…men who are strong and powerful. Being seen. For who I am. Not as the boring pastor's daughter."

"I see you. Believe me."

She smiled again, down into her coffee cup, and took another sip. "I confess, my tastes have strayed into being a little bit more outside the box of late."

"Yes?"

"Well, you know. I told you. I always liked the idea of…rough. I started reading books that took it further. Showed pain and domination being pleasurable and it… I like the idea of a powerful man, but that isn't about wealth or status."

Interest fired his blood. "Yeah?"

"No. It's about…" She met his gaze. "I love how strong you are. I knew I would."

He knew she was talking about sex. And hell, the sex was fantastic. But he couldn't remember anyone ever loving a damn thing about him ever. And ever saying it.

"I love how soft you are."

The words felt foreign on his tongue, and he couldn't say he didn't like them. They were nice enough words.

They just weren't normal. Not for him.

"I want to show you something."

He hadn't planned on this. But she was here, and he hadn't gotten much work done yesterday and he'd have to do some today. It seemed like not the worst idea in the world to show her.

"Oh…okay."

"You don't have to get dressed, not unless you want to walk through the whole forest bare-assed."

She wrinkled her nose. "I'll get dressed."

She did, and he watched, because she was sexy as hell and he loved to watch her. He was just going to go ahead and use that word.

Because it was new, and he felt old. Because it was fresh, and he felt jaded.

Then they walked out of the house together, and she was at his side. And he had the strangest urge to reach out and hold her hand. So he did.

And it sent a strange, uncomfortable surge through his chest.

This was new.

What in his whole tired life had felt new? Nothing. For a long damned time.

He looked down at her just as she looked up and smiled at him. They couldn't be more different, except one thing was the same. They'd both gotten off their paths, and they were on new ones.

And right now, they were walking on the same one together, which was, in this tired world, in and of itself a miracle, Zane thought.

They pushed through the trees until they came to the clearing, and the view that overlooked the world. The cabin, of course, hadn't been built on the edge of a view like this because everything his dad did had to be done in the dark, in secret.

Everything.

It was a metaphor. They'd had this whole glorious property, and had lived in a dark corner of it.

The house he was building was no more than a frame right now. But it was there, tall and pretty damned spectacular if he said so himself.

"What is this?" she asked.

"I'm building. Something new."

"Are you going to live here?"

He knew a moment of sadness. "I wasn't planning to. I just wanted to get a new place built so I could sell the land for more. I…own a few properties, a few houses."

Her eyes widened.

"Oh," he said. "You thought this little cabin was all I had."

"Well, you *were* in prison."

"I've been out for twelve years, Shayna. I've had time to sort myself out." He hadn't though, not really. He'd lived a transient existence, even if it had been comfortable. He'd made friends, he supposed, but it was shallow. He'd been moving, constantly, and never letting grass grow under his feet and he couldn't rightly say why.

Because he'd been waiting for this place? It was almost impossible to say.

That couldn't be it, because he was going to sell it. He needed to.

He needed to draw a line under this life, this existence, and move the hell on.

"This is beautiful," she said, taking a step forward, a step into the house.

And his chest did something weird. Completely unexpected. Almost like what he felt a heart attack would feel like, except it didn't feel terrible. It felt almost good. Watching her admire his work, seeing her standing there in the house he was building.

"You're doing this by yourself?" she asked.

"I do everything by myself."

She shook her head. "Not anymore." She tilted her head back and sun spilled over all that glory. "It's Sunday," she said. "I never miss church."

"And I never have someone with me." She smiled at that and he took hold of her chin and tilted it up toward him. "Think you'd mind missing it today?"

Her cheeks turned pink. "I've always felt like this place, the woods, was where I really felt the most spiritual, the most connected. Maybe that sounds silly."

"Other than the times your dad helped me out—and he did help—I've never been to a church, so thankfully,

I don't think it sounds silly at all. The one good thing about living out here, even with my dad, was that not even he could erase the beauty of all of this."

"No, it's way too powerful for that."

"I agree."

He dropped his hand back to his side. "So, you'll stay here today?"

She looked thoughtful for a moment. "Yeah. Yeah, I will."

CHAPTER EIGHT

"You haven't been around much lately."

Shayna looked over at her dad. She had just finished serving him dinner. She hadn't wanted to cancel their regular time, because she didn't want to...

She was trying to remind herself that what was happening with Zane was not permanent. No matter how much she might want it to be.

Zane was gorgeous. Wonderful. More than she could have ever hoped for in a man. But he was a different sort of man. Way too different than she was.

At least, that was what she kept trying to remind herself. They didn't talk about the future, and she tried not to think of it. But she knew that he didn't intend to stay at the Fox property, and she couldn't blame him. His intent was to leave. He was hardly going to change that for her. Nor could she ask him to. It wouldn't be fair.

It wouldn't be fair.

And so, she had sought to maintain her life, even though she spent nearly every night up at his cabin, exploring her desires, and his.

Touching him, tasting him.

Learning all of these new parts of herself. Who she was, and where her limits were. What was best left as a fantasy, and what lit her reality on fire.

But she knew that she couldn't hollow out her existence, because when he left, she needed a life to go back to.

It would be changed. She knew that. Just as she would be. It wasn't a terrible thing. Just something to keep in mind.

It was odd, though, the way that she had known her wallflower status would go on forever if she didn't do something. The way that she felt her life with Zane couldn't go on forever.

"I've just been keeping myself busy," she said.

Her father's gaze became far too keen. But then, of course it would. He knew people. Knew all about them. The flattering and the unflattering, and nothing much seemed to faze him.

But still. He knew her. And she imagined that it wasn't terribly believable that she was just suddenly busy. Though, she didn't think it would be terribly believable that she was engaging in a red-hot affair with a man who was never seen around town. A man who was only rumored to be back.

"You seem happy," he said.

"I am," she said. "I have been. I mean… I am."

"I'm glad of that, Shayna. You don't have to tell me everything that goes on in your life, not until you're ready. But your happiness is the only thing that I care about."

"I appreciate that."

"You also don't have to stay here in exhaustive service to me or to the church."

"I know that."

"Do you?" He looked concerned all of a sudden. "I feel that it has been impressed upon you that you were supposed to be filled with gratitude to me for raising you. But it was never a favor to you. I love you. You are the child that I prayed for, and one that I never thought I would have. You are a miracle to me. And you owe me nothing. All I want is for you to go and have the life that makes you happy. If that's here with me, I'm glad of it. If it takes you somewhere else, I would be glad of that too. Because you were happy."

"Thank you," she said.

And she meant it. Though, there were certain things her gentle father did not need to know, and the fact that she was enjoying glorious nights with a man who left his fingerprints on her skin was probably one of them.

But she was happy. She was happy.

She dropped a kiss on her dad's cheek. "You have never made me feel like I owed you anything."

"I'm glad of that."

But she could see that he looked a bit emotional. And she found herself blinking tears away.

They finished dinner, and she made the trip up to Zane's cabin. She had taken to driving up his driveway, which was faster. It had been a few weeks now.

He was just wonderful. He told her stories about his time in prison, and they could be bracing. Though honestly, not worse than the stories of his upbringing. Which was altogether more disturbing because the violence that he'd suffered was at the hands of his own father.

She talked about the way she had wished for her mother with a detached kind of wistfulness that had nothing to do with reality.

How when she had gotten older she'd realized she was lucky to have a father who loved her as much as hers did, and how most people couldn't claim to have that kind of love even if they had two parents.

She told him that she secretly dreamed of traveling abroad, but had never taken the steps toward it.

He confessed to her that he had never dreamed.

And she had broken just slightly for him.

They shouldn't connect.

He was ten years her senior, and jaded by the world. And yet she had never found another person that she felt quite so connected with. There was something about him. He didn't try to give her advice, even though he had lived a great deal more than she had. He was never derisive of her lack of experience, or her innocence. He didn't believe all the same things she did, and yet he never mocked her.

She had never found quite that combination in another person, and plus, he was... Incredible. Fantastic in bed and demanding. Stern when she wished him to be, and commanding as it aroused her.

To be with someone who respected her, didn't sell her short, understood her and was also not...easy on her... That was something she hadn't known existed. Something she hadn't known she needed. There were other men, she knew, who would've treated her like she was breakable, or like she was a sacred object because her father was the pastor. He managed to make her feel sacred while igniting her with pleasure, and there was something about that which thrilled her in ways she had not anticipated.

She pulled up to the house and got out, and she was secretly thrilled because she was wearing underwear that was entirely different to what she normally did. She knew that he enjoyed her plain underclothes. Because there was something about her innocence that aroused him, but she was in the mood to play seductress tonight. To push his boundaries.

They were all about testing boundaries.

As she approached the door, he opened it, and stood there, wearing nothing but a pair of low-slung jeans, his chest bare, the curve of his mouth dangerous tonight. As if he was waiting for her. As if he had something in store for her.

She shivered in anticipation.

The more that she got to know him, the more trust they built outside of the bedroom, the sharper an edge their play took within it. Because there was trust. It had been delicious to be with him when he was a stranger, because that in and of itself had carried with it a hint of the dangerous. But it was better now. Better the more intimate they became. The more they entwined around one another.

"I've been waiting for you."

"Good. I'm glad."

"I was beginning to wonder if you were going to come tonight. I might have had to punish you if you'd decided not to show."

She wondered if she should stay away one night, just to see what would happen.

To test. To push.

And at the same time, the idea filled her with dread. Because how could she skip a night knowing that their nights together weren't endless?

How could she miss a chance to fall asleep in his arms?

She wanted him. No one else but him.

The desperation of that need frightened her.

He reached his hand out. She loved to hold his hand.

Whether he was leading her to the bedroom, or through the forest for a walk.

He was the same man in both places. Hard, beautiful. A caregiver, and masterful at all times.

He drew her inside slowly, and her heart thundered just a little bit harder than usual. As if she sensed that tonight was different. It felt special to her, even though she couldn't say why.

She was ready. For something. Something more.

"Take your clothes off for me," he said.

It stunned her, the way that he knew. Because he had to know. That she had a surprise for him. That she had something special in store, he had to know.

Because he was the sort of man who did. He could probably see it in the way she held herself. He could probably see it in the way she stood.

That she had on lace instead of cotton.

He was the sort of man who knew such things.

She unbuttoned her dress, slowly, and revealed the black lace bra with glittering red gemstones she had beneath the dress.

The sound that escaped his throat was a growl.

Then her dress dropped down past her hips, and revealed the underwear, and the garters that held up her stockings. Also glimmering with gems.

"Little Red," he said. "You came looking every inch the feast tonight."

"I wanted to please you," she said.

"You have."

A shiver of satisfaction went through her. He did not withhold praise. It was another glorious thing about him.

He made her feel beautiful, and like more than

enough. Like she was wonderful. And like she could do anything. Like she was already flying.

He was wearing a belt, and she knew it was simply because the sight of him undoing one sent a shiver of anticipation through her body. And when he began to slowly undo the buckle and work it through the loops, the temperature inside of her began to rise.

She felt like it was a fever. And she was not sad about it. Not in the least. She was happy to be held in his thrall.

Slowly, he slid the belt out of the loops on his jeans, the side of the leather wrapping around his hand making her throat dry.

He set it down, then undid the button on his jeans and lowered the zipper.

"Get on your knees."

She obeyed, clad in the black lace, and reveling in it.

She kept her eyes on his as she dropped to the ground. He exposed himself, the long, thick length of him familiar now, but exciting all the same.

"You know what I want. Your mouth. On me."

She nodded, and leaned in, curving her hand around his hardened arousal, taking the tip between her lips, slowly, very slowly, taking in as much of him as she could. He was far too big for her to handle all of him, but she loved the taste of him. Loved that in this submissive pose, she could make him shake. Bring him close to the edge.

It was the thing she found to be one of the more exhilarating truths about sex.

That it was the one in the pose that would be described as weak to the outside world that usually held all the power.

That as heady and delicious as it was to be under his command, he only had that command because she gave it to him. Because there was a line, and he would not cross it. Because there was no coercion, only joyful, willing submission.

Because if she refused, then he would be the one left standing there, vulnerable, having asked for what he wanted most, and being denied it. The one who conducted the dance was the one who risked the most.

It made her feel sheltered, cherished and protected that he took that role.

And pleasuring him like this made her feel strong.

She sucked him down, and then slowly released him, moving her hand along his shaft before sliding her tongue from tip to base and back again.

She drew him back into her mouth, watching as the muscles on his stomach tightened, shifted with the effort that it was taking him to keep it together.

She did this to him. She, who had been a virgin up until a few weeks ago, could push him here. Could take him to the brink.

It was beyond belief. The most glorious thing she could have ever imagined.

It still wasn't enough.

He began to thrust his hips forward in time with her movements, the tip of him touching the back of her throat.

And she took him.

Because he wanted her to. And that made her strong.

He cupped the back of her head with his hand, and she was lost. Consumed by him.

"Enough," he said, pushing his fingers through her

hair and grabbing hold of it, drawing her head away, pinpricks of pain dotting her scalp.

"I want all of you."

She nodded. She agreed. Without even asking what that meant. Because she didn't care. Because it didn't matter. Because she would give him whatever he desired. She was his.

She was his.

And somehow that still felt like not enough.

He guided her to her feet, and they looked at each other. He had a cool, remote gaze in his eyes, and she knew it was a game. The part that he played when they were in the space. And there was something about that that locked him into place. That made her not feel like he was quite so distant. That made him feel close. That made this feel real.

She looked down. Because that was her role.

And she could feel his satisfaction coming off of him in waves.

"Go to the bedroom," he said.

And as she walked into the room, she could feel his gaze on her.

She stopped when she got into the room. Because on the bed, coiled at the center of the mattress, was some shimmering black satin. Like a necktie, but longer.

"I told you. I want all of you. I want you to trust me."

"I do," she said.

If she didn't trust him she wouldn't be here.

"I need you to trust me," he said, his voice taking on a hard edge. "I know what I am. And I know what you are. You've never done a damn thing wrong." He moved to her, and she didn't look at him as he gripped her chin and slid his thumb over her bottom lip. "You're such a good girl. You always have been. Until me. I made you bad. And I made you mine. Anyone could trust you. But not me. I was in prison. I was a criminal. That's who I was. That's still in me. I need you to understand that."

She nodded. "I do."

"And I need you to trust me anyway. I need it."

She felt compelled to look up at him. "I do," she said.

He squeezed her chin. "Good."

Then he reached down toward the bed and picked up the length of silk, wrapping it around his hand as he'd done with the belt earlier.

He took the silk and draped it around her neck, crossing it at the front, pressure on her throat sending a thrill through her body. And then he moved it down the length of her arms, wrapping it around her forearms and wrists in an intricate design that left her hands bound together. It was comfortable. Soft. Nothing about it was painful. And no part of her was afraid.

She was his, though. Wrapped up like a gift with a bow on the end.

Just for him.

"Lay down on the bed."

"Of course."

"Hands above your head."

She obeyed. And as she did, lifting her hands up tightened the silk just a bit around her throat. Just that edge of danger. That little bit of a rush that she got with him.

It was easy to trust him. He didn't need to do this, but he could. She would do whatever it took to prove that she trusted him. That she was his. Always.

She lay there, and he moved his mouth to her nipples,

sucked them in deep. She gasped at the friction of his bristly jaw against her soft skin.

He kissed her. Everywhere. And then moved between her legs, taking one long stroke through her woman's flesh with his tongue.

He consumed her, until she couldn't breathe. Until she couldn't speak. Until everything was him, and he was everything.

She reached down to grab him, but couldn't quite because of the way her hands were tied.

"Above your head," he ordered. And so she did.

It was like having his hands on her, even as he gripped her hips. On her throat, pinning her wrists. It was a way for him to keep control even while he concentrated on giving her pleasure.

And he did give her pleasure. Until she was sobbing with it. Mindless with it.

And then he gripped her hips, and positioned himself at the entrance to her body, thrust home.

She was lost in it. The wildness of it. Of him. The sound of their bare flesh meeting, the hoarse, animalistic cries they made.

She had never had shame with him. And she knew that she never would.

And it wasn't enough.

Somehow this wasn't enough.

Pleasure began to build within her, building, to a peak. The very top point of a wave. And she knew that it had to break. Because that was how all things in nature worked.

There was an end.

And this would have to end too.

But as that wave crashed over her, endless wave after wave of pleasure, it wasn't the end that she saw before her.

"I love you."

She sobbed it. That truth. And it flooded through her. A certainty in a truth that went beyond trust. That went beyond sex. That went beyond fantasy. And that. Only that, was enough.

And after that wave crested within her, after she felt her need subsiding, he unbound her wrists, slid the slick silk away from her, and drew her up close to his body.

He gazed down at her, his eyes fierce.

"Are you all right?"

It was the height of care. The way that he checked in on her after. Even though he already knew the answer. That wasn't the point. He did it to show that he cared.

And she answered because she knew that it mattered.

"Yes."

"I was nine," he said, looking down at her. "The first time my father hit me. The first time I remember it. Because he did it with a closed fist. Because he did it in a way that was sure to leave a mark because he was never afraid of the consequences."

"Zane…"

"You must know. You need to know. Because this is who I am, and it's what made me. And you have given me the greatest gift. In you. But you must know exactly who I am. I remember camping outdoors as often as I could, anything to keep from coming home. Because it was miserable here. Damn, it was so miserable here. Just so… Bleak. I didn't even mind so much when he hit me. It was easier to go to a place inside of myself. To shut it off. It was when he hit my mother, that was what was much harder. And you know, my older brothers… They were cruel like he was. I thought I was better than him. I really did. But then it was nicer sometimes to drink out of the still than it was to be conscious of where we lived and how little we had. And that was something I quit doing, when I started becoming aware that my mother was using the meth. And what it did to her. She used to be really pretty. She used to be sweet. She just got vacant. She was so beautiful. Then he broke her. He ruined her. Every part of her." Something changed on his face, something shifting in his gaze. "I don't want to ruin you. I don't ever want to do that. I treasure you. Do you know that?"

"Yes," she said. "You showed me that. Over and over again."

"Good. Good. Shayna… By the time she left she was a shell of a woman. And I'll tell you, part of me wondered if she really left, or if he did something to her. Because I wouldn't put it past him. I wouldn't put anything past him. Not ever."

He took a breath. "Death is what comes from places like this. My brothers were never arrested, not given jail time like I was. And I think it's why they're dead. Because they never stopped. Not for one moment. To think. To get themselves on a different path.

"I had to. And that changed me. But I am this place. And I have been. And you are someone who was brought up in love. I was brought up by fists. Fear."

"It isn't who you are, though," she said softly. "I see who you are. You're the man who went to prison and decided to read. You're the man who got out and looked for a job."

"Yeah. I made friends with a rough crowd. And I... You know I was with a lot of women."

"It's okay." It hurt a little bit. But she knew, without even having to ask, that those women didn't have the connection with him that she did.

That what they had was unique, even if he had been with other people before.

"I need you to understand," he said again, his voice rough.

She was trying to figure out why. What. She loved him. Hadn't she declared that? But maybe it wasn't enough. Maybe that was what he was trying to tell her. That it didn't change his plans, that he still had to leave. That this was too broken for him to ever try to piece it back together. She did understand that. She did.

But she wanted it to be different.

But she had already changed so much in the last few weeks, and she didn't know if she had one more shift left in her. To become strong enough to tell him that. Not when she'd already said that she loved him. And he hadn't given her a response.

He did. This is it. He's giving you more of himself, either to make it so you don't love him, or to explain why he can't love you.

She nodded. "I understand that the past hurt you. But I think you and I have both learned one thing and learned it well since our childhoods. And that is that... You don't walk on any path you don't choose to walk on. Being on the same one, well, that's a choice, isn't it? I chose to be the same for all those years. Until I chose to be different. And now... I can choose anything. And so can you. We both can."

He didn't speak. Instead, he kissed her. Drawing her

against his body, and when they made love again, it was furious and fast. Against all odds, especially given how close together their pleasure was.

He didn't withdraw after, and she didn't want him to. She just held him. Until they went to sleep.

CHAPTER NINE

HE DIDN'T SLEEP. But he watched her. Curled up there on the bed, until the sun came through the window again.

He did that. Every night. He dozed for a little while, and then he watched her sleep.

He didn't know why he had that horrendous sense of time being short.

Perhaps because he had all of his life. Because that was what happened when you felt old by the time you were eighteen. The idea that time was short was prevailing.

It was constant, and relentless.

And she made him want to fight against it, rather than live a life in weary acceptance.

He'd come to this place to fix it up, so that he could leave it. He didn't even know why he had decided to fix it up instead of raze it to the ground. Maybe it was because he wanted the money, but it was more than that. He had money.

Yeah, he wanted to make the place a ranch, a place for himself. Someday.

But he didn't need the money from this place to do that. Not every last penny that he was planning on getting out of it, so what was the point really?

Why was he really here?

As he looked at Shayna, her red hair spilled across

the pillow that she was sleeping on, he thought he might know the answer to that, but his stomach went tight in rebellion at the thought.

She was too beautiful. To perfect, too soft. It was what he had been trying to tell her when he explained about his life.

He was not the kind of man for her.

Except… How could they be so right, then? How could they fit like this?

How could he have found a woman who called to the darker things in him, and asked them to come out and play? Who seemed to delight in them, in spite of the fact that she had been an innocent before they'd been together.

It was like she'd been waiting for him. And suddenly, his heart jumped in his chest, and he had the strangest sensation that he had also been waiting for her.

Just for her.

He got out of bed, without thinking. He pulled on his jeans, and took a last look at her as he headed out the front door.

He walked slowly down the path that took him to the house he was building.

And he looked out over the view.

The view. The view his father hadn't been able to enjoy. The view they hadn't had, because they had been carrying on misdeeds in the darkness. He'd had all these thoughts. He'd confronted this already. What was the lesson? Because there was a lesson.

He knew that there was.

And most of all, there was Shayna. And she was glorious and beautiful and everything that he'd ever wanted.

But there was this place. This place. Where his father had terrorized them all, where they had been built on a foundation of moonshine and violence.

When he had gotten to the point that he had decided to agree to rob a store with his father because he couldn't see a way off of the path until he had been pushed from it. Until he had been arrested. Until he'd been sent to prison. Then. And only then.

It didn't make sense. None of this did.

How he had gone from there, to here. To her.

And how he could...

She said she loved him. Love. That word had captivated him from the first moment she'd said it. And that first time she hadn't even said she loved him. But he'd felt it all the same. Like a balm for his soul.

And he had toyed around with saying it near her, about other things, because it made him feel something light.

But he couldn't imagine ever being the kind of man who could love another person. Who could be loved.

But she was here.

Here of all places.

He looked around at the wooden frame that he had built with his hands.

Yes. This was the same land. That cabin that she slept in was the same cabin. The very same one, where so much of his trauma had taken place.

But she was there now, so it was different. And it was as if a key had turned in the lock inside of his chest. A dawning realization moving over him.

It was the same house. But it was different because of her. Because the same house could become a home as long as Shayna was inside of it. And his heart, the one that his father had tried to twist with violence, insults, his poison, could be like it had never been damaged as long as it loved her.

They had gotten off the path that they were set on. And the important thing was that now they move forward. Onto a path of their own making, and where they went, they would decide.

Because this place... This place didn't have to be sold. He didn't have to run from it. It wasn't defined by what his father had made it. Not any more than he was. He wanted her. And as he stood there, he could see her standing beside him in his mind's eye, round with his child. And the very idea just about took him out at the knees.

That he could have a wife?

A baby.

No. Those were things he never thought he could have. He thought he had taken it from himself. He thought his father had taken it from them by violence from the time he was a child. He had not thought that he could be repaired. He had not thought that he could be whole. That this place, this place, could be the site of his redemption was the most beautiful thing that he had ever conceived of.

And there was an echo of some song in the back of his mind. He makes all things beautiful in his time.

And he didn't know what he thought about that. If he believed it, but he knew that Shayna did. She had made this beautiful, that he was certain of. And she was everything that he needed.

She loved him. She loved him.

Rough and dirty and broken. While she was sweet

and soft and whole. But she wanted what he had. He needed who she was.

He took off running, back toward the house. As fast as his legs could carry him, and he threw the door open, just as Shayna came walking out of the bedroom, naked.

"Shayna," he said.

"What?"

And then he crossed the space between them and pulled her into his arms, twirling her around in a circle. "I love you too."

She grabbed hold of his face, her eyes wide with shock. "What?"

"I love you too. I needed a minute. To figure out what that meant. No one's ever told me they love me before."

"I love you," she said again, as if it was a reflex. "I love you. I love you, Zane Fox. I love you."

"Say it again," he said.

"I love you."

"I love you too. I want to have babies with you. I want to marry you. I want you to be my wife. My woman. My forever. Shayna. I fucking love you so much. I didn't even know that these feelings could exist inside of me. I didn't know that I could dream. Baby, because of you I dream. I was down at the house, and I saw it. You beside me and pregnant. I want that."

"I want it too. I do. I... Zane. I love you so much. You are everything I have ever wanted. Everything. A fantasy that I didn't know I could have. I just thought I had these... These thoughts late at night that turned me on and I didn't think they had anything to do with love. But you are everything. You are my adventure, my fantasy. My heart. And who on earth is so lucky to have all of those things? Who? I love you."

He held her close, and kissed her. And it was like the light had gone on inside of him for the very first time.

"I think… I think it's time for you to meet my father."

And that made him a little bit afraid. "All right. I'm ready."

SHAYNA WAS STILL buzzing when they drove down the hill together, to her father's house.

They opened up the doors of the church, and found him there, standing in the sanctuary.

"Dad…" She took Zane's hand, and led him forward.

Her dad smiled, a smile lighting up his face.

"Well hello there, Zane Fox. Welcome home."

EPILOGUE

IT WAS HOME. Truly. Spectacularly. More than he had ever imagined possible, more than anything he had ever dreamed.

He and Shayna finished building the house—he actually hired somebody because he was in a hurry. They got married quickly, too, because while her father was deeply accepting of Zane and all of his past mistakes, it was clear that he was anxious for Zane to make an honest woman out of Shayna. And that was fine with him, because he was more than willing to do so.

It was a good thing too, because it wasn't long after she walked down the aisle that the pregnancy test turned positive.

The house still wasn't quite finished, but it would be by the time the baby was born.

He kissed her stomach as they lay in bed that night, and it was the strangest thing to be able to imagine a future. A real future. With her.

"It's a good thing you came back after running away, Little Red," he said, stroking her hip.

"Of course. I couldn't have stayed away from you. I guess I was always drawn to a big bad wolf."

He looked up at her. "You're the strong one, you know. And in many ways, I think I was the one who was innocent."

"I *know* that isn't true. You corrupted me."

"Maybe. But you showed me what love was. And I think that love is the most powerful, dangerous thing of all, don't you?"

"Maybe. Just maybe."

She stared up at the ceiling, a smile on her lips.

"What are you thinking?" he asked.

"Oh, just that… Only a few months ago I was thinking that things couldn't go on like this. And now I hope they go on like this forever."

* * * * *

Do you love romance books?

JOIN

on Facebook by scanning the code below:

A group dedicated to book recommendations, author exclusives, SWOONING and all things romance! A community made for romance readers by romance readers.

Facebook.com/groups/readloverepeat